EXTRICATING
OBADIAH

By JOSEPH C. LINCOLN

AUTHOR OF

"Mary Gusta,"   "Thankful's Inheritance,"
"Kent Knowles, Quahaug,"   Etc.

A. L. BURT COMPANY

Publishers   New York

Published by arrangement with D. APPLETON & COMPANY

Printed in the United States of America

EXTRICATING OBADIAH

CHAPTER I

DINNER at the Mansion House was over. The smells of fried "plaice-fish," fried potatoes, fried onions, fried doughnuts and fried "turnovers" were a trifle less pervasive in the parlor, now that the dining room door was shut. On the porch the aroma had changed to that of strong tobacco smoked in stronger pipes. From the direction of the kitchen came the sound of washing dishes.

Yes, dinner at the Mansion House was over. Mrs. Euphemia Hobbs, hostess of the establishment, declared to Miss Ethelinda Doane, who washed dishes and waited on the table, that she was thankful for it. "I'm always thankful," said Mrs. Hobbs, "when another meal's done with and out of the way." Miss Doane said that she, too, was thankful.

"I try to be thankful for whatever comes along in this world," she added, "but sometimes a person's thankfulness gets an awful jolt. I've always been thankful that I had a pretty name. I think Ethelinda's real sort of cute and pretty, don't you, Mis' Hobbs? Um-hm. Well, t'other day I happened to hear Mr. Clifford talkin' at the table and he said every person's name meant some-

I

thin'; 'twas took from some furrin language and had a meanin'. I asked him what Ethelinda meant and he said if I looked where it said 'Names of Women' in the back of the big dictionary I could find out; said the language 'twas took from would be in what he called 'brackets' right alongside of it. So I went and looked in your dictionary in the parlor—I know you wouldn't care, Mis' Hobbs—and, sure enough, I found it. I kind of hoped it might mean 'lovely' or 'beautiful' or 'true,' or somethin' like that; there was a lot of 'em that did. But what d'you suppose it did mean?"

"I don't know, I'm sure," said the landlady, absently. "Look out for that platter, 'Linda; you'll have it onto the floor in a minute."

"No, no, I shan't neither. I'm hangin' onto it just as careful. Well, I guess you *don't* know what that name meant, Mis' Hobbs! When I see it I pretty nigh give up. It means 'noble snake.' "

"Noble which?"

"Noble snake. My-y soul! And for anybody hatin' snakes the way I do! If I see one a mile off a body could hear me yell to glory. But to be *named* after one, and a noble one, too. My-y soul! But there 'twas, right in black and white. And the language 'twas took from was the Tee-utt language."

"The *what* language, for mercy sakes?"

"The Tee-utt language. Any way that's how it was spelt inside them brackets—T-E-U-T. *I* never heard of it, did you, Mis' Hobbs?"

"No, I'm sartin sure I never did."

"Neither did I. Sounds like some kind of Indian talk

to me. But to be called after a noble snake! Noble—
that means a critter about nine foot long, I presume
likely. Ain't that the *worst!* I'm goin' to ask Mr. Clifford about that Tee-utt language soon's ever I get a
chance. . . . Oh, my land! did that plate break? Why,
I put it down just as easy. Must have been awful tender, seems to me. I'm *so* sorry, but 'twan't my fault,
was it, Mis' Hobbs? Findin' out you're named for a
snake makes anybody terrible nervous. You don't cal'-
late Mr. Clifford knew 'Ethelinda' meant 'noble snake,'
do you, Mis' Hobbs?"

Lack of breath caused Miss Doane to pause just here,
which afforded her employer an opportunity to express
her opinion of the plate breaking and of Ethelinda's carelessness in general. Ethelinda replied, of course; if she
had failed to reply at any time and to any remark those
who knew her well would have been tempted to send
for the doctor. Mrs. Hobbs was, herself, by no means
taciturn, so the subject was most effectually changed, and
neither the "noble snake" nor Mr. Clifford was again
mentioned during the dish washing.

Meanwhile, the gentleman responsible for the re-
search in "Tee-utt" nomenclature was standing on the top
step of the porch, smoking an after-dinner cigar. Upon
one point he was in perfect agreement with the landlady
and her helper—he, too, was glad that dinner was over.
He had been as glad when breakfast was at an end; he
knew he should be equally pleased when supper was finished. The conclusion of a meal at the Mansion House
was, to Irving Clifford, a time for mild rejoicing; it

3

was a satisfaction to feel that he would not be called upon to face another for several hours at least.

He stood there upon the porch smoking and thinking. It was a fine October day, clear and cool. The sky was blue, the sea a deeper blue, the fields and hills brown or gray in their autumn dressing. In summer they were green, but now the grass was dead, the leaves of the bayberry and beach-plum bushes fallen, the reeds at the edges of the ponds broken and rusty. Only the clumps of pines, scattered here and there over the knolls behind the houses bordering Trumet's main street, flared green and bright, defying the coming winter. The street itself was almost empty of life. In July and August Trumet was a gay village and at this time of day the sidewalks would have been decorated with groups of summer people, radiant in flannels and sport suits, bound for the post office and the noon mail. Now there was no one, or at the most only an occasional someone. The group of two or three "regular boarders" seated on the Mansion House porch behind Mr. Clifford carefully noted each passer-by. It was not often that they could enjoy the privilege of sitting on the piazza in October. Cape Cod Octobers are usually too chilly for that.

Captain Ezekiel Penniman, retired shipmaster, now selectman and person of consequence, leaned forward in his chair and looked, as he would have said, a point or two up to wind'ard.

"Who's that comin' along?" he demanded, addressing the company in general. "Some of you young folks with deadlights that's fit to see through tell me who that is."

The only young person on the porch was Mr. Clifford.

The others, besides Captain Penniman himself, were old Mr. Laban Bassett, commonly called "Uncle Labe," and Mr. Peleg Bearse, the fish peddler. Their "deadlights" were no more reliable than the captain's.

"Don't ask me, Zeke," said Uncle Labe. "My eyes ain't no good more'n ten foot off nowadays. Ask Peleg, maybe he can tell you."

"Huh!" grunted Mr. Bearse, disgustedly, "don't ask me nothin' just now. I busted my spectacles yesterday and since then I've sold my fish by guess and by godfreys more'n I have by sight. I can tell a plaice-fish from a cod 'cause they ain't the same shape, but when it comes to tellin' a cod from a haddock, there you've got me. All I can see is that somebody's comin' up street—two somebodys, nigh's I can make out. Who be they, I wonder?"

Mr. Clifford, thus addressed, looked in the direction indicated.

"One of them," he said, "is Mr. Griggs—Mr. Balaam Griggs. The other is a stranger to me."

"Eh? A stranger?" Captain Penniman leaned forward; so, too, did "Uncle Labe" and Peleg.

"A stranger, eh?" exclaimed the latter. "I want to know! What sort of a lookin' feller is he, I wonder? Never mind, they'll be abreast here in a minute. Then I can see for myself."

The stranger, on closer inspection, proved to be a little man, dressed in what was obviously a brand-new suit of clothes, topped by a brand-new hat. He walked beside Mr. Griggs, looking up into the latter's face and talking eagerly. Mr. Griggs was long-legged and thin

5

and his companion's gait was almost a trot in the effort
to keep up. As the pair came abreast the Mansion
House Mr. Griggs was speaking.

"You leave it to me, Mr. Burgess," he was heard to
say. "You leave it to me, sir. I take a pride in such
things and it won't be no trouble at all for me to do
it for you. You just leave it to me and——"

They passed out of hearing. Captain Penniman
nodded.

"Ya-as," he drawled, "you leave it to him and you
won't have much left yourself, I cal'late. Who in time
has Balaam got in tow now?"

Uncle Labe shook his head. "Burgess—Burgess," he
repeated. "Where have I heard that name lately?
Humph! Burgess?"

"Say!" Mr. Bearse evidently had an idea. "Say,"
he cried, "I wonder if 'tain't the feller that owns the
Badscom place downtown there, the one that lives up
to Wapatomac and has had that place willed onto him.
Seems to me I heard he was expected down most any
day now, and Mirandy Hedge's girl has been in there
cleanin' house. I wouldn't wonder if 'twas him, I
snum if I would! Mirandy give out that that feller's
name was Birdgrass or some such foolishness, but she
never gets nothin' straight. Burgess—humph! I'll bet
that's who 'tis."

Captain Zeke sniffed. "Well," he observed, "if Bale
Griggs has got him in his claws, he won't have nothin'
much *but* his name in a week or so. Of all the con-
trivin' schemin' old— What are you kickin' me for,
Labe? Can't you keep your feet to home?"

6

"I—I wasn't kickin' you, Zeke," protested Mr. Bassett, hastily. "I was—was just crossin' my knees, that's all."

"Crossin' your knees! Crossin' telegraph poles! What was your knees doin' way over here in the next county? I— Eh? Oh!"

Both Uncle Labe and Mr. Bearse had winked expressively and jerked their heads in the direction of Irving Clifford. Captain Zeke saw a light.

"Um—yes, yes," he said slowly. "It's a nice day, ain't it. Goin' back on the job so soon, are you, Irve? Back to the cold-storage so quick?"

Clifford, who was at the foot of the steps, turned as he answered.

"I'm not going directly back to the storage plant, Captain," he said. "I have an errand over at the machine shop in South Trumet. I had at first intended asking Seth Bailey to take me over in his car, but the fine weather has tempted me and I think I shall walk."

The three "regular boarders" stared at him in amazement.

"Walk?" repeated Captain Penniman.

"Walk!" exclaimed Uncle Labe. "Why, how you talk!"

"Walk!" cried Peleg. "Man alive, don't you know it's all of three mile?"

Clifford laughed.

"You fellows down here might almost as well have no feet," he said. "You never use them to take you anywhere. You ride, if it is only to call on a neighbor."

Captain Zeke shook his head. "Well," he observed, "I cal'late I *wouldn't* have no feet if I walked six miles **on**

7

'em in one afternoon; cal'late I'd wear my legs down to stubs, if I did that. However, don't let my legs interfere with yours. Heave ahead and walk your six mile, if you want to."

The young man laughed again.

"Evidently you don't believe in exercise, Captain," he said.

"Yes, I do—for other folks. Why don't you walk another six mile for me and Labe and Peleg? That kind of exercise might do us good; eh, boys?"

The fish peddler and his companion doubled up in hilarious appreciation, and Irving Clifford waved his hand in farewell and strode away down the path to the gate. Uncle Labe peered after him.

"Humph!" he grunted. "He's goin' to the east'ard, ain't he? How's he cal'latin' to get to South Trumet that way?"

Mr. Bearse answered. "Wa-al," he drawled, "he can get there that way by goin' around the lower road, I presume likely."

"The lower road! Yes, so can a feller get to the North Pole by goin' south, I cal'late, but he'd have to travel clear around the world to do it. Why, the lower road's another three-quarters of a mile, good, out of his way."

Captain Zeke grinned. "Maybe so," he observed, "but if he went straight, same as you and I'd go, Labe, Balaam Griggs' house would be three-quarters of a mile out of *that* way, wouldn't it?"

Peleg chuckled and looked wise. Uncle Labe rubbed his chin.

"I see," he said. "Yes, yes, I—see. Mary Barstow, eh?"

"Sartin sure. Can't you remember the time, Uncle Labe, when it took more'n three-quarters of a mile of walkin' to keep you from your girl? I can, if you can't."

"I can remember that all right, Zeke Penniman, old as I be. But how do you know there's anythin' in all this talk? Why should a smart, likely, promisin' young engineer feller like Irve Clifford be hangin' around Balaam Griggs' stepdarter? 'Tain't for money; Mary, nor nobody else, 'll ever get a cent of that, long's Balaam lives. For gettin' cash and hangin' onto it he beats anybody ever *I* see."

The captain nodded.

"I wouldn't trust Bale Griggs' spirit on the golden streets up aloft," he observed; "not if the pavement was anyways loose, I wouldn't. But Irve Clifford ain't after no Griggs money. If he's after anything of Balaam's, it's the stepdaughter. Mary Barstow's pretty and she's a mighty nice, smart, able girl. If Irve gets her for a wife, he'll get a good one. I don't know's he wants her, or she him, but there's been consider'ble town talk lately."

"One thing makes me think there may be somethin' in it," put in Bearse, "is the way Balaam acts. He's as cranky as all get-out. All you've got to do is heave out a hint about Irvin' Clifford takin' consider'ble many walks down the lower road lately and away goes Balaam up in the air, hollerin' out that it's all a passel of lies. What makes him so anxious to call it a lie if it ain't the truth? Most of his own truth is lies, I know that."

Mr. Bassett borrowed a match from Captain Zeke.

9

relit his pipe and said: "You can't tell much by that, Peleg. Balaam acts the same way whenever anybody gets beauin' around Mary. You'd think he'd want to get her married and off his hands, she bein' a stepdarter and with no money fur's anybody knows; but he don't act as if he did. Just mention Mary Barstow's name along with some feller's and Balaam gets sorer'n a stubbed toe. I can't understand it, and neither can a whole pile of folks. But I'll tell him this for his own good—he won't find any better young chap than Irvin' Clifford. He's one chance in a thousand, that's what he is."

At that moment Mr. Clifford, quite unconscious that he and his most personal feelings and aspirations were subjects of discussion, was turning from the main road into the lower road. The corner of the main and lower roads is Trumet's business center. Snow's "Dry Goods, Notions and General Store" is there, and Lathrop's "Drugs, Toilet Articles, Ice Cream, Soda and Cigars," and Wixon's "Boots, Shoes, Rubbers, Corn, Hay and Feed." The post office used to be there before the change of administration switched it from Mr. Hezekiah Wixon's lingering grasp and bestowed it upon Philander Cahoon a half mile to the "west'ard."

In summer the corner is a busy place, but in October it, like the rest of the town, is quiet and almost deserted. Irving Clifford saw no one as he turned into the lower road, but at least four pairs of eyes saw him, eyes peering from the windows of the various stores, and four tongues made sarcastic observations concerning his probable destination. It may be true that Love is blind; it seems to be equally true that all the rest of creation has its eyes wide open to watch the sightless god upon his way.

The lower road, at first bordered by the usual story-and-a-half Cape Cod houses, with thick red chimneys and green blinds, curves away to the south and southwest until, after about a mile of curving, it rejoins the main road again at Eldridge's Corner at the western end of the village. For the most part its way lies over the hills and along the bluffs bordering the bay, and land on the bay front, once worthless except for pasture, is now valuable as the site of summer homes.

Irving Clifford strode briskly along the lower road until he reached the foot of the slight eminence known locally as "Knowles' Hill." At the crest of this hill on the landward side stood a good-sized white house, surrounded by a picket fence, and with two big silver-leaf trees in its front yard. A dingy sign attached to the picket fence read: "Balaam H. Griggs. Real Estate, Insurance, Money Loaned on Mortgages, etc., etc. Genuine Antiques Bought and Sold." At the bottom of this sign a pasteboard placard was nailed, upon which was lettered in black crayon the words: "FRONT DOOR LOCKED. Come Round Back."

It might have been noticed—in fact, it was noticed by Miss Sarepta Hatch, nearest neighbor on the right, and Mrs. Elvira Ginn, nearest neighbor on the left—that, as Mr. Clifford approached the foot of Knowles' Hill, his hitherto brisk stride became a trifle slower. It slowed still more as he climbed the hill until, when he reached the center of the sidewalk before the house with the white picket fence, it had become very slow indeed.

Also it might have been—and was—noticed that the young man's glance seemed to rest wistfully, almost hopefully, upon the side door of the white house. And then that door opened and a young woman came out.

She did not appear to be aware of Mr. Clifford's proximity; in fact, she was almost at the gate in the picket fence when she raised her eyes and saw him. And she was, plainly, very much surprised to see him. And it was equally plain that he was very much surprised to see her.

"Why, Miss Barstow!" he exclaimed. "Good afternoon!"

Miss Barstow was just a little confused, but she smiled —an operation distinctly not unpleasant to witness—and held out her hand.

"Why, good afternoon, Mr. Clifford," she said. "You did decide to do it, after all, then?"

Clifford shook hands with her and opened the gate.

"Yes," he said, closing it after she had come out, "I decided to walk. It was such a beautiful day I couldn't resist the temptation. I came around this way because— er—because it made the walk a little longer, you see. And you—you were going for a walk, too?"

They fell into step and, quite oblivious of the fact that a window pane in Miss Sarepta Hatch's residence and one in the front hall of the house occupied by Mrs. Elvira Ginn were flattening the noses of eager watchers, walked onward together. Miss Barstow's eyes were brown and their lashes were long and brown, and the cool breeze from the bay fluttered a strand of her brown hair so that the October sunlight shining through it made it look like spun silk, or threads of gold, or something else equally shining and fascinating and pretty. All of which Irving Clifford may or may not have noticed.

"Yes," she said, answering his question, "I couldn't resist the day, either. I had that errand up at the dressmaker's and, although Mr. Griggs told me I had better harness the horse, I decided to walk. You remember I told you I thought I might."

"Oh, yes, so you did. I remember you said something about it."

"Yes, I did. And you spoke of walking all the way to South Trumet. But of course I didn't think you meant it."

Now that very morning, after breakfast, at the post office, these two young people had met by chance, and there Miss Barstow had spoken of her errand to the dressmaker's and of her intention of walking instead of riding, and that she should probably start for the walk about half-past one that afternoon. And Mr. Clifford had suddenly discovered that it was a beautiful day for walking and that he might walk to South Trumet that same afternoon. And, although neither of them mentioned it, both were aware that Miss Carrie Cahoon, the dressmaker, lived on the South Trumet road about half a mile from the village. And now, when all this conversation had, according to the admissions of both sides, been, if not forgotten, at least not taken seriously, they had met almost at the hour named, half-past one, and were walking together. Amazing coincidence.

They talked of the weather, of course, and of other equally safe and sane topics. Miss Barstow asked how the work at the new cold-storage plant was progressing. She supposed they would be installing the engines pretty soon. Mr. Clifford said that only portions of the engines had arrived as yet, and that the installation would not begin for at least a fortnight.

"How long will it take?" asked the young lady.

"I don't know," was the answer. "I presume it will be necessary for me to be here in Trumet for nine or ten months more, perhaps. Ten months should finish the plant and give me time enough to test it, I should say."

"Oh, and then—where will you go?"

"I don't know. Wherever the firm sends me, I suppose. I'm not anxious to go anywhere. If the railroad people lost the engines in transit and it took a year to find them, I should bear up under it."

"Really! Why? Don't you like your work, Mr. Clifford?"

"Like it? I'm crazy about it. I wouldn't do anything else for any amount of money. I didn't mean what I said exactly, Miss Barstow. Of course, I shouldn't want the engines to be lost and I do mean to get my job here finished on time, but——"

"But what?"

"I'm not very anxious to leave Trumet, that's all."

This remark seemed to put a stop to conversation for a moment. When Miss Barstow next spoke it was concerning a different subject. They had reached the next hill on the lower road. It was a higher hill than "Knowles'," and from its top there was an expansive view of bay and shore, stretching for miles in either direction. Upon the water side of the road, standing in a good-sized plot of ground, was an old-fashioned, rambling house, much out of repair. It had been in its day a very roomy, comfortable house, and the possibilities for comfort were in and about it even yet; but the whitewash was peeling from the shingles, the shingles themselves, some of them, were dropping off, here and there a blind hung on one hinge, and the dead grass and weeds in the yard were a foot high. The house looked as if it had been shut up for years, as, in fact, it had. But now a door and several windows were open and smoke was rising from the kitchen chimney.

"It will seem good to see that house open," said Mary Barstow. "It has been closed ever since I came here to Trumet to live. When I was a little girl I used to be frightened to go by it at night, it looked so deserted and spooky. But as I grew older I came to like it, rather. It seems so—so—what shall I say?—homey, or as if it ought to be made a home again. I like the way it is spread out, long and low, you know; and the way all the ells and extensions and barns and henhouses cuddle up to it. I am ever so glad it is going to be opened and lived in. I only hope the new owner won't improve it too much, not enough to spoil it, anyway."

"Who is the new owner?" asked Clifford.

"His name is Burgess; and his Christian name is as queer as—well, almost as queer as my stepfather's. It is 'Obadiah'—Obadiah Burgess. Haven't you heard of his falling heir to the old Badscom place and coming here to live?"

Irving nodded. "Yes," he said, "I have. I heard something about it, although I paid little attention. But

I think I saw Mr. Burgess. A little chap, isn't he; with a sort of round, red, moony face and grayish hair?"

"That is Mr. Burgess. Did you meet him? He came only yesterday."

"No, I didn't meet him. I saw him on the street just now. At least Mr. Peleg Bearse said it was he. He was with Mr. Griggs—your father."

Again there was a momentary silence. It seemed to Clifford as if his companion looked troubled; but she said: "Yes, I believe Mr. Griggs is attending to some business matters for him. Isn't this a wonderful after-noon? See how clear everything is. See that schooner's sails, so clean-cut against the sky, and yet her hull is below the horizon."

But Irving Clifford did not mean to be sidetracked by the clearness of the atmosphere or the beauty of the view. The dressmaker's house, Miss Barstow's destina-tion, was not so far ahead—they had passed the corner and were now on the main road—and there was some-thing he wished to say before they reached there. So he summoned his courage and began:

"Miss Barstow," he said, "I hope you'll forgive me for saying this, but it has troubled me a little, and I determined to ask you about it. It may be my fancy, but it has seemed to me of late that your father doesn't —doesn't—well, as if he had a sort of prejudice against me. Almost as if he disliked me. Have you noticed it?"

For just a moment she hesitated. Then she said: "I am not sure that I know what you mean, Mr. Clifford. I didn't think you and my—father were well acquainted."

"Why, we're not, you know, not very well acquainted.

16

I—well, to be frank, he doesn't seem to care for my acquaintance. On the last two or three occasions when we have met he has scarcely spoken to me. I couldn't imagine how I had offended him. I can't yet. Can you, Miss Barstow?"

Again she was silent for a moment; then she said:

"Mr. Griggs is somewhat peculiar, as perhaps you have noticed—or heard."

He had heard at least that. In fact, of all the stories of Balaam Griggs, his characteristics, manners and methods he had heard since he came to Trumet, not one was to Balaam's credit. And he knew she must, to some extent, be aware of this. Yet he tried to make his answer as diplomatic as possible.

"I have heard," he said, "that he was—er—eccentric."

"Yes, he is. He has few friends; says he doesn't care for them."

"Humph! that's odd; I'm sorry."

"Why?"

"*Why?*"

"Yes, why? Do you wish to become a friend of his?"

This was a direct question, certainly. Irving Clifford was surprised and rather embarrassed. But he would not help smiling.

"Well," he answered, "since you ask me so very plainly, I don't know that I do, particularly. If Mr. Griggs wishes to dodge my acquaintance he has that privilege, I suppose. But I do value your friendship, Miss Barstow, and because I do and hope that it may continue I shall be sorry if your father's eccentricity takes the form of dislike to me."

17

They had reached the whitewashed fence, the gate of which supported the sign: "Miss Caroline Cahoon, Modiste and Dressmaker. Plain and Fancy Sewing Done Here or Out by the Day." Mary paused, her hand on the gate. She seemed to be considering, to be making up her mind. When she spoke it was evident that that mind was made up.

"Mr. Clifford," she said, quietly, "you know, of course, that Mr. Griggs is not my own father, my real father."

"Yes; yes, I knew that he was your stepfather. I had been told so."

"He is. My own father died when I was a little girl. My mother married Mr. Griggs while I was away at school, and I remained at that school until just before her death, four years ago. During her last illness I came here to her home—Mr. Griggs' home—and I have been here ever since. My mother asked me to stay here with him, for a time at least, and I have done as she asked.

"I am telling you this," she added, "because I want to make plain to—to all my friends that my stepfather's personal prejudices do not influence me in any way, either in my feelings or my acts. Mother asked me to stay here with him and make him a home as long as I felt it right to do so. That I have done and am doing, but my friendships are my own. Good afternoon, Mr. Clifford. I have enjoyed the walk ever so much."

She entered the dressmaker's yard. Irving Clifford resumed his walk, his head high and his spirits equally so. What did he care for the eccentricities or prejudices of Balaam Griggs? If he had met the dealer in real estate, insurance and mortgages just then he would have felt like snapping his fingers in the latter's face.

So he walked on, increasing his pace and whistling cheerfully. As he left Trumet behind him the houses were more widely scattered and there were stretches of woods, pines and scrub oaks. The road became more winding and crooked and the hills and hollows more frequent. In summer, particularly on Saturday or Sunday, there would have been a procession of automobiles on that road; now, in October, there were very few.

He had covered perhaps two of the three miles separating South Trumet from its parent town when he heard the raucous squawk of a motor horn. The sound seemed to come from beyond the summit of the hill on the road before him. The hill was rather high and long, for a Cape Cod specimen, and the road, curving gently upward to its top, disappeared behind a clump of sturdy old pines, their foliage feathery and green against the afternoon sky. At the foot of the slope, beside and to the left of the road and almost opposite where Clifford was walking at that moment, was a hollow and a little pond, the latter perhaps fifty yards in width. Between the road and the pond was a stretch of rickety rail fence.

The squawking of the motor horn was so loud and insistent that Clifford looked up the slope with some interest, wondering what sort of vehicle might be attached to that horn and why its progress was announced with such preliminary trumpetings. He expected to see at least a seven-passenger limousine shoot from behind the clump of pines and descend the hill at a speed of seventy miles an hour.

EXTRICATING OBADIAH

But the car which did appear was not a limousine. It was a runabout containing a single passenger. The passenger, who was also the driver, was a man, and he was humped over the steering wheel, his elbows well out and his hat on the back of his head. Clifford had little time to observe what the man looked like; his attention was centered on the car itself. The latter was small and "tinny," also it glittered in the sunshine as only a very new car can glitter. It turned the corner by the pines to the accompaniment of brazen squawkings and came down the hill, gathering speed as it came. It edged over toward the right-hand side of the road until the watcher at the foot of the hill feared he might be crowded off the highway altogether. Then with a violent jerk it shot diagonally across to the left, where in turn it was yanked from the very edge of destruction and sent to the right again.

Clifford, standing in the middle of the road below, was very anxious to get out of the way of this erratic equipage. but there was some difficulty in knowing which way to jump. If he went to the left, the car was just as likely to go there too, and the right was equally dangerous. However, a sudden swoop of the approaching motor to the right decided him, and to the left he sprang, shouting a warning as he did so.

The shout reached the ears of the driver, apparently, for he looked up from the macadam directly at the end of the radiator, the spot upon which his gaze had hitherto been fixed as if glued, and saw the fellow human in his path. Then he, too, shouted, or roared, or bellowed, and, twisting his body to one side, turned the steering wheel with it. The runabout swerved sharply to the left, Clifford leaping out of its way just in time, crossed the road, smashed headlong through the rickety rail fence and splashed hub deep into the little pond, where it stopped short.

Irving, as soon as his bewildered senses were able to grasp the situation at all, jumped over the splintered ruins of the fence and ran to the rescue. The auto, surrounded by agitated rings of mud and water, seemed to be safe enough. At any rate, it was standing on its four wheels. As for its driver, he, too, appeared to be safe and sound. Clifford, who unheedingly had run ankle deep into the mud and water himself, voiced his anxiety in a hail:

"Are you hurt?" he asked.

The man in the auto turned a red and somewhat dazed face in his direction. It was a big face, for he was a big man, and there were strands of iron-gray hair tumbled across the forehead, and a gray-sprinkled, pointed chin beard and mustache. It was a strong face, one which looked as if it had faced many climates, many weathers and many different kinds of human beings. Clifford, of course, noted all this later; just then he noticed very little except that the man himself appeared to be uninjured.

"Eh?" gasped the stranger in the auto.

"I say, are you hurt?" repeated Irving.

"Eh? Hurt? No, I guess I ain't, but I ain't sartin. I wouldn't swear to nothin' definite just this minute. You're the feller that was there in the road off my bows, wan't you? Are *you* hurt?"

"Not a bit. I'm sorry I startled you. I yelled and tried to get out of your way, but——"

"That's all right; that's all right." He looked Mr. Clifford over and a smile twitched the corner of his lip. "As for gettin' out of my way," he added, "your intentions was all right, son, but your judgment was bad. You'd ought to have stayed right in the middle of the channel. I've hit 'most everywhere since I left Province-town in this dratted thing, but I ain't hit the middle of the road yet. Where am I, anyhow?"

He peered over the side of the car. Then he shook his head.

"Water, ain't it?" he demanded. "Blessed if it ain't water! Tut! tut! Son, is there any other pond or water hole within two mile of here?"

Clifford laughed; he could not help it. "So far as I know this is the only one," he said.

"*I* bet you! And I got into it! If there's any water, salt or fresh, on top of this earth anywhere you can 'most generally cal'late on my gettin' in it—or on it. 'Twas *some* prophet in our family that named me Noah. . . . Well, son," he added, after another look over the side of the auto, "what do you think? Is the Ark stranded for keeps here on Ararat; or can I kedge her off?"

CHAPTER II

THE term "kedge her off" did not convey a great deal of meaning to Irving Clifford's mind, but he had spent sufficient time in Captain Zeke Penniman's society to realize that nautical phraseology contained many terms non-understandable to a landsman. And it was, of course, plain that the man in the runabout was, or had been, a sailor. "Sea captain, active or retired," was written all over him. So Mr. Clifford took a chance.

"I think we can get the car out," he said. "We must be prompt, that's all, before it settles into the mud. You sit where you are, sir, and I'll wade in and see how much damage is done."

He stepped back to dry land and bent to the laces of his dripping shoes. The man in the car roared a protest.

"You shan't do nothin' of the kind," he declared. "You stay ashore there and keep dry. You've had enough trouble on account of me, as 'tis. I pretty nigh run over you; 'tain't likely I'm goin' to drown you, is it? You stay right there, I tell you, and keep your feet dry."

Clifford laughingly shook his head. "I couldn't keep them dry if I wanted to," he replied. "My shoes and

23

stockings are soaked through already. You sit there and I'll— Oh, great Scott! what did you do that for?"

The question was uttered in a tone of protest and amazement. The man had quietly opened the car door, stepped out, and was now standing in the pond, the muddy water reaching his knees.

"What did you do that for?" repeated Clifford.

"Well, you said we'd have to be prompt, or she'd settle. This was the promptest way to be prompt I could think of. She wouldn't have stopped settlin' any quicker with my two hundred and fifty pounds roostin' on deck. Besides, I wan't any good there; I may possibly be some here."

"But why in the world didn't you take off your shoes and stockings?"

"Son, when you get to my age and tonnage you'll realize that, when it comes to makin' a choice between gettin' wet and takin' off your shoes and socks in a two by four space like the cockpit of that automobile, you'll get 'em wet every time. There! now we're both in the briny deep, as the feller said. What do you think of her? Know anything about that kind of craft, do you?"

Clifford had waded in and was standing beside him. "Yes," he answered. "A little. But the first thing is to see if we can push it back out of this mud hole. If we can't we shall have to hunt up some one with a horse; and there isn't a house, as far as I know, for a mile either way."

"To say nothin' of a barn, eh? I cal'late we can shove her, if she ain't too deep in. Don't weigh much more'n

24

a termatter can, she don't. That's what I told the feller
I bought her of: 'If she springs a leak,' I says, 'I can
put her in my pocket and take her down to the tinsmith's
to be soldered.' There! now I'll shove one stern wheel
and you the other. Got everything fixed, have you? Say
when you're mad! Now! *Heave* and she goes!"

Clifford having adjusted the clutch as best he could,
they "heaved" together, and the light little car pulled out
of the mud and bumped and wallowed and splashed to
the shore. They ran it back until the forward wheels
were clear of the water. Then they stopped for breath.

"Whew!" panted the big man, rubbing his coat sleeve
across his forehead. "Say, I'm glad the tinsmith ain't
hollerin' for her now. Perhaps he is, though; him or
the undertaker. Land knows how her engines are after
that souse. Better take off the hatches and have a look,
hadn't we? Not that I'd know any more after I had
looked; but you said you would know, eh, Mister?"

"Yes. I am an engineer. Looking after engines of
various sorts is my business."

"You don't say! Well, well! Every man to his job,
as the tipsy feller said to the snake charmer. So you're
an engineer, eh? Well, son, I *have* showed a little mite
of judgment in this fool business, after all, ain't I? I
knew who not to run over. How does she look? Any
chance short of the scrap heap?"

The young man had removed the hood and was inspecting the engine. His examination was brief but
thorough.

"She is not badly hurt," he said, after two or three
minutes of testing and peering. "That is, she is not in-

jured seriously. If you hadn't gone into that pond quite so far she wouldn't have been hurt at all."

"Sho, sho! And I was thinkin' 'twas lucky I hadn't gone in all under. She is hurt some, I judge. What's the damage?"

"Well, that cold water has cracked one of your cylinders."

"The devil!"

"Oh, that isn't such a dreadful thing."

"Ain't it? I didn't know. I just said 'the devil' on the chance. Then 'tain't very bad, eh?"

"It's bad enough. With a big car it might be very bad; but with this little one, of this particular make, you have only to wire the Boston agents, and new parts will be here in a day or so."

"Humph! A day or so! What'll I be doin' while I'm waitin'; settin' here on the edge of this pond whistlin' for hornpouts to swim in for supper?"

"Ha, ha! Not unless you want to. I think I can get your car going so that it will limp on three cylinders as far as South Trumet. There's a good garage there where you can leave it and it will be well looked after. I'll go with you, if you wish; I was bound there, anyway. Unless, of course, my company will inconvenience you."

"Humph! Yes, 'twill inconvenience me about as much as a square meal would inconvenience a starvin' man. I don't know how I'm goin' to thank you for all this, Mr.—Mr.——"

"Clifford is my name, Irving Clifford."

"Mine's Newcomb—Noah Newcomb. Well, Mr. Clif-

'ford, I won't waste time tellin' you I'm pleased to meet you, because I hope you've seen enough of me by this time to give me credit for havin' a teaspoonful of common sense. In spite of the way I handled that automobile just now, I give you my word that there's times when I'm as rational as other folks. I'm mightily obliged to you, Mr. Clifford, I am so. Now what's the first thing you want me to do? I warn you right now you'll find me about as handy at this job as a clam is at climbin' a tree."

Clifford, who was finding his new acquaintance rather amusing, replied that there was nothing for him to do at the moment. "Just sit down and watch me, Mr. Newcomb," he said. "Or should I say 'Captain Newcomb'?"

The big man grinned. "Smell the tar on me strong as all that, can you?" he inquired. "Yes, you can call me 'Cap'n,' if you want to. Most folks do, I notice. I ain't done much seafarin' for quite a spell, but for pretty nigh twenty years at a stretch I got my livin' on salt water. Last part of it I commanded one of the Clay Line boats, runnin' to Porto Rico."

Clifford was interested at once. "Porto Rico?" he repeated. "I know Porto Rico pretty well, myself. I was at San Juan for nearly two years installing the engines and setting up the plant of a big sugar company."

"You don't say! Why, I know San Juan same as I know Portland, Maine, and Portland's where I've been livin' for the past twelve year or more, ever since I gave up steamboatin'. So you've been to Porto Rico, eh? Well, well! I want to know!"

8   27

EXTRICATING OBADIAH

There was little doubt that he did want to know, also that he intended to find out. While the young man busied himself with the engine of the automobile, Captain Newcomb, hands in pockets and apparently quite oblivious of the fact that his garments from the knees down were soaked through, walked up and down asking questions. Having learned that Irving Clifford was a mechanical engineer, that his home was in Ohio, that he had been educated at Cornell, and that his reason for being on Cape Cod was the installing of the mechanical equipment at the new fish freezing and storing plant at Trumet, the captain proceeded to impart a little information about himself.

Irving learned that his companion was a Cape Codder by birth, having been born in that very town, Trumet. That he left school and went to sea when he was fourteen. That his sister, whose name, it appeared, was Dorcas, and who married a man named Cornelius Dillingham, had lived at Ostable until her husband's death, which occurred some time in the early nineties.

"I used to come down and visit 'em every once in a great while in the old days," explained Captain Noah. "Used to call Cape Cod my home then. 'Twas as much my home as any place. Fellers that go sailorin' and steamboatin' don't have any home, rightly speakin', and I was in the Pacific trade then, mate on a tramp freighter. No, I never went square-riggin', that was afore my time, but I've schoonered and steamboated from here to Glory and back. Well, Dorcas had a lot of trouble here on the Cape; her baby died and then Cornelius got drowned fishin' on the shoals down by Orham. So Dorcas begged

28

me to take her away somewhere. I was with the Clay
Line folks then, in active service, so I took her to Boston and she lived there a spell. Then they made me port
commander of their line of steamers runnin' from Portland to the West Indies, and my sister and I moved to
Portland and we lived there ever since."

"Is your sister there now?" asked Clifford absently.
He had heard very little of his new acquaintance's chat-
ter; the engine was occupying most of his attention.

"She's dead. Died last spring; pneumonia 'twas that
took her finally, but she'd been ailin' a long spell. After
she died I didn't seem to care to hang around there much
longer, so I settled up my affairs and got out. I'd laid
by a little bit, had some lucky investments and one thing
a'nother, and I cal'late I've got enough to last me through.
I've got to put in one more winter at Portland—I promised the Clay Line folks I'd stay with 'em while they
broke in a new man—but after that—well, after that
your Uncle Noah's goin' to cruise on his own hook."

"Where?"

"Eh?"

"Where are you planning to cruise, Captain?"

"I don't know. Anywhere I take a notion, I guess;
so long as it don't cost too much."

"You want to look out for the fences and ponds."

"Eh? Ho, ho! you're right, son, so I do. Well, I
presume likely you're wonderin' what I am doin' down
in these latitudes in a craft I don't know any more about
than I do that one; eh?"

"Well, I—I confess I did wonder a little. This is a
brand-new car, isn't it?"

"It was yesterday noon, when I took command of it. My buyin' that auto is quite a yarn. Show's that you can't judge much by the looks of a feller's outside. Anybody to look at me would say I was fairly strong and able, wouldn't they?"

"They certainly would."

"Yup. Well, they'd make a mistake. I'm feeble under the hat and the right kind of man can toll me along with soft soap until I do most anything. Oh, it's so, I've just proved it. Four days ago I hadn't any more idea of buyin' an automobile than I had of puttin' peppermint and molasses on my head and sellin' it for a cough drop. I was up in Boston and I met a feller I used to know, a feller that used to live in Portland. I asked him where he was livin' now and he told me down to Provincetown here, on the Cape. Well, of course, anything about the Cape interests me—I was a boy here and I always did like it better than anywhere else on earth—and we talked and talked a long spell. He was goin' back the next mornin' on the boat and I'm blessed if, the first thing I knew, he hadn't coaxed me into promisin' to go along with him, just for the trip. I didn't have anything particular to do, you understand, and the Old Harry finds some mischief still for lazy folks to run afoul of, as the Good Book says.

"So down to Provincetown I went, just to look around. Stopped at this feller's house—his name was Ryder, by the way—over night. Next day he took me down to his place of business, and it turned out he was in the automobile trade. I rode around town some with him and then he says, 'Noah,' he says, '*you* ought to have one of these things.' 'Yes,' I says, 'I know. And I ought to have a sealskin sack and a diamond breast-pin, but I ain't got either of 'em.' 'They don't cost much of anything,' says he. 'A car like this now, why, they almost give it away.' 'If they did give it away,' I told him, ' 'twouldn't help me any; I couldn't pilot it.' 'Yes, yes, you could,' he says; 'of course you could. It's as simple as A B C. Why, just you look here.' I looked and—Ho, ho! Well, what's the use of pickin' the funeral *all* to pieces? That was the first day; the next day I bought the car."

"Well, I think that was pretty good judgment, Captain Newcomb. I'm sure you'll get a lot of fun out of it."

"Eh? Land, yes! I've got a shipload of fun out of it already. The same kind of fun the boy had that thumped the hornets' nest to see if 'twas holler. I cal'-late he got stung, and I know I did. And yet, by time, I *did* learn to run that auto! I run it all around Provincetown this very mornin'."

"Well, Captain, if you can do that you should be able to run it anywhere. To run a car through those narrow streets is quite a feat."

"Yes, but I run it all right. *Only,* son—and here's where the difference comes in—that Ryder man was right at my elbow all the time. 'Twas the difference between goin' into a strange harbor with a pilot and goin' in without one. This noon, when I left Provincetown, I had a chip on each shoulder. I was perfectly sartin I could navigate that automobile to China, if 'twas necessary. Well, ho, ho! I made a try at it. If that pond had been deep enough to reach clear through, I'd have fetched up in Hong Kong, I shouldn't wonder."

"What was the matter? What set you to going wrong?"

"Everything, son; everything and every livin' critter I met on the road. The further along I got the wider I turned out to pass. When I was runnin' through Provincetown yesterday I wouldn't have given a cow more than six inches clearance room. This afternoon I was liable to give a cat half a mile. I did think all the nerves I had had been washed out of me by Pacific Ocean typhoons, but I guess I've grown a new set. When I got to navigatin' this last string of hills and hollers I knew my finish was just ahead somewheres. I had so many different things to think of, that was the trouble. Ho, ho! I had to think of what to do with my hands, and with my feet, and with my eyes, and about the brake and the clutch and the whistle and—and—land knows what else. And then, every time she'd strike a steep place, I'd get to thinkin' about my past life, because the way I looked at it I'd soon be landed where I'd have to give an account of it. Ho, ho! . . . Good godfreys mighty! What's she doin' that for?"

Clifford had at last reached the point where he was ready to attempt starting the engine. He had been "cranking" for a minute or more. Now his efforts were rewarded by a series of gasping barks and explosions.

"*Fsst! hoo-hoo! Fsst! hoo-hoo!*"

"Got the phthysic, ain't it?" queried the car's owner, anxiously. "Sounds like somethin' catchin'. Liable to do that long, think?"

EXTRICATING OBADIAH

"Until we get to the garage, I'm afraid. Jump in, Captain, and we'll see how she goes."

She went, but that was all that might be truthfully said concerning her progress. She crept barking and spitting up the hills and spitting and barking down the slopes. Clifford had taken the steering wheel and Captain Newcomb sat beside him on the seat. After a few minutes the latter spoke.

"Would it be doin' anything unsafe or sacrilegious," he asked, "to let you and me change places? Don't think I'm altogether loony," he added, apologetically. "The only thing is I—I hate to give up. I started in to learn this car and I do hate to have the thing lick me. I'm goin' to run her afore I get through or die a-tryin'. Sounds foolish, don't it, for a grown up man to be so sot and childish, but I can't help it, it's the way I'm made. Will it be all right for me to take the wheel now?"

Irving laughingly assured him that it would be all right, and the change was made. From that moment until they reached the door of the South Trumet garage conversation was dispensed with. Captain Noah's energies were otherwise employed.

The garage man received the little car cheerfully and philosophically, as garage men usually welcome the crippled fish which come to their net.

"Well, 'tain't so bad as it might be," was his optimistic observation, after inspection of the damage. "Nothin's so bad but what it might be wuss. We mustn't forget that; eh, Mister?"

Captain Noah regarded him with eager interest.

"Thank you, Commodore, thank you," he said solemnly. "I'm much obliged to you for remindin' me. 'Nothin's so bad but what it might be worse.' That's a wonderful comfort, that is. That, and 'Birds of a feather gather no moss,' and 'It's an ill wind that blows nobody—blows nobody's whiskers,' or whatever 'tis, that's the kind of talk that reconciles us to everything, Commodore; you're dead right. Thanks. I'll do as much for you some day. Now about how soon might I reasonably expect to have this craft back again?"

The proprietor of the garage stared at his customer as if he had strong doubts of the latter's sanity. The captain, however, was so mild and bland that the bewildered business man decided to chance a reply.

"If we have luck," he said, "them new parts ought to be down here tomorrow night. Then you can have her, maybe, two afternoons after that."

"Um-m. Yes, yes. Well, I tell you, Commodore, you just help that luck along all you can, will you? Remember, 'A burnt child dreads the—er—pain-killer.' I'll be here sharp day after day after tomorrow afternoon. Well, son," turning to Clifford, "what do you say? Shall we be cruisin' along?"

Irving explained that his errand in South Trumet had been to that very machine shop and garage. "It will delay me only a minute, however, Captain Newcomb," he said. The captain said he would wait and, taking his handbag from beneath the seat of the runabout, strolled outside, where, at the corner, Clifford found him soon afterward. The big man was chuckling quietly to himself.

"I cal'late," he observed, with a backward jerk of his head, "that feller in there thinks I'm all ready for the asylum, don't he?"

His companion laughed.

"Well," he replied, "he did ask me how long you had been this way."

"Ho, ho! I bet you! Well, son, I don't know why 'tis, but proverbs and sayin's and such always kind of stir me·up the wrong way. I ask that chap in there how bad the auto is hurt and he looks wise as a cross between King Solomon and a cage full of owls, and tells me not to forget that nothin's so bad but what it might be worse! Muttonhead! However, I gave him one or two proverbs of my own, didn't I? Ho, ho! Well, if he thinks I'm crazy now he wants to look out for me when I come back. If that car ain't done on time I'll be violent . . . and in the meantime, son, is there a hotel in this place?"

Clifford shook his head. "No," he said, "there isn't. But there is one, such as it is, at Trumet, and that is only three miles away."

"Um. Such as it is, eh? You know somethin' about that hotel, I take it."

"I ought to. I put up there myself."

"So? Well, you look pretty toler'ble husky. I cal'-late I can stand it for a couple of days, anyhow. Suppose likely they'll have room for me?"

"I'm pretty sure they will."

"Good enough. Let's heave ahead for Trumet. 'Twill seem like real old times, stoppin' in Trumet will."

The young engineer had used so much time in adjust-

ing the auto after its bath in the pond and in getting it
to the garage that he felt obliged to give up his contem-
plated walk home. Moreover, his new friend was not
at all in favor of walking. "Iron's cheaper'n leather
these hard times," was the way he put it. "No use
wearin' out our own shoes when we can coax a horse to
wear out his for us."

They were not obliged to "coax" a horse, for the
owner of the garage agreed to drive them in his own
car to Trumet for two dollars. As they entered the village Captain Noah's interest grew more and more keen.
The town hall was new to him, so was the grammar
school, but the Congregationalist meeting-house received
the greeting of an old friend. The Mansion House was
new, of course, having been built within the past ten
years. He was introduced to Mrs. Hobbs and shown
to his room by Ethelinda. Afterward he sat between
Mr. Clifford and Captain Ezekiel Penniman at the supper table. When the meal was over he confided to the
former that he had "struck another old acquaintance."

"Captain Penniman?" asked Clifford.

"No, no; never met him afore. It's that apple pie
I'm talkin' about. If I ain't awful mistaken I had a
slice off that same apple pie the night afore I left my
granddad's house in this town and run away to sea.
'Twas one of the things made me run. Course it *may*
not be the same pie," he added, "but if 'tain't then the
children's children take after the old folks amazin'. No,
I'll gamble it's the same one; the crust is a little mite
tougher, but age would account for that. I'm tougher'n
I was, myself."

He asked Irving what the "main excitement of the evenin'" might be about town.

"Don't want to risk anything *too* wild-eyed and divilish," he explained, "but I should like to do somethin' to make me forget that pie. Is there anything to go to? Any 'time' at the town hall or anything?"

"No, Captain, I'm afraid not. There are moving pictures here twice a week now, but this is not one of the nights. The mail gets in about eight o'clock and almost every one goes to the post office. If your system craves excitement, I imagine that is where you are most likely to find it. It's not so fevered as to be dangerous."

"Well, that's a comfort. I remember 'twan't what you'd call delirious in the old days. My, my! how long ago it seems since I lived here. I cal'late I will go to the post office. I might meet somebody there I remember, though that ain't hardly likely. Won't come along, will you?"

But the engineer had work to do that evening. He therefore excused himself and went to his room. Captain Newcomb lit a cigar and strolled slowly toward the post office, staring about him as he walked and trying to pick out places or buildings which he remembered. But it was too dark to see plainly, and his attempts at seeing only caused him to walk into posts or off the edge of the sidewalk. In fact, he almost collided with a pair of pedestrians just ahead of him, a couple too deeply absorbed in their own conversation to notice his approach. They were both men, and all the captain noticed concerning them, except their imminent proximity, was that one was tall and the other short. He pulled up just in time to avoid bumping into the taller one, and stepped off the sidewalk to pass. As he did so he heard the other, the short man, say:

"Well, I don't care, you know. I—I—I don't care much. A dollar or so more or less d-d-don't make much difference. If you say it's all r-r-right, I'd just as soon go ahead and b-b-buy it."

That was all Captain Noah heard. The tall man, suddenly aware of the stranger at his elbow, drew aside and pushed his companion further toward the fence at the inner edge of the walk. The captain moved on, but, as he moved, the scrap of conversation which had reached his ears kept ringing in them like an echo from the past. Not the subject matter, not what had been said, but the voice which said it. That voice, its high pitch and the funny little stutter, seemed oddly familiar. When had he heard that voice, or one very much like it, before? Sometime, somewhere, a voice like that had been familiar to him; somewhere he had known someone who squeaked and stuttered in just that way. Someone he had once known, in the village of Trumet, of course, it must be, but who? And why should the voice seem so *very* familiar? He felt as if he must have known the speaker very well indeed.

CHAPTER III

NOT until he reached the lowest step of the post office platform did the solution of the puzzle come to him, and then he smiled disgustedly. The solution was not a solution at all. He remembered now who squeaked and stuttered in just that way, but the person who did so had never lived in Trumet, nor, so far as he knew, had ever been within a hundred miles of the place. The similarity of voices was a coincidence, that was all.

However, it was a satisfaction to have run down and located the memory, the fancied echo of which had so tantalized him, and Captain Noah entered the post office with the feeling of contentment possessed by one who has guessed a riddle. He glanced about at the faces of the crowd, but, if there were any there whom he had once known, the years had changed them beyond his recognition. And no one appeared to recognize him.

The mail was "in," but it was not yet sorted. Interest seemed to center about a counter at the rear of the office where the evening newspapers had just been put on sale. The captain bought a *Boston Herald* and, with it in his hand, retired to a corner to read. There was a

39

chair in that corner and, for a wonder, it was unoccupied. He sat down, his bulky form squeezed between the corner of the shelf, which was offered the public as a substitute for a writing desk, and a peach crate, which did duty as a waste basket. There he unfolded his newspaper and essayed to read.

By and by the raising of the postmaster's little window made evident the fact that the mail was sorted. The crowd pushed forward, some to get in line at the window, others to unlock private letter boxes. Captain Noah, who, naturally, expected no letters, remained where he was. His toes were trodden upon rather often, and his nose had more than one narrow escape as a hurried discarder of circular or paper wrapper took a flying shot at the waste basket. But the captain read on. The editorial he was reading flayed the Democratic party in a thoroughly satisfactory way, and he wished to follow the process to its tormenting finish.

But the cuticle had not been entirely removed when his reading was interrupted. Just before him and not much higher than his head, as he sat in the chair, he heard again the squeaky voice which he had heard on his walk to the office.

"All right, Mr. G-G-Griggs," it stammered. "I'll wait right here. You get your mail, if you w-want to. I ain't exp-p-pectin' none."

The captain looked up. As he did so the man who had just spoken looked down. He had a round, cherubic little face—he was a little man—with a tuft of gray beard on the chin and a clean-shaven upper lip. His eyes were a light, watery blue, and as he stared down into the captain's face they opened wide and wider. Then his mouth opened also.

"Wh-wh-wh—" he panted, like a toy engine getting up steam; and then exploded with a *"Why!* Cap'n Noah Newcomb!"

Captain Noah threw down his paper and rose to his feet. He towered above the little man like a floating derrick above a tug boat. His big hand closed over the other's small one and swallowed it up.

"I declare to man!" he cried, in huge astonishment. "Obadiah Burgess! Then *'twas* you I heard when I was comin' along down. What in the world are you doin' here in Trumet?"

Mr. Burgess did not seem to grasp, even if he heard, the question. He was staring up into the captain's face with an expression of huge astonishment coupled with delighted reverence.

"Cap'n Noah Newcomb!" he repeated. "Cap'n Noah! Well, I snum! And I don't know's I ever expected to see you again. I'm awful glad, I am so!"

"Much obliged, Obe. I'm glad, too. I don't know's I *never* expected to see you again, but I sartinly never expected to see you here. When I heard that voice out yonder just now, thinks I: 'That sounds natural, that voice does.' And then afterwards I remembered 'twas your voice it sounded like. But here in Trumet! You don't live here, do you?"

"No, sir, I don't. That is, I do. Anyhow, I ain't; but I mean I'm g-g-goin' to."

Captain Noah shook his head. "You don't and you do and you ain't but you're goin' to. Little mite foggy, that is, ain't it, Obe? Cal'late I'll have to have a chart if I'm goin' to navigate through that. Do you mean you haven't been livin' here, but you're goin' to now?"

"Th-th-that's it, sir. You know about my gettin' the place and the money, don't you? About Aunt Sarah's willin' 'em to me, sir?"

"Never mind the 'sir,' Obadiah. We ain't on board the old *Flyaway* now. Goodness gracious, how long ago that seems—and is! So somebody's willed you a place and money, eh?"

"Yes, sir. Yes, Cap'n. I thought likely you'd heard of it. 'Twas put in the newspapers."

The captain repressed a smile. Mr. Burgess' pride in the fact that the news of his good fortune had been "put in the newspapers" was so very evident.

"I must have missed the paper that day, Obe," he said. "But tell me about it. How much was it? Who was your Aunt Sarah? How did you come to be here in Trumet? Is the place you're talkin' about here?"

"Yes, sir—yes, Cap'n, I mean."

"Call me Noah. Never mind the handles."

"All r-r-right, sir—Cap'n—Noah, I mean. Yes, the place is here. You see, Aunt Sarah, she——"

"Wait a minute, Obe. Heave to. This ain't a very good place for us to talk, is it? Too much competition. Come on round to my room at the hotel. We can talk there in comfort. Come ahead."

But Mr. Burgess hung back.

"I can't, Cap'n Noah," he said. "I forgot. Mr. Griggs is here w-with me. He's round here somewheres. Oh, here he is! Mr. Griggs!"

EXTRICATING OBADIAH

The captain turned and looked over his shoulder. A tall, thin man was standing in the corner by the chair he had just vacated, reading a letter. He was a long-legged, stoop-shouldered individual, whose sharp-featured face was sparsely decorated with a scattering pair of sidewhiskers, and whose long nose supported a pair of spectacles worn not more than half an inch from the tip. The expression on the sharp-featured face was not at the moment a pleasant one. Something in the letter seemed to annoy its reader. As Captain Newcomb looked at him he tore the letter into strips and dashed the pieces savagely in the direction of the waste basket.

"Mr. Griggs!" called Mr. Burgess once more.

The tall man turned, looked over the spectacles, and, seeing who had called, nodded and smiled.

"I'm a-comin', Mr. Burgess," he said. "Shan't keep you waitin' another minute. Had a little mail to look over, that's all."

"Mr. Griggs," said Mr. Burgess, excitedly, "I want to make you known to Cap'n Noah Newcomb, of—of— Where are you livin' now, Cap'n?"

"Portland was my last home port, Obadiah."

"Yes, yes. Portland, Maine. I've been there. Cap'n Newcomb used to be my skipper when I use to go sea-cookin'. I went many as seven v'yages with him, didn't I, Cap'n? And I cooked to s-s-suit you, if I do say it; eh, Cap'n Noah?"

"You sartinly did, Obe," agreed the captain, cheerfully. "And this is Mr. Griggs, I take it."

"Yes, sir; yes, Noah, I mean. Mr. Ba-Ba-Bub-Bub-Bub——"

43

"Balaam," put in Mr. Griggs himself. "Balaam Griggs, my name is. It's a kind of hard name to say. Pleased to make your acquaintance, Cap'n Newcomb. Any friend of Mr. Burgess' is a friend of mine, right off."

"That's good." Captain Noah and Mr. Griggs shook hands. "And you're another old chum of Obadiah's, I judge, Mr. Griggs."

Mr. Griggs seemed a little disconcerted, but he rallied promptly. "No, not that—not exactly an old one. Hey, Mr. Burgess? He! He! But I hope him and I are goin' to be chums, as you call it. If we ain't 'twon't be my fault."

"Mr. Griggs has been awful generous and obligin' since I got here," put in Obadiah. "Yes, even afore I come. Why, I d-d-don't know how I'd got along with all there was to bu-bu-buy and hire around that new house of mine if it hadn't been for him. No, sir-ee, I don't!"

Captain Noah gave Mr. Griggs an appraising glance. He decided that the thin man's looks must belie him. There were, certainly, no exterior indications of either the obliging nature or the generosity.

"You in business here, Mr. Griggs?" he asked.

Balaam nodded and fumbled in his vest pocket, producing a battered memorandum book, from between the pages of which he took a printed card.

"Real Estate and Insurance, etcetery and so on," he said, handing the captain the card. "Wasn't thinkin' of buyin' and settlin' amongst us, was you, Cap'n Newcomb? You might do worse. Trumet's a growin' town."

The captain shook his head. "No," he said, "not this minute. Just now I'm mighty interested to find out all about Obe here and his good luck. I judge likely there's quite a yarn and I want to hear it. Can't you come round to the hotel now, Obadiah?"

Obadiah hesitated. Mr. Griggs looked doubtful. "Course I wouldn't interfere with your plans for nothin', Mr. Burgess," he said; "but if you was cal'latin' to look over that bedroom set, tonight would be an awful good time to do it. I told John we'd most likely be down this evenin', so he'll probably wait in for us. However, don't let nothin' I do put you out. No, no."

Mr. Burgess looked troubled. "I'd like awful well to come round and see you, Cap'n Noah," he said. "You and me have got a lot t-t-to t-t-talk over, all these years. But, you see, Mr. Griggs here is helpin' me buy some furniture for the house, and—and we've got an appointment, kind of. How long you goin' to s-stay, Cap'n?"

"Couple of days, I guess. That's all right, Obe, come and see me tomorrow. No, hold on! I'll come and call on you. Give me a chance to see this property of yours as well as yourself. On the lower road, you say? All right, I'll find it. Be down pretty soon after breakfast. Good night, Obe. Good night, Mr.—Mr.—Briggs—no, Griggs."

He glanced at the Griggs business card. "Balaam," he read. "Say, that's a good old Scriptur' name, ain't it? We're a kind of Scriptural bunch, come to think of it, Obadiah—and Noah—and Balaam! Ho, ho, ho!"

His laugh caused the postmaster to look out of his little window.

EXTRICATING OBADIAH

"Obadiah and Noah and Balaam," repeated the captain. "That's Old Testament for you! Ho, ho! You'd have to hunt some ways to get a fourth name to match up with them; eh? Ho, ho! Well, good night, good night. See you tomorrow, Obe. You, too, maybe, Mr. Griggs. Good night."

After they had gone Captain Noah turned back to the corner, picked up the *Herald* from the top of the waste basket where he had thrown it when he rose to greet Mr. Burgess, crumpled it up, stuffed it into his pocket and walked back to the hotel.

In his room he took off his coat, vest and shoes, lit a fresh cigar and settled back in a rocking chair to finish the editorial. As he unfolded the *Herald* a piece of paper fluttered to the floor. He stooped and picked it up.

It was an oblong strip of cheap note paper, evidently torn from the bottom of a letter. There was writing upon it. Scarcely realizing what he did the captain read these words:

> sending you every cent ju
> omptly as ever I can. For
> d's sake remember how hard it
> n't put Joash, poor boy, in states prison

Captain Noah turned the bit of paper over. The other side was blank. He wondered where in the world it had come from. Then he remembered that his newspaper had lain across the top of the post office wastepaper basket and, doubtless, someone had torn up the letter of which this was a part and tossed the fragments, as he or she supposed, into the basket, but really

46

on the paper. When he picked up his *Herald* he picked
up the fragment with it.

He was about to throw it down again when the name
"Joash" caught his eye. He laughed aloud. His remark concerning Old Testament names had been to the
effect that one would have to hunt some to find a fourth
name to compare with "Obadiah" and "Noah" and
"Balaam." Now, without hunting at all, here was a still
more odd name brought to his attention within the half
hour.

"Joash!" He repeated it aloud. Then he laughed
uproariously and, going over to the hook upon which he
had hung his coat, took his pocketbook from the inside
pocket and put the bit of note paper inside. The name
"tickled" him immensely. He had never heard it before. He knew where, in the Bible, to look for "Noah"
and for "Balaam"; he would not have dispaired of finding "Obadiah." But where to find "Joash" he had not
the slightest idea. But, as this was New England, and
Cape Cod in particular, he would have been willing to
bet that "Joash" was a Scriptural name. He meant to
"stump" the minister with it, after his return to Portland. Whatever else was written upon that bit of paper
he had forgotten already, but that name he did not
intend to forget.

"Joash! Ho, ho!"

So he put the piece of paper in his pocketbook as a
reminder. And, therefore, having shifted responsibility
from his memory to his pocket, he, naturally, proceeded
to forget all about both paper *and* name.

CHAPTER IV

C'APTAIN NOAH had hoped to meet his new acquaintance, Irving Clifford, at the breakfast table and ask a few questions concerning Balaam Griggs. But when he entered the dining room the next morning he found that Mr. Clifford had already breakfasted and gone. Mr. Laban Bassett explained that the young man had a habit of leaving the table earlier than the rest of the boarders.

"This mornin' he didn't eat scarcely no breakfast at all," declared Uncle Labe. "Hardly ever has but one cup of coffee, but this mornin' he didn't drink more'n half a cup. A body'd think 'twan't good, the way he went off and left it."

Captain Noah tasted the slate-colored beverage in his own cup. "A feller must be crazy that goes off and leaves coffee like that," he observed, hastily putting the cup down again.

Uncle Labe nodded. "That's what I tell him," he affirmed. "Especially this mornin'. Why, today's Wednesday, and Mis' Hobbs makes it fresh every Wednesday and Saturday. Don't catch me leavin' none of mine settin' round."

The captain rose. "That's right," he said. "We can't be too careful; some child or innocent person might get hold of it. Well, so long."

He walked out of the dining room, leaving the puzzled Mr. Bassett to ask Ethelinda, when that young lady appeared to clear the table, who that "big, hulkin' critter—that Newcomb one—" was, anyhow.

"I dunno," replied Ethelinda, cheerfully. "Mr. Clifford fetched him here last night, and he's got the room Mr. Moses Tidditt died in. That's all I know about him."

Uncle Labe looked doubtful. "Well," he said, "maybe he ain't touched in the head, but he talks mighty queer for a sane person. Asked Cap'n Zeke how long he'd been boardin' here, and, when Zeke told him three years, he wanted to know if he was cal'latin' to get anything off for good conduct. I can't make no sense out of that; can you, 'Linda?"

"No, I'm sartin sure I can't, Mr. Bassett. He talks the same way to everybody, though. I think he's loony myself, but I suppose 'tain't none of *my* business, long's he pays his board."

The captain, whistling blithely if not tunefully, walked along the main road to the corner, where he turned into the lower road, just as Clifford had done the previous afternoon. He looked about him with interest as he walked, for the morning was a fine one and, in spite of the Hobbs coffee, he was in good spirits. He found himself rather enjoying his enforced stay in the village of his boyhood. That village had changed greatly, it is true, but its location had not changed; the sea and the air and the sky had not changed, and more and more of the old places became familiar to him as his memory brought them forward through the years. Along that lower road his bare feet had stubbed many and many a time on the way to the bay and the "swimming place." In that house there—it had no dormer windows then and the porch was new—had lived the girl who was his "first choice" at parties. The gray, tumble-down abandoned shanty back in the field yonder had been the home of old Captain Joshua Phinney, who, when himself a twelve-year-old, had been cabin boy on a ship boarded by pirates. That barn over there was new, but on the very spot where it stood, behind the clump of willows that used to be there, he and Abe Cole, the minister's son, had fought over a stolen watermelon. And he had blackened Abe's eye. He wondered where Abe was now; wondered if he was living; if he felt as kindly toward his old enemy, Noah Newcomb, as that one time enemy now felt toward him.

The view of the bay from the slope of Knowles' Hill was distinctly satisfying. It was much as he remembered it. The summer places along the shores and on the knolls were new, of course, and the boats at anchor were, for the most part, of the motor instead of the sail varieties. But, generally speaking, Tiumet Bay looked as it used to look, as he felt it ought to look.

It must be somewhere along there that Obadiah Burgess' property, that of which he was in search, was located. He decided that he had better stop at some house on the way and ask particulars concerning that location. Then, as he reached the crest of the hill, he saw the name

"Balaam Griggs" on the sign topping the white picket fence, and decided to ask Balaam himself.

Following instructions given by the placard at the bottom of the sign he did not knock at the locked front door, but went "round back" as directed. There were several doors there, but the farthest had chalked upon its upper panels the words "Genuine Antiques Here," so Captain Noah, although he had no desire to buy any antiques, thought it possible that Mr. Griggs might be with his stock and rapped on that panel.

The person who answered the knock was decidedly not an antique, genuine or otherwise. On the contrary she was a very attractive young woman, with a dust cloth in her hand and a sweeping cap upon her brown hair. In answer to the captain's question she said, in a voice as pleasant as her appearance:

"No, Mr. Griggs is not in just now. He has gone over to the village, I believe. Is there anything I can do for you? I am his daughter."

Captain Noah asked for and received directions concerning the location of Mr. Burgess' legacy, the "Badscom place."

"I can point it out to you from the other window, the one at the back here," said the young woman. "Won't you step in?"

The captain stepped in and followed his guide through a tangled maze of scarred bureaus and seatless chairs and crippled tables to a window which commanded a view of the bay and the further windings of the lower road.

"That is the Badscom place," said the young woman,

pointing. "The old, low, whitewashed house at the top of the hill."

"Thank you, thank you very much, Miss Griggs," said the captain. Then, as he picked his way through the leggy tangle of chairs and tables, he added, "My! you've got a lot of old things here, ain't you! Sell consider'ble, I presume likely, in the course of a year; eh?"

He was sorry the moment after he said it, realizing that he had himself opened the way to a dissertation on "antiques" and a probable attempt to display choice pieces. But his forebodings were groundless. The young woman did not appear even interested.

"Mr. Griggs sells a good deal," she answered.

"Mostly to the summer folks, I suppose?"

"I presume so. I know very little about it."

She was obviously so anxious to avoid the topic, and her attitude was so decidedly unlike that which one would have expected a daughter's attitude toward her father's business to be, that Captain Noah was puzzled and curious. He tried again.

"That's a fine-lookin' old—old—er—bureau," he observed, pointing to a battered and blackened relic before him. "How much is that worth now?"

She shook her head. "I don't know," she said. "You will have to see Mr. Griggs about that."

"Yes, yes, of course. But I don't know when I've seen a bureau like that. Kind of a unusual—er—specimen, ain't it?"

She looked at the "specimen" and then at him.

"It would be—if it was a bureau," she answered, "but I'm afraid it's a sideboard."

Her eyes twinkled. The captain put back his head and laughed heartily.

"Kind of gettin' out of soundin's that time, wan't I?" he observed. "Well, it don't make much difference, long's you can't tell me what it's worth."

They had reached the door by this time.

"I can't," she said, her hand on the latch. "But if you can come back in an hour or two, I am sure Mr. Griggs will be glad to tell you—what it sells for."

She closed the door. Captain Noah walked out of the yard, a broad grin on his face. Balaam Griggs' daughter was strikingly unlike her father, so it seemed to him, unlike him in every way. The long-legged dealer in real estate and "antiques" had not impressed him over favorably at their meeting the night before. But to the daughter, in spite of her deficiency or indifference as a saleswoman, he had taken a fancy at first sight. He had his own opinion of the "antique" business, as too often conducted, and he believed this young woman's opinion was much like his. The slight hesitation between the "you" and the "what" in her last sentence had not escaped his notice. He was still chuckling over it when he entered the gate of the "Badscom place" and found its new owner awaiting him on the threshold.

That Obadiah was glad to see him there was no doubt; also there was no doubt of the little man's tremendous pride in his new possessions. He refused to sit down or to tell the story of his good fortune until he had shown his former skipper over the house, from its queer circular, cemented pit of a cellar to the long, dark attic with the rows of old chests and trunks under the eaves. The

captain liked the old house exceedingly. The bedrooms,
with their sloping ceilings, so convenient for head-bump-
ing; the parlor, with its quaint wall paper, the "spatter
painted" floor of the dining room—all these reminded
him of the house where he had lived as a boy. And the
view from the windows overlooking the bay was really,
exceptionally fine.

"You've got a tip-top place here, Obe," he said, heartily. "You'll be as snug and comf'table here as a moth in
a flannel shirt. All you need is a piazza out back here
to pace the quarter-deck on, and a whale-walk and a spyglass on the roof, and I don't see but you're fixed for
life."

Mr. Burgess' cherubic face beamed.

"That's what I say," he declared. "That's what I tell
Mr. Griggs. 'There may be b-b-better places on top of
the airth,' says I. 'Them Rockyfellers you read about,
and the Old Doctor Bellows' Bitters man that built the
castle over t-t-to Wapatomac, may have more f-f-fancy
houses and grounds, but *I* wouldn't swop with 'em. No
sir-ee,' says I, 'I wouldn't, not if they come beggin' me to
on their b-b-bended knees.' "

"That's the way to talk, Obe. I'll warn any millionaire
that asks me 'tain't any use wearin' out the knees of his
trousers on your account. I don't wonder you're tickled.
This *is* better'n the galley of the old *Flyaway*, I will
give in. But I want to hear all about how you got it.
Can't we come to anchor somewheres now, and talk?"

They "came to anchor" in a pair of rocking-chairs in
the sitting room. Captain Newcomb reached into his
pocket for his pipe, but his host prevented his filling it.

"When you come to my house, C-C-Cap'n Noah," he said, proudly, "you have to smoke m-m-my cigars."

He produced a box of cigars, large, fat cigars, gaudily banded and with the likeness of a robust young woman patriotically clad in the Stars and Stripes on the inside of the cover. The captain took one of the cigars and eyed it respectfully.

"I didn't know you smoked cigars, Obadiah," he said. "You didn't used to when you sailed with me."

"C-couldn't afford to," was the prompt reply. "Now I can. I'm worth t-t-twelve thousand dollars and this house and land. That's better'n bein' cook on a three-masted schooner, even on one of your schooners, Cap'n Noah. Ain't it, now? He, he! Light up and I'll tell you all about Aunt Sarah's willin' it onto me."

Captain Noah lit up, as ordered, and the fortunate legatee proceeded to tell his story.

For seven voyages Obadiah had, as he told Balaam Griggs at the post office, sailed as cook and steward on the three-masted schooner *Flyaway* under Captain Noah Newcomb. During that time he had learned to almost worship his big skipper, certainly to reverence and respect him beyond all other men. And the captain, for his part, liked the little man, although he, of course, realized the very obvious fact that his cook was far from being a Solomon.

"Obe's head rattles a little mite," he used to say, "and the rattle gets into his talk, as maybe you've noticed. He ain't anybody's fool exactly, but it ain't so very hard to fool him. His best gifts are cookin' and stutterin'; I'd back him to cook and stutter with anybody. And another thing, he's clear grit, as nobody knows better'n me. If it hadn't been for Obe Burgess I wouldn't be here now."

Which was a reference to the time when, in a Central American port, Captain Noah was seized with yellow fever and, when his mates and crew having run away, he was nursed back to health by loyal Obadiah, who could not be coaxed to leave him.

After Captain Newcomb gave up command of sailing vessels and had entered the employ of the Clay Line, he and his former cook had drifted apart. Obadiah had cooked on a number of coasters and fishermen, had worked in a restaurant on Atlantic Avenue in Boston, had cooked for two winters in a Maine lumber camp, and then, at his Aunt Sarah Badscom's solicitation, had gone to live with her at her house in a Boston suburb, where he took care of the lawn in the summer and the furnace in the winter and acted as a sort of general housekeeper for the old lady, who was his mother's half-sister.

"Then," explained Obadiah, "Aunt Sarah she went to work and c-c-caught pneumonia and up and died. Course she'd been tellin' me she was goin' to p-p-pup-provide for me all right, but I never thought nothin' of it. I knew she was well off, but I cal'lated her Cousin Nathan Daniels, that lives d-d-down to Augusty, Maine, would get everything. Well, he did get the heft of it, but Aunt Sarah she willed me this old house, that belonged to B-B-Bethuel Badscom, her husband, and his dad afore him, and she left me twelve thousand along with it. Well, sir! don't talk! you never see such an upset critter in your born days as I was when that lawyer told me. I recollect it was a consider'ble spell afore I'd believe he hadn't made a mistake and that 'twan't twelve dollars instead of t-t-twelve thousand. But, by mighty, 'twas so, 'twas so, Cap'n Noah! And here I be, with a house of my own and rich b-b-besides. Here, have another cigar, won't ye? That one's gone out, ain't it?"

His guest looked at the stump of the cigar between his fingers. He had not been smoking it for some time.

"No, no more, Obe, thank you," he said, hastily.

"Better have another, hadn't you? Take another, take a couple. I can afford 'em. I ain't sea-cookin' any more these days. Ho, ho! Smoke right up, Cap'n. I like to see you. Good cigars, ain't they? The 'Liberty Maid,' that's what they call 'em. Balaam Griggs says there ain't no better five-cent cigar made. He buys 'em for me. Ever smoke a 'Liberty Maid' afore, Cap'n?"

"No."

"Sure? Balaam says they're awful popular; maybe you've forgot."

The captain shook his head. "No," he said, emphatically, "if I'd smoked one afore I shouldn't have forgot it. So this Griggs man buys your cigars for you, does he, Obe?"

"Land sakes, yes! He knows how, you see; I never had no experience buyin' cigars. Nor not much else neither. Never had much of n-n-nothin' to buy with. But Mr. Griggs he's helped me out somethin' wonderful. I don't know what I'd done if it hadn't been for him. He's been a real friend, he has."

"So? Well, real friends are scarce. You want to hang

on to 'em—after you're good and sure that they are real.
Known him a long while, have you?"

"No, only a little spell. That's what makes his kindness so wonderful, you understand. He see in the
p-p-pup-paper about Aunt Sarah willin' me the house and
the money and all and he wrote me a letter. Said he was
down here in T-T-Trumet, right on the ground, as you
might say, and if there was anything he could do to help
me here—as a neighbor, you understand—he'd be glad
to do it. I wrote him I was c-c-comin' down to look her
over and he met me at the depot. I d-don't know what
he ain't done for me. Hired a woman to clean house
here and b-bought dishes for me and f-f-furniture
and——"

"Wasn't the house furnished?"

"Only part. Hadn't anybody lived in it for years and
years. There was lots and lots of stuff needed. Balaam
he bought most of it for me."

"Where'd he get it?"

"Oh, I don't know. Some he had himself, part of it
was. You know he sells antiques and such to the summer folks. Some of his best t-t-tables and bureaus and
things that he was holdin' for high p-p-prices he let me
have at cost."

"Did, eh? How do you know 'twas cost?"

"He told me so, himself. That come straight enough,
didn't it? And what he didn't have himself he went out
and hunted up for me. Last night, now, after I met you
at the p-p-post office, Cap'n, him and me went up to
John Bangs' and bought a bedroom set for forty-two dollars that Mr. Griggs says couldn't be duplicated for less'n

a hundred and eighteen. Solid black walnut, 'tis, same as
Aunt Sarah had in her spare room, and the only way
you'd know 'twan't brand-new is that one of the cut-out
bunches of grapes on the bow end of the bedstead is
nicked s-s-some and there's a leetle mite of a crack in
the m-m-marble top of the commode. Balaam Griggs
says that ain't nothin'; he says he can show me grave-
stones right here in the Trumet cemetery that are cracked
more'n that commode, and in the b-b-best lots, too."

Captain Newcomb laughed aloud. "You couldn't ask
anything better'n that, Obadiah," he said. "Where is
that set? Has it come down yet?"

"No, but I expect it 'most any time. Balaam's gone
up with his team to get it. He helped me out there, too.
He says 'twould cost me two dollars to hire a horse and
truck wagon at the livery stable and he'll take his horse
and borrow a wagon and 'twon't cost me but a dollar and
a half. That's the kind of friend to have, ain't it, Cap'n
Noah? I tell you I'm thankful I run afoul of him the
way I did. I only wisht you knew him better."

"Humph! I'm beginnin' to wish I did, myself. I
stopped at his house just now to ask the way here. That
daughter of his is a mighty pretty and nice-appearin'
girl."

"She ain't his real daughter. She's the daughter of his
second wife; her name's Mary Barstow. I'm afraid she's
a kind of trial to him."

"So? She don't look it. I could find a schooner load
of men in an hour that would be glad to take the trial off
his hands, I shouldn't wonder. What's the matter with
her?"

"Oh, nothin' special, I cal'late, only she's kind of spiled and sot in her ways, I judge. Mr. Griggs don't want young fellers hangin' around her yet awhile. She's too young for that, he thinks."

"He does, eh? I don't believe he'd want to leave that question to a referee. She's twenty-one, ain't she?"

"Just about, I cal'late. That young cold-storage engineer, Clifford his name is, would like to keep company with her now, I cal'late if her pa would let him."

"So? Irving Clifford, the young chap that has rooms at the Mansion House? I've met him."

"That's the one. Mr. Balaam he says he's afraid that young man ain't much account."

"Humph; I want to know! I liked what I'd seen of him first-rate. Your friend Balaam must be particular. Well, Obe, tell me a little more about yourself. Made any plans about what you're goin' to do down here, have you?"

Obadiah crossed his knees. "Well," he said, with a self-satisfied smirk, "I don't know's I'm goin' to do anything 'special. I cal'late I'm as well f-f-fixed as ever I want to be; enough sight more'n I ever *expected* to be, I know that. Nice house and land, p-p-plenty of money, and my health. What more do I want?"

"Yes, I know. You've got enough to keep you—if you keep *it*. Who's goin' to take care of your house for you?"

"Cal'latin' to do it myself. May have a woman come in once a week or so to do the scrubbin' up. Mr. Griggs he thinks that would be a good idea. He cal'lates he can coax this same woman, this Hedge one, to do it for a spell."

"Um-hm, I see. He'll do the hirin' as well as the coaxin', I presume likely, won't he?"

"Yes. He saves me a lot of trouble. I don't know how I'll ever pay him back."

"I wouldn't worry about that—much. Is this twelve thousand of yours pretty well invested, Obadiah?"

"Six per cent. Seven hundred and twenty a year I get out of it. Gosh t' mighty! I've *worked* many's the year for enough sight less'n that. And now I just set down and they come and hand it t-t-to me, as you might say."

"Yes. Well, you take my advice and let 'em keep on handin' it. Don't get ambitious and help yourself to more out of the principal. And don't let anybody talk you into doin' it, either."

"Oh, I shan't. I wouldn't touch that principal for nothin'—that is, except to buy a little furniture for the house, you know; I had t-t-to do that, of course. No, I'm goin' to be savin' as ever I was, Cap'n Noah; don't you worry about me. But s-s-s-some day I'm goin' to travel. A sea-cook don't get no chance t-t-to see nothin' of the world except the wet places in it, and I mean to go everywhere—Niagary and M-M-Mum-Mammoth Cave and White Mountains and Syracuse, New York."

"Syracuse? What in the nation do you want to go to Syracuse for?"

"Cause I've heard so much about it; what an elegant p-p-place 'twas and all. After I left you, Cap'n Noah, I sailed along of a second mate that hailed from Syracuse and he was always talkin' about what a fust-class t-t-town 'twas. Always goin' b-b-back there end of every cruise, he was. I guess likely he would only he spent all his money for rum and p-p-pup-police fines and never had enough left to pay fare. He—why, you ain't goin', be you, Cap'n? Don't go. I was kind of hopin' you'd give up the hotel and come down and visit long with me for a spell."

"I'd like to, Obe, but I can't just now. I may have to go over to South Trumet this afternoon and see how the Commodore's gettin' on with that automobile of mine. But I'll see you again afore I go. Yes, I promise that. . . . Hello! here comes your self-sacrificin' friend with the new second-hand bedroom set. Is that the horse he rented to you for a dollar and a half? Why didn't you pay him a dollar more and buy the critter?"

"Eh? B-b-*buy* him? Wh-what kind of talk's that? You can't buy a horse for t-t-two dollars and a half? N-n-not unless it's a dead one."

"Can't you? Well, maybe you're right, Obe. And that one ain't much more'n half dead, is he? Well, so long. Hello, Mr. Griggs! Good mornin'!"

The Griggs welcome was effusive. Balaam had had the opportunity to talk with Mr. Burgess concerning the latter's nautical friend, and Obadiah had spoken largely of the friend's wisdom and ability and wealth and influential connections. The wealth was largely imaginary, but this Mr. Griggs did not know.

"How do you do, Cap'n Newcomb, sir?" he cried, his tone and handshake exuding cordiality. "How do you do, sir? Been lookin' over Mr. Burgess' property, have you? *Some* property, I call it, sir—*some* property."

"Yes, seems to be; some property and the rest sand. Good day, Mr. Griggs. So long, Obe; see you later."

On the way out of the yard he paused for a moment to inspect the "solid walnut bedroom set" which Obadiah had been able to purchase, through the help of his agent, at such a bargain. Whatever he thought of the bargain, he said nothing. Mr. Burgess, himself, came running from the house.

"Gosh!" he panted, "I 'most forgot. Have another 'Liberty Maid' to smoke on your way along. Light right up. I b-b-brought the matches."

Captain Noah appeared to hesitate momentarily. Then he took the proffered cigar, bit off the end, lighted the other end, and with a "Thanks, Obe," strode up the road, puffing like a tugboat. The puffing continued until he was out of sight from the house. Then he tossed the "Liberty Maid" into a ditch, made a face, and walked on. It was evident, from his preoccupied manner, that he was thinking deeply and that his thoughts troubled him a bit.

He did not, of course, go to South Trumet and the garage that afternoon, but that evening he did telephone to his proverb-quoting acquaintance, the "Commodore," and learned with satisfaction that the needed "parts" had arrived on the night train. The car would be ready two days later, as promised.

CHAPTER V

H E spent the next day and a half in wandering about Trumet. At Irving Clifford's urgent invitation he accompanied the latter to the scene of his labors, the half-completed cold-storage warehouse. Clifford took him over the big building, explained where the engines were to be placed, how the ammonia pipes were set and arranged, and described quite thoroughly the equipment and the process used in freezing fish. The captain was much interested.

"Humph!" he grunted, musingly. "Just freeze 'em and keep 'em forever and ever, amen; eh?"

"Pretty nearly that, Captain."

"Yes, I presume likely now if I should drift into one of these rooms after you got her started and laid down and went to sleep I'd freeze up same as a herrin', eh?"

"Much the same, I imagine."

"Sho! And, if nobody disturbed me for a hundred year or so, my great-grandchildren, if I had any, could step in any time and see what the old man looked like. That's a queer thing to think about, ain't it?"

"Ha, ha! Yes, it certainly is."

"Um-hm. Say, son, I believe I've met and talked with

64

folks that have had somethin' like that happen to 'em. They must have been froze for a couple of generations and only just woke up. That would explain why they're walkin' around here in nineteen hundred and so on and thinkin' and reasonin' back in eighteen hundred and forty. I've always wondered why it was, and now I know, they've been in cold-storage. It's a great comfort to strike on a satisfyin' explanation, ain't it?"

Clifford, much amused, said it certainly was.

"*I* bet you! I've been to more'n one church in my time and had to listen to a cold-storage sermon."

He and Clifford spent the evenings together. The engineer enjoyed his new friend's society and wished he were going to stay longer. Congenial male friends the young man had found rather scarce in Trumet and, although he had known Noah Newcomb so short a time, he liked him. There was a marked difference in their ages, Clifford not yet thirty and the captain just past the half-century mark, but so far as spirit was concerned one was not more youthful than the other. And if there were any physical deterioration in the big frame of the older man, no evidences were visible. They had occasion to row across the bay on the morning of the third day and Captain Noah insisted on handling the oars. There was a strong head tide, but when they reached the wharf at the other side the captain's breathing was as full and regular as when they started.

He asked a good many questions concerning people and village affairs, but he asked none concerning Balaam Griggs or his stepdaughter. None of Clifford, that is, but at the Mansion House Captain Zeke Penniman and

EXTRICATING OBADIAH

Uncle Labe Bassett were systematically "pumped," although they themselves were quite unconscious of the process. One item picked up from Mr. Bearse, the fish peddler, was also of interest. Captain Noah had led the conversation to the subject of "antiques." Peleg waxed sarcastic and profane.

"I ain't got no patience with the whole d——n foolishness!" he declared. "If I had my way I'd have the law onto it; I'd put a stop to it some way. The way them summer folks spend money on—on old busted crockery and chairs with the shakin' palsy is sinful—yes, sir, sinful! Why, I had a old blue platter that my wife used to keep soap fat in out in the woodshed. Bale Griggs he see it one day and he says, 'That's a good-sized platter, ain't it,' he says. 'I been wantin' a platter like that to feed my hens on.' 'To feed your *hens* on!' I sung out. 'Do you feed your hens on Chiny dishes, for the Lord sakes?' 'I don't mean my hens, my big hens,' says he. 'I mean my little chickens; I've got slathers of little chickens this spring. Want to sell that old platter, do you?' 'I don't know's I do,' says I. 'It's kind of handy to have round. What'll you give for it?' 'Oh,' he says, 'I don't know's I ain't crazy to give anything for the old thing, but maybe I'd give twenty cents or a quarter, maybe.' Well, we haggled around some and finally I let it go for forty cents, figgered I was in about thirty-eight and a half cents at that. And a month later, by godfreys! just one month later, blessed if he didn't sell that same platter to a Chicago loon that was stoppin' down at the big hotel, for twelve dollars. Twelve—*dollars!* My godfreys! Wan't that a crime? Wouldn't you think he'd have been ashamed? Eh, Cap'n Newcomb, now wouldn't you?"

"Yes."

"So would I. And what makes me so mad is that I knew that Chicago man just as well as he did and, more'n likely, I could have sold the platter for twelve dollars to that same feller—if I'd only known he or anybody else would have paid it. But Balaam Griggs knew all right. You bet *he* knew!

"He's always snoopin' round buyin' things to sell again," went on the irate Peleg. "Why, I see John Bangs day afore yesterday and he told me he was cal'latin' to sell Balaam a black walnut bedroom set he had up garret. Said Bale had offered him twelve-fifty for it, but he was holdin' out for fifteen. Yesterday mornin' I see Balaam drivin' down along with a bedstead and a bureau and commode in his cart, so I cal'late him and John made a dicker. I'll bet you Griggs sticks some poor trustin' idiot twenty dollars or more for that same set."

Captain Noah rubbed his chin.

"I shouldn't wonder," he said, slowly. "I shouldn't wonder a bit—and then some."

But neither of this nor of other information gathered from the regular boarders at the Mansion House did the captain speak during his next call upon Mr. Burgess. It was a short call; he had received word from the garage that his car was ready, and that afternoon he was to start —to *start*, he emphasized the word strongly when stating his intention to Clifford—for Boston in it. And in accordance with his promise, he came once more before leaving to the old house cn the hill.

67

Obadiah and he shook hands and said good-by at the gate.

"Well, Cap'n Noah," said the little man, "I'm awful glad I had the chance to see you this much, but I'm awful sorry you can't stay longer. If you'd only stay and make a little visit along with me I'd be tickled. But I've asked you and asked you and you keep on sayin' you won't."

The captain shook his head. "You're wrong, Obadiah," he answered; "I keep on sayin' I can't—not this time. But I tell you, some of these days I'm comin' back to Trumet again, and when I do maybe I'll make that little visit you've said so much about."

"Well, I hope you will, but I don't know. A busy man as you are ain't likely to find much in Trumet to interest him."

"Oh, I don't know. I can see one or two things developin' here now that are liable to be pretty interestin' afore they finish. I cal'late you'll see me, Obe; sooner'n you expect, maybe. And now let me tell you this: There's my address on that card I gave you. A letter or a telegram or anything sent to me there will reach me sooner or later. If ever you need me, Obe—that is to say, if you're in trouble or in a tight place and don't know how to get out, if you want help or advice or anything— why, don't you hesitate to send for me. Don't you hesitate a minute. If I'm on top of this earth anywheres I'll come."

The ex-cook looked up into his former skipper's face with the old expression of doglike regard and reverence.

"That's awful kind of you, Cap'n," he said; "it is so. I thank you a thousand times. But 'tain't likely I shall need any of them things. Looks to me as if I wan't liable to get into any trouble; way I figger I'm out of it for k-k-keeps and 'twill be smooth sailin' for me to the end of the v'yage."

"I know, but you can't always tell, Obe. Sometimes there are rocks and shoals that ain't down on the chart. Remember now, if you want me just give me a hail. Promise."

"Land yes, I'll promise, Cap'n Noah. You're just as good-hearted as you used to be, ain't you. I never could see why you was so good to a little no-account sort of critter like me. I can't see it n-n-now, either."

"Can't you, Obe? Well, maybe you've forgot the time when that same little no-account stuck by me when every other hand afloat or ashore skipped out and left me to fight Yellow Jack alone. I say maybe you've forgotten it, but I ain't—and I ain't likely to. Well, so long, Obe. Good luck and a fair wind. So long."

That afternoon Irving Clifford robbed the cold-storage company of time sufficient to accompany the captain to South Trumet and to ride back as far as the Mansion House in the little car. During the three-mile ride he had given the owner of that car all the advice in his power, advice concerning driving, steering, stopping and even slight repairing. At the walk in front of the hotel he alighted, rather reluctantly it must be confessed.

"I must leave you, Captain Newcomb," he said, "and, to be honest, I hate to do it. I hate to see you start for Boston."

The captain chuckled.

"I know you do," he said. "I can see it in your face.

Well, now, I'm goin' to tell you this, son: I'm not only goin' to start for Boston in this craft, but I'm goin' to get there in her—some time or other. She and I may go in swimmin' together two or three times more, if there's ponds enough handy, but never mind, *when* we get to Portland I'll be boss of the ship. I've handled a ten thousand ton steamboat in my day, and no tin dingey on wheels is goin' to beat me, if I know it. And all this doesn't mean that I ain't more obliged to you than I can tell, Mr. Clifford. I am, and I hope you know it. I'm sorry I can't stop and have you give me more lessons in pilotin', but I can't, haven't the time. Don't you worry about me, though. I'll drop you a line from whatever port I make tonight and so on as I navigate up the coast."

Clifford smiled. "I'm not greatly worried about your safety," he said. "I'm pretty sure you'll get through without trouble. But I do hate to have you leave Trumet. My offer to give you lessons in driving wasn't entirely unselfish, you see. I have enjoyed your society very much and I wanted more of it, that was all. I hate to lose you, Captain."

Captain Noah was plainly much pleased. He leaned from the car and shook the young man's hand.

"Well, now, I'm much obliged to you," he declared, heartily. "And it's the same here and many of 'em. But you ain't got rid of me yet. It's about a hundred to one shot that some of these days you'll see me comin' down here again. Well, it's time to cast off, I cal'late. All ashore that's goin' ashore! So long, son."

The little car buzzed down the main road. It disap-

70

peared, taking a wide sweep around the bend. Clifford, watching it, wondered if he should ever see it or its driver again. He hoped so, certainly. He had meant what he said—he hated to lose Captain Noah Newcomb.

CHAPTER VI

THE following day he received a post card from a town midway between Trumet and Boston. The little car and its driver had reached that point the previous night without, so Captain Noah wrote, "running on the rocks or sinking any of the channel traffic." The captain hoped and expected to make the city before another nightfall. That he had done so, a second post card proved. There came a third, this time from Portland. "Safe, sound and considerable astonished on account of it," wrote Noah. Clifford wrote a note in reply. That ended the correspondence. No more letters came from the Maine metropolis, and in Trumet the engineer's time was, between work and purely personal interests, fully occupied. He did not forget his salty pupil in the art of auto piloting; he thought of him occasionally and wondered where he might be, even resolved to write and find out, but being very busy at the storage plant and somewhat worried by the personal interest just mentioned, his resolutions never became performances. And the winter passed, spring came and went, and summer was at hand.

It was a beautiful June forenoon when the little car

once more appeared on Trumet's main street. And, as on the occasions of its former appearances, Captain Noah Newcomb was at the helm. But now he did not crouch over the wheel, his hands bent in a petrified clutch at its circumference and his eyes glaring at the road just ahead. Indeed, no. The captain leaned back against the upholstery and his clutch upon the wheel was light but confident. He did not glare at the road; he smoked a cigar and looked easily about him. And in the wake left in the dust by the tires of that little car there was not to be discerned one nervous "jiggle." It was plain that Captain Noah had become, as he had sworn to become, "boss of the ship."

He sailed down the main road at a twenty mile an hour clip, and as he passed the platform of the Mansion House he looked hopefully up at it. But the only person visible was Ethelinda, who was dusting the piazza chairs. Her glance was fixed upon the manly beauty of Izzy Thacher, the grocer's boy, who was delivering a basket at Mrs. Copeland's across the street, and she had eyes for no one else. However, the captain paused long enough to hail.

"Hello! Hi!" he shouted. "Is Mr. Clifford on board, do you know, sis?"

Ethelinda heard him, but it suited her to pretend that she did not. The grocer's boy was looking on and Ethelinda felt that she had a dignity to maintain. She went on with her dusting.

"Hi!" shouted the captain again. "Hi, you—er— what's your name—Shindy? Windy? Oh, Lindy; that's it. Say, Lindy, do you know whether Mr. Clifford's inside there or not?"

'Linda, nose in air and conscious that Izzy across the road was grinning broadly, condescended to reply.

"Was you speakin' to me?" she drawled, crushingly.

Captain Noah looked at her with eager interest. "Yes, I was," he said. "You guessed it the very first time. My, but you're a smart girl! Now see if you can guess what I asked you."

Izzy burst into a delighted "Haw, haw!" Ethelinda flounced into the hotel to inform Mrs. Hobbs that that crazy man that was here last fall had come back again and was ravin' worse than ever. The captain, quite unperturbed, turned to Mr. Thacher and asked the latter if he knew where Mr. Clifford might be found.

"Down to the cold-storage, I cal'late," replied Izzy. "He was a spell ago, anyhow, 'cause I see him."

So to the cold-storage plant went the little car, piloted by Captain Newcomb. The plant, now almost ready to open for business, was situated on a point at the mouth of Trumet Bay on the southern shore. Several workmen were busy on the roof of the engine-house extension searching for a leak which had developed during the winter's storm-beating. The captain pulled up in front of the building and alighted.

"Mr. Clifford around?" he asked, hailing the workmen on the roof.

"Don't know," was the careless answer. "Ain't seen him lately. Maybe he's inside somewheres."

The captain entered the engine room. The engines were in place now and the room seemed ready for occupancy. Even the big fire hose connected with the pressure tank hung coiled on the wall. There was no sign of Clifford, however, and Captain Noah, after a look around, emerged from the building to find another visitor standing by his automobile and regarding it with an expression of amused condescension.

This visitor was evidently not a Trumet "native." In fact, he looked as much out of place down there on the beach amid the bundles of seaweed rolled in by the winter tides, the clam shells and the defunct "horsefoot" crabs, to say nothing of the shavings and chips and builders' débris, as an orchid might have looked in a potato patch. He was a rather undersized, slim person, with a closely trimmed, waxed mustache, a fancy waistcoat, spats and a bamboo walking-stick. He was smoking a cigarette in a meerschaum holder. As Captain Noah approached he languidly lifted one gaitered foot to the hub of the auto's wheel and tapped the radiator with his cane.

"Who owns this—er—Panhard?" he asked, addressing the workmen on the roof. "Clifford hasn't been going in for jewelry, has he?"

One of the workmen replied. It was the same fellow who had answered the captain's inquiry, and now, as he spoke, he was unaware that the captain himself was standing in the doorway beneath him. "No, 'tain't Clifford's," he said. "Belongs to a feller that came here lookin' for him. Some flivver, ain't it, Mr. Wentworth? Got her dolled up regardless, ain't he?"

The slim gentleman deigned to smile. "Rather," he admitted, and tapped the radiator again.

Now the glistening varnish on that car was the pride of its owner's heart. During the trying period of his initiation into the science of driving it had received some severe scratches and humps, but these scars had all been covered, the nickel was polished each morning and no mud was permitted to cake upon the wheels. Various improvements the captain had added during the winter—electric lights, a self-starter and a clock were some of these. And now to see this lofty stranger carelessly thumping upon the hood, upon the polished shirt-front, so to speak, of his pet was a little too much. Captain Noah uttered a mild protest.

"Excuse me, Mister," he said, coming forward, "but perhaps you wouldn't mind hittin' not quite so hard. That paint on there's kind of 'fresh—I had her revarnished a little spell ago—and so I— Well, you see, I'm kind of fussy. Excuse me, won't you?"

The stranger turned and looked him over. So far as consideration for the captain's feelings went he might have been inspecting a wooden image.

"You see," went on the latter, "I—I—er—well, perhaps you'll think I'm too particular about that car, but —er——"

The slim person interrupted. "Where's Clifford?" he demanded, addressing the workmen on the roof.

"I don't know, Mr. Wentworth. Ain't he inside? I thought he was. He," pointing to Noah, "was in there just now lookin' for him. Did you find him, Mister?"

"No, didn't seem to be there. Hi! Whose dog's this?"

A brindle bull terrier had suddenly made his appearance and was sniffing hungrily at the captain's ankles.

"Hi! get out!" commanded Noah, uneasily. "Say, whose dog is this, anyhow?"

The person addressed as Mr. Wentworth smiled slightly. The captain's uneasiness appeared to amuse him.

"He's mine, I believe," he drawled.

"He is, eh? Well, does he bite?"

"Sometimes."

"I want to know! Well, do you cal'late he'll bite *me?*"

"I hope not, but you can't always tell. Sometimes he isn't very particular."

A smothered giggle came from the roof. Captain Noah, glancing up, saw that the workmen had stopped hammering and were enjoying the tableau below.

"Call the critter off," he commanded, sharply. Mr. Wentworth languidly snapped his fingers.

"Here, Sport!" he said. The dog left off sniffing at the captain's ankles and trotted to his master, wagging an abbreviated tail. Noah smiled, apologetically. "Always makes me nervous to have a strange dog smellin' around my legs," he observed. " 'Tain't likely he meant anything, you know, but—er— What kind of a dog is he? What you might call a watchdog, eh?"

Mr. Wentworth smiled again. His was a queer smile, a lazy smile, a sort of tired smile, which lifted one corner of his mouth but did not disturb the rest of his countenance. The countenance as a whole looked tired also; it was pouched a bit under the eyes and lined from the nostril to the corner of the jaw; a sophisticated, weary sort of face, one which looked as if it might have seen a great deal of life—some kinds of life.

"Why, yes," drawled Mr. Wentworth, "I presume you might call him that—if you cared to. He's a pretty good watcher, at that. If I told him to watch anything I rather think he'd watch it."

"You don't say!"

"Yes, I do. For instance." He strolled over and rapped the step of the automobile with his cane.

"Guard, Sport," he said. Sport trotted over to the car and sat down by the step.

"Guard," said Mr. Wentworth again. Then he turned on his heel and walked to the corner of the building, where, pausing for an instant, he looked up at the group on the roof and dropped his left eyelid significantly. Then, whistling a popular melody and cutting the tops of the beachgrass clumps with his cane, he turned the corner and disappeared.

Captain Noah did not see the wink at the corner; in fact, he did not notice the disappearance. The promptness with which the dog had obeyed pleased him and he was regarding the animal with a growing respect.

"Sho!" he exclaimed. "Takes orders like a second mate, don't he? I declare, he's more of a dog than I thought he was. Had him quite a spell, have you, Mister?" Then, hearing no reply, he turned. "Why, where's he gone to?" he demanded.

The talkative workman answered. "Gone to hunt up Mr. Clifford, I guess likely," he said.

"Sho! Why, I told him Mr. Clifford wasn't there."

He ran over to the corner and called: "Hi, Mr.—What's-your-name—Mr. Wentworth!" But Mr. Wentworth was out of sight and, apparently, out of hearing. So he returned to the front again.

"Say," he said, addressing the group on the roof, "I can't wait any longer. If Mr. Clifford comes back afore dinner time tell him Cap'n Newcomb, Cap'n Noah Newcomb, was here and will see him at the hotel. Get the name straight, now—Noah Newcomb. He'll remember, I cal'late. I— Here, you dog, get out of my way, will you?"

But the dog seemed to have no idea whatever of getting out of his way. As the captain approached the car the animal stood in front of him. The captain stepped to one side and the dog stepped likewise. Captain Noah raised his foot to put it upon the auto's step. The dog raised his head and opened his mouth, displaying a beautiful set of teeth.

"Why, what ails the critter?" demanded Noah. "Hey, you, Sport! Clear out, will you?"

Sport's answer was a further display of teeth. From behind the teeth came a menacing rumble, like the sound of moving something heavy in a cellar.

"Well, I swan to man!" exclaimed the captain. "I do believe he ain't goin' to let me get in my own car. Here, Mr.——"

He had turned and had raised his voice, intending to summon the dog's owner. But just then another giggle came from the roof. And that giggle brought enlightenment to his mind.

Wentworth had ordered the dog to "guard" the car.

79

After giving that order he had walked away. The dog was guarding the car. The group of workmen on the roof had stopped working and were watching. Nine chances out of ten Wentworth also was watching somewhere. The joke was on him, Noah Newcomb, and they were watching to see the fun.

Captain Noah looked at Sport and rubbed his chin. Sport showed his teeth and growled. Another giggle sounded above.

For perhaps a minute the captain stood there seeking ways and means. He could go into the building, find Wentworth and make the latter call off his dog—that he could do, of course; and, also, he inwardly vowed, that he would *not* do. Slowly he rubbed his chin.

Then, suddenly turning, he walked to the open door of the engine room and entered. When he came out he was holding the nozzle of the fire hose in his hands and the hose itself was unwinding from the reel as he walked. He walked on until the hose was unwound its entire length. Then he laid the nozzle upon the ground and turned again toward the door of the engine house. The group on the roof had watched this performance with astonished interest.

"Hi!" cried one, the one who had done all the talking. "Hi, Mister, what are you goin' to do with that hose?"

Captain Noah, who was humming a hymn, looked up.

"I was just noticin' how dusty my auto'd got this mornin'," he cried. "Cal'late I'll wash off a little of it; 'twon't do any harm."

He walked into the engine house, humming. "Land ahead, its fruits are wavin'."

A moment later the water spurted from the nozzle of the hose, tearing a hole in the sand and sending the pebbles flying. The captain reappeared. Stooping, he picked up the nozzle; the force of water was so great that he was obliged to hold on with all his strength.

"'Drop the anchor, furl the sail,'" hummed Captain Noah. He turned the stream of water in the direction of his car. It struck the road just behind the rear wheels. The flying mud and spray spattered about Sport's clipped ears. The dog closed his mouth and swallowed uneasily; nevertheless, he still maintained his position.

"'Drop the anchor, furl the sail,'" sang the captain. The stream of water from the hose moved close to the rear tires.

Then a window on the second story of the cold-storage building was thrown up and a voice called:

"Here! What are you doing?"

Captain Noah did not appear to hear. He sang on: "'We are safe within the vail.'"

"Here! D——nation! What are you doing? Don't turn that hose on my dog. You'll kill him."

The captain turned his head. "Eh?" he queried. "Who's that? Oh, it's you, Mr. What's-your-name. Yes, yes. Been lookin' over the plant, have you? Interestin' kind of place, ain't it?"

Mr. Wentworth's usually placid countenance was now anything but that.

"What the devil are you doing?" he demanded. "Do you want to kill my dog?"

"Kill your dog? What dog?"

"What dog! Why, my dog there. Haven't you got any sense? If that water hits him there's force enough to kill him."

"Oh, no, no! I guess not. I was just cal'latin' to wash my car. He'd get out of the way afore the water hit him. You just watch now and see if he wouldn't."

"*Stop!* Don't point it at him."

"Well, just as you say. Better call him off, then, hadn't you? He's right in the way and accidents do happen, sometimes."

Someone on the roof burst into a roar of laughter. Mr. Wentworth looked as if he would have enjoyed murdering a certain individual. The captain, serenely innocent and unconscious, began another hymn.

" 'These are they that have come out of great tribulation.' "

"Sport," ordered Wentworth, "come here."

Sport, who had been eyeing the hose with sidelong glances, needed no second command. He left his sentry post before the auto's step and dashed over beneath the window from which his master leaned.

"Come here, you fool!" shouted Wentworth. The dog ran around the corner of the building. Captain Noah sighed.

"After all," he said aloud, "I don't know's 'tain't kind of foolish for me to wash this car. Might just as well have it done at the garage."

He tossed the streaming nozzle from him, climbed into the car and pressed the starting button.

"Just shut that water off, one of you, please," he said, "when you get time. Don't forget to tell Mr. Clifford I was here. Good mornin'. Mornin', Mr. Wentworth."

During the ride up to the village he chuckled more than once. When he entered the front hall of the Mansion House he was still chuckling. Mrs. Hobbs, in spite of Ethelinda's unflattering opinion of the captain's sanity, was glad to see him.

"Real glad to have you back, Cap'n Newcomb," she said. "Are you goin' to stay with us for a spell? Would you like your old room? It's empty."

Captain Noah replied that he didn't know how long he should stay. "Maybe quite a spell, maybe only this afternoon," he said. "If, with that understandin', you'd be willin' to give me a room I'd like to have it fust-rate. Where's Mr. Clifford; is he 'round?"

It developed that Mr. Clifford had left the hotel only a few minutes before Captain Newcomb's arrival. He had been down at the cold-storage plant in the morning, as usual, but had come back unexpectedly, asked for and eaten an early luncheon, and had taken the eleven o'clock train—for Provincetown, Mrs. Hobbs believed.

The captain was disappointed; he had wished to see Clifford. However, as he could not see him until evening, he decided to make the best of it and asked to be shown to his room.

"You tell 'em to leave my car right out front here," he said. "I'll most likely be usin' it again pretty soon."

EXTRICATING OBADIAH

Alone in his room, he took from his pocket a crumpled envelope containing a letter. Adjusting his spectacles he read the letter for the fourth or fifth time.

CAPTAIN NOAH NEWCOMB.

DEAR FRIEND: I take my Pen in hand hoping these **few** Lines will find you the same. When you was Here **you** said if I neded you to Write. I don't know wether I **nede** you or not but sometimes seems as if I did. I have got some things on my Mind. I would like to of had a Chance to talk to you if you was Here but I guess likely **you** are to Busy to come. So I shant ask you. I Hope **you** are first rate as to Helth. I am to. We dident have much Snow here this Winter and the spring is coming in Good.

Yours truly,

OBADIAH B. BURGESS.

The letter was dated six weeks previously. After reading it he sat for a moment in thought, then, shaking his head as one who gives up trying to guess a conundrum, he put it back in his pocket, and, shortly afterward, went down to luncheon. Again he regretted Irving Clifford's absence. Before calling upon his former cook the captain had hoped, by asking some judicious questions, to learn a little of what had transpired at the "Badscom place" during his absence. By getting an outside opinion concerning these happenings and then hearing Obadiah's own story of them Captain Noah believed he might be in a better position to judge that which Mr. Burgess himself seemed unable to decide—namely, whether or not the latter needed his friend's counsel and help. And the captain, having some knowledge of character, believed Irving Clifford's opinion would have been the best obtainable. He had a mind to wait for that opinion, even if waiting entailed delaying his call upon Obadiah until the following morning.

CHAPTER VII

BUT before luncheon was over he changed his mind. The only one of the regular boarders present at that meal was Mr. Laban Bassett. A conversation between Ethelinda and "Uncle Labe" attracted the captain's attention.

"I see Joe Kenney goin' down street a spell ago, Mr. Bassett," said Ethelinda. "He had his paintin' tools with him. Guess likely he's goin' to make another picture of somebody's cow or somethin'. He, he!"

Uncle Labe sniffed disgust.

"Pesky foolishness!" he declared. "If I was his aunt I wouldn't let him waste his time that way. If he wants to paint why don't he paint houses or whitewash fences or somethin'? There'd be some sense to *that*."

Ethelinda tossed her head. Her opinion of art and artists was much like Mr. Bassett's, but she liked to tease the old man.

"Oh, I don't know," she said; "some of the things Joe Kenney paints are awful pretty. I saw a picture of the bay that he done t'other day and 'twas fine. So bright and gay, sort of. Hang one of them pictures up on the wall and you couldn't look at nothin' else."

"Humph! I cal'late you couldn't; lookin' at that would put your eyes out. And as for the crayon enlargements he does—my soul! Did you see the one he done of Obadiah Burgess himself? Well, I did. Frank Hammond had it down in his store, puttin' a frame onto it. Didn't look no more like Burgess than—than a monkey does—or I do—or anything. A sight, I called it. And why Mr. Burgess lets him live there everybody says is a mystery. Great hulkin' feller like him. I hear he don't pay a cent of board."

"Why should he? He's Mrs. Mayo's nephew, and they tell me he's lived with her ever since his ma died. So when she came to live along of Mr. Burgess and keep house for him 'twas natural enough for Joe to come, too. Seems that way to me, anyhow."

"Well, what did Obadiah Burgess need a housekeeper for, anyway? Wan't nobody to housekeep for but just he, himself."

Before Ethelinda could reply Captain Noah asked a question.

"What Burgess is this you're talkin' about?" he asked. "The one that had the—what do you call it?—Badscom place left him?"

"That's the one. Know him, do you, Cap'n?"

"Yes, pretty well. You say he's got a housekeeper? A reg'lar one, that stays there all the time?"

"Sartin. And her nephew, Joe Kenney, stays there, too."

"What sort of woman is she? Come from round here, did she?"

"No; somebody Balaam Griggs fetched from down

Cape Ann way. She's some relation of Balaam's, they tell me. As for the sort of woman she is—well, she seems to be a good enough sort. I never heard nothin' against her, as I know of."

"She's real sort of good-lookin', I think," put in Ethelinda. " 'Course she's old——"

"She ain't neither," interrupted Uncle Labe. "Ain't more'n forty, I bet you."

"*Forty!* Well, ain't that old, for mercy sakes?"

"*Old!* Is the gal crazy? I'm sev— Well, I'm more'n forty, and I don't call myself old yet."

"How long has Obe—Mr. Burgess, I mean—had this housekeeper woman there?" asked the captain, who was not particularly interested in the age question. Ethelinda answered.

"Oh, most two months now," she said. "Folks don't know but he may be cal'latin' to marry her; good many rich folks do marry their housekeepers, you know. And they say Mr. Burgess has got lots of money."

Captain Noah somehow seemed not to like this remark. "Humph!" he grunted, and frowned.

"She and that Joe Kenney nephew of hers came to Burgess's just afore Mr. Wentworth did," went on Uncle Labe. "When Burgess told Balaam that Mr. Wentworth was comin' to live with him——"

"*Who* was comin'?" The captain turned in his chair. "Who was comin' to live with Obe Burgess?" he demanded.

"Why, Mr. Wentworth, Mr. Calvin Wentworth, of New York. He's some sort of relation—cousin or somethin' of Obadiah's, seems so. Seems he's been ailin' for a long spell and the doctors said Fifth Avenue and the like of that would be the death of him if he stayed there and he'd have to go to the country. So——"

"So he came," finished Ethelinda, evidently greatly excited at the mention of the Wentworth name. "Mr. Griggs says he's awful rich and he's goin' to leave everything to Mr. Burgess when he dies—and he's liable to die 'most any time. I heard him tell Mis' Hobbs he was expectin' it any minute. And——"

"What sort of a lookin' feller is he?" interrupted Noah.

"Oh, he's an awful fine man. He's just my idea of a gentleman, same as you read about in books. He's got a mustache just like that 'Count Somebody-or-other' that was in the movin' pitchers last week. And he talks so sort of slow and—and—and proud, as you might say. And he 'most generally carries a cane; and——"

"Heave to a minute. Does he own a dog; a kind of pepper-and-salt critter, with a jaw like a muskrat trap?"

"He's got a full-breeded Boston bull terrier. Its name is Sport. I just love that dog."

"Humph! so do I. And this Wentworth man is livin' at Obe Burgess'; *livin'* there for keeps?"

"Um-hm. . . . Why, where you goin'? You ain't through, are you? You ain't had your pie yet."

But Captain Noah did not wait for pie. He strode out of the room. A few minutes later he was on his way to the Badscom place.

The house and its surroundings were much improved since he saw them last. The missing shingles had been replaced, the loose blinds rehung and the house and out-

buildings whitewashed. The fence had its full comple-
ment of pickets and it, too, was spotlessly white. The
captain entered the front gate and walked around to the
side door. Being a Cape Codder by birth and early
breeding, he had an instinctive repugnance to front
doors.

The door was opened, in answer to his knock, by a
woman. She was a rather plump, matronly sort of
woman, plainly dressed and wearing a white apron. The
apron was spotlessly clean. She looked the captain over
and waited for him to speak.

"Good afternoon, ma'am," he said. "This is where
Mr. Burgess lives, ain't it?"

He knew it was, of course, but the intentness of the
woman's gaze disconcerted him the least bit, which was
unusual, for, generally speaking, it took a good deal to
disconcert Captain Noah Newcomb.

The woman nodded.

"Yes," she said; "Mr. Burgess lives here."

Captain Noah waited for her to say whether or not
Obadiah was in. As she did not, nor in fact anything
more, he was obliged to ask.

"Is—er—is he to home?" he inquired.

"No."

"Sho! Liable to be gone long, do you think, ma'am?"

"I can't tell you. He didn't say how long he'd be
gone."

The captain shifted his feet uneasily. He was getting
replies to his questions, but he was not getting anything
more. On the whole, he felt inclined to give it up for
the present.

"Humph! Well, all right, ma'am," he said, turning away. "I'll see him later, I presume likely."

The woman still looked at him intently. She seemed to be inwardly debating some question or other. He had taken perhaps three steps toward the corner when she spoke again.

"Just a minute, if you don't mind," she said. "Of course this isn't really any of my affairs, but Mr. Burgess asked my opinion about it and I gave it to him. To be real up and down honest, I think he's gone out so as not to see you when you came."

Captain Noah stared at her in amazement.

"Gone out?" he repeated. "He's gone out so as not to see—*me?*"

"Yes. He didn't say so, but I imagine that's it. He has made up his mind not to take it."

"Not to *take* it? Take what?"

"Why, the land—the property, whatever it is you've got. He says he told you he'd got all the property he wanted, says he told you that at the very beginnin'. I suppose it's a part of your business to keep on tryin', but, honest, it does put me out of patience sometimes to see how you people pester and torment the poor man. Between agents and peddlers and promoters and——"

"Now—now—now," broke in the captain, incoherent in his astonishment. "Now—now—hold on a minute, ma'am, if you'll just please. I ain't a peddler. I ain't got any land to sell. I'm an old friend of Obadiah's and I've come here to see him, that's all. That's all, I give you my word."

7   91

Her gaze was just as intent as ever, but there was a shade of doubt in her voice when she spoke.

"Ain't you the man from the Indian Hill Development Company over at Mashpee?" she asked.

"Not guilty. Never heard of the—what is it? Injun Hill crowd—in my life. I'm an old shipmate of Mr. Burgess'. He used to sail cook for me one time. My name's Newcomb—Noah Newcomb—and——"

But now the woman interrupted him. Her expression changed entirely.

"Not Cap'n Noah Newcomb of Portland?" she cried.

"That's the one, ma'am."

"Mercy on us! And I've been talkin' to you as if I'd caught you breakin' into the henhouse! I don't know *what* you must think of me. Come right in, Cap'n Newcomb. I'm sure Mr. Burgess'll be back pretty soon. Yes, come right in and wait. I'm Mrs. Mayo, the housekeeper. Dear! dear! and how I did talk to you!"

Two minutes later the captain was seated in the rocker in the Burgess sitting room. Mrs. Mayo, the housekeeper, was still apologizing.

"I ought to have known, I suppose," she said, "but maybe I had a little mite of excuse. I hope I did, anyhow. You've no idea, Cap'n Newcomb, how Mr. Burgess is plagued and pestered by people who want him to buy somethin' or take shares in somethin', or subscribe to somethin'. You've no idea of it, you can't have."

Captain Noah nodded.

"I can imagine it," he said. "Where the carcass is the—er—er—dogfish are gathered together. I don't know's 'dogfish' is the right word, exactly, but maybe you understand what I mean, ma'am."

There was just a hint of extra emphasis in the last sentence, but the housekeeper did not seem to notice it.

"Yes, I know what you mean," she said. "The papers here on the Cape have had a lot to say about Mr. Burgess fallin' heir to this place and a lot of money, and consequently there's a perfect swarm of those 'dogfish,' as you call 'em, schoolin' around the poor man about every minute of the day. If Mr. Burgess would only say no once in a while—if he'd only put his foot down and keep it down—but I'm afraid he don't know how to do that very well. It's so easy to take advantage of him."

"Is it?" asked the captain, innocently. He would like to have added, "Do you find it so?" but he thought it better policy to wait. Besides, this woman puzzled him. She was not the sort of woman he expected to find there, not the sort he would have expected Balaam Griggs to provide. That is, she did not look like that sort of woman. She looked and spoke like a sensible, straightforward New England matron, comfortable, competent, honest and aboveboard. She did not act or appear like a schemer, nor an agent of schemers. Appearances, however, are often deceitful, and the captain, being a bachelor, was especially distrustful of feminine appearances. And there was one point in which Ethelinda was right; Mrs. Mayo was good-looking for her age. This, of itself, was suspicious.

The lady went on. "I hope you won't think I'm talking about Mr. Burgess behind his back," she said. "I don't mean to run him down, that's sartin. He's as

93

good-hearted, well-meanin' a soul as ever I saw in my life. It's because he is so good and kind that I hate to see him taken advantage of and I try to save him from it all I can. Last night he was tellin' me he met a man —this Indian Hill development man—down street somewheres, at the club or the post office or some such place —and the man got after him to buy some land the company had. Mr. Burgess didn't want to buy the land, he didn't want even to hear about it, but the man kept talkin' and talkin' and finally said he'd be around here after dinner today to talk some more. Mr. Burgess was real worried, said he didn't want to see him and how could he get out of it and all that, so I told him I'd help him out. Says I, 'You go and take a walk and when the man comes I'll send him to the right-about-face in a hurry. What's he look like?' Well, he said he was a big man with a beard, and so when you came knockin' at the door, I— Well, I do hope you'll forgive me, Cap'n Newcomb."

"Oh, I'll forgive you, Mrs.—Mrs.——"

"Mayo. Melissa Mayo, my name is."

"Yes, yes, I remember you said 'twas Mayo. So you're keepin' house for Obadiah now; eh, ma'am?"

"Yes. I'm here nearly two months."

"Did you use to live on Cape Cod; after you came here, I mean?"

"No, my home used to be on Cape Ann, down near Pigeon Cove. I lived there when my husband was alive and, after that, with my sister and her boy. She was a widow, too."

"Pigeon Cove. Yes, yes. That's quite a ways off

94

from Trumet. How did you happen to hear of Obadiah's needin' a housekeeper? Used to know him afore, did you?"

For the first time the housekeeper's pleasant, whole-some face clouded. It was but a slight cloud, neverthe-less Captain Noah, who was on the lookout for weather symptoms, noticed it.

"No," she said, "I never knew Mr. Burgess before I came here." She paused, and then added, "I got the position through Mr. Griggs—Mr. Balaam Griggs, here in Trumet. Mr. Griggs is a sort of relation, a second cousin of mine."

"I see, I see. I met this Mr. Griggs last time I was down here. He and Obadiah are great friends, I under-stand."

The cloud upon the housekeeper's face had not lifted.

"Yes," she said, simply, but made no further com-ment. A moment later she added, "Perhaps you'll ex-cuse me now, Cap'n Newcomb. I've got some bakin' in the oven and I presume likely I ought to look at it. Make yourself right at home. Mr. Burgess'll be here in a little while, I'm sure."

Without waiting to receive his permission she left the room. Captain Noah, rising, walked about the apart-ment on a tour of inspection. It was neatness itself, no dust anywhere, windowpanes shiningly transparent, no lint or threads upon the carpet, no crumpled newspapers upon the table, each picture hanging perfectly straight.

Speaking of pictures, there was one which the visitor found interesting. It was a crayon portrait of—of—yes, of Obadiah Burgess himself. The captain decided it must be intended for Obadiah, because he could think of no one else whose likeness it could be. And, besides, there was a sort of far-off resemblance to the ex-cook in the petrified image hemmed in by the ornate gilt frame. If Obadiah had undergone a long, wasting illness and had then slowly and painfully ossified he might look like this, perhaps. The name of the criminal responsible for the outrage was printed in the corner of the canvas and Captain Noah, bending to read, read, "J. Kenney, Trumet." Then he remembered; "J. Kenney" must be "Joe Kenney," the housekeeper's nephew, the young fellow who, so Uncle Labe and Ethelinda had said, was living with his aunt at the Badscom place. Mr. Bassett had spoken of a "crayon enlargement."

He was still looking at the picture when he heard someone enter the room behind him. Turning he faced Mr. Burgess himself. And the Burgess eyes and mouth opened as they had that night at the post office.

"Why—why, Cap'n Noah!" gasped Obadiah.

The captain put out his hand.

"Yes, Obe," he said; "here I am. Told you all you had to do was set the distress signal and I'd get here soon as I could. I'd have been here a month ago only I didn't get your letter. Went down to Porto Rico on a sort of farewell business trip and only been home a fortni't. Had to settle up matters with the old Clay Line and then I came to you. I'm through with 'em for keeps now; retired millionaire, I am, like yourself. Only one thing lackin' to make me so—that's the million. . . . Well, Obe, what's the matter? Ain't you glad to see me?"

EXTRICATING OBADIAH

Mr. Burgess, who had been standing staring at his former skipper, a curious expression on his face, seemed suddenly to wake up. He took the proffered hand and shook it.

"Yes, yes, course I'm glad to see you, Cap'n Noah," he declared. "Course I b-b-be. 'Tain't likely I wouldn't be glad to see you, is it? Sit d-down, won't you?"

Captain Noah grinned.

"Why, yes," he said, "I think maybe I will set down, long as you're so pressin' about it. Considerin' that I've been cruisin' all the way from the State of Maine to see you, I guess likely I'll set a spell after I've got here. Better set down yourself, hadn't you?"

Obadiah, thus urged, sat. His friend looked at him.

"Well, Obe," he said, "you sent for me and I have come, as the feller in the old theater show used to say. What's the matter? What's wrong?"

Mr. Burgess shuffled his feet. "Why—why, Cap'n," he said, "I guess there ain't nothin' wrong. I guess likely there ain't. I'm real glad t-t-to see you, I am so. Goin' t-t-to stay a spell, be you? How's things up to P-P-Portland?"

The captain smiled. "Things up to Portland are up there," he said. "Suppose we don't bother 'em for the present. There's enough down here in Trumet for us to talk about, I should think. Come, come, Obe! you wrote me you needed me. What do you need me for?"

More foot shufflings. Obadiah seemed oddly embarrassed. His friend's questions and scrutiny were evidently making him very uneasy.

"Why—why—why, Cap'n Noah," he said, "I guess I

don't want you for nothin'. That is, I mean I don't
need you. You see—you see——"

"Oh, yes, I see. You don't need me and that's why
you wrote you did. That's about as plain to see as a
flea's eyebrow is to a blind man."

Obadiah's uneasiness increased. "I—I didn't write
you that—that I needed you for sartin," he said. "Course
I'm awful glad to see you, you know that, Cap'n Noah.
'Tain't that I ain't glad to see you, b-b-but—but——"

The captain held up his hand. "Never mind, Obe,"
he said. "Let it stand for a minute. Tell me about
yourself and your doin's here. You've got a housekeeper, I see. Seems like a capable woman. How long
have you had her? Where'd she come from?"

The ex-cook, evidently glad of the opportunity to
evade further questioning concerning his letter, began to
talk volubly of the housekeeper. She was a "real smart"
woman; she was lively as a cricket, there was no shift-
lessness where she was, she could cook——

Captain Noah interrupted.

"I thought you was goin' to do your own cookin',
Obadiah," he said. "And most of your own housework;
that's what you told me the last time I was down here."

Obadiah coughed, cleared his throat, and shuffled his
feet again.

"Well, I was," he said, "but—but, you see, after we
heard— Well, after I got word Calvin was comin',
Balaam he thought we'd need somebody, so——"

"We'd need somebody? Who was 'we'; you and who
else?"

"Why—why, nobody. Just me and—and Balaam, that's all."

"Balaam? Balaam Griggs doesn't *live* here, does he?"

"No—no, he d-d-don't live here, exactly, but—but he comes in so often and helps me out so much that—that seems almost as if he was one of the family. I don't know's you'll understand that, Cap'n Noah, but——"

"Yes, yes, I guess I can understand that much without callin' in the schoolteacher. Who's Calvin?"

"Why, why, he's Calvin Wentworth, my cousin from New York. I guess most likely you ain't heard about him, Cap'n Noah, have you?"

"No, I ain't *heard* much about him, but I saw a little of him this forenoon, unless I'm mistaken. Tell me about him. How did he come here?"

Calvin Wentworth was a third cousin of Obadiah's. His father had made money in some lucky ventures many years before, had moved to New York and made more. He died, reported to be worth a good many thousand dollars, and Calvin was his only heir. Obadiah and he were utter strangers. The lives the two lived were as wide apart as the poles. Calvin was reported to be a New York "swell." Obadiah was a sea-cook.

"Land sakes!" exclaimed Obadiah, "I never thought of seein' him. I'd almost forgot there was such a relation of mine in creation. And then—and then, by godfreys! right out of a clear sk-sk-sky, as you might say, sprouted up this letter of his sayin' he was all alone in the world except me, and his health was 'debilitated'— whatever in time that was—he couldn't live but a year or two longer, anyhow, and he wanted to come d-d-down to Trumet and die on me, so to speak. Did you ever hear such a thing in your life? What did I want anybody d-d-d-dyin' on me for? I wasn't no hospital, was I? No, nor no graveyard, neither.

"Soon's I fetched my breath I took the letter over to Balaam. No, come to think of it, he was here when I got it. He 'most always is here, somehow. The amount of meals I've provided for——"

He stopped, looking rather foolish and startled as if he had said more than he intended. Then he went on with his story.

"I showed the letter to Balaam," he said, "and when he read it he showed me a part, a postage—no, a post-script part that I hadn't read. In the postscript Calvin says he'd made up his mind, he bein' all alone in the world, providin' I let him come and d-d-die on my hands same as he said, to make a will in my favor, leav-in' all he had to me, his only relation and dear cousin.

"Well, sir! somehow or 'nother that postscript made a turrible impression on Balaam. He asked more'n a deck load of questions about how rich I cal'lated Cal-vin was and all. I didn't know how rich he was, but I said thirty or forty thousand anyhow. He ought to be worth that, even if he's b-b-blowed in a thousand every year of the fifteen years since his pa died. 'Then,' says Balaam, all het up and excited, 'you must t-t-take him in and let him die onto you. It'll be dum good business to do it.' 'I won't,' says I, right up and down. 'By god-freys, I won't! S'pose I'm goin' to cook his meals? Didn't I g-g-give up goin' to sea just on purpose not to cook meals for other folks?' 'But he won't last more'n

a year or two, feeble as he is,' says he, 'and then we—
you, I mean—'ll get the thirty thousand. And as for
cookin'—*you* needn't cook. You get a housekeeper and
let her d-d-do it. By time! I'll get one for you. I've
been thinkin' of that very thing. I know just the woman
for you. I'll write her today.'

"I vowed he shouldn't, but he did. And that's how
Mrs. Melissa Mayo came here. She's a relation of his;
you see——"

"Yes, I know; she said she was. She's got a nephew,
I hear. He's livin' here, too, ain't he?"

"Yes, yes. Who told you that? Did she?"

"No. I heard somethin' about it up to the hotel.
What sort of a man is the nephew?"

"He ain't a man, just a boy, that's all. Ain't eighteen
yet."

"What does he do for a livin'? What's he workin'
at?"

"Well—well, he ain't—er—he ain't exactly workin' at
anything, as you m-m-mum-might say. Not just now, he
ain't. He's a-a painter, a hand painter."

"*Hand* painter? What kind of a critter's that?"

"Why, he paints things with his hands, you know."

"With his hands? Don't he use a brush?"

"Course he does. I don't mean that. I mean he—he
hand-paints. You've heard of hand-paintin', Cap't Noah;
hand-painted dishes and such. Like that, he is, only he
d-d-don't paint dishes; he paints folks' faces."

The captain burst into a laugh.

"I always cal'lated that folks who had paint on their
faces generally put it there themselves," he said. "Never

mind, Obe, I guess I know what you mean. He did that,
didn't he?" pointing to the "crayon enlargement" on the
wall.

Mr. Burgess regarded the "enlargement" with com-
placency, not to say pride.

"Yes," he answered, "Joe done that. It's pretty fine,
too, most folks think. Know who 'tis, don't ye, Cap'n?
What do you say to that for a picture, eh?"

Captain Noah regarded the work of art solemnly.
"I wouldn't dare say anything to it, Obe," he answered,
with feeling. "Does—er—this Joe Kenney, whatever
his name is, pay you much board?"

"Board? No. Course he d-d-don't pay board. He's
Melissa's nephew; didn't I tell you?"

"Yes, you told me. . . . Humph! And this other feller—your Cousin Calvin—he don't pay any board either,
does he?"

"No. I told you about his bein' sick and comin' down
here to——"

"Yes, you told me. Balaam Griggs don't pay for the
meals he gets here either, does he?"

"*Pay* for 'em! Why, how you talk, Cap'n! Why
should he pay for 'em? I ain't runnin' a boardin'-house."

"Ain't you? Well, maybe you ain't, Obe, maybe you
ain't. . . . And now do you want to tell me why you
wrote you rather guessed you needed me?"

The troubled look returned to Mr. Burgess' face. He
tried to change the subject.

"Land sakes!" he exclaimed, "I ain't asked you to
have a smoke. What was I thinkin' of? Got a new
box of them Liberty M-M-Maids, Cap'n."

"Keep 'em," ordered Noah, hastily. "I've sworn off smokin'—until after supper—today I have, anyhow. Come, Obadiah, come! What was it you wanted to talk to me about?"

"Why—why, 'twan't nothin', Cap'n. For a spell I—I thought—I thought . . . but 'tain't nothin'. I'm sorry I done it. Course I'm real glad to see you, though," he added, hurriedly.

"Thanks. Did you write me because this Wentworth man was comin'?"

"No."

"Or because the housekeeper and her hand-painted nephew was comin'?"

"No. No, 'twan't nothin', Cap'n Noah, honest!"

"And you're not in trouble at all? Haven't been in any and ain't in any now?"

It took longer for the ex-cook to answer this question. When he did answer it he was looking out of the window, not at the questioner.

"No," he said, after a moment, "there ain't any trouble; I'm all right."

Cap'n Noah rose.

"Well, I'm glad of it," he said, heartily. "I'm real glad of it, Obe. Now I can go back to—er—Boston, or wherever I want to go; and have nothin' to worry about."

Obadiah turned from the window.

"You're goin' away?" he demanded.

"Why, yes. I came down here 'cause I thought you needed me. Now you say you don't need me."

Again Obadiah hesitated. Then he said, "No, I—I—No, of course I don't need you, only——"

He did not finish the sentence, but turned and looked out of the window again. Captain Noah, stepping quietly to a position where he could see the little man's face with the afternoon sunlight upon it, regarded him intently. Then he reached over and laid a hand upon his shoulder.

"Lord love you, Obe," he said, heartily, "what an innocent you are! 'Tain't any fun to fool you, it's too easy. I ain't goin' away. I'm goin' up to the hotel and I'm goin' to stay there over night; but tomorrer mornin' I'm comin' down here bag and baggage. Didn't you ask me over and over again, when I was here last fall, to come and make you a visit? Course you did! Course you did, old man! Well, I've come to do it. That 'goin' away' talk was just foolin'. You couldn't drive me away. Tomorrer mornin' I'm comin' here—to stay—for a good long spell, just as you asked me to. There! Now ain't you glad?"

Obadiah did look glad, really glad. But he also looked troubled and, so it seemed to his former skipper, frightened.

CHAPTER VIII

THAT evening Captain Newcomb and Irving Clifford sat on the Mansion House porch until nearly midnight, smoking and talking. The smoking was done by both, but the captain did most of the talking. Clifford was very glad indeed to see his friend of the previous fall and especially glad to learn that the latter had decided to stay in Trumet for some weeks at least.

"Might just as well," explained Noah. "I'm a kind of wanderer on the face of the earth just now. No home, no job, no nothin'—but my health and a tin automobile. I used to like Trumet when I was a little shaver; I liked it just as well when I was down last October. Now I'm goin' to give it a real try-out and, if I keep on likin' it, I may settle down here for keeps. Got to have some kind of moorin's to tie up to when you get too old to cruise in deep water."

He said nothing to Clifford about the summons he had received from Obadiah Burgess. He thought it best to keep that a secret at present, even from Irving, whose judgment he regarded highly. He did ask some roundabout questions concerning Mr. Burgess and his affairs, but the engineer seemed to know little about either.

Everyone spoke well of Mrs. Mayo, he said. He had met her once or twice and liked her.

"How did she impress you, Captain Newcomb?" he asked.

"Why—why, she impressed me fust-rate," was the answer. "Yes, fust-rate. I couldn't find any fault anywheres. That's the — Humph! Well, never mind. How about her nephew? I ain't met him."

"Young Kenney? Oh, he's all right enough. He'll never set the river afire, I guess. Rather visionary and dreamy, they say; his artistic temperament, no doubt. He paints; lid you know that?"

The captain grinned. "Um-hm," he said. "Have you seen the picture he made of Obe, Burgess, I mean?"

"No. Was it a good likeness?"

His companion's grin became a chuckle. He rubbed his knees.

"I don't know's you'd call it a good likeness, exactly," he said. "If you put it behind bars in a dark room the average child would hanker to feed it peanuts. All it needs is fingers on its feet and a tail. Ho, ho! But Obe thinks it beautiful. How about this other feller—the one that wears the wristers on his ankles?"

"The what?"

"Garters—or gaiters, I believe they call 'em. I mean the feller that sharpens the ends of his mustache with a file. The one with the sportin' guard dog, or the guardin' sport dog—Wentworth, how about him?"

Clifford laughed aloud. The captain had told him of his adventure at the cold-storage plant that morning; he had heard the carpenters' version also.

"Mr. Calvin Wentworth is—well, he *is* something of an enigma," he observed.

"Somethin' of a what? You don't mean to say he's got colored blood in him? I'd never have guessed it."

"Ha, ha! No, indeed. You misunderstood .ne, Captain. I say he is something of a riddle—a puzzle. It seems strange that a city swell like him should be content to live here in Trumet the year round; not here on business either, but just existing, that's all. When I knew him in New York he showed no fondness for a rural life, the reverse, rather."

"When you knew him in New York? You used to know him there then?"

"Yes, slightly. Shortly after I left college I was in New York for a time. I belonged to a rather good club then; reckless extravagance on my part, of course, but I was young and foolish. Wentworth belonged to the same club; he resigned afterwards."

"What made him resign?"

"I don't know. Too tame an organization, perhaps. He had the reputation of being rather a high roller in those days. I certainly was surprised when I met him here in Trumet. He says his health is poor and that is why he is here. I never should have guessed that he was an invalid."

"Humph! What did he used to do for a livin' when you knew him over to New York? What was he workin' at?"

"I don't know. I never inquired. He and I were never friendly—slightly acquainted, that's all. You seem very much interested in him, Captain Newcomb."

"Do I? Well, maybe I am. When you've got a line out for herrin' and hook on to a goldfish, it's enough to interest the average feller, seems to me. How did you fust meet this Calvin man; somebody at the club introduce you, did they?"

Clifford's expression changed. His answer was curt, almost sharp.

"No," he said.

But Captain Noah was persistent. "You met him somewheres else then?" he said.

For an instant the young man hesitated. Then he said: "I met him at the home of a mutual—er—acquaintance. I hadn't seen him for years until he came down to the cold-storage plant a month or more ago. He calls there occasionally, just as he did this morning, to smoke and chat. I presume he finds it dull here in the village at this season of the year. I should think he might. I should die if I had no work to do."

"Humph! Well, maybe he'd die if he had. His health's bad, you know. This house where you met him; belonged to a friend of yours, you say?"

"Yes."

"This friend, then, he was a friend of Wentworth's, eh?"

"She was an acquaintance, I presume, like myself. Suppose we change the subject, Captain. You won't mind, will you?"

"Mind? No, no, course I shan't. Look here, son, have I been makin' a nuisance of myself, askin' questions when I hadn't no business? I snum I'm sorry! I ask your pardon."

EXTRICATING OBADIAH

"No necessity for apology, none in the least. There are some unpleasant memories connected with that period of my life and I dislike to speak of it, that's all. That's why I suggested changing the subject."

Captain Noah nodded. "It's a good suggestion, too," he agreed, heartily. "I've had about enough of friend Wentworth myself for now. He's a kind of a hothouse plant, judgin' by the looks of him, and the air in a hothouse never did agree with me for long at a stretch. What'll we change the subject to? If 'twan't that I might be afraid of gettin' my foot in it again, I'd be tempted to ask how that nice girl was, the one who wouldn't sell me a sideboard for a bureau. What was her name? Mary Barstow, that's it. I liked her fust-rate. Is she pretty smart?"

Irving looked at him quickly. The captain's face was innocence itself.

"Miss Barstow is well, I believe," replied Clifford.

"So? That's good. Don't know when I've seen a young woman I took a shine to so quick. Good thing for the young sparks in this town that I'm a hundred and eighty instead of twenty-five. Speakin' of age and antiques and such, how's old Leviticus, her step-pa? Balaam, how's he?"

"He's all right. At least I haven't heard that he was not."

"See much of him, do you?"

"No."

There was a finality about this which caused the captain to change the subject again. It was quite evident that Irving Clifford was no more desirous of discussing

Balaam Griggs than he had been of recalling memories of his New York sojourn.

The talk thereafter dealt with a variety of topics. Just before they separated for the night the younger man said:

"So you have come down here—just to make us a visit, Captain Newcomb."

"Ye-es, I guess likely. To make my old shipmate—and you—a visit. Ain't you glad to see me?"

"Of course I am."

"Um-m. But you have your doubts, eh?"

"Doubts? Why, did you—did I say——"

"You didn't say anything, son—except '*just* to make a visit.' You think maybe I've got some other reason up my sleeve, eh? Well, perhaps I have, perhaps I have."

Clifford was confused and embarrassed.

"Captain Newcomb," he said, "I beg your pardon. I certainly did not mean to imply that I doubted your word. Of course your reason for coming here is not in the least my business. It was only that something you said—your manner—led me to infer—I beg your pardon."

Captain Noah laid a hand on his knee. "That's all right, son," he said, heartily, "that's all right. No need of beggin' pardons between us, I hope. Some of these days I'll most likely tell you more about my reasons for comin' here. Just now I——"

He stopped, and remained silent for a moment, puffing at the stump of his cigar. Then he rose from his chair.

"Son," he said, again, "do you remember that yarn in the Bible about the feller that went down to—to somewhere or 'nother and fell amongst thieves?"

"Yes, certainly, I remember it, Captain."

"Um-hm. What happened then? The thieves sprung up and choked him, didn't they?"

"Why, not exactly, I believe. The——"

"Yes, yes, all right. I was gettin' my parables snarled up together, wan't I? Ho, ho! Anyhow this feller that fell amongst the thieves was in bad shape till another chap that was cruisin' in those latitudes came along and helped him out."

"Yes; the good Samaritan."

"That's the feller." He drew two or three more big puffs and then tossed the stump of the cigar over the porch railing. "I cal'late everybody has to be a Samaritan once in a while," he said. "Good night, son."

CHAPTER IX

THE next forenoon, "bag and baggage," according to his promise to Obadiah, he arrived at the Badscom place and the visit began. Mr. Burgess welcomed him effusively; if he still felt the doubt and uneasiness of the previous night he concealed the feeling. Mrs. Mayo also seemed glad to see him, and although he suspected that her gladness was a pretense, her manner and behavior furnished no excuse for the suspicion. His room was a good-sized one overlooking the bay and, like the rest of the house, it was neatness itself. The housekeeper might be, and probably was, acting with an ulterior motive, but she could keep house, even Noah was obliged to admit that.

And she could cook, also. Dinner that noon was the best meal the captain had had for many a day. At that meal he met for the first time Joe Kenney, Melissa Mayo's nephew, he of the "artistic temperament." Young Kenney was a freckle-faced youth with a blue eye and a healthy appetite. Joe seemed to be rather bashful, said little during dinner and, after bolting his share of the dessert, hurried off. In answer to the captain's question he explained that he was over at Mr. Griggs' that day helping the latter "pack up some stuff."

"Does your nephew work for Mr. Griggs, ma'am?" asked Noah, addressing the housekeeper. The question, innocent enough, seemed to embarrass the lady somewhat.

"Why—why," she stammered, "he doesn't exactly work for him. Not all the time, that is. He does sometimes, like today."

"Good, strong, healthy lookin' boy," said Captain Noah. "I suppose he's plannin' to do consider'ble in this world, ma'am."

Mrs. Mayo seemed more confused than ever. "Yes—yes," she said, "Joey plans a good many things. He wants to go West awfully. He's a great reader and he's read a lot about the West."

"So? I had an idea maybe he was cal'latin' to be a picture painter. Obe, here, showed me the picture he did of him."

"Oh, he likes to do pictures, too, but he does those mostly for fun. If he could have his way he'd like to go out West and work on a ranch, a cattle place, you know."

"I should think he'd go, then. He ain't so young but what he can take a chance. At his age I wasn't doin' much *but* takin' chances."

"I know, but—but he can't go, just yet."

"Oh, he can't, eh? I see, I see. That's too bad. Ah, how do you do, Mr. Wentworth. Glad to see you again, sir."

Mr. Calvin Wentworth, debonair as ever, had just strolled into the dining room. He was very late for dinner, in fact the others had almost finished, but he appeared not in the least perturbed. One might have surmised that it took much more than tardiness to perturb Mr. Wentworth. · But he was capable of astonishment, and Captain Noah's presence in that house and at that table evidently astonished him hugely.

"Eh?" he exclaimed. "Why—who——"

"Newcomb," exclaimed the captain. "Noah Newcomb, my name is. Met you down to the cold-storage plant yesterday mornin'. Glad to see you again. How's that smart dog of yours? That's as good a watchdog as I cal'late I ever saw. Goin' to guard that automobile of mine till doomsday, he was. Ho, ho!"

Mrs. Mayo and Mr. Burgess looked at each other.

· "Why!" exclaimed the former. "Was it *your* car Mr. Wentworth's dog was guardin', Cap'n Newcomb? Now ain't that funny! Mr. Wentworth was tellin' us about that last night. Wasn't you, Mr. Wentworth?"

"Yes," put in Obadiah. "Cousin Calvin said that if he hadn't t-t-took pity on the old g-g-guy that owned the car and called Sport off, that auto would have been out of commission yet. But we didn't know 'twas your auto, Cap'n Noah."

The captain nodded.

"I was the guy," he said, simply.

The housekeeper, looking first at Noah and then at Mr. Wentworth, smiled slightly and her eyes twinkled. Obadiah went on.

"That Sport is s-s-some dog," he declared, "some dog. When he sets out to guard anything he's like a mud t-t-turtle—he won't let go till it thunders. I cal'late you

114

was glad, Cap'n Noah, when Cousin Calvin took p-p-pity on you. 'Tain't thundered yet, you know, now has it?"

The captain's eyes met Mr. Wentworth's and the captain smiled. It was evident that, in his story-telling the previous evening, Cousin Calvin had omitted to mention the fire hose.

"You're right, Obe," said Noah, with a nod. "It ain't thundered, but—well, there was one spell when Mr. Wentworth seemed to think 'twas goin' to rain. Even the dog seemed to think so, didn't he, Mr. Wentworth?"

Cousin Calvin nodded, muttered something or other, and sat down at table. The housekeeper, who had kept his dinner warm in the kitchen, served it deftly and promptly. Evidently she was used to his habits. He did not thank her. He paid little attention to anyone; something, possibly the memory of the fire hose, had put a damper on his powers of conversation. Mr. Burgess introduced his friend and former skipper, and paid glowing tributes to the latter's character and his skill as a seafaring man. Mr. Wentworth nodded acknowledgment of the introduction and managed to restrain his enthusiasm when told that Captain Newcomb was to be, for some weeks at least, a member of the household. When the captain, who was urbanity and politeness personified, addressed him, he answered with chilling hauteur.

But before the day was over he found an opportunity to get his Cousin Obadiah aside and question him concerning the new arrival.

"Who is the old card?" he inquired. "Where does he come from? What is he doing here?"

Mr. Burgess' answer was fluent and lengthy. Cousin

Calvin gathered from the mass of information one or two items which seemed to interest even his bored metropolitan mind.

"So he's got the stuff, has he?" he asked. "Well fixed, eh? A million, should you say?"

Obadiah, who had not the slightest ground for estimating his friend's fortune, nor even for assuming that there was such a fortune, other than the fact of the captain's retiring from business, admitted that there most likely wasn't quite a million.

"Half a million?"

"Wa-al, maybe not quite——"

"Gad, I thought he must be a Rockefeller, you were so reverent when you mentioned his money. What has the old guy got; a hundred thousand?"

Obadiah, making a loyal guess, opined that he shouldn't wonder a mite.

"Huh! Well, does he ever let go of it? Is he a tight-wad?"

Mr. Burgess, whose education in up-to-date slang had been neglected, but who judged that a tightwad was an undesirable person, stoutly declared that his friend was not that.

"No sir-ee!" he affirmed. "I've seen him out of sight of land for a week at a time and he wasn't never no t-t-tightwad."

Cousin Calvin strolled away, hands in pockets, and a meditative expression upon his face. At supper that evening he unbent toward Captain Noah; was, in a condescending way, almost genial.

Mr. Balaam Griggs dropped in for supper; "just hap-

pened to be goin' along by," he said. Balaam had heard
the news of the visitor at the Badscom place. He greeted
the captain like an old friend returned after a long and
agonizing separation, and the captain's greeting of Mr.
Griggs was, if not as effusive, still very cordial and
friendly.

The next day Obadiah underwent another questioning
concerning Captain Noah. This time Mr. Griggs was the
questioner. He asked, not directly, of course, but by
various roundabout methods, the size of the captain's fortune, his past and probable future and, more than all, his
reasons for coming to Trumet and staying there.

Now, as it happened, before retiring the night before
Noah and Obadiah had had a long chat and the captain,
usually rather reticent when dealing with his own plans
and intentions, had seemed willing, almost anxious, to tell
his host about those plans. They were rather vague
plans, not defined as yet, but they centered about the idea
of buying Trumet real estate as an investment. "Got to
put my money somewheres," said Captain Noah, "and,
the way I feel now, Trumet real estate looks good to me.
Course I came down here really just to see you, Obe, but
there is no harm in lookin' around while I'm down here,
is there?"

All of which, Balaam, by judicious questioning, managed to extract from Mr. Burgess. And Mr. Burgess
confessed as much to Captain Noah later on.

"They're all awful curious about you, Cap'n," he said,
proudly. "Makes a feller feel g-g-good to have a visitor
all hands takes such an interest in. And they like you,
too. Why, I ain't seen Cousin Calvin so social and folksy

with anybody sence he's been here as he is along of you."

"Well, well, I want to know! I ought to be real flattered, hadn't I, Obe?"

"Why, yes, I suppose you had," was the answer, given very seriously. "Cousin Calvin has been used to livin' amongst the highest k-k-kind of society, he says so himself, and it means somethin' to have him t-t-take a shine to you. There ain't many he does, I tell you that."

"Um-hm. Well, I must try not to get *too* sot up about it."

"And Balaam, he thinks you're a fine man. Says he don't know when he's seen such a able, fine-spoken man. Him and Calvin has asked more'n a thousand questions about you!"

"Hum! Well, I *shall* get stuck up if I don't look out. And this Mrs. Mayo now; I cal'late she's asked a lot about me, too—eh?"

"Why—why, no, she ain't."

"Ain't, eh?"

"No. She likes you, I guess, but she don't ask me questions about you and about how much you're worth and all, same as the others do. G-g-guess likely that's 'cause she is a woman; women ain't interested in how much m-m-money a feller's got, same as men are."

"Oh, ain't they?"

"No, stands to reason they ain't. And Melissy she don't ask hardly any questions about you. Just kind of seems to t-t-take you for granted, as you might say."

Captain Noah had no comment to make on this statement, but a week or so later when, during a call upon Irving Clifford at the cold-storage plant, Irving happened to ask him how he enjoyed his visit at the Burgess home, he made this enigmatical answer, if it can be called an answer:

"Son," he said, "did you ever do one of them cut-out picture puzzles, same as young folks like to play with nowadays? Um-hm. Dorcas, my sister, she wan't what you'd call young, but she liked to fuss with those things and I used to tackle 'em occasionally. Sometimes you got a piece that wouldn't seem to fit in anywheres. Seems almost as if it didn't belong in the puzzle. I'm havin' that kind of trouble just now. Most of the pieces in my puzzle fit all right—I've got their number, as the boys say—but there's one that don't, I can't seem to make her —it, I mean—fit. Seems almost as if that piece had got in by mistake."

Clifford, who did not understand, except vaguely, was tempted to question, but he judged it wisest not to do so. His acquaintanceship with Captain Newcomb had progressed sufficiently to teach him that the captain told what he wished of his affairs, and that it was poor policy to press for more.

"Perhaps the piece did get in by mistake," he ventured.

Captain Noah shook his head.

"I don't believe it," he said, "I don't believe it. It's just that I ain't got the right way of lookin' at it yet. It must be—it must be, or else what's it doin' in with the bunch? But—but, I snum, son, it's got me so fur."

CHAPTER X

I T continued to "get" him more and more as the days and weeks passed. He was now a prime favorite at the Burgess home. Balaam Griggs, whose calls and little friendly "droppings in" for meals were at least as frequent as ever, now addressed him by his Christian name and slapped him on the back when they met. Balaam had confidentially taken the captain into his confidence concerning two or three exceptional bargains in Trumet land which he, Balaam, alone knew of, but which knowledge, owing to his love for his new friend, he was willing to impart to the latter provided "nobody said nothin'."

Captain Noah was tremendously interested in these bargains. He accompanied Balaam on tours of inspection during which Mr. Griggs invariably spoke in a whisper and kept looking cautiously about for fear someone might see them looking at the land together, "smell a rat" and seize the wonderful opportunity—before the captain did. The fates were kind in this respect, the opportunity remained unseized, although Mr. Griggs declared that he woke up each morning "cal'latin'" to find them lots snapped up ahead of us."

EXTRICATING OBADIAH

They spoke of other investments also, of business matters in general. The captain usually led the conversation in this direction and Balaam followed the lead. They discussed the "antique" business, and Mr. Griggs, after the friendship had developed sufficiently to warrant a degree of confidence on his part, mentioned a few good trades he had made. He did *not* mention the chamber set which Obadiah had acquired through his "kindness"; that he neglected entirely.

From all these interviews and talks Captain Noah gathered enough information concerning Mr. Burgess' "best friend" to strengthen the impression he had already gained concerning the latter's character. And he assisted Balaam in confirming the idea that he, Noah, was a man of means, guileless, trustful and decidedly worth cultivating.

Mr. Calvin Wentworth, of New York, was an absolutely different proposition. Cousin Calvin did not slap the captain on the back, nor hail him by his Christian name. His manner toward the former skipper of the *Flyaway* was still lofty and condescending, but he unbent sufficiently to joke with him, to smoke his cigars and, on one or two occasions, to borrow small sums of money. Trifling accommodations, these were, until his dividend checks arrived, so he said. Captain Noah seemed so eager, almost grateful for the opportunity of forestalling the "dividend check" that Wentworth's amusement was scarcely repressed. The "old card" was certainly queer, although a convenience. He was in such good humor that, in answer to Noah's inquiries concerning New York life, he told a few anecdotes of his own adventures in the metropolis. To these the captain listened with awe-stricken admiration. He made mental notes as he listened, and, later on, in the quiet of his own room, he transferred these notes from his mind to paper. 'Also he wrote a letter to his nephew in New York City. In this letter the Wentworth name was mentioned more than once.

So, in doing his "picture puzzle," the parts labeled "Calvin Wentworth" and "Balaam Griggs" were, in the captain's mind, coming into place satisfactorily. He believed that he was, as he told Clifford, "getting their numbers." But the pieces of the puzzle which he was finding it hard to put where they belonged were the two which should, it would seem, have been easiest; they were Mrs. Melissa Mayo and Obadiah Burgess himself.

The idea of there being any mystery connected with meek, stammering, peaceful little Obadiah seemed absurd on the face of it. The idea that Obadiah could keep a secret long enough to cover up a mystery was just as absurd. But apparently he was doing it. Captain Noah was more than ever convinced that his former cook had not told him the whole truth, that he was keeping back the real reason, the real trouble, which had caused him to write asking his friend and ex-skipper to come to Trumet. Obadiah insisted that this was not so, that he had written because he was "kind of worried about the Cousin Calvin business, whether to have him die on me or not," and had wanted his friend's advice. This explanation was plausible enough, so far as it went, but it did not go far enough. It did not explain why Mr. Burgess appeared so guilty and embarrassed when Captain Noah mentioned the letter, why he seemed so uncomfortable, even wretched, when questioned concerning it, and least of all did it explain why the captain so often found him moping alone in his room or on the bluff by the shore, with an expression of abject, hopeless misery on his face. That queer, round little face had so shone with pride and happiness when Noah saw it during his first visit to Trumet that the contrast was particularly disturbing.

The captain had come to the Burgess home with a fairly well-defined idea in his head, an idea which, he believed, would prove the solution of this part of his puzzle. He had believed that Obadiah's odd behavior and embarrassment were due to the fact that he and his housekeeper were entangled in some sort of matrimonial engagement, that he had proposed to her, or, which would be more likely, she had proposed to him and they were to be married. He surmised that, after this had happened, Obadiah had lost his nerve and had written for help in order to break off the relationship. Captain Noah, knowing that Griggs had been responsible for the hiring of Mrs. Mayo as housekeeper, summoning her all the way from Cape Ann to take the position, had, even before he saw her, labeled her a clever, designing woman who, like the rest, was after the Burgess money.

His first impression had, in spite of this prejudice, been a favorable one. This favorable impression upon further acquaintance had deepened. If things had not been as they were, if he were not perfectly sure she was pursuing some underhand plan or other—that she *must* be, there could be no other explanation of her presence, she, a relative and protégée of Balaam Griggs—if he were not so stubbornly determined that this must be so, he would have declared long ago that he liked and respected her. He did give up the idea of there being any love affair between her and Obadiah. It was perfectly evident there was not. There were no signs of it on Obadiah's part, and she treated him with the same good-humored, managing sort of kindness with which she treated her nephew, young Kenney. There was nothing sentimental in her manner, nor was she kinder to her employer, or more attentive, than to any other member of the household.

So the captain gave up the idea that she was planning to marry Obadiah. And, as the time passed and he and she became better acquainted, he found his other suspicions wavering. She was capable, she was good-humored, she enjoyed a joke almost as well as he did. She could be sympathetic, and, when Cousin Calvin's dog, Sport, got into a fight and came home, limping on three legs, a badly chewed canine, her bandaging and nursing of the suffering creature seemed to prove that she had a kind heart. And she possessed a wonderful fund of Noah's most prized faculty, New England common-sense.

He and she would have been the best of friends by this time, were it not for his feeling that no relative of Balaam Griggs could be honest. Even in spite of this he found himself liking her against his will, but, with customary "sotness" he tried all the harder to discover some underhand reason for her being there. And, at last, he believed he had discovered something, a straw showing which way the wind blew. He discovered that Obadiah had with customary easy-going carelessness intrusted the buying of the household supplies to his housekeeper and that she was buying them of Mr. Griggs, who seemed to be acting as a sort of broker—a broker who exacted a liberal commission, the captain had no doubt.

One of the local grocers gave him the hint which led to this discovery. The grocer asked Captain Noah what they lived on down at the Badscom place. "Must be east wind puddin' with fresh air sass," declared the man. "Nigh's I can find out Burgess nor his housekeeper don't buy much of anything of anybody. Not in this town they don't, anyway."

So the captain investigated and learned from the station agent that Balaam was receiving a good many packages and bundles by express from Boston grocers and provision dealers. He questioned Obadiah and found that the latter knew little or nothing about the matter. "Melissy, she does the buyin'," explained Obadiah.

"Does she do the payin', too?" inquired Noah, tartly.

"Eh? Yes, sartin she does. She tells me how much money she needs every week and I g-g-give it to her. It's the easiest way; saves me a lot of trouble."

Captain Noah shook his head. That afternoon he waited his chance until the housekeeper was alone in the kitchen. Then he went in and sat down in the chair by the window. The lady was standing by the kitchen table rolling pie crust.

"Mrs. Mayo," said the captain, suddenly, "how much trade do you give Crowell Brothers in the course of a week, do you think likely?" Crowell Brothers was the name of Trumet's leading grocery firm.

The housekeeper looked at him.

"Not very much," she said.

"Oh, I want to know! Trade with Solon Baxter, I suppose, eh?"

"No; or, at any rate, no more than I do with Crowell Brothers."

"Sho! Is that so? Send way over to Bayport, do you? That's a pretty long way to go, seems to me."

"I don't trade at Bayport, Cap'n Newcomb."

"Then——"

Ever since his first question she had been watching him intently and now she interrupted him.

"Just a minute, Cap'n Newcomb," she said. "You've found it out, haven't you? I wondered how long 'twould be before you did."

Captain Noah stared at her.

"Found it out? Found what out? I don't know what you mean, Mrs. Mayo."

"Oh, yes you do. I mean you've found out that my cousin, Balaam Griggs, sells me about everything in the way of supplies that comes into this house. He does. Now what else have you found out; anything?"

The captain swallowed hard. This was decidedly not the way he had expected Mrs. Mayo to act. He had expected to lead up to his discovery of her dealings with Balaam and then listen to a variety of explanations and excuses. To have her answer his question before it was asked and then ask one of her own along the same line was a staggerer.

"Why—why—" he stammered, "I——"

She wiped the flour from her hands with her apron and, crossing the room, sat down in a chair facing him. Her expression was very grave, and the captain noticed that her hands, now folded in her lap, trembled just a little. She seemed to be fighting something, agitation, distress, alarm—something of the sort. Yet her tone was calm enough.

"Cap'n Newcomb," she said, "you're a great friend of Mr. Burgess's, ain't you?"

"Eh? Why, yes, I suppose I am. I like him and he seems to like me pretty well."

"Likes you! My soul and body! He thinks you're a sight bigger man than the President, and he worships the ground you tread on."

"Oh, now, Mrs. Mayo, don't——"

"Cap'n Newcomb, don't let's waste words. I ain't got any to waste just now and I don't feel like complimentin' anybody; you can be sure of that. You know what I just said is true. Now then, if you are such a friend of his, why do you let things go on as they are? Why do you?"

"Why—why—I don't just get what you mean, Mrs. Mayo? I don't understand."

"Don't you? Well, if you don't, then you're a lot more stupid than I give you credit for bein'. Cap'n Newcomb, do you know what I thought, or more than half thought, when you came to this house to live? I thought maybe you, bein' such a good friend of Obadiah Burgess, had come here on purpose to try and help him out of his trouble. That's what I thought. Did you come for that?"

Captain Noah stared at her in amazed silence. Before he could decide how to answer, or even to answer at all, she went on.

"Well, never mind tellin' me," she said. "If you did come for that you wouldn't want to tell me anyhow, I suppose; and if you didn't, why—well then it don't make any difference. But that was what I thought, anyway. I'm sure of one thing, though, and that is that you're an honest man. And if you are an honest man and an honest friend of Mr. Burgess, why don't you help him? Why do you stand by and see the poor thing imposed on and—and cheated—yes, and robbed, for that's what it amounts to? Why do you do it?"

Her agitation was suppressed no longer. She had risen to her feet and her eyes were snapping. The captain breathed heavily and shook his head.

"I declare!" he exclaimed, "if this ain't— Look here, Mrs. Mayo, if you don't mind, suppose you answer me this: Who is it that's imposin' and cheatin' and—and murderin'—or whatever 'tis? Who?"

He smiled, but the housekeeper did not smile.

"You know who," she asserted. "Why do you ask that? Are you blind?"

"Well, I never thought I was, but—but— And it's Obadiah that's bein' murdered, you say?"

"He's bein' swindled, done out of his money, imposed on. Don't tell me you don't see it; you must. You've known him all your life, Cap'n Newcomb. You know he ain't much more than a good, kind-hearted, innocent, simple sort of child. Anybody can get the best of him; anybody can impose on him; he'll trust anybody, and swallow anything they say for gospel truth. You know it—you must know it. He's had a little money left him; not very much, I guess, but some. However much it was —or is now—he won't have it long. Can't you *see* he won't?"

Captain Noah pulled his beard, and looked up at her from under his brows.

"Humph!" he grunted. "Well, supposin' I can see it —or guess it, which is the next best thing, what would you expect me to do about it?"

"Do? Stop it. Tell him what's goin' on. Prove it to him."

"Um-hm. And who shall I tell him is doin' the—er—swindlin'?"

"Everyone. This Wentworth man for one."

"Sho! Cousin Calvin? Mercy, how you talk, Mrs. Mayo! Why, Cousin Calvin is an invalid. He's sick and down here for his health, Cousin Calvin is."

"Sick! I've done consider'ble nursin' in my time, Cap'n Newcomb, and if he's sick, then you and I are in the last stages ourselves. He eats as much as both of us together. Sick! He's sick of lookin' out for himself, maybe, but—Oh, you know he isn't sick!"

"Well, he says he is. And, besides, he's goin' to leave Obe all his money when he dies."

"He won't. Mr. Burgess'll die forty years ahead of him."

The captain laughed. "But your own relation, Balaam Griggs, was dead set on Obe's gettin' him here," he said.

"I know it. But that makes no difference. My *relation,*" with bitter emphasis on the word, "is responsible for lots of things, but that don't make 'em right. He's responsible for my buyin' the groceries and things from him instead of from the stores, and payin' half again as much, for all I know—I haven't tried to find out. And here am I—spongin' my livin' and my nephew's livin'

from Mr. Burgess. Oh, Cap'n Newcomb, why don't you
do it? Get rid of the Wentworth man, get rid of Balaam,
get rid of me—get rid of us all. We're all cheats and
swindlers—all but Joe, and he doesn't realize, poor boy.
Pitch us all out, neck and crop; it's what we deserve."

She paused, her bosom heaving. Then she turned
away.

"There!" she said, "I guess I've said too much, more
than I'd ought to, I'm sure. There's times when a body
can't hold in any longer. I don't know what you think
of me—but it doesn't make any difference. Nothin'
makes much difference, so far as I can see."

She turned and, leaving her pie crust unfinished,
walked toward the door of the dining room. Captain
Noah, rising from his chair, strode after her.

"Just a minute, Mrs. Mayo," he said. "You have said
a good deal, I will give in. Some of what you've said I
understand, cal'late I've been understandin' it better
every day I've been here. But some I don't. You tell
me you're here spongin' your livin' off Obadiah. I can't
see what you mean by that. You're housekeeper here and
I hope you won't mind my sayin' that you're a good one,
as good a one as ever I saw. You earn your wages, whatever they are. Now why do you call that 'spongin'?'"

She turned quickly.

"Because it is," she said, fiercely. "Not now, perhaps,
with all this tribe in the house, but it would be if they
weren't here. Obadiah meant to live here alone, he's told
me so, himself, more than once. He can cook; it used
to be his trade. He doesn't need a housekeeper; all he
needs is a woman to come in twice a week or so and help

with the cleanin'. He can't afford to pay me—or I don't believe he can. And I'm sartin sure he can't afford to feed and lodge Mr. Wentworth and me and Joe, to say nothin' of Balaam one meal out of every three."

"And me," put in Noah.

"You ain't permanent, same as we are. And you ain't here for *business*," with scornful emphasis. "You're clean and aboveboard and honest. Oh! *why* don't you get rid of us all? Throw us all out—and wash your hands afterwards? . . . There, please don't say any more to me. Please don't!"

But the captain would not let her go.

"Only one more thing, Mrs. Mayo," he said; "just one. If you feel that you ain't needed here, what makes you stay? When you found you wan't needed, or really needed, why didn't you leave them? If you think you're 'spongin'' a livin'—that was your own name for it, not mine—why don't you quit the ship this minute? Just hop overboard and go? Why not?"

And now it was she who hesitated. And when she answered it was without looking at him.

"I—I—you mustn't ask me, Cap'n Newcomb," she said, with a choke in her voice. "There are some things we can't— There! please don't talk to me any more."

She hastened into the dining room. The captain, a greatly disturbed and thoroughly puzzled individual, stood in the middle of the kitchen floor, tugging at his chin whisker, and muttering exclamations indicative of mental disturbance. A minute or two later, he tiptoed to the door of the dining room and looked in.

The housekeeper was sitting in the rocker by the window. The afternoon sun was shining in through the panes and the light glistened upon her wet cheeks. She had been crying. Something, pity or sympathy or some other strong feeling, gave a tremendous twist to the captain's heartstrings. He felt an unreasonable but almost uncontrollable desire to walk in and tell her not to cry, that everything was going to be all right for her, that he would see that it was.

Of course he did not do anything of the kind. What he did was to step back and knock at the panel of the half-opened door. The housekeeper turned her head.

"I—I just wanted to say I was goin' down street a spell," stammered Noah. "I'll be home 'long about supper time. And—and—er—er—Mrs. Mayo——"

"Yes?" wearily.

"You—you needn't worry about what you said to me; it's all right. And I'm mighty glad you and me had this talk."

It was a considerably disturbed and troubled Captain Noah Newcomb who walked thoughtfully down to the village. Before reaching the Corners he turned to the right and, with hands in his pockets, walked on along the Bay road to the cold-storage plant. Just before he reached the new building he saw a man striding rapidly toward him. As they approached each other he recognized Mr. Balaam Griggs.

"Afternoon, Balaam," said the captain.

Mr. Griggs' response was a brief nod and morose grunt, as different from his usual suave greeting as could be imagined. He was scowling savagely and he strode on without waiting to shake hands or exchange a word. Captain Noah could not understand it.

He found Irving Clifford standing by the door of the engine room at the cold-storage plant. Irving, himself, looked a trifle ruffled.

"Humph!" exclaimed the captain, after a look at his friend; "you and Balaam been passin' the compliments of the season, have you?"

Clifford stared at him in astonishment.

"How in blazes did you know?" he demanded.

"Oh, I just put this and that together, same as the old woman made the mince pie," was the answer. "I met Balaam a minute ago and I noticed his face had turned sour, and when I got here I found yours was some curdled. So I judged maybe you and he had been swappin' regards."

"Humph! Well, you are right, we have. That is, he has given me his. What is the matter with the old fellow; is he crazy?"

"No-o, no. Whatever else Balaam Griggs is he ain't crazy. Crazy folks are apt to do things that haven't got any reason in 'em. And whenever our old messmate Balaam does anything you can bet your hull and cargo there's a reason for it—and most generally it's a reason that you can get interest on. What ailed him this afternoon? Of course," he added, hastily, "if it's anything that ain't any of my business, why just tell me to clap on hatches and heave ahead to Jericho. I ain't tryin' to shove my jibboom into your affairs; I hope you understand that."

The young man colored a little and looked rather embarrassed. "Of course I understand that, Captain New-comb," he said. "And—and— Oh, well, I don't know why I shouldn't tell you. I suppose you've guessed it, anyway. Mr. Griggs and I disagreed concerning my visits to his house. He doesn't seem to care for my society."

"Or he doesn't care for his stepdaughter to care for it, eh? . . . And I know *that* ain't any of my business, either. Excuse me, will you, Irve? I have a habit of talkin' too much, even when I'm asleep."

"That's all right, Captain. It's no secret, I imagine. It's pretty hard to keep a secret in Trumet. Yes, Mr. Griggs disapproves of my calling upon or even speaking with Miss Barstow."

"Told you so just now, did he?"

Clifford smiled. "He did," he said. "He told me at least that."

· "Sho! I want to know! And what did you tell him? If that ain't askin' too much."

There was a crisp sharpness in the tone of the young man's answer, although he was smiling still.

"I told him," he said, "that so far as calling at his house was concerned I should not, of course, do so in the fu-ture; but that I should continue to meet and speak with Miss Barstow until the young lady herself told me not to."

Captain Noah grinned.

"That must have been as soothin' to him as a dose of blue vitriol tea," he observed.

"It was. He said a good many more things then."

"Shouldn't wonder. And you?"

"I didn't say so many. The conversation was rather one-sided."

He ceased speaking and looked off across the bay. The captain, after a glance at his face, made another remark.

"Say, son," he queried, "how bad would you damage my hull and standin' riggin' if I should ask you somethin' that was less my business than anything I've asked yet?"

Clifford laughed shortly. "I should probably not attempt damaging it at all," he replied. "After my success in holding in during my recent conversation with Griggs, I have considerable confidence in my powers of suppression. 'Ask whatever you please, Captain. I don't promise to answer.'"

"That's right, that's right. Don't never sign articles till you know where the ship's bound. I've got a reason for askin', and whatever you say, if you do answer, will never get out from under my decks. I may talk a good deal, but when it's needful I've got as good a keep-stiller as any man you ever saw."

"That's all right. I know you fairly well by this time, Captain Newcomb. Ask your question."

"Well—er—well, son, is—is there anything serious between you and Mary Barstow? I mean are you just friends and cal'latin' to be, or—or—Lord! It sounds more cheeky to say out loud than it was to think. Don't you answer a word, Irve; just tell me to shut up and then forget I said it."

The engineer was silent for a moment, still gazing out across the bay. But his answer, when he gave it, was conclusive enough.

"If Miss Barstow will have me," he said, quietly, "I mean to marry her."

The captain nodded. "Bully for you, son!" he said. "Judgin' from the little I've seen and the lot I've heard you're goin' to get a mighty fine young woman. I sartin do congratulate you."

"You'd better wait. I haven't got her yet."

"Well, then, I'll wait. But I'll tell you why I asked. First, though, I'll ask another question. Does Balaam know how you feel?"

"I told him just now."

"And 'twas after that that he blew the safety gauge clean off his biler, I presume likely."

"It seemed to make him absolutely furious."

"Um-hm. Now why? You're a respectable young man—barrin' that you keep company with me, of course. And your wages are good, and your prospects better. You can support a wife, can't you?"

"In moderate comfort, I hope—yes."

"Humph! As much comfort as she's liable to get in Balaam's Windsor Castle, I shouldn't wonder. Now then, why don't Balaam want you to marry her?"

"I don't know. Doesn't like me, I suppose."

"No reason why he shouldn't. And besides you ain't the only one he hasn't liked. Don't you flatter yourself, young feller, that you're the only young male critter that's been tryin' to keep company with Mary Barstow. Nigh's I can learn you're the only one she'd look at more'n once, but there's been others fishin' on the Griggs shoals. And Balaam had the same row with each one of them that he's had with you. There ain't anything

personal in it; he ain't got anything special against you.
It seems to be that he don't want his stepdaughter to
marry anybody. Now why don't he?"

"Don't know, I'm sure. Probably he doesn't want to
give her up."

"Don't you believe it! Balaam never had anything yet
that he wouldn't give up for money. He'd sell his under-
flannels and try to grow wool on his shoulder-blades if
you paid him enough for it. He's always complainin'
about what an expense Mary is and how cheap he could
keep house if he didn't have her. Anybody, knowin'
him, would naturally cal'late he'd be tickled to death to
have a nice, promisin' young chap like you take her off
his hands. But he ain't. Why?"

"Oh, don't ask me, Captain Newcomb. I tell you I
think he's crazy."

"Then your thoughts are sprung out of plumb, my
son. Balaam ain't crazy, don't you think he is. No,
there's a nigger in *that* woodpile, too, same as there is in
the one I'm anchored alongside of. That pile of mine
is full of 'em, a darky to every stick. And just as I think
I've got hold of the foot of one of 'em I—I find I ain't
at all. Just now, for instance, I had a— Look here,
son; you've been tellin' me some of your private affairs.
Do you want to hear some of mine? I've just *got* to
talk 'em over with somebody. Do you want to have me
tell you just why I'm down here in Trumet; the real
reason; the whole of it? All right, then, you listen, and
if *you* see any light in the darkness, sailor, as the hymn
tune used to say, for thunder mighty's sake, sing out.
I'm lost in the fog ahead and astern."

He began and told the whole story. Of Obadiah's letter, of the ex-cook's mysterious reticence and evident trouble, of Balaam and Cousin Calvin, then of his own suspicions of Mrs. Mayo, and finally of the interview he had just had with that lady, the impersonal parts of it, that is.

"So you see," he said, in conclusion, "here I am worse off than I started. I figgered, naturally, that she must be crooked and, like the rest of 'em, was there to work poor old Obe out of his last cent. And, just as I was congratulatin' myself that the puzzle was 'most done— She was the piece that wouldn't fit; the one I spoke to you about, remember— Well, just as I was pattin' myself on the back that I'd got her at last where she belonged, she turns to and upsets the whole checkerboard again. She orders me to do what I've been workin' to do from the beginnin', chuck the whole crew of 'em over the side, herself along with the rest. Orders me to do it —*she* does! Why? I ask you why?"

Clifford shook his head. "It's a queer business," he said.

"*Ain't* it now? It's as queer as old man Patterson's cat, and that slept in the chicken coop and barked like a dog. Don't you see, Irve? Don't you *see?* I've been all wrong—about her, I mean. She ain't crooked at all. She never did act anything but honest and I used to think that was funny or else just her smartness. But it wan't either; 'twas just her natural way of actin'. She *is* honest! I'll bet my mittens and wear my hands barefooted if it ain't so. She's an honest, square woman, and a mighty fine one. She knows Obe is bein' skinned;

138

she believes she's helpin' skin him. And yet—and yet, by thunder mighty, she stays right there! She won't quit, but she tells me to put her out. Why? Why? Why? Oh, this shakes my confidence, this does. A little more of it and I'll go back to Porto Reek and climb a palm tree and swop my head for a cocoanut. Tut! tut!"

Irving slapped his friend on the back.

"Cheer up, Captain," he said. "You'll get the answer by and by. It's a good thing for your friend Burgess that you *are* his friend; that's evident. And," he added, reflectively, "have you thought that—well, she is related to Griggs; he brought her to fill the position of house-keeper there. Have you thought that possibly he—that there may be something——"

Noah interrupted him. "Have I *thought?*" he repeated. "Son, I've thought my upper deck loose and started the plankin' in the hold. But in my opinion you've put your finger on the right button and it's got 'Balaam Griggs' lettered on it. Maybe it'll jingle some day or other when I press it the right way. But don't it beat all," he added, "how deceivin' appearances are sometimes? Here's this little single-sticked, cat-rigged town of Trumet; you'd never think a mystery could be hid anywheres aboard of it, could you? And I've been here only a month or so and I've bumped into no less than three already. Three and a half, you might say.

"The first," he went on, "is Obe himself. What's he got up his sleeve? What's his trouble and why is he hidin' it from me? Number two is the Mayo woman. She's honest, she's capable, she knows she shouldn't be workin' Obe or workin' for him. Then why don't she quit? Is Balaam makin' her stay there? She ain't the kind, or don't act like the kind, to be scared of him or anybody else. And number three is this queer business of Balaam's along of his stepdaughter. Why don't he want her to get married? There's a nice netful of picture puzzles, ain't it? Let's see you put 'em together, son."

Clifford laughed. Then he said: "You spoke of three and a half mysteries, Captain. What is the half?"

"The half? Oh, Cousin Calvin is the half. Why should a swell club feller like him be down here in Trumet loafin' around, towin' a dog on a chain? His health? Bosh! Oh, well, he don't fret me any. I'll have *his* measure most any time I want to take it, I cal'late. There, son," he added, drawing a long breath, "let's forget the whole three and a half for a spell. You're through work for the afternoon, ain't you? Good! Let's go up to the garage and get that car of mine, that— What was it Wentworth called her first time he saw her? Pancake? No, Panhard, that was it. Let's go get the Panhard and take a ten-mile cruise around the roads. Maybe 'twill blow some of Balaam's fog out of our heads. What do you say?"

CHAPTER XI

IT was on the morning following this discussion between Captain Noah and the engineer that two of the people discussed, namely, Mr. Balaam Griggs and Miss Mary Barstow, had a conversation of their own. It was a spirited conversation on Balaam's part and a provokingly cool and determined statement of fact on the part of the young lady.

"You'll do as I tell you!" shouted Griggs. "You won't see nor speak to that feller again."

His stepdaughter did not answer. She was clearing away the breakfast dishes and did not even glance in the direction of the irate Balaam.

"Do you hear?" repeated the latter, angrily.

No reply.

"Do you hear, I say?" roared Mr. Griggs.

Mary went on collecting the dishes on the table.

"Yes," she said, calmly, "I hear. So do the neighbors, I should imagine."

"Darn the neighbors! That's what I say about them."

Miss Barstow smiled slightly. "I wonder if you ever heard what they say about you," she observed.

Balaam choked and, figuratively speaking, clawed the

air, seeking to grasp a satisfactory retort. Failing to lay hands upon such a one he changed his tactics. After all, it was best not to quarrel.

"Now—now, Mary," he pleaded, "why don't you act nice and not so cross-grained and unlikely? Why do you always want to do just what I don't want you to do?"

Mary, having carried the silverware and dishes to the kitchen, paused momentarily in the doorway.

"Why do you always want me not to do what I wish to?" she asked.

"I don't! I don't! You can do anything you want to—anything in reason, that is. All I ask is that you just—just do same as I want you to, that's all. That's all I want."

The young lady laughed, merrily. The laughter served to bring back all of Balaam's irritation. His florid face blazed redder than ever.

"Laugh, will you?" he demanded. "Laugh?"

"I certainly shall when you make such ridiculous speeches."

"I want to know! Well, the last time I see that Clifford—er—er—sculpin *he* wan't laughin'. I told him what I thought of him. I told him if I ever see him hangin' around this house and tryin' to coax you into marryin' him I'd——"

"You *didn't!*"

Miss Barstow was not laughing now. She had entered the room and was facing her stepfather. Her eyes when they met Balaam's seemed to promise anything but humor.

"You didn't say that!" she repeated. "You *didn't* say that to him!"

Balaam was a bit nervous, but his anger was so great that it overbore his prudence for the moment.

"Yes, I did, too!" he shouted. " 'Twas last night I said it to him. Says I, '*I* don't want you round there and my daughter she don't and——' "

Miss Barstow interrupted, and her tone was so cold and clear that each syllable falling upon Mr. Griggs' torrid temper should have sizzled like a water-drop on a hot stove.

"I think you and I may as well have a final and complete understanding," she said. "It is evidently quite time. I have been keeping house for you, as you know, because my mother asked me to, asked me when she was very ill, just before she died. I have tried to make you comfortable, or as comfortable as I could with the means you provided."

"Yes, yes, that's all right, Mary, I ain't sayin'——"

"Wait. I have put up, for Mother's sake, with a great deal of annoyance and humiliation. You have assumed a sort of—of guardianship over me which I do not recognize in the least——"

"Guardian! Why, Mary, if I ain't your guardian, who is?"

"No one—now. I am twenty-one."

"Don't make no difference. I'm your father, ain't I?"

"No, you are not. And you have no control over my actions or my friendships. I shall do exactly as I please and I shall see and speak with whom I please. This house, I know, is yours. My only right here is that you

143

have begged me to stay. Now I think it best that I
should go."

"Go? Go where?"

"I don't know. To Boston, perhaps."

"To—to Boston! What for? What—what'll you
live on?"

A disinterested listener might have noticed a note of
eager anxiety, almost of fear, in Mr. Griggs' tone as he
asked this question.

"What have you got to live on, in Boston or anywheres else?" he repeated.

"Why, nothing."

"I guess nothing!" The note changed to triumphant
relief.

"But I can earn my living. I have friends there who
will help me to find employment. I think I should enjoy
working there; it would, at least, be a pleasant change
from this sort of thing. I think we may as well consider it settled. I shall go."

She turned and walked into the kitchen. Balaam
glowered after her and stood in the middle of the dining
room floor tugging at his whiskers. He was evidently
thinking hard and his thoughts were disturbing. After
a few moments of thought and whisker pulling he shuffled over to the kitchen door.

"Say, Mary," he said, "I—I'm sorry I said that about
young Clifford. I guess maybe I was a little mite hasty
there. You ain't goin' to leave me and go up to no Boston, course you ain't."

Mary, busy at the sink, answered without looking at
him.

144

"I am," she said.

"No, no, you ain't. What'll I do if you go? Didn't your ma make you promise you'd stay here and look after me? She thought a sight of me, your ma did. She used to say to me, 'Balaam,' she'd say, 'Mary's a good girl; she'll look after you in your old age.' She knew what a turrible lot of store I set by you, Mary."

"Yes, that is very evident."

"Well, now, 'tis. That's the reason I can't bear to think of your gettin' married to Irve Clifford, or anybody else. I can't bear to have you go off and leave me, Mary. If your ma knew—if she's where she can see us and knows you're cal'latin' to leave me, she——"

"Oh, don't!" wearily.

"Well, 'twould break her heart, same as the very idee of it is breakin' mine. You think it over now, Mary. And—and as for this Clifford feller—well, we won't talk about him."

"No, we will not," with decision.

"If—if you want to see him once in a while——"

"I shall see whom I wish, when I wish."

"Yes, yes. Well, we won't fight, anyhow. And you won't go to Boston and leave your poor old dad here alone. Your mother, she——"

"Stop! If you don't stop I shall go now."

"All right, I'll stop. Er — er — Mary, I'm going to Ostable today. Got some business over there. I shan't be back for dinner. You be a good girl now, won't you? Don't do nothin' foolish, nothin' you'll be sorry for later on."

His stepdaughter's answer was brief but, from his viewpoint, scarcely satisfying.

"It will not be necessary," she said, dryly. "I have enough to be sorry for now."

Balaam emerged from the house, angry through and through. As, swearing under his breath, he slammed the door behind him, a whiff of cigarette smoke tickled his nostrils and, turning, he saw Mr. Calvin Wentworth seated on the washbench below and to the right of the kitchen window. Cousin Calvin was, as usual, a miracle of raiment and *savoir faire.* His appearance would have struck envy to the souls of the young men pictured in the ready-made clothing advertisements.

"Morning," observed Mr. Wentworth, cheerfully.

Griggs grunted. He wondered how long the immaculate New Yorker had occupied the washbench. The kitchen window was open and the recent conversation with his stepdaughter had been of a somewhat personal nature. He looked suspiciously at Cousin Calvin, and the latter gentleman regarded him with languid self-possession.

It was Mr. Wentworth who spoke next. He blew a ring of cigarette smoke into the air and observed: "Sorry I haven't my card with me. I seem to remember my name; is your face familiar?"

Balaam's lower jaw dropped. "Eh?" he demanded. "What are you sayin'? What kind of talk—I don't know's I just understood you, Mr. Wentworth."

Cousin Calvin rose from the bench. "Oh, you do remember me, then!" he drawled. "Charmed, I'm sure."

"Remember you!" stammered the bewildered Griggs.

"Course I remember you! Why shouldn't I remember you, for the land sakes? 'Twas only last night I see you. What are you doin'; havin' fun with me, or what?"

Mr. Wentworth rose and tossed away his cigarette. "Judging by your face, old scout," he said, "I couldn't have fun *with* you; you wouldn't go halves. You look peeved, Uncle, peeved. What is it; the usual morning dark-brown? Hang-over from the Trumet Midnight Frolic, and all that sort of thing?"

Mr. Griggs smiled sourly. "You're a funny feller, ain't you?" he said. "Got up airly, didn't you? Thought you was goin' to meet me down to Ziby's?"

"I was, but I rose with the lark this morning. 'Double up, Lucy, the sun is in the sky' and that sort of thing. I strolled down to the gentle Ziba's—holy smoke, what a name!—laid violent hands on his new benzine bus and here I am. Shall we start?"

"Sho! Got the car already, have you?"

The car was Mr. Ziba Rogers'. Balaam, who had business at his lawyer's in Ostable, had arranged to borrow it for the day. The automobile was almost new and Ziba had not been keen for lending it. But Mr. Griggs, along with his other antiques, possessed a mortgage on the Rogers homestead. Therefore Ziba's disinclination to lend yielded under discretionary pressure. Having secured the car, Balaam found himself in need of a driver. Mentioning that need in the Burgess sitting room an evening or two before he had been somewhat surprised when Cousin Calvin volunteered his services. Wentworth had driven and owned numberless cars, so he gave the company to understand; he fancied he might rather enjoy taking a flier on the road again. Captain Newcomb solicitously asked if he cal'lated his health would stand it. Cousin Calvin opined that it would.

The car was now standing in the road by the Griggs front gate. Mr. Wentworth led the way toward it and Balaam followed. The pair climbed to the seat, Cousin Calvin took the wheel, pressed the starting button, and they began to move. In three minutes they were moving much faster, in five faster still, in ten——

"Hold on!" protested the alarmed Mr. Griggs. "What in time are you doin'; tryin' to fly? Don't! Hold on, I tell you!"

The car whizzed up a hill, turned a corner on two wheels, and shot along the next level.

"Hold on!" roared Balaam again. "Don't you hear me? I say, hold on!"

Mr. Wentworth took one hand from the wheel in order to find and open his cigarette case. "Good advice," he drawled. "I am holding on, rather. Are you?"

Lighting the cigarette necessitated a momentary pause in the car's cyclonic progress. The passenger availed himself of the opportunity; he opened the door.

"By godfrey's domino!" he panted, mopping a perspiring forehead, "don't you dare to start up that thing again. You hold still now till I get——"

He paused, his foot groping for the step. His driver regarded him with interest.

"Get where?" he asked.

"Out!" roared Balaam, throwing off the laprobe and standing erect. "Out of this everlastin' machine!"

EXTRICATING OBADIAH

"What are you getting out for? Tired of riding?"

"I'm tired of ridin' with a crazy lunatic. My godfrey's domino! Why, we never missed that last fence-post by more'n two inches!"

"So? Well, it isn't your fence, is it?"

"Ain't my *fence!* Ain't my—— By time, you *are* crazy!"

He turned and strode off. Cousin Calvin indulged in a quiet chuckle and then called after him.

"Here!... Uncle!... Griggs!" he shouted. "Wait! Come back!"

Balaam answered over his shoulder. "You go to the devil!" he snarled.

Wentworth's foot pressed the accelerator; in a moment the car was beside its former passenger.

"Better go there with me, hadn't you?" suggested Cousin Calvin. "What's the use of walking to the devil when you can go in. up-to-date fashion, with bells on? There, there! don't bend your face like that, it might crack. Jump in! I was only trying the machine out a bit. I'll slow down, of course. Anything to oblige."

Balaam hesitated and was inclined to argue, but as his companion solemnly promised not to drive faster than twenty miles an hour and offered to let the passenger guess the speed himself, he reluctantly consented to try another short stretch. "Just to see whether you're permanent loony, or only by spells," he explained.

Apparently the lunacy was merely temporary, for the car's progress for the next five miles was at a perfectly safe and sane rate of speed. Balaam was too nervous and apprehensive to offer anything in the way of conversation, and Mr. Wentworth, although unruffled and debonair as always, was not loquacious. It was not until they entered the four mile stretch of woods between Bayport and Denboro that he became talkative.

"Uncle," he observed, cheerfully, "I'm sorry to say it, but I'm disappointed in you, I am, really."

"Eh? What's that? What's comin' now, more craziness? How have I disappointed you, for mercy sakes?"

"You have. Uncle——"

"I ain't your uncle, nor no other relation, as I know of."

"Aren't you? Gad, that's a blow! Well, never mind; you've disappointed me, uncle or not. I thought you were a dead-game sport, and I'm afraid you are a four-flusher."

"A what? Now look here, Mr. Wentworth, you've been callin' me names all the mornin'. A joke's a joke, but——"

Wentworth calmly interrupted. "I thought you were a sport," he went on, "and you're not, not for a minute. I speed up this tin Lizzie here a bit and you want to get out and walk. For a man who is supposed to hunt the wild antique in its lair, as you have the reputation of doing, I—well, I'm shocked."

Most of this airy persiflage passed high over the Griggs head, but a little of it flew low enough to make a slight impression. Balaam looked rather foolish.

"Well, I tell you, Mr. Wentworth," he said, apologetically, "maybe I am a little mite extry nervous this mornin'. That—that daughter of mine, she does rile me when she sets out to. She and I had a—a little mite of a difference of opinion just now that— What are you laughin' at?"

Cousin Calvin was smiling. "Oh," he replied, carelessly, "nothing in particular, except that— Well—er— when you and she have a *real* row I wish you'd let me know, will you? I should like an orchestra chair; the performance should be interesting."

His passenger regarded him sourly. His suspicions concerning the open kitchen window and the washbench were confirmed. He had a huge respect for the New Yorker, or rather for the large fortune which the latter was supposed to possess; but there were limits to the liberties which even a rich man might take—especially on this particular morning.

"Humph!" he grunted. "So you heard the fuss, did you? Listenin', I presume likely."

"No, it wasn't necessary. I could have heard it if I had been asleep. I could have heard some of it if I had been dead."

He chuckled. Balaam gritted his teeth. "Humph!" he observed, tartly; "sounded funny to you, I presume likely. Other folks' business is liable to sound queer to —to folks that ain't got no business with it."

This shot glanced harmlessly from the Wentworth armor. Cousin Calvin calmly steered the car between a vegetable peddler's wagon and cart loaded with stove wood, missing each by a scant three inches. During the accomplishment of this feat, which called forth spirited and personal comments from the drivers of each vehicle, the condescending smile did not once leave his face.

"Peeved again, Unc— *So* sorry—Griggs, I mean.
Peeved again, eh?" he observed. "Very foolish, very
foolish. No use in getting fussed, my boy; although I
admit you did have a good excuse. She surely did make
you look like a lead dime, and when a dime is good it
isn't worth but a third of thirty cents. I'm afraid you
haven't had much experience with women, old scout."

"I want to know!" sarcastically. "And you have, eh?"

"Oh, a bit, here and there."

"Is that so! Well, you never had no experience with
one like that Mary Barstow, leastways *I* never did, and
I've been married twice."

"What's the matter with her? She's a clever girl;
seems to have a mind of her own. *And* she's a good
looker. She's the nearest approach to the blue ribbon
winner in the peach exhibit that I've seen in *this* county
fair. You can't drive a girl like that, Griggs. Your
only hope would be to coax her, or to work the diplomatic racket somehow. Well, you won't be troubled
with her much longer, I imagine. Your responsibility
in that direction will be relieved."

If the latter portion of these remarks had been intended as an additional irritant to the already raw temper of Mr. Griggs, they achieved their aim.

"What?" snarled Balaam. "Won't be troubled? Responsibility? What do you mean? What are you talkin'
about?"

Wentworth glanced at him from the corners of his
eyes.

"Oh," he observed, lightly, "I meant simply what I've
heard—what everyone says, you know. You know what

I mean; you and she were discussing it in that little family—er—difference of opinion you mentioned. From all I can gather she'll be taken off your hands soon. Our cold-storage friend—er—Clifford, you know—he—"

He got no further. Mr. Griggs proceeded to express his opinion of Irving Clifford, volubly, forcibly and at length. His companion listened until the typhoon had spent a little of its force, then he broke in to ask another question.

"What's the matter with Clifford?" he asked. "He seems a decent enough chap—for a burg like this. Why have you got it in for him?"

That didn't make any difference. Irving Clifford was a—etcetera, etcetera. And he should *not* marry Mary Barstow.

"Why not?" inquired the blandly persistent Wentworth. "She's bound to marry someone some day. Gad, man, you can't expect to keep her always, you know. Not her variety—not on your life, not any. Why not Clifford as well as the next in line? Why not the cold-storage candidate?"

Mr. Griggs proceeded to give other reasons. They were noisy but not very convincing. Boiled down, the objections seemed to center less on any particular suitor than on suitors in general. Cousin Calvin noted this.

"I see," he said; "I'm on. You don't want the girl to get away from you at all; want her to stay at home with you and do the clinging vine and sturdy oak business, prop of your declining years and all that. I see; yes, yes. Old scout, you lose; you can't win."

"Why? Why? Ain't I givin' her all the comforts and—and—clothes—and——"

"Back up. Clifford will give her all the clothes and comforts, I imagine—glad of the chance. Say," turning with a whimsical grin in his passenger's direction, "this is a revelation to me, Griggs, really it is. I didn't know you were such a fond parent. Just dying to sacrifice your all for the girl, eh? My ducats for my daughter! Gad, the young lady doesn't seem thrilled with your self-sacrifice. Judging by some of the jolts she handed you this morning——"

"Damn her!"

"Eh?"

"Damn her, I say! She's a sassy, impudent, money-spendin' critter. I wish she was to thunder and gone! I——"

"Whew! Wait! I don't just get you. I was all set to catch a blessing and you toss over a damn. You wish she was—where?"

Balaam told where he wished his stepdaughter might be transported, shouted it, in fact. His rage had boiled over at last and he was forgetting everything in the joy of expression.

"I see. Well, why don't you give her to Clifford and tell him to take her there? It would be less expensive, wouldn't it? Of course, when I thought you loved her so devoutly I——"

"Loved nothin'! If 'twan't for that darned will she could take Clifford or anybody else and go to Joppa for all I care. *I* wouldn't shed no tears."

He paused, out of breath. Wentworth waited almost

a minute before he spoke again. When he did his tone was very quiet.

"What will?" he asked, gently.

Balaam started. All at once he seemed to realize that his anger had gotten the better of his discretion. The red slid down from his forehead and cheeks; for an instant he was almost pale. He glanced apprehensively at his driver, but the latter was innocently scanning the road ahead.

"Oh, nothin', nothin'," stammered Mr. Griggs. "There, there!" he added, testily, "let's change the subject, for godfrey's sakes. I'm sick of talkin' about women's foolishness."

So the subject was changed. Only indirectly, and then only when they were within a few miles of Ostable, was Miss Barstow's name again mentioned. Cousin Calvin, who had done most of the talking during the latter part of the journey, had been inquiring concerning the old families of Trumet. The Griggs family, so brilliantly represented by its present head, was one of the oldest. Balaam knew every cousin, second, third or fourth, for two generations, and had much to say, generally of an unpleasant nature, concerning each.

"Your wife, too, came of an old Trumet family, didn't she?" asked Wentworth.

"My first wife did, she was a Bassett, same tribe as Uncle Labe Bassett. My second wife, though, Mary's ma, she wasn't a Trumeter. She belonged up to Wapatomac, all her folks came from there."

"How did you happen to meet her? Are you acquainted in Wapatomac?"

11   155

"Ain't now, much. I used to be. I knew her husband that was."

"Miss Barstow's father, you mean?"

"Sartin, Ira Barstow; I knew him fust-rate. Done some real estate tradin' with him. Good while ago that was."

"Did he ever live in Trumet?"

"No, no. Lived in Wapatomac most all his life. Died there, too. I helped his widow straighten out some of the real estate deals he had—that was his business, you see. She and I got acquainted then. 'Twas five year afterwards we got married, though. The Barstows wan't Trumet, not a bit of 'em. But the Pennimans, there's another old family. Why——"

He discoursed concerning the Pennimans until they turned into the Ostable main street and stopped before his lawyer's door.

"I'll be in here for quite a spell," he informed his companion. "Got a lot of fussin' and red tape about foreclosin' a mortgage. Want to come in and wait, do you? I guess likely you can, if you want to, but 'twould be kind of stupid for you, I should say."

Cousin Calvin declined this cordial invitation. He would walk about the town and see the lions, he said. Balaam informed him that the "nighest things to lions or any other menagerie critters in Ostable are them two cast-iron deers up on Judge Baxter's grounds." Mr. Wentworth said no doubt they would do and strolled away.

He did not visit the Baxter grounds, however. Instead, he walked up the main street until he reached the

County Court House. Entering the building, he sought the office of the Clerk of Probate. The clerk was out, but the young man in charge was willing to oblige.

"You keep the records here, don't you?" asked Mr. Wentworth. "Deeds and copies of wills, and so on? I thought so. Well, I'm from the—er—from the West, you see, and I am looking up some old family records. I am interested in the Barstow family; the branch which used to live in Wapatomac, I believe. There was a John Barstow and a—an Edward Barstow and—and a—oh, yes, an Ira Barstow. It occurred to me if I could look over some of the Barstow wills it might help me to trace——"

And so on, smiling, urbane and graciously polite. The youthful representative of the Clerk of Probate felt quite flattered to be on such friendly terms with so distinguished a visitor. When that visitor handed him a cigar —one Captain Newcomb had given him, Wentworth, that very morning—he was ready to turn the entire records of the county over for inspection.

"The only thing is," he said, "these kind of things are all dated. If you knew about what years some of these Barstow folks died, Mister, I guess we could locate 'em."

Mr. Wentworth did a little mental arithmetic. Mary —he had heard her say so—was twenty-one. He had heard from other sources that she was but a young girl when her mother married Balaam Griggs. He added, substracted, and then took a flying shot.

"Suppose we begin by looking up one of them," he said. "John— No, he would be too far back. Edward would come later, but— No, we'll see if we can find

Ira. Please try and find the will of Ira Barstow of Wapatomac, who died in—well, in 1905 or 6 or 7, or thereabouts."

When Cousin Calvin emerged from the Court House he was smiling and there was a satisfied look on his face. He had inspected Ira Barstow's will, also the will of Martha Briggs, formerly Martha Barstow. He had been unable to locate the wills of several other Barstows, John and Edward among them, but he bore these disappointments bravely. He was in serene good-humor when he returned to the spot where he had left the motor car and found Mr. Griggs waiting for him on the lawyer's steps.

Balaam, too, was in good-humor. The business at the lawyer's had been entirely satisfactory. He had secured a desirable piece of property at a small cost to himself and, if the former owners would be obliged to give up what had been the family home for two generations, that, obviously, was not Mr. Griggs' fault.

He and Mr. Wentworth boarded the car again and they moved out of Ostable once more. Then, on the Bayport road, the driver slowed down to a surprisingly moderate rate of speed and began to talk.

"Griggs," he said, "are you really serious in your objection to Clifford's marrying your stepdaughter?"

"Eh? Am I serious? Good godfrey's domino! Have I been talkin' as if I was enjoyin' it? Am I serious! What in the nation?"

"Oh, all right! Keep your kimono on, Uncle. You'd like to break off the intimacy between them, then?"

"Would I? You show me how to do it and then see!"

"It shouldn't be so very hard."

_ "Oh, shouldn't, eh? Humph! Talk's cheap. Any kind of a job's soft to the feller that don't have to do it."

"Yes, and nothing's much harder than a bonehead. If it were up to me I'd guarantee that she tied the can to our friend Clifford inside of a month."

"I want to know! Huh! Well, then, I wish 'twas up to you, that's all I've got to say. How would you do it?"

"Oh, I'd do it."

"Yes, you would—like a hen!"

"I beg your pardon?"

"Eh! What for? You ain't done nothin' to me, have you? I said you wouldn't do what you said you'd do, that's all."

"No, you didn't. You said I would do it like a—like a chicken, wasn't it? What on earth did you mean by that?"

"Eh? I said like a hen. That means you wouldn't do it at all."

Cousin Calvin shook his head. "Griggs," he observed, "your conversation is scrambled. I could do it. Would you like to make a sporting proposition of it? What will you bet that the—er—friendship between Miss Barstow and Clifford isn't ended inside of a month? Come, now, be a dead game one. Name your figure."

Baalam regarded him with suspicion.

"You're foolin' again, ain't you?" he asked.

"Not a bit of it. What will you bet?"

Mr. Griggs scratched his chin.

"I don't never bet," he said, after a moment's reflection. "I don't believe in it, 'tain't moral."

His companion laughed heartily. "Griggs," he exclaimed, "you're a wonder. You're too good to be real; there ain't no such animal. Do you know, just for that I'm inclined to help you out of your scrape. Do you want to get rid of Clifford very much?"

"You bet your life I do!"

"Here, here! Careful! Betting isn't moral. Well, then, I'll— Yes, I'll get rid of him for you."

"You will? You *will?* Humph! What for?"

"Oh, just for love. Who could help loving you, old scout? 'None knew him but to love him, none named him but to——' "

"Aw, shut up your foolin'! What are you goin' to help me get rid of Irve Clifford for?"

"What for? . . . Oh, you mean for what?"

"For what? For how much? That's what I mean."

"For nothing."

Mr. Griggs sniffed disdainful unbelief. "I know a dum sight better," he declared. "Nobody in this world does anything for nothin'. What do you want for doin' it? Takin' it for granted you can do it at all," he added, "which I doubt."

Wentworth whistled a few notes of a popular song. "I don't want anything," he said, "except——"

"Ah, ha! Yes—except——"

"Except the fun of doing it. Perhaps I don't love brother Irving myself—perhaps."

"You don't! I thought you and him was kind of chummy. You go to see him down to the cold-storage, and all."

"I have to go and see someone, occasionally; and in this God-forsaken hole choice is limited. But I knew

him in New York and— Well, never mind that. Do
you want me to can him for you?"

"Yes, sir-ee!"

"Good! It's a deal. Shall we shake on it?"

He took one hand from the steering wheel and extended it in his passenger's direction. Mr. Griggs' huge
paw reached forth and surrounded it.

"And now," demanded the owner of the paw, "how
are you goin' to do it, eh?"

Cousin Calvin whistled another verse of the song.
Then he said:

"That, my old college chum, is my business for the
present. Yours is to keep quiet and wait. When it is
your turn to jump I'll pull the string."

Balaam nodded.

"All right," he agreed. "I'll be quiet, don't you fret.
But—but I wish I knew what in time you are settin'
out to do this for."

His driver sang a line of the song he had been
whistling.

"'It is you, my darling, it is you,'" he hummed,
sweetly.

That evening he wrote a letter and, the next morning,
posted it.

CHAPTER XII

MR. BURGESS threw down the book in disgust. "Well, I snum!" he exclaimed. "If that don't beat all! Advertise from Dan to Beersheby that when you read one of these b-b-bub-books you'll know more'n Dan'l Webster and Moses and the Ten Commandments rolled into one, and yet—and yet, by cu-cuk-cracky, the fust word I go to look up ain't in it at all."

Captain Newcomb, sitting in the rocker by the window and looking out over the bay, rosy with the after-sunset glow, turned and regarded the little man.

"What book's that you're heavin' round so reckless, Obe?" he asked.

Obadiah kicked at the discarded volume.

"Encyclopedy," he replied, crossly. "Cost much as two or three dollars a p-p-piece, them books do, they tell me, and there's about forty of 'em in a set; come in schools, they do, like b-b-bluefish. And there ain't nothin' in 'em! By cracky, it does m-m-make a feller mad the way he's skinned out of his money."

He gave the book another thrust with his foot.

"Humph!" observed Noah. "There's lots of things in this world that cost money but ain't much use. A good many rich men's sons would fill *that* bill. But I wouldn't kick the thing, if I was you; playin' football with a three-dollar book seems to me kind of an expensive game.

Mr. Burgess sniffed. "Oh, 'tain't my book," he said. "I b-b-borrowed it off the Methodist minister."

However, he stooped and picked it up.

"What word was you lookin' for?" asked the captain.

"Copper. That's a common enough word, ain't it? Ought to be in any decent cyclopedy, hadn't it?"

"It sartin had. I guess likely 'tis, too. Let's see that book. Humph! 'tis the C. one. I thought maybe you was huntin' for it under K."

Obadiah's feelings were hurt. "K! the idee!" he exclaimed. "I guess I shouldn't hunt for c-c-copper under no K. I've been to school same as you have, Cap'n Noah."

His companion nodded. "Cal'late that's so, Obe," he said. "However, I judge you didn't hunt very far for it under C. Anyhow, here 'tis, two or three pages of it."

Mr. Burgess rose and looked over his friend's shoulders. "Why, it's got *two* p's in it!" he declared, with evident astonishment. "Sho!"

He took the book from the captain's hands and sat down to read. Noah watched the process, a slow and apparently painful one, for a few moments. Then he chuckled quietly and asked: "Obe, what set you to readin' up about copper?"

Obadiah absently raised his head.

"Eh?" he queried.

"What are you studyin' up about copper for? Cal'latin'

to buy a few mines, was you? Or have you been specu-latin' heavy in stock lately?"

These questions were intended as jokes, but Mr. Bur-gess did not laugh, nor even smile. On the contrary, he straightened in his chair, the book slipped from his knees to the floor, and he sat there, pallid, and staring at his friend as if the latter's harmless and rather feeble at-tempt at humor had been a pistol shot fired at his head.

Captain Noah in return stared at him.

"What in the world?" he demanded.

Obadiah's chin quivered. He essayed to speak.

"I—I What— What?" he faltered.

The captain sprang to his feet.

"He's got a shock!" he cried. "He's had a stroke! Mrs. Mayo! Mis' Melissy!"

But Obadiah waved both hands in frantic protest.

"Don't!" he begged. "Don't—don't holler! I—I—I——"

"Holler! I'll do more'n holler."

He was on his way toward the kitchen, but Obadiah seized his coat tail.

"Don't! Don't!" he commanded. "'Tain't nothin'. I'm all right! I be, honest! I——"

"All *right?* Why, you're white as my shirt this min-ute. You're sick! Anybody can see that. What is it? Where does it hurt you?"

He was bending over his friend, hastily trying to un-button the latter's waistcoat. Obadiah pushed him away.

"It don't hurt me," he protested. "There ain't nothin' to h-h-hurt. I'm all right."

"You are, eh?" Noah stopped and looked into his face.

"Humph!" he grunted, after a brief inspection; "well, you do seem to be little mite more human and less like a —a jelly fish. What in the nation set you off that way?"

Burgess was obviously struggling to get control of himself. He reached for his handkerchief and mopped his perspiring forehead.

" 'Tain't nothin'," he explained, avoiding his companion's eye. "It's just a—a—a kind of—of a spell as you might say. I'm—I'm s-s-subject to 'em."

"Oh, you are!" Captain Noah regarded him with suspicion. "Subject to 'em, are you? Well, Obe, if *I* was subject to anything like that I'd get a doctor—or a keeper —or somethin'. How long have you been subject to 'em? This is the first attack you've had since I've been here."

Mr. Burgess, still dabbing at his forehead with the handkerchief, explained that he hadn't had none lately. "It's—it's somethin' I eat," he added. "Don't talk about it. Hearin' you makes me nervous."

"Want to know! Well, *seein'* you makes me nervous. What did you swallow that set you to shakin' like that— an earthquake? There, there, don't go. I won't pester you. Stay where you are."

Obadiah stayed, although, judging from his manner, he would have preferred to go. He picked up the encyclopedia once more and pretended to read, although the deepening dusk made reading more and more impossible Captain Noah filled and lit his pipe and, leaning back in his chair, regarded the little man steadily. At last the latter spoke again.

"Cap'n," he said, fidgeting with the leaves of the volume in his lap, "—er—er—what made you ask me that question?"

"What question?"

"Why—why, that question about my b-b-buyin' stocks or such foolishness? That was a f-f-funny thing to ask, seemed to me."

"Um. Yes, I could see it seemed awful funny to you, Obe. I never saw anybody get so much fun out of anything as you did out of that."

"Ha, ha!" Obadiah's laugh was rather forced. "I know," he went on, "but I didn't mean f-f-funny, I meant queer. Queer you should ask me if I'd bought stocks. Who told you such a thing as that?"

"Told me! Nobody told me, of course. I was just foolin' with you, that's all."

"Was you?" Mr. Burgess seemed to doubt the statement. "Was you? Yes, I presume likely you was. But —but co-cuk-copper stock, that was a queer thing to think of. Who put that silly notion in your head?"

"Nobody. It came there of itself; saw there was a loft to let and moved in, I shouldn't wonder. By the way, you haven't answered my question. What set you to lookin' up copper in that book?"

"Nothin', nothin'. I just took a notion, that's all." He put down the encyclopedia and rose. "I cal'late I won't read any more," he said, hastily. "Guess likely I'll go— go down to the p-p-post office or somewheres."

"Shall I go along with you, Obe?" suggested the captain.

Obadiah apparently did not hear; at all events he made no answer.

EXTRICATING OBADIAH

For a few minutes after he had gone Captain Noah sat there, puffing at his pipe. Then he stood up, put the pipe in his pocket and walked briskly to the kitchen. Mrs. Mayo was just wiping the last of the supper dishes.

"Obadiah's gone to the post office, ain't he?" asked the captain. "Notice which way he went?"

Joe Kenney came into the kitchen just then and it was he who answered the question.

"I don't think he's gone to the office, Cap'n Newcomb," he said. "I saw him walkin' along the path back of the barn just now."

The path behind the barn skirted the edge of the bluff above the bay. It was a short cut to the beach and the fish houses, but it most certainly did not lead to the post office. Captain Noah climbed the low fence by the pigsty and set off along the path. It was quite dark now and very quiet. The ripples splashed and chuckled on the shore below, and except for the barking of a distant dog, there were no other sounds.

The captain walked briskly on. He meant, if possible, to overtake his friend before the latter reached the village. He climbed another fence, descended a little hill, and there stopped short. At the top of the knoll before him, where the path wound close to the cliff edge, some one, a summer resident probably, had at some time or other erected a rustic seat. On that seat, his huddled form silhouetted against the evening sky, was a man. And as Noah stood there, looking and listening, he heard the sound of a groan.

The captain tiptoed carefully up the little hill, bent over

167

the figure on the rustic bench, and gently laid a hand on its shoulder.

"It's all right, Obe," he said, quietly. "Don't be scared. It's just me; it's all right."

Mr. Burgess was scared, or at least tremendously startled. He would have fallen from the seat and, as likely as not, over the edge of the bluff, had not the captain's big hand held him fast.

"Steady, Obe, steady," said Noah. "Set right where you are. I was in hopes I'd catch you afore you got too fur, and now that I have, I ain't goin' to let you go. Set still, shipmate. It's high time you and me had a talk."

Obadiah gasped and stammered. He had been in a highly nervous state before his friend's unexpected appearance; now he was on the verge of collapse.

"Steady as she is, Obe," ordered the captain. "As I say, it's high time you and me had a talk. 'Twas plain enough you had a load of trouble under your hatches, but you would persist in keepin' those hatches closed. Now that I've got one peek at your cargo you might as well let me go over the whole manifest. What kind of copper stocks have you been buyin' and how much money have you lost?"

Obadiah turned, stared at him, and then, before his companion realized what he was about, leaped to his feet and started to run. Fortunately for Captain Noah's plans, made during the recent few minutes of meditation in the sitting room, he did not get entirely free. The captain pulled him back, forced him down upon the seat and held him there.

"No use, Obe," he said. "I ain't been towin' my rheumatiz so fur across these damp fields just to start it after you on another lap. You set still and tell me all about it. Set still, you little shrimp! I swan to man, you've got more wiggles to you than an eel in a barrel of sweet ile! Hold still! don't be so foolish."

Mr. Burgess held still, that is, he was held, but his protests were voluble. For the first time during their acquaintance, as Captain Noah said afterwards, he did not have time to remember to stutter.

"Let me go," he ordered. "Let me go, Cap'n Noah. What have you been followin' me this way for? What are you hangin' onto me for? Let me go, I tell you."

His captor was imperturbable. "Sorry I can't oblige, Obe," he said. "I don't know as it's really soaked down through your main deck yet, but I'm doin' my best to be your friend. That's what I came to Trumet to be, and it's the job I've had on my hands ever since. I'm goin' to find out what sort of a scrape you're in, and then, if I can, I'm goin' to help you out of it. Seems to me that now's as good a time as any for you to tell me the yarn. What do *you* think?"

Whether this appeal to reason had the desired effect or not is immaterial, for something did. Mr. Burgess ceased struggling and began to groan.

"I—I know you think I'm a p-p-plaguey fool," he wailed. "I know you do. I—I s'pose Balaam told you about my buyin' it and—and——"

"Sshh! Balaam told me? Balaam Griggs ain't told 'me anything. What's he got to do with it?"

"He sold it to me. He must have told you, else how did you know? I never said——"

"Wait a minute! Heave to! What was it Balaam Griggs sold you?"

"Why, the copper stock, the hundred shares Ostrich Minin' and Smeltin' of Lake Superior Company. Fifty dollars a share I paid and—and he said 'twas liable to go to a hundred and f-f-fifty 'most any minute."

"Did, eh? Um-hm. Well, maybe 'twill—if it don't get off the course. Sometimes those sure-thing clippers run on the rocks."

"Eh? On the rocks! Oh, *don't* talk so, Noah! Don't! I—I put five thousand dollars into that stock. Five *thousand!* You don't cal'late anything's goin' to happen to it, do you? My—my Lord above, if it does, what'll I do? I don't sleep none nights thinkin' of it. I got scared soon as I done it. That was why I sent for you. Oh, Cap'n Noah, I—I can't get along and p-p-pup-pay my bills as 'tis; I'm runnin' astern every minute. If I lose that money— O, o-oh!"

He wrung his hands. The captain patted his shoulder.

"There, there, Obe!" he said. "You ain't on any rocks yet, maybe; perhaps you ain't goin' to be. You may be on your way to millions, for all I know. There, there! stop wavin' your flippers and spin me the yarn; tell me the whole of it from stem to stern."

So Obadiah told it. The telling took a good while, owing to the narrator's tendency to stammer and his fondness for repetition and ejaculation. It seems that the purchase of stock had been made about a month before Noah received the letter summoning him to Trumet. Mr. Burgess and his friend Griggs had discussed financial matters, incomes, dividends and the like. "We talked

about them kind of things pretty often," explained Obadiah. "Balaam he had money and he knew I had,
too——"

"Knew how much you had, I presume likely?" interrupted the captain.

"Sartin. I told him. Bein' wuth twelve thousand and
more ain't nothin' to be a-sh-sh-shamed of, is it?"

"No, no. Long as you are worth it, it ain't. Heave
ahead with your yarn."

When Mr. Griggs learned that his friend was receiving
only six per cent interest on his money he was shocked
and pained, particularly when told that Mr. Burgess
never was tempted to do what he, Balaam, termed "turn
it over."

"He said he was always 'turnin'' his money over," declared Obadiah. "Never let it lay idle, as you might say.
He just kept her busy, turnin' over and turnin' over, and
whenever he see a g-g-good investment he turned it into
that. Understand what he meant, don't you, Cap'n?"

The captain nodded. "Um-hm," he said. "I cal'late
I understand what _he_ meant. Go on."

"I'm a-goin'. Well, of course, hearin' all that talk made
me kind of—of uncontented myself. I kind of got to
hankerin' to t-t-tut-turn over some of my capital."

"Some of your what?"

"Some of my ca-ca-capital. That's what Balaam calls
it, means money and—and such, you know. He says
rich folks never call their money money, always call it
capital."

Obadiah had yearned for the "turning over" of his
capital, also for the eight, ten and twelve per cent divi-

dends his financial mentor spoke of as so plentiful provided one was, like himself, "in on the know." Then he spoke of lucky turns in the stock market, of doubling one's investment, of mines—and, at last, of the Ostrich Copper and Smelting Company of Lake Superior. "If a feller had the ready money to put into it," whispered Mr. Griggs, in the strictest confidence, "and could get a holt of—say—fifty or a hundred shares of that Ostrich Minin'— Whew! But," he added, sadly, "it's turrible scarce and hard to get a holt of."

He showed Burgess clippings from New York papers stating that it was rumored in the Street that wealthy and influential parties were negotiating for the Ostrich property. He showed him records of sales on the Curb. Those sales recorded the advance of Ostrich Common from thirty to fifty—yes, even sixty—dollars a share. And at last he came to joyfully whisper the news—when speaking of money or its equivalent Mr. Griggs was accustomed to whisper reverently—that he believed he could "get a-holt" of one hundred of Ostrich Common at fifty.

"He said 'twas a chance wouldn't come more'n once in a lifetime," went on Obadiah. "He'd been just dyin' for me to h-h-have such a chance and here 'twas. He'd done it just out of friendship."

"Oh, *he* wan't goin' to buy no—er—Zebra—Ostrich, or whatever 'tis, then?" the captain broke in to ask.

"No, he couldn't. His money was all tied up where 'twas gettin' such big interest he dasent disturb it. But he'd h-h-heard of the chance and thought of m-m-me and——"

"Yes, yes, I see. Well, you bought it and paid five thousand for it. Where'd you get the money?"

"Sold some of the stocks Aunt Sarah left me. They wan't p-p-payin' but six, you see."

He named some of the securities he had sold. Captain Noah groaned when he heard their names.

"Don't tell me any more," he said. "You've got your —your Spread-Eagle—Mackerel Gull—your Ostrich, I mean? Got the certificate, have you?"

Yes, Mr. Burgess had that at home. He would be glad to show it to his friend.

"It's all made out, Cap'n," he declared. "Got my name on it and all, it has. It's a awful pretty c'tif'cate."

Noah grinned. "Well, I'm glad to hear that," he said. "That's a great comfort. If you'd paid five thousand dollars for a homely certificate my heart *would* have been broke. Well, Obe, I've heard so much, but I ain't heard why you sent for me. Wanted me to help spend the extry cash you've made, was that it?"

It was rather cruel sarcasm. Poor Obadiah almost wept. "I—I—I ain't made none," he faltered. "That is, I don't know's I ain't, but I don't know as I have. I—I—I don't know nothin' about it. You see, I—I've been lookin' in the papers every day, in the p-p-pup-places Balaam showed me, but it ain't there."

"What ain't there; your profits?"

"No. Nothin' ain't there. Ostrich ain't. Fur's I can make out by them newspapers nobody ain't buyin' any Ostrich, nor sellin' of it neither."

"Humph! That's funny. You say there was sales in the paper."

"Sartin! Every day there was. Balaam, he showed me 'em."

"Sho! Did you—er—notice the dates of the papers he showed you? Whether they was that day's papers or last year's?"

"No, I never noticed that. Oh, Cap'n Noah, you don't cal'late——"

"I don't cal'late anything yet, Obe. Any sort of worth while cal'latin' takes time. You ain't heard a—a squawk from your Ostrich, you say? Got any dividends?"

"No."

"Humph! What's Balaam say about it? A man that's 'in on the know' the way he figgers to be ought to give you news right straight from the Ostrich—er—roost, so to speak. What kind of comfort does he give you?"

"Why, he says he cal'lates it's goin' to come out all right. Give it time, he says. Takes time for them big d-d-deals to go through. He keeps tellin' me to keep c-c-cuk-cool and not to say a word about it to a soul."

"Especially me, eh? Ever mention not tellin' me?"

"Well, he did just happen to say that—that—maybe I'd better not worry you with it."

"My, I'm grateful to him. Anyhow, your conscience is clear; you didn't tell me; I guessed. But you *ain't* told me why you sent for me."

And then Obadiah's remnant of self-control left him. The tears which he had thus far held back rolled unrestrained down his cheeks. He sobbed forth his woes. He was worried almost to death. His income would not half meet his expenses; he was running into debt; he didn't know *what* would become of him.

"It was hard enough to get along afore I sold my other stocks," he wailed. "Even then, the way things cost nowadays, I—I—I couldn't hardly see my way clear. Not after Cousin Calvin came I couldn't, and Melissy and Joe and—and——"

"And me," finished Noah.

"But—but you're different. I sent for you. I thought 'twould be a good notion havin' C-C-Calvin come, 'cause he was a invalid and s-s-so rich and liable to die and all. Then I had to have a housekeeper to t-t-tut-take care of the tribe of us and I had to have her nephew 'cause she wouldn't come unless he did. But Calvin he d-d-didn't d-d-die and I d-d-dud-d——"

The succession of d's was too much for him; the final "didn't" proved a hurdle which seemed likely to throw him altogether. Noah came to the rescue.

"Sound as if you was runnin' with your cut-out open, Obe," he said. "Let me sing the rest of the tune for you. You couldn't get along on what you had—not with all creation signed to sail with you—so when Balaam told you about this Hummin' Bird—this Ostrich, I mean—you thought you saw a chance to make a lot more. Then after you'd bought it you got cold feet, got scared you'd done the wrong thing, and wrote to me to come and tell you you hadn't. Then, after I had come, you got cold feet again, got scared to tell me for fear I'd tell you that you'd made a fool of yourself. That's about it, ain't it?"

Mr. Burgess nodded, miserably. "That's it," he groaned. "I don't see how you knew it, though."

"Oh, I'm awful smart, Obe. My middle name ought

to have been Solomon. Well, 'twas pretty much as I suspected; I knew there was somethin' up. . . . Humph!"

He paused, evidently reflecting. Obadiah looked fearfully up at him.

"Have I?" he faltered.

"Have you what?"

"Made a f-f-fool of myself, same as you said?"

The captain started to speak and then evidently thought better of it. A moment later he said:

"Obe, my dad used to tell about old man Jotham Hallett that lived somewheres down this way. Jotham and his wife used to squabble six days in the week and every other Sunday. One time he took the cover off the cistern, so's to see how much water there was in it, and fell in. His wife heard the splash and came runnin'. There was Jotham standin' on tiptoe with just his face above water. 'Why, you old numskull!' she says. 'I'd like to know how you ever got in there.' Jotham blew the water away from his mouth and sputtered back: 'Don't you worry about how I got in, woman,' he says. 'It's goin' to strain what little brains you've got to know how to get me *out.*' That's the way I feel about this Ostrich business of yours, Obe—that and the rest of it. We know you're in, that's sartin. What we'll worry about now is gettin' you out."

"But—but Cap'n Noah——"

"Ss-sh! There, there! Don't get yourself all worked up again. Your beloved messmate, Griggs, gave you one good piece of advice, no matter what the heft of his counsel may amount to. He told you to keep cool, didn't he? Um-hm. All right, you keep cool, Obe; cool *and* quiet.

Don't you mention one single word to a soul about havin'
this talk with me. If you do I'll—I'll—I swan I'll clear
out and leave you the minute I hear of it."

"Oh, I won't, Cap'n. You know I won't. I'll swear
it on the Bible. I——"

"Never mind that. There won't be any swearin'
done unless I think it's necessary—and then I'm afraid
'twill be another kind. Now you heave ahead to the post
office, or wherever you want to go. I'm goin' up to my
room and think. Thinkin' is a kind of hard exercise for
me and I need elbow room to do it in. See you later,
maybe. Good night."

"But—but Cap'n Noah, you ain't told me about that
Ostrich stock. You don't think——"

"Yes, I do, but I try not to talk until I have thought.
So long, Obe."

The little man made one more attempt.

"Oh, Noah," he pleaded, "you will try to help me,
won't you?"

The captain's patience was plainly at an end. He
turned quickly. But when he saw the simple childish
face upturned to his, he relented somewhat. He shook
his head.

"Obe," he said, with elaborate gentleness, "I'm sorry
I didn't tell you that. I meant to have told you that
when I left you last fall I told you I'd help you any time
you needed help. And I likewise meant to have told you
that about every day since I came back here I've been
tellin' you I'd come to help you. It's too bad I ain't told
you how much I've told, isn't it? Well, I'll tell you now.

177

You want to know if I'm goin' to try to help you, do you? Good! Listen and I'll whisper it."

He stooped, put his lips close to Obadiah's ear, and shouted "Yes" at the top of his lungs. Then he strode down the hill and back to the house.

CHAPTER XIII

UPSTAIRS in his room and with the door shut he sat down to do what he had told Burgess he intended doing—that is, think. His temper was still rather ruffled. Not that he had been greatly surprised at the nature of his former cook's trouble; he had from the first suspected something of the sort. He had told Clifford in one of their conversations that Obadiah Burgess was about as fit to be trusted with money as a year-old child was with the front parlor lookin'-glass and a hammer. But having one's forebodings realized is not necessarily pleasing. He was irritated to think Obadiah had been such an idiot, and furiously angry with Balaam Griggs for taking such a mean advantage of the little man.

There was, of course, no doubt in his mind that such advantage had been taken. The Ostrich mining stock was, in all human probability, worth little or nothing. If it had been very valuable Balaam would have kept it himself instead of procuring it for his "friend." However, there was a chance that it might not be entirely worthless, and the first thing to do, he decided, was to find out what it was worth or likely to be worth, to find out, in fact, the history and probable future of the Ostrich Mining and Smelting Company of Lake Superior. Having that information he could better decide what to do for Mr. Burgess and to Balaam Griggs.

He had a relative in New York, a second cousin, who was a broker downtown. This cousin, whose name was Chase, had helped him before with advice concerning financial matters. Noah had always consulted him when making his own investments. He took from his bureau drawer pen, ink and paper and sat down at the table to write a letter.

DEAR GEORGE: [he began] I want to know something. There are times when even as clever a feller as one of your relations comes to realize that he is off his course and has to speak for his latitude and longitude. I want you to tell me what you know about a copper stock called Ostrich Mining and Smelting. I have a notion that last name ought to be "Smelling" because, unless I am a whole lot mistaken, one deal that has been put through in it is pretty rank fishy. You need not telephone the asylum, George, because I ain't the one that was in the deal. But——

He had written so much when there came a knock at the bedroom door.

"Cap'n Newcomb," said Mrs. Mayo, "Mr. Clifford is downstairs and he says he'd like awful to see you. He says if you've gone to bed——"

"To bed! Land sakes, no! I ain't gone to bed yet. What does he think I am, a pullet? Course I'll see him, glad to."

"Then I'll tell him you'll be right down?"

"No, you tell him to come up aloft here, if you'd just as soon."

When Irving entered the room the captain greeted him with a broad grin.

"Glad to see you, son," he said. "I was just thinkin' I'd have somethin' to tell you when I did see you. Looks as if I'd fitted in another piece of that puzzle of mine. I. . . . Eh? Why, you look as if you had somethin' to tell *me*. What's the matter, Irve?"

The young man certainly did look as if he had something to tell and as if that something was anything but pleasant. He threw himself into the chair his friend pushed forward, but waved aside a proffered cigar.

"No, thanks, Captain," he said, gloomily, "I don't feel like smoking."

"Don't, eh? Well, now, don't you think if you tried it you'd feel more like it? My troubles are kind of like a ham or a herrin', they're better smoked. Perhaps yours'll be."

Clifford smiled in recognition of the pleasantry, but the smile was a faint one. However, he took the cigar, gripped it between his teeth and, having lighted it, puffed savagely.

"Bad news?" asked Noah, after a short silence on the part of both men.

Clifford shook his head. "I don't know that one could call it news exactly," he said, "but it's bad enough."

"Humph! Nobody dead, but somebody ought to be. Is that it?"

"That's it. Or part of it."

"Sho! Feel like tellin' me who?"

"Can't tell you. I don't know. If I only did I'd——"

His fists clenched. The captain regarded him sympathetically, but asked no more questions. It was Clifford
himself who resumed the conversation.

"Captain," he said, "you're a good fellow, did you
know it? Nobody but you would have let me lug my
grouch in here and behave in this way without worrying
me to death to find out what it was all about. The reason I haven't told you yet is—is——"

"There, there, Irve! You ain't got to tell me, you
know."

"I know, but I'm going to. That's what I came here
for; I've *got* to talk it over with somebody. I can't go
away tomorrow, to Chicago, and leave things as they are,
without a word to anyone. I can't! I won't!"

Captain Noah was surprised. "You're goin' to Chicago—tomorrow?" he cried.

"Yes. I told you I should have to go soon, you remember."

"Sartin, but I didn't think 'twas as soon as all that."

"Neither did I until I got the telegram this morning.
Yes, I must go, and I shall probably be there for some
time. The firm has a big contract there and the chap
who has been in charge is ill with typhoid. So they sent
for me. The work here can be left all right. I shouldn't
mind going ordinarily, but now——"

He did not finish his sentence, but relapsed again into
silence. His expression was proof sufficient that his
trouble, whatever it might be, was serious.

"Well," he resumed, a moment later. "I may as well
begin, I suppose. It's confoundedly hard to tell. It

isn't a thing a fellow would tell, ordinarily, unless it might be to his father or brother or someone like that. However, my father is dead and my only brother is in Frisco. And you—well, I haven't known you very long, but—but——"

The captain helped him out. "Why don't you adopt me as—as a—well, as sort of a step-uncle, Irve?" he suggested. "That is, if you're needin' relations just now, as you say you are. I'll be proud and you won't be obliged to tell anybody, you know."

Clifford laughed shortly. "I'll accept," he said, "all but the 'step' part of it. I've just had an experience with a step*father*, and that's sufficient."

Noah nodded. "Um, I see," he said. "Balaam again."

"He is only part of it. If he were all—— But there, I'll tell you and get it over with."

That afternoon while he was at the cold-storage plant a boy had brought him a note the contents of which surprised him greatly. It was from Balaam Griggs, and requested him to call at the Griggs house immediately, as the writer had something important to say to him. Considering that Balaam had forbidden him the house and he had not been there for a fortnight, the invitation seemed strange. However, he went.

Balaam had received him in the sitting room. Mary, too, was there.

Griggs looked very severe and self-righteous; his step-daughter angry and indignant. Before the former could say a word the young lady burst out with a denial that she had had any part in summoning him, Clifford, there.

"I want you to understand, Irving," she said, "that I do not believe a word of it, that I know it is not true and that I am sure the whole thing is merely a ridiculous attempt on Mr. Griggs' part to bring about a quarrel between you and me."

Here Clifford, having told so much, reddened a little, appeared confused and then blurted out: "You see, Captain Newcomb, I— Well, perhaps I ought to say—ought to tell you that since our former talk on this subject Miss Barstow—Mary—and I have had—had had—well, we had reached an understanding, and she—she——"

The captain waited to hear no more. He sprang from his chair and, smiling broadly, extended a hand.

"Good enough, son!" he cried, heartily. "I congratulate you! Shake!"

But his visitor refused to shake. Instead, he frowned and said gloomily: "Better keep your congratulations until you hear the rest of the story. Thank you just the same, of course."

Mary's declaration had stirred Balaam to high indignation. He scorned her base insinuations, not in those words, of course, but in his own. When she announced her intention of leaving the room he commanded her not to do so.

"I tell you to stay right here," he said. "You don't believe what this letter says is true, eh?"

"I know it's not," scornfully.

"No, you don't. Why, you ain't read it yet. And we don't either of us know it *is* true, neither, but we'd ought to know. All I want is for this young feller himself to tell me whether 'tis or not. That's the first thing I want. If he says 'tain't true, then——"

Irving had interrupted here. "Look here, Mr. Griggs," he said, crisply, "perhaps we might get on faster if, instead of preaching a sermon beforehand, you told me the text. Apparently that letter has something to say about me. What is it? Don't go, Mary; I want you to stay."

So Mary stayed. And Balaam, after loftily proclaiming that he might read the letter aloud, but he wouldn't "demean" himself to do so, handed it to Clifford, with the command that he read it in that manner.

"Read it right out loud," he ordered. "It's about you, and I'm givin' you the chance to see all the testimony and prove yourself not guilty if you can. And let me tell you, young feller," he declared, " 'tain't every father would do that. Now you read."

Here Captain Noah's visitor seemed to find the telling of the story particularly hard. His embarrassment increased and he picked nervously at the table-cloth as he proceeded.

"So I took the letter," he went on, "and—well, as soon as I looked at it I recognized the handwriting. And I guessed, or I partially guessed, what was coming. It was a surprise to me, of course, and I was angry anyway, and—and— Well, confound it, I imagine I must have looked and seemed like a crook caught with the goods. For a minute I just held the letter and stared and stuttered and turned red. . . . Oh, hang it all, Captain! the telling of this thing is pretty nearly as hard as the thing itself."

"Don't tell unless you want to, Irve," cautioned Captain Noah, sympathetically.

"But I do want to. I came here to tell, to see if you couldn't help me out. I took the letter and. . . . Well, after a while I began to read it. It was from a woman in New York, a woman I used to know, to know well, and she—she had written it to Griggs because, so she said, it had just come to her ears that I was contemplating marriage with his daughter and she felt both the young lady and her father should know me as I was, see me in my true colors, and all that sort of melodramatic rot. She went on to say that I had. . . . Well, what's the use? I can't tell you all the stuff in detail. It makes me furious now, it made me that and more then. And the consciousness that I was standing there, with Griggs gloating over my confusion and Mary looking at me as if—as if— Oh, hang it, Captain! I threw the letter down before I had finished it."

"You did, eh?"

"Yes, I did. I wish now I hadn't, but I did. And I turned to Mary and I asked her if she believed it."

"What did she say?"

"Nothing then. Before she could answer that confounded Griggs asked me why I hadn't read it through. There was more of it, he said, and if it wasn't true why was I afraid to read it. He would read it for me, now that he had given me the first chance and I had refused. He did read it, too. It accused me of having been engaged to marry this woman, of breaking off the engagement, of deserting her, of—of about every dishonorable thing you can think of, or, if it did not actually accuse, it intimated. The old man read it all. Then he turned to me and he said:

" 'Now, young feller, is what she says true?'

"Of course, if I had had time to think, if I had had time to decide, I should have answered him fully then. But I was so angry and so anxious to relieve Mary's mind, or to relieve my mind concerning her attitude, that I didn't answer him at all. Instead, I asked her again if she believed what the letter said."

"Sho! I want to know! What did she say?"

"She said of course not. But—but——"

"But all the same you could see she sort of did. Well, son, I ain't surprised. Mary Barstow's a mighty good girl and a sensible one, 'cordin' to all accounts, but good and sensible women are like the other kinds in one way: they'll stick to a man through thick and thin, they'll see him accused of murder or houseburnin' or piracy or anything else, and with all the evidence in creation against him they won't believe a word of it, they'll hold him innocent against the world. But when there's another woman mixed up with him, no matter if the yarn of the mixin' is so thin and slimpsy that a Nauset marsh muskeeter could fly through it anywheres and not foul a wing, then—*then*, my son, look out for squalls. I've never had a wife, but I've had an only sister. So Mary said no but looked yes, eh?"

"She looked doubtful and disturbed, or so it seemed to me. Then Griggs began to cross-question. He asked if I knew the woman. I was obliged to say I did, of course. Then he asked me if I was engaged to her. I said—I was getting more angry every minute—I said,

13   187

finally, yes, I was engaged to her at one time. And next he asked if I had told Mary that."

Captain Noah interrupted with a whistle of involuntary admiration.

"Whew!" he exclaimed. "*That* was a shot in the biler! I didn't know Balaam was so spry a cross-examiner. Sounds almost as if somebody had put him up to that. I—er—presume likely you hadn't told her?"

"No, I had not. Of course I should have done so, at some time or other. There was no reason why I should not. Look here, Captain," he added, sharply, as the thought occurred to him, "of course you thoroughly understand there was nothing I might have told which was in any way a reflection upon me in the matter."

"Oh, sartin, sartin! Never thought for a minute there was, Irve."

"There was not. I had not told Mary simply because I hadn't, there was no other reason. But Griggs' question sounded as if—well, it put me in the light of deliberately keeping something hidden from her, something I was ashamed to tell."

"I see, I see. And of course you realized that and that made you act and look as if you *was* ashamed."

"Precisely. And because there was no reason to be ashamed the whole affair made me angrier than ever with myself, with Griggs, and — yes — with Mary for looking a doubt even if she hadn't expressed it in words."

"I understand. Well, how did the whole business end?"

"It ended pretty soon after that. Griggs repeated his question. I answered pretty sharply that I had not told

Mary because I hadn't thought the affair of sufficient consequence."

"Humph! And then——?"

"Then Mary spoke. 'You have told me so many things concerning your past life, Irving,' she said. 'Some that seem, to me at least, of no more consequence than this. Why did you keep this from me?'

"I think I should have answered in a fairly temperate spirit if it had not been for Griggs. He nodded his head and sneered. 'Find that a kind of hard question to answer, I judge; eh, young feller?' he said.

"Then—then I lost my temper completely. I told him I objected strongly to his tone and manner. I was not a criminal on trial and I did not propose to be treated like one. I should answer no more questions. He might believe what he chose, that made little difference to me."

"So? Well, that was—er—plain, if not very judgmatical. And how about Mary? Say anything to her, did you?"

"Why, yes, I did. I told her that I thought she should have sufficient confidence in me to require no explanations."

"Um. Well, I don't know's what I said about your remark to Balaam wouldn't fit that, too. What did she say?"

"She said—she said she had had such confidence. But now she could not help wondering. I had kept one secret from her. Were there others?

"I said of course there were no others.

" 'But there was this,' she said. And then her— No, I won't call him her father—Griggs broke in again.

'And he ain't told you, Mary,' he said, 'why he broke off bein' engaged to this New York woman. *She's* told us, but he ain't.'

" 'Will you tell me, Irving?' Mary asked.

"And then, Captain Newcomb— Well, then I made a fool of myself. I realize it now, but then all I could think was that, in spite of my asking her to trust me, she was still questioning, she still did not believe. I'm a pig-headed idiot at times; I was one then. I stiffened, I suppose, like a ridiculous wooden Indian, and told her I would tell her nothing under compulsion; she must take me on trust, or words to that effect. She looked at me for a minute without speaking. Then she said, 'I am sorry, Irving. Good-by,' and left the room. Old Balaam brayed joyfully, like a modern edition of the animal that spoke to the Balaam in the Bible, and I hurried out for fear I should be tempted to knock him down, old as he is. That's the story; an inspiring thing, isn't it?"

He relit his cigar and scowled vindictively at the carpet. Captain Noah nodded in sympathy.

"Tut, tut, tut!" he said. "Sho! so you and she have squabbled and parted company, eh? Humph! Well, 'tain't so bad but what it can be mended, I guess likely. There's always tomorrow, you know."

"Tomorrow, and for a good many tomorrows, I shall be a thousand miles from here."

"That's so, so you will. That does complicate matters some, don't it? Well, what did you do after you left Balaam's?"

"I went back to the storage plant, but I couldn't work, so I went to my room at the Mansion House. I've been

there ever since—thinking and thinking. And the more
I think the more puzzled I get and the more angry at
myself. I can see now that I did the worst thing possible, but now it is too late."

"Ye-es. Well, son, I will say this—you did swim into
the net head, gills and back fin."

"You think it was a trap, then?"

"Sartin sure. And pretty well set, too. Our dearly
beloved Balaam *may* have been the only hand that set it,
but I have my doubts."

"Who could have helped him?"

"Suppose we take that up a little later. You haven't
told me why you came to me."

"Because I had to come to some one, and you are the
one, here in Trumet, whom I seem naturally to go to
with my troubles. Captain, I can't give Mary up. I
won't. If I were to remain here I should see her, I
should make her see me and listen to me. But she
wouldn't see me now—tonight, and Griggs is there to
prevent it as well. Tomorrow I go on the early train.
I can write—I shall, but will she receive and read my
letters? I don't know. Sometimes I think I will wire
the firm I will not go to Chicago. Then I'll stay here
and fight it out. If they discharge me— Well, there
are other firms, I suppose."

"So there are, but I wouldn't give this one its clearance papers just yet. Let's take an observation first,
anyhow. Humph! I don't wonder it looks pretty thick
ahead to you, son, but there never was a night so thick
but what a feller could see a light if he got nigh enough
to it."

"Perhaps, but I don't see any."

"Don't you? Well, maybe I don't, either, but it does seem as if there was a spark—yes, sir, a glimmer of a spark. Whether it's a lighthouse or a lightnin'-bug remains to be seen. Son, long's you've told me so much would you mind tellin' me a little more? Would you mind tellin' me the whole story—not the Griggs letter one, but the true one—about this New York woman you was engaged to? Oh, 'tain't just curiosity, I've got my reasons for askin'. I'm kind of hopin' it'll fetch us a little nigher that light I think I sight in the offin'."

Clifford waited some time before replying. It was very evident he did not relish the idea of telling the story. At last, however, he seemed to make up his mind.

"Oh, all right, Captain," he said, "I'll tell it. It's unpleasant but not disgraceful—to me, at least. And, as you say, I've told so much that a little more won't hurt. I knew this woman when I was a young fellow just out of college. I was in New York then and I met her at a concert given by some acquaintances of mine. Her name was Emmons, Madeline Emmons, and she was a widow about five years older than I. Her husband had been in the navy, I believe."

"You believe? Don't you know?"

"I believed it then, because she said so. I would have believed anything then. He was a naval officer, so she said, and died abroad. She lived in a pleasant apartment uptown and seemed to have many friends. I got in the habit of calling there. We became more intimate and, later on, we were engaged. That's about all, isn't it?"

Captain Noah's eyes twinkled. "Yes," he said, "that's about all, except the way you got disengaged."

His friend frowned.

"It was a miserable business," he said. "I hate to speak of it because it makes me appear so like a simple idiot. I was just that, a simple, innocent young cub, and she— Oh, she used me and made a fool of me, that's all. I found out, after a while, that she had been playing with me, that she never had really cared two straws for me, that I had money to spend and lend and she needed money and so— Oh, it's plain enough, isn't it?"

"Does seem to be, that's a fact. So you give her the go-by, eh?"

"Yes. If it had been the money alone I shouldn't have cared. It left me head over heels in debt, but that was nothing. I found out other things, things about other men that— Well, that's all. I don't care to say any more. Just forget it, will you, Captain?"

"Sartin, sartin. But afore we forget it altogether, son, seems as if we'd ought to clear the fog a little mite, if we can. You and she quarreled, of course? She didn't bear you any good-will, naturally?"

"No."

"No. And she'd be rather glad to do you a bad turn, if she could?"

"I suppose so. Considering what she *has* done we might take that for granted, I should say."

"Um-hm. But how did she know how to get at you to do it? You never told her you were comin' to Trumet to work?"

"No, certainly not. I have neither seen her nor written her for six years at least."

"So? But her letter was addressed to Balaam and she knew all about you and Mary. Humph! There's been a mutual friend at work somewheres, that's sure. Can't guess who 'tis, can you, son?"

The young man's fists clenched. "I cannot," he affirmed. "If I could, that 'friend' and I would have an interview."

"That so? Well, Irve, here's another thing: When we was talkin' 'tother day you told me you first had the honor of makin' Cousin Calvin Wentworth's acquaintance at the home of a friend in New York. That friend didn't happen to be this Emmons lady, did it?"

He received no reply in words, but he needed none. The expression upon Irving Clifford's face was sufficient. Captain Noah burst into a laugh.

"Irve," he said, "that spark of light I thought I sighted a spell ago is gettin' brighter every minute, ain't it? We'll begin to see how to steer pretty soon, I cal'late."

His companion rose to his feet. "Wentworth!" he exclaimed. "Wentworth! He would know, of course. If I thought he did— But why should he?"

The captain shook his head. "Why, that's the sticker, I give in," he admitted. "Nine and three-quarters chances out of a scant ten he's the swab that put Balaam up to this. But why should he? that's the question. Here! Where are you goin'?"

Clifford was on the way to the door. "I'm going to see him and find out," he said, with savage determination.

"No, no! Here, heave to, Irve! Don't be foolish

194

'Can't you see that's just the way *not* to find out? All
he'll do is deny everything and make you look like a
fool. You can't prove anything on him now. Wait
until you can. That's it; you think it over. Here! set
down again. You can think better that way."

The young man reluctantly sat down in the chair he
had just vacated. It was quite evident that postponing
the interview with Wentworth appealed more to his
judgment than his inclination.

"The blackguard!" he exclaimed. "If I were only
sure! But I can't believe it. He's been friendly enough
down here. Why should he do such a thing?"

"That's it, why should he? Well, let's see. How was
it in New York; were you good chums there?"

"We weren't chums at all. I knew him, but very
slightly."

"He wasn't one of the fellers you hinted at in connec-
tion with your ex-lady friend?"

"No-o, no. That is, he appeared to know her well,
but——"

"All right. I only meant there was no reason why he
should be jealous of you or anything like that?"

"No."

"No. And you and he never had any row, or quarrel
or fuss or anything?"

"No. We disagreed once or twice, and once I declined to second the proposal of the name of a friend of
his for club membership. I was frank enough about it,
told him I didn't know the chap well enough to second
him. As a matter of fact, Captain, I didn't like Went-

worth or his set very well, although I tried not to show my feelings."

"Humph! Yes, yes, I see. Maybe you didn't try quite hard enough, son. However, even if he don't love you like a brother, his comin' to call on you a dozen times or so down at the cold-storage proves he don't hate you. If he's responsible for sickin' the Emmons woman onto you—and I'll bet he is—there must be some better reason than just a halfway grudge. Of course, there's Mary. If we thought he would like to get her for himself, why then— But he don't."

"Of course he doesn't. Why, he scarcely knows her."

"That ain't the reason. Once get you out of the way and he could get to know her quick enough, especially if he stands in with Balaam. But, unless I'm way, way off in my reckonin', Cousin Calvin won't ever marry unless he can feather his nest. If Mary had money then I should say we had the answer, but she ain't, has she?"

"No. She told me once that she was dependent upon her stepfather, while she lived here at least. But Wentworth doesn't need money; he's wealthy."

"Is he?"

"Everyone says he is."

"Yes, I know, but— However, there's no use guessin' when waitin' will give us a sartinty. I expect a letter most any day that will settle Cousin Calvin's ratin'. But this I'll stand pat on: He ain't the kind to marry for love, and if Mary Barstow won't bring him any money then it ain't her he's after. So why does he help Balaam get rid of you?"

"I give it up. I don't believe he is doing it."

196

"Don't you? I do. For one thing, he and Balaam have been pretty thick lately. I've noticed it, and so has Obadiah. I cal'late Calvin's in it, Irve, but why I own up I can't see. And I can't for the life of me see why Griggs don't want his stepdaughter to get married. Find that out and we might find out all the rest. And we will find it out; we will. It may take time, but——"

"But in the meantime I go to Chicago to stay for months."

"Eh? So you do, so you do. That does make it harder, as the boy said when he made up a riddle and put in a lot of extra questions that had nothin' to do with it. But, Irve, *I'm* goin' to stay by the ship, you know, and if you *want* to let me play stevedore, why—why I'll do my best to look after your property and I'll undertake to say that nobody—Wentworth or anybody else—runs off with it. That ain't much comfort to you, maybe, but it's about all I can say just now."

Clifford seemed to find a little cheer in it. He thanked his friend cordially. Then, with an obvious effort, he attempted to change the subject.

"Captain," he said, "when I first came in here you said you had something to tell me, something about your puzzles, I think it was. I've been filling you full of my worries and haven't shown the slightest interest in yours. But I am interested, I am really. What was it you had to tell me?"

Noah smiled. "Why, nothin', Irve," he said. "That is, nothin' except that I've fitted in one little piece in one of my picture puzzles, that's all. I ain't at liberty to tell you what 'tis; all I can say is that it fits. By and by I'll tell you more."

His visitor said good night shortly after this. His tone, as he said it, was anything but hopeful. The captain laid a hand on his shoulder.

"Brace up, son," he counseled. "Mary's a good girl, a sensible girl. She's a little mite put out with you now, but when she comes to think it over she'll feel different. You write her a good, straight, honest letter, tell her the whole truth and nothin' but the truth. Then you'll see."

Irving still looked dubious.

"I doubt if she ever gets my letters," he said. "I imagine old Griggs will see that she doesn't."

"He will, eh? Well, you put 'em inside another envelope and address that envelope to me. Then *I'll* see that she does. And I'll see you tomorrow mornin' before you start for the train. Maybe I'll— Why, yes, I will: I'll take you up to the depot in my 'Pancake.' We'll both have slept on our troubles by that time and they may not seem so hard. Good night, son. Much obliged to you for comin' and tellin' me about it."

After his visitor had gone Captain Noah sat down once more beside the table. He took up the letter to his New York cousin, that which he had been writing when Irving's coming interrupted him. He read what he had written, reflected, then tore the letter up and began a fresh one. This one was long. It ended as follows:

And so here is what I want you to find out for me——

EXTRICATING OBADIAH

Number one—Find out all you can about Ostrich Mining and Smelting Company.

Number two—Find out all you can about Calvin Wentworth, who used to belong to the New Amsterdam Club. I wrote asking about him once before and I did not get a peep out of you. If you don't hurry up and answer I will transfer my business to another broker next time I invest a couple of hundred dollars. I hate to be cruel as all that but I have got to get a letter out of you somehow.

Number three—Find out all you can about a widow woman name of Madeline Emmons. She was a friend of this Wentworth fellow's and lived——

Here the captain paused, remembering that he had not asked Clifford where Mrs. Emmons lived when he knew her. He decided to wait, get this information from the young man when he took him to the station in the morning, and finish his letter afterward.

He blew out the lamp, moved his chair over beside the open window, and sat there looking out. It was a fine starlit night, and there was little wind. The lights in the houses across the bay were for the most part extinguished, but the distant lighthouse was a fiery spark, and on the horizon a pinprick of fire marked the position of a tug or schooner.

Captain Noah leaned back in his chair, crossed his knees and meditated upon his curious position there in Trumet. If anyone had told him, two years before, that he was destined to spend so much time and mental energy trying to solve the difficulties of people not related to him in any way, he would have laughed at the idea. And now here he was, neck deep in those difficulties, like old

EXTRICATING OBADIAH

Jotham Hallett in the cistern. And, as if Obadiah's troubles were not sufficient, here was young Clifford in a tangle, which he, Noah, had undertaken to straighten.

At the Clifford tangle, however, he was inclined to smile. A lover's quarrel, with Balaam and Wentworth as its fomentors, so he appraised the affair. But the situation would require tact and careful handling. As for Obadiah's investment in copper stock, that was likely to be more serious. Poor Obadiah! his Aunt Sarah's legacy had not been an unmixed blessing. One fact was shaping itself clearer and clearer with each new development, that was that Mr. Balaam Griggs was a good deal of a scoundrel as well as a sharp trader. Curious that a woman like Melissa Mayo should be helping him in his schemes. No, of course she was not helping him, for she had more than hinted her disapproval of those schemes. But why was she mixed up in them, or why did she remain as housekeeper when— Oh, hang the "picture puzzles"! they were altogether too disturbing to the mind. And, after Clifford had gone, there would be no one to confide in, no one to help discuss or conjecture. For the first time since he came to Trumet Captain Noah felt lonely.

A window in the ell opposite his own lit up. It was the housekeeper's room. A moment later the window shade was raised and the captain saw Mrs. Mayo standing by the window, looking out. He was in the dark, of course, so she did not see him, but the light from the lamp which she held in her hand shone full upon her face. It was a kind face, a wholesome, comely face. To a woman with a face like that one might—or ought—

to turn for counsel, for help, for comradeship, for stead-
fast, cheerful courage through the shadows as well as
the sunshine. If things were other than as they were,
if she were not a part of the mystery he was trying to
solve, how natural it would seem to go to her for advice
in the solving. But she was a part of it. And, so far at
least, it was such a mean, mercenary mystery. A group
of people conspiring to cheat an innocent, guileless fel-
low-mortal out of his few dollars.

Captain Noah, leaning back in the dark behind his
open window, gazed across at Melissa Mayo's face in
the lamplight and once more vowed, mentally, his belief
in her honesty. She *was* honest, she was true and square
and above board. He would stake his last cent on it.
But she was in trouble, deep trouble. She looked sad
and careworn. Again the captain felt that strong desire
to help her, to comfort her, to——

Just here Mrs. Mayo pulled down her window-shade.
Captain Noah suddenly came out of his reverie, rose, lit
his own lamp, pulled down *his* window-curtain and prepared for bed.

It was high time, he decided. Sitting in the dark
made one think foolish things. He was past fifty and
at that age a man's thoughts should be sane and his head
hard. If the thoughts were foolish and ridiculous it
was, probably, a sign that the head was in danger of
softening and needed the restorative of rest.

So Captain Noah went to bed.

CHAPTER XIV

NEXT morning, true to his promise, he called in the little motor car to take Irving to the railway station. Not to the Trumet station; that, the captain declared, was "too nigh a port." He had turned out early, he said, in order to have time enough for a good talk with his friend before the latter boarded the train, and as that train might be boarded just as well at Bayport as Trumet, and as Bayport was a ten-mile ride, to Bayport they went.

During the run over, the Griggs-Barstow-Wentworth situation was thoroughly rediscussed. The captain was just as certain as he had been the previous evening that Cousin Calvin was responsible for the Emmons woman's letter to Balaam. Clifford was inclined to agree with him, but was not so sure. The reason why Wentworth was helping Griggs in the latter's schemes, if helping he was, was still a mystery.

"I've guessed till I've strained a plank in my guesser," declared Noah, "but the right answer is always round the next p'int and out of sight when I get there. And then there's the other question: Why don't Balaam want Mary to marry? Well, maybe when we get one answer

we'll get the other. They may be strung on together, like
herrin's on a stick. Anyhow, son, I'll keep my weather
eye on Cousin Calvin and the antiquer. Don't you worry
about that."

Irving did his best to appear cheerful as they stood on
the station platform waiting for the train, but his best was
not a huge success. Their interview was interrupted by
an acquaintance of Clifford's, a Mr. Philander Badger.
Mr. Badger was a lawyer, with an office in Ostable, but
he occasionally visited Trumet on professional business.
While in the latter village he was accustomed to make his
headquarters at the Mansion House, and it was there that
Irving had met him.

He was not especially delighted to meet him now, but
Badger, quite unaware of this, chatted, laughed, was introduced to Captain Noah, and generally gave evidence
of a determination not to go elsewhere for the present at
least. He had come down to Bayport the day before and
was awaiting the arrival of the "down" train.

"Got to go over to Harniss," he explained. "A half
hour's business over there and I have to wait an hour and
a half for a train to put me where I can do it. My auto's
in the repair shop or I shouldn't be marking time on this
depot platform. However, what can't be cured must be
endured; so why worry? Isn't that good logic, Cap'n
Newcomb?"

"Sartin is," observed Noah. "Only it's a pretty good
idea to make sure there's no cure in sight afore you start
the endurin'. Now in your case, Mr. Badger, I've got a
prescription. My car's right out yonder, and soon's I've
put this young feller aboard the train, I'm goin' to head

14

'for Trumet. I can go by way of Harniss just as well
as not, and if you want to— Eh? Who said the days of
miracles was past? Here's the up train a-comin' and
she's *on time!*"

He accompanied his friend to a seat in the car, shook
hands with him once more and then stooped and whispered in his ear.

"Irve," he whispered, "send those letters right along,
those you and me spoke about last night. I'll see she gets
'em, every last one. And don't you fret yourself a single
mite, son; everything's goin' to come out fine."

Clifford smiled dubiously. "I wish I had more of your
optimism," he said. "However, I won't give up hope."

"You bet you won't! Neither will I. We may get those
two schemers' fingers squeezed in the jaws of the jib yet.
And if we do we won't slack up the tackle in a hurry,
neither. Now you write me, won't you? I know you'll
write other places, but— Eh? Oh, all right, conductor,
I'm a-comin'. So long, Irve. Fair wind, safe passage and
a quick v'yage home again. Good-by."

He stood on the platform watching the train until it
was out of sight. Badger touched him on the shoulder.
He started and turned.

"Oh!" he exclaimed. "Land sakes, Mr. Badger, I forgot all about you."

The lawyer grinned. "So I thought," he said, "but I
hadn't forgotten about you. Anyone who offers to save
me an hour's wait in this fag-end of creation and give me
an automobile ride besides on a morning like this is too
precious to be forgotten. Hope you haven't repented of
your bargain, Cap'n."

"Nary a bit. Ready, are you? That little satchel all
the dunnage you got? Sho! you travel pretty nigh as
light as old Barney Gould used to, eh? Folks down this
way when I was a boy, visitin', used to say that the only
change Barney made was to put on a heavier coat of sun-
burn in the summer. Here's my nine-cylinder dust-dis-
turber. All aboard."

There was a good deal of conversation on the way to
Harniss, but only just as the car was entering that village
did Mr. Badger make a .emark which particularly impressed his pilot. The talk immediately leading up to this
remark was as follows:

"I can't tell you how much obliged I am to you for this
lift, Cap'n Newcomb," said the lawyer. "Now the next
time you come to Ostable you call and see me, will you?
I want you to meet Mrs. Badger and have dinner with
us."

The captain thanked him, but observed that he was
afraid he should not get to Ostable very soon; it was a
good way from Trumet.

"Oh, not so far! People with cars don't count twenty-
odd miles nowadays. Why, a couple of your Trumet
neighbors were over there in a car only a fortnight ago.
Mr. Griggs—Balaam Griggs—was one. Know him, do
you?"

Noah nodded. "Um-hm," he said. "I know him."

Badger chuckled at the tone. "I judge you know him
well," he said. "He was over at Judge Baxter's fore-
closing a mortgage. The Judge told me that if Griggs had
a mortgage on an island in the brimstone lake at the bottom of perdition, he believed the old fellow would put on

asbestos gloves and try to collect the interest. The Judge doesn't often talk that way about his clients, but I imagine he would shed mighty few tears if Griggs hired another lawyer."

Captain Noah laughed. His companion laughed also, and continued.

"Who was the chap he had with him, I wonder?" he asked. "Do you know him, Cap'n? A slim, citified fellow with a little black mustache and a sort of smooth, smart-Aleck way. A good deal of a dude. I saw him getting out of the car he and Griggs came over in, and if he and Balaam weren't a contrast then I never saw one."

The captain nodded. "That," he observed, gravely, "was the Honorable Calvin Wentworth of New York City. Balaam likes to ride in automobiles when he can get somebody to drive 'em free and he's usin' somebody else's gas and ile. Cousin—I mean the Honorable Calvin—he likes the fun of drivin' 'em, I cal'late. That's how the combination hitched up together, I believe. Some color scheme, though, them two, eh? Match up like a pogy scow and a steam yacht."

The lawyer seemed to find the comparison amusing. "Ha, ha! that's good, Cap'n," he said. "So our citified friend is from New York. Humph! then young Baker at the Probate office must have made a mistake. He said the fellow came from the West somewhere and was looking up his family records, old wills and that sort of thing."

This was the remark before referred to, that which made a particular impression upon the captain's mind.

For a moment he made no answer at all. Then he said:

"What was that, Mr. Badger? You say Wentworth give out that he was from the West and was down to the Clerk of Probates' lookin' up old wills?"

"So young Baker told me. He said this man— It certainly was the one you call Wentworth, that is, if Wentworth came in the car with Griggs that day."

"He did. I know it for a fact. And Balaam himself told somebody afterwards that Calvin had drove him to Ostable in Ziby Rogers' auto—Balaam borrowed it off Zibe—and that he'd never seen such hair-raisin' drivin' in *his* life."

"Yes, well, Baker told me that this swell Western man came in to the Probate office while he was there alone and gave him a good cigar and then spent fifteen or twenty minutes looking over old wills, wills of people who had lived in Wapatomac, I believe. He was tracing family records, he gave Baker to understand. But I told you that, didn't I?"

"Um—yes—yes, I believe you did. Lookin' up wills of Wapatomac folks, eh? Um—yes, yes. You don't happen to remember whether the Baker chap said whose wills, do you?"

"Yes, I think he did say. I think he said—let me see— Why, yes, he said they were the wills of some of the Barstows who used to live over that way. Ira Barstow and his wife and that lot. . . . Eh? Did you speak, Cap'n?"

If Captain Noah had spoken he did not speak again. In fact, for the last five minutes of their ride together he was remarkably quiet. Only when the car drew up before the door of the Harniss residence, which was Mr.

Badger's destination, did he offer more than a mono-syllabic grunt. Then, in answer to his passenger's thanks and repeated invitation to call upon him at Ostable, he said:

"Well—well, you can't tell, Mr. Badger, I may get over there sooner than I expected. When I do I'd kind of like to go down to that Probate office and have you introduce me to that Baker feller. Had you just as soon? Thanks, thanks. Don't say a word. Pleasure's been all mine. Mighty glad to have had your company. So long."

All the way home he sat at the wheel of the little car preoccupied and thoughtful. When he ran the car into the Burgess barn there was a twinkle in his eye and a smile at the corner of his lip. He looked more confident and satisfied with himself than he had for some time.

Two days later he received a reply to the letter he had written his New York cousin. The broker wrote that he was having an investigation made of the Ostrich Mining Company and its affairs and would send those particulars a little later. But in the present letter he gave some other information which Captain Noah seemed to find interesting and satisfying. The day after receiving this letter he left the house in his car soon after breakfast and remained away until supper time. The following day he was gone quite as long. When Obadiah, the ever curious, asked him where he had been, he said:

"Been? I been out takin' the air, Obe. Been soakin' in the ozone. Cruisin' round through the scenery and doin' picture puzzles. You'd ought to try it some time,

Obe; strengthens the lungs, lights, liver and appetite, like old Doctor So-and-So's Spring Bitters."

Obadiah grunted. "How you do talk, Cap'n Noah," he said. "Doin' picture puzzles ridin' round in a a-a-au-automobile!"

"Sure thing. Best way to do 'em in the world; anyhow I seem to get better results that way. Obe, have a cigar, won't you? By the way, seems to me I ain't seen you burnin' up so many 'Liberty Maids' lately."

Mr. Burgess groaned. "I can't afford 'em," he said. "Them nor no other kinds. I'm on my way to the poorhouse, I cal'late, and p-p-pup-paupers don't smoke cigars."

Noah clapped him on the back. "Cheer up, Obe," he said. Then, as a hen cackled loudly behind the barn, he added: "Hark! there's one of your Shanghai ostriches laid an egg; maybe that other Ostrich of yours'll lay one, too, some of these days. Hello! I just noticed how dressed up you are. Ain't goin' to be married tonight, are you?"

Obadiah's expression of discouragement was succeeded by one of disgust.

"Married!" he repeated. "Married! What do you think I be, a d-d-d-dud——"

"Don't say it, Obe. There's no fun in swearin' when it takes as long as that."

"Swearin'! I wan't cal'latin' to swear. I was askin' you if you took me for a d-d-dud-dud-dumbhead. There; I got it out finally. I've got my Sunday clothes on 'cause me and Balaam are goin' down to lodge meetin' tonight. Goin' to put a couple of new candidates through, they be. It'll be a lively doin's, I cal'late, 'cause one of em's Ezra Paine and he ain't very p-p-pop-pop'lar, Ez ain't."

Captain Noah reflected. "Humph!" he grunted. "So Balaam's goin' with you, is he? Sure of that?"

"Sartin. He's goin' to call for me on his way along."

"How long'll you be puttin' those poor victims through, think?"

"Couple of hours, anyhow; more likely three."

"I see. Well, Obe, I hope you enjoy their sufferin's."

Obadiah nodded with gloomy satisfaction. "I'm cal'-latin' to," he affirmed. "A feller's bound to get a *little* comfort out of life."

Mr. Griggs called for him just before eight o'clock and they walked away together. Captain Noah watched them go. Then he, too, left the Burgess premises, although his walk was in the opposite direction. It was a short walk, merely to the Griggs front gate and along the path to the side door. Upon that door he knocked and Mary Barstow opened it.

The young lady looked, so it seemed to the captain, rather pale and careworn. However, she smiled when she recognized the bulky figure on the stone step.

"Why, good evening, Captain Newcomb," she said. "I'm awfully sorry, but Mr. Griggs isn't in. He has gone to the meeting of the lodge, I believe."

Noah nodded, cheerfully. "There's one p'int where I've got the advantage of you, Mary," he observed. "You only believe he's gone and I know it. I saw him go. Fact is, I was waitin' for him to go afore I came around to see you. Thank you, I guess likely I will come in, seein' as you're so pressin'."

Mary laughed. She and the captain had become pretty well acquainted during the month just past and she was getting used to his eccentricities.

"I don't know that I ought to invite you in after such an outrageous speech as that," she declared. "However, I suppose I must this time. Do come in and sit down. That's it; now let me take your hat."

The captain relinquished the hat with apparent misgiving.

"Don't take it too far off, Mary," he cautioned. "It's a kind of touchy and particular business I've come about and—er—well, there's no tellin' how soon you'll be showin' me through that door again. I'd feel easier in my mind if that hat was where I could grab it in a hurry."

The young lady was plainly puzzled by her caller's manner. She looked at him questioningly.

"Touchy and particular business?" she repeated. "I don't understand. Oh, I know! it's about the lodge supper. I told Mr. Burgess that I would bake a cake, but I couldn't do anything more, I was too busy. So if he has sent you to ask me, Captain Newcomb——"

"He ain't, he ain't. I didn't come beggin' cold vittles this time, Mary, not even for the lodge. I'm more of a postman than I am a tramp. I've got a letter for you."

He took the letter from his pocket and handed it to her.

"A letter for me?" she repeated. "A let— Oh!"

There was a sharp change in her tone as she saw and recognized the handwriting. Noah, in writing of the interview to Clifford, declared: "Right there the glass fell from 'Fair and Sunshine' to 'Clouds, Squalls and Ice-bergs.' " She handed back the letter unopened.

"Thank you," she said, coldly. "I don't wish to see it."

"What? Don't wish to see it? Ain't you goin' to even look and see what's inside?"

"No." She rose from her chair. "If the particular business you mentioned," she said, "has to do with the writer of that letter, then I think——"

She did not finish the sentence, but Captain Noah finished it for her.

"Then you think I'd better be reachin' for that hat you took away just now," he suggested. "Well, all right, Mary; I get you, as the boys say, but I ain't goin'—not yet. The only way you can coax me out of this house for the next fifteen or twenty minutes is to fire me out by main strength, and I know you're too much of a kind-hearted lady to do that. You are, ain't you? You wouldn't lay violent hands on an old derelict like me, I'm sure."

His expression and tone were so anxiously solemn that Mary, disturbed and irritated as she was, could not repress a smile.

"Please don't be absurd," she said. "I don't feel in the least like joking on that subject, and if Mr. Clifford sent you to me——"

The captain held up his hand. "Just a minute, Mary," he said. "Don't take too much of the channel for granted; better wait for the pilot. Irve Clifford didn't send me to you. He don't know I'm here. He didn't know that I intended comin' here."

"But he sent that letter by you."

"He sent it in my care because I asked him to. I knew he'd want you to get it, or any letters he might write. And if those letters wan't sent care of me, or somebody else he could trust, there was a pretty fair chance you never would get 'em."

Miss Barstow did not answer. She was gazing at him intently, evidently trying to make up her mind whether or not he was serious. He went on, slowly and earnestly.

"Mary," he said, "I'm responsible for Irve's sendin' that letter inside another envelope with my name on it. I didn't want that letter to get in the hands of the gang that are tryin' to keep you two apart."

She had been standing during the last few minutes; now she sank slowly into her chair again.

"The gang?" she repeated. "The gang who are trying to keep—Captain Newcomb, what *are* you talking about?"

Noah shook his head. "I ain't any more crazy than I've always been, Mary," he vowed, answering her thought rather than her words; "I know I'm talkin' like a movin'-picture play, gangs and plots and all that. Course I don't mean that anybody's layin' schemes to murder you or kidnap you and such. But I do mean that there's a plan on to keep you from marryin' Irve Clifford."

Once more the young lady rose. "I think you had better go, Captain Newcomb," she said, firmly. "To be very frank, I consider that you are attempting to interfere with matters which are my own and personal. I shall not talk of those matters with you or anyone else."

She took a step toward the door, but her visitor remained seated, imperturbable and determined as ever.

"If you will not go," observed Miss Barstow, crisply,
"then I shall. Good night."

"Mary," he commanded, "you stay here. Stay here
and listen to what I've got to say. If you go and don't
hear it you'll be sorry all the days of your life. You can
take my word for that: All the days of your life you'll
be sorry. Now will you come back here and sit down,
like a good, sensible girl, and listen? I'm old enough to
be your father; I haven't got any ax to grind, for myself
or anybody else; I've found out some things you ought to
know, that's all. Will you listen while I tell you what
they are?"

His tone and words made an impression this time, as
he intended they should. She hesitated, then she slowly
came back and took her seat once more.

"I will listen," she said.

"Good enough! I knew you had common sense. Mary,
I haven't known Irvin' Clifford so very long, but I've
known *men* all my days, made it my business to know 'em
and judge 'em. I liked young Clifford when I first met
him; I've been likin' him better ever since. If I know
anything, I know that young feller couldn't do a mean,
dishonorable thing to anybody, man or woman. He hasn't
been dishonorable to you; he wasn't to that other
woman."

Her eyes flashed. "It is evident," she said, scornfully,
"that Mr. Clifford has made you his confidant. I don't
care to discuss his character, nor that of his—friends. If
this is all you have to say——"

"It ain't. It's only the beginnin'. But it's leadin' up to what I've got to say. Yes, Irve did tell me about the trouble between you and him. The poor chap was all upset and torn to ravelin's about it; he didn't have any-body but me to go to, he was leavin' town the next day, and—well, he came to me and spun his yarn and asked my advice. I didn't have much to give him, but I said I'd try and find out some things and I did tell him to write you care of me. Then at least the letters would have a fair chance, *which*," with strong emphasis, "they might not have had if they'd been sent direct to this house.

"After he'd gone," continued the captain, "I set down and wrote to my cousin in New York. He's a broker and one of them society fellers the papers tell about. Also—and this was about as important as anything—I knew he was a member of a club Irvin' used to belong to there in the city. I thought likely he might know somethin' about Clifford and this Mrs. Emmons, the widow. I asked him about her and about Irve and about—some-body else I was interested in. His answer came yesterday mornin'. It's pretty interestin'. Maybe you'd like to read it. Here it is."

He took it from his pocket and would have handed it to her, but she made no move to accept it. He looked disappointed, but he laid it on the table beside him and went on.

"Perhaps you'll feel different about lookin' at it by and by," he said. "I kind of hope you will. But whether you do or not hasn't anything to do with the rest of what I've got to tell you. Mary, has it ever struck you as funny the prejudice your stepdad has against your gettin' married?"

She made no reply, but it was evident the question aroused her curiosity.

"Has it?" repeated Noah. "Not to Clifford alone, I don't mean, but isn't it true that Balaam has been dead set against you havin' young men friends at any time? Hasn't he been more or less insultin' to those you have had and done his best to keep 'em away from here and from you?"

Mary reflected. "Why, yes," she said, "he has seemed to object to my having such friends, but his objections have not influenced my friendships. I do not consider myself under obligation to Mr. Griggs."

"Sho, sho! course you don't, course you don't. But it's kind of funny he should be so anxious to keep you from meetin' and knowin' young men. You might say 'twas because he didn't want you to marry and go and leave him, but—but he could get another housekeeper for at least as little as your clothes and upkeep cost him, and as for his lovin' you—well, you'll excuse me, but your stepfather don't bear the reputation of bein' an over-sentimental man."

Miss Barstow smiled faintly. "He isn't," she said. "And yet when I told him of my intention of going to Boston and earning my living he objected strongly and told me how much he cared for me."

"Did, eh? Humph! Was that after you and Irvin' parted company or before? Excuse me for askin', but it's all part of what I'm on the track of."

The answer was not given immediately, and when given was briefness itself.

"Before," said Mary.

"Yes, yes, I see. And—and what made you tell him you thought of leavin' him? Course you needn't tell any of this unless you want to. It *ain't* just nosiness, honest it ain't."

"I told him because—well, because he attempted to order me to break off my acquaintanceship with Mr. Clifford."

"*I* bet you! It all fits in. Yes, sir, it all fits in. He didn't like the idea of your goin' to Boston, either, did he?"

"No. But, really, Captain Newcomb——"

"Just a minute now, just a minute. Gettin' clearer every minute. We'll be out of the fog pretty soon. Now, Mary, here's another somethin' for you to think of. How did your stepdad come to know of this Emmons woman? *Please* don't get mad. I won't talk very much about her, I promise you. How did he come to know?"

"She wrote him. Surely Mr. Clifford must have told you that."

"Yes, but why did she write him? Who told her there was such a person as Balaam Griggs? Or such a girl as you? Or that Irve Clifford was here in Trumet? He hadn't seen her or heard of her for six years. Who gave her all these particulars? Have you thought of that, Mary?"

Her expression showed that she thought of it, and that it had puzzled her. She was interested now; her gaze did not leave his face. He noticed this and chuckled triumphantly.

"Curious, to say the least, her writin', wan't it?" he said. "Balaam didn't know her, nor of her. He never mentioned her afore he got that letter, did he?"

"No."

"No. Looks almost as if somebody who did know her and had known Irvin' had given both Balaam and her the tip. Eh? Looks that way to me. And it looks, too, as if that somebody might be helpin' your stepdad to get rid of Clifford. Don't that sound kind of reasonable? Think, Mary, think."

Mary was thinking, there was no doubt of that.

"But who?" she said, slowly. "Who? You know more than you have told me, Captain Newcomb. Who was it?"

The captain's eyes snapped. "Mary," he asked, "has Mr. Calvin Wentworth been a little mite more neighborly here lately than he used to be?"

Mary slowly leaned back in her chair.

"Mr. Calvin Wentworth?" she repeated.

Captain Noah nodded. "Um-hm," he said, "Mr. Calvin Wentworth, late of New York City, dog fancier, gaiters wearer and general lily of the field. Hasn't he been a little mite thicker with your stepdad than he used to be? Ain't he been a little mite more—er—contagious, as you might say, in these latitudes durin' the last week or so? What do you think about it?"

Instead of answering his question she asked one.

"Captain Newcomb," she demanded, "what do you mean? What reason have you for thinking Mr. Wentworth has—has——"

The captain broke in without waiting for her to finish.

"I tell you my reasons in just a minute, Mary," he said, "but first you just please tell me: *Hasn't* Wentworth been more—er—numerous, prevalent—whatever you want to call it—round here durin' the last week?"

Mary reflected. "Why, yes," she replied, somewhat doubtfully, "I—I think he has. I have seen him with Mr. Griggs several times recently; he has called here twice this week. He was here last evening for an hour or so, but——"

"Just a minute, Mary; just a minute. Has he been—er —well, a little mite more sociable with—er—excuse me, with you—with *you* than he was?"

"With *me?* What do you mean?"

"Well, it's kind of hard to make it plainer without runnin' the risk of havin' to grab for that hat of mine. What I mean is, has it occurred to you that—that possibly Cousin Calvin might be a candidate for—for—well, for Irve's—er—vacant chair, as you might say?"

The color rose in Miss Barstow's cheeks.

"Captain Newcomb," she said, "you are—really, you are——"

"Yes—yes, Mary, I know I am. But, honest, I can't help it, I've got to be—now. *Has* he shown a willin'ness to be more folksy and companionable with you? Has he, now you come to think it over?"

"No," indignantly; "of course he hasn't. That is, he— Well, he called last evening, and one or two evenings before, but it was to see Mr. Griggs. Of course it was. Why, I scarcely know Mr. Wentworth."

"Sartin. I understand that, but unless I'm so far off

soundin's that I couldn't get bottom with the Atlantic
cable, he means you shall know him better afore long.
Mary, I may as well tell you now that I've had my eye
on Cousin Calvin—that's what Obe Burgess calls him,
you know—ever since I landed here. And he's been
somethin' of a mystery. He's an invalid, so he says, but
he don't act—or eat—like one. He's a New York society
high-roller, 'cordin' to his accounts, but he's spendin' his
summers and winters rollin' in this little sand pile. He's
rich as Aunt Tabby Small's Sunday dinner puddin', and
that was made out of a half cup of flour and the rest
shortenin'. Yet rich as he's supposed to be, he don't
spend a cent, unless he can borrow it, and *when* he bor-
rows it the only way you can tell the loan from a present
is by sewin' a tag on it. Now why should a rich man and
a society man, even if he is an invalid, pick out Trumet
to die in and Obadiah Burgess to die on? I couldn't see
why, for the life of me I couldn't. And because I was a
friend of Obe's and because I owed the little feller my
life, as you might say, I set in to find out.

"In that letter from the broker cousin of mine—the
one I told you about, Mary—there's consider'ble interestin' information about Cousin Calvin. Information that
clears the skyline consider'ble. He——"

The young lady interrupted.

"Captain Newcomb," she said, "unless you can prove
to me that Mr. Wentworth's personal affairs have some
bearing upon mine I can't see why I should be told their
details. Admitting that he is a mysterious person—what
of it? As I told you, I scarcely know him."

"And as I told you, you're in a fair way to know him

a whole lot better. Now if you'll let me read you this broker feller's letter——"

"I can't see that that is necessary."

"Can't, eh? Well, then I'll have to prove to you that 'tis. We'll leave that letter one side for another little spell and instead of tellin' you what I've found out, I'll tell you first what I guessed. As I said, if Wentworth was rich and a society pet and all, then I couldn't make him fit down here. But if he wan't rich and only a has-been, a gone-to-seed sunflower, so to speak, who was too lazy to work, but havin' heard of relation Obadiah's comin' into house and money, got the idea of spongin' a soft and easy livin' by pretendin' to be a well-off invalid who was goin' to will Obe every cent when he died, *then* I could make him fit like a tender foot in an old shoe. And that's the way I had him entered in my log—waitin' information from my broker cousin, of course—when this new development, this one with you and Balaam and Irve Clifford in it, bobbed up to stump me.

"When Irvin' come to me in his trouble, poor chap, and told me of your stepdad's facin' him with the letter from the Emmons woman, it was plain enough that somebody else, some cleverer critter than Balaam, had had a hand in it. And suspicion p'inted right off to Cousin Calvin because he was from New York, had known Irve over there, and was in a position to know somethin', very likely, of Irve's bein' engaged to the woman and all the rest of it. But, as you yourself said when I first hinted at it, why should he want to make trouble between you and Clifford?

"With a different man to deal with there might have

been two or three answers. He might have hated Irve, had a grudge against him or something, and wanted to get even. Well, in a small way maybe he has, but Irve's perfectly sure it ain't a big enough grudge to make as lazy a man as Wentworth go out of his way to square it. He might—you'll have to excuse me, Mary—have fell in love with you and wanted to get you for his own."

"Captain Newcomb!"

"Sartin, he might. I should be tempted myself if I was a hundred and odd year younger. However, knowin' Cousin Calvin, I didn't believe that was it. No matter how much he might be in love with you or anybody else, he was too much in love with his precious self to undertake to care for and work for a wife. If that wife was liable to bring him money, even if 'twan't a very great deal of money, *then* again I could see. But you, I understood, weren't wealthy in your own right; eh, Mary?"

Miss Barstow smiled faintly.

"Scarcely," she said.

"Excuse me for askin', but have you *any* money of your own?"

"A few dollars in the savings-bank, that is all."

"And you never have had any, or never was told that you was liable to have any?"

"Of course not. What *do* you mean?"

The captain's only reply was a satisfied nod.

"So that seemed to settle that answer to the riddle," he said. "But on the other side, there was Calvin and your stepdad chummin' round together more and more, thick as—well, perhaps we won't say thick as thieves 'cause that wouldn't hardly be polite, but thick as hasty-

puddin', anyhow. What made 'em so thick all at once?
They ain't any more alike than a clam and a hummin'-
bird. I couldn't see any reason, and yet all the time I
was sartin there was one. Well, Mary, today I found
the reason."

Mary gasped, "You found—what?" she cried.

"I found out the reason why Calvin Wentworth should
want to get you away from Irvin' Clifford. Not only
that, but I cal'late I've found out why Balaam Griggs is
so dead sot against the idea of your marryin' at all. As
I kind of suspected, both of the reasons hang together.
Eh? Now what do you say to that?"

She did not say anything, in words, but her eyes asked
all sorts of questions. The captain chuckled.

"I don't suppose you'd care to hear what those reasons
was, would you?" he inquired. "Long's you didn't want
to read that broker's letter, why——"

"Captain Newcomb!"

"Oh, all right! all right! Don't look at me that way,
I've got weak nerves. The way I found out, Mary—
or, rather, what put me on the track of findin' out was
just dumb luck. I met a feller named Badger, a lawyer
from Ostable he is, and somethin' he said gave me the
end of the string."

"What was it? What did he say?"

"Why, he told me that your stepfather and our friend
Wentworth had been over to Ostable ten days or so ago,
together, in an automobile."

"Was that all? Why, I could have told you that; Mr.
Griggs borrowed Mr. Rogers' car and Mr. Wentworth
offered to drive it for the fun of doing so. There was

no secret about their going. Mr. Griggs had some business there, something about a mortgage."

"Um-hm, so Badger said. But Cousin Calvin found some other kind of business to keep him busy while your stepdad was mortgagin'. He went perusin' down to the Probate Clerk's office and put in his time pretendin' to be a travelin' Westerner interested in the wills of dead folks."

"Wills? Mr. Wentworth was interested in wills? What wills?"

"Well, now, that's what I asked, Mary, and the answer I got sent *me* to Ostable will chasin'. I went over there yesterday in my Pancake—my auto, I mean. I found the will Calvin was so interested in and I made a copy of it. Here is the copy."

He took a folded sheet of paper from his coat pocket. Mary stared at the paper and at his face.

"But what is it, Captain Newcomb?" she begged. "What is it? Has it anything to do with me?"

The captain nodded solemnly. "Um-hm," he said, "it has a whole lot to do with you. It's Ira Barstow's will, Ira Barstow that used to live in Wapatomac."

"My father? Is that my father's will?"

"It's a copy of your father's will, or of a part of it."

"But—but are you sure? I never knew that he left a will."

" 'Pears that he did. 'At any rate I found this one recorded over there to Ostable. Here it is, Mary. I warn you," he added, solemnly, "that it's goin' to surprise you some. Leastways it did me."

She took the paper from his hand and, wonderingly,

began to read what was written upon it. She read on for
a few lines and then uttered an exclamation.

"Oh!" she cried. "Why——"

Captain Noah grinned. "That's what I said," he observed, "and then some."

Mary read the writing through to the end. Her face,
when she looked up, was pale.

"Why—why!" she stammered. "It—it can't be, Captain Newcomb! It isn't true, is it?"

"True as preachin', I believe," he said, with a brisk
nod, "and a good deal easier to prove true than some
preachin'. That's a copy of your father's will, Mary.
When he died he left you that much money in trust to be
yours when you come of age or married. Twenty-five
thousand ain't enough to buy a fleet of ocean liners, I
give in to that, but it is enough to keep the wolf away
from the door and even out of sight from the upstairs
windows."

She put her hand to her forehead. "But are you sure,
Captain Newcomb?" she pleaded. "Are you sure? Did
father ever have any such sum to leave? I never heard
that he did. My mother would have told me, wouldn't
she? Isn't it possible that father was—was mistaken—
was——"

"Was crazy, or somethin' like that, you mean? Well,
Mary, that's one of the first things that run across my
mind after I see the will. And so today the Pancake and
I took another cruise, to Wapatomac this time. I asked
some questions around and made it my business to meet
some of the folks that used to know your folks when they
lived there. I found out that your dad was generally

reported to be quite comfortably off, to have made some money and saved it. I found out, too, that you was the apple of his eye, so 'twas natural enough that he should take care to provide for you when he died."

"But—but why was I never told of this money? If there is any such sum, or ever was, why did my mother never speak of it?"

"That's a good, sensible question. You'd have made a first-rate lawyer, Mary. The answer to that, I cal'late, is in another part of that will, one I didn't take the pains to make a copy of. In that will the persons your twenty-five thousand was put in trust with was your mother *and* Mr. Balaam Griggs of Trumet, Mass. They was joint executors so named."

"Mr. Griggs! Mr. Griggs was executor?"

"Yes. Seems he and your father had been tradin' in real estate together. Balaam's business shrewdness, I cal'late, had made consider'ble impression on your pa. Probably he thought 'twould be a good idea to have a business man's advice to help your mother in her managin', and where could a body find a better business chap than Brother Griggs? See, don't you?"

Mary evidently did not see clearly.

"But why didn't Mother tell me?" she repeated.

"That was Balaam, as I look at it. You were a little girl then, and, naturally enough, they wouldn't tell you of money that would be yours when you was twenty-one or got married. Either happenin' seemed a long ways off then. And Balaam's influence over the family probably kept gettin' stronger and stronger. Five years later

'twas strong enough to get the widow to marry him.
What 'twas after *that* you know better'n I do, Mary."

Mary, leaning forward, her chin on her hand, was
thinking hard.

"She was almost his slave," she said, slowly. "He
seemed to have the faculty of making her do anything he
wished."

"Um-hm. Sartin, so I judged. He told her, probably,
never to mention will or money to you and so she never
did."

"I remember once, during her last sickness, she told
me that she was happy knowing that I was so well provided for. I thought she meant provided with a home
and," bitterly, "Mr. Griggs' society. She may have meant
—this."

"Don't doubt she did, poor woman. Course Balaam
had told her he should turn over the money to you soon
as you came of age."

Miss Barstow drew a long breath. Some of her color
had returned, but she was still agitated and excited.

"It doesn't seem as if it could be true," she declared.
"Perhaps it isn't true now. Perhaps the money has gone,
has been spent or lost in speculation. Perhaps that is
why he has never told."

Noah shook his head.

"Don't you believe it," he said. "No, it ain't been
spent. Balaam Griggs wouldn't spend twenty-five thousand dollars, not in twenty-five lifetimes I was goin' to
say. And the only speculatin' in any deal he goes into
is just a speculation as to how much the other feller
loses. No, he's got it safe and sound."

"Then you think he means to steal it. He must, for my twenty-first birthday was nearly a year ago."

"He wouldn't call it stealin'. If you taxed him with it he'd most likely say he was just keepin' it for you. [And the longer you don't know about it the longer he *can* keep it and the five or six or seven per cent interest along with it. And you see now why he's been so dreadfully anxious you shouldn't marry, don't you?"

"I—I don't know that I do."

"Sartin sure you do. The minute a husband comes along there's a new and mighty dangerous figure in the cal'latin'. That husband, for one thing, takes you out from under your stepfather's wing, out where you may hear somethin' or learn somethin' about this will any day. Or the husband may learn. *And* the said will puts a double knot in the halliard where it says the money shall be yours when you marry. Balaam'll shave the wind'ard side of the law close enough to blister the paint on his plankin', but he don't enjoy takin' a double risk of jail any more than anybody else. The single 'comin' of age' risk is enough to keep him worried, I rather guess. *Now* you see, don't you?"

Mary did not answer, although the expression of her face proved that she saw and understood. If Mr. Griggs had seen that expression, he, too, might have understood —and trembled.

"And Mr. Wentworth?" she asked, after a moment.

"Yes, indeed; mustn't forget Cousin Calvin. *How* he got on the track of the will I don't know. Very likely Balaam dropped a hint and he picked it up. But that don't make any real difference; we know he went to the

Probate Court and saw the will, and we know, too, that not very long after that your stepfather got the letter from the Emmons woman. If you was a poor girl, real poor, it probably wouldn't have been worth the Honorable Calvin's while to interfere along of you and Irvin'. But twenty-five thousand, although it ain't a kerosene ile fortune, is good enough for——"

"Stop! stop! don't say any more, please. I can't bear it. Captain Newcomb, you said you had a letter from a friend of yours in New York which gave some information concerning this—this man we have just been speaking of."

"Cousin Calvin? Yes, indeed; tells a lot about him."

"May I see the letter?"

Considering that it had been offered her twice already, the question was rather superfluous. However, Captain Noah made no mention of the offers nor her refusals. Instead, he handed her Mr. Chase's letter with satisfaction and alacrity. Others than Calvin Wentworth were mentioned in that letter, and this the captain, wily man, knew.

Mary read the letter through, her companion watching her intently as she did so. Then she rose to her feet. Her face was pale no longer. Now there was a crimson flush on her cheeks and an ominous flash in her eyes.

"Well, Mary," queried Captain Noah, "what are you cal'latin' to plan to do?"

She turned and faced him. "Do?" she cried, fiercely. "I don't know what I shall do now. But tomorrow morning I shall tell my stepfather what I think of him and

leave his house forever. After that I shall consult a lawyer concerning the recovery of my money, I suppose."

The captain shook his head.

"I hope you won't, Mary," he said, quietly. "Won't
go away from here, I mean. I know you want to, I
know 'twill be a trial to you to stay; but I'm hopin' you
will stay for a little while longer anyhow."

She looked at him scornfully, incredulously.

"Stay here?" she repeated. "Stay *here,* with that man?
Captain Newcomb, what do you think I am?"

"I think you're a sensible girl. I think you'll want
to do the right thing, right for all hands. And I think,
Mary, that maybe, after you've come to think it over,
you'll be willin' to put yourself out a little mite for—well,
if for no other reason than just because I ask it as a personal favor."

Her expression changed. She held out her hands to
him impulsively.

"Please forgive me, Captain Newcomb," she begged.
"I haven't even thanked you. You have taken so much
trouble for me and——"

"Now, now, now, Mary, don't make any mistake. What
I've been findin' out wan't entirely on your account. I'm
mighty glad I did find it out, if only for you; but I had
other reasons for wantin' to learn the workin's of the
Griggs and Wentworth combination. I'm tryin' to help
poor little Obe Burgess out of his troubles, you remember. Yes, and—er—there's another friend of mine, a
young feller that I believe has been pretty badly used.
Not by you," hastily. "No, no, no, not by you, of course;
you just misunderstood. But by that same combination.

Now, as I told you in the beginnin', Mary, I've got a letter from that young feller in my pocket and it's got your
name on the envelope. If——"

But she interrupted.

"What was your reason for asking me to stay here?"
she asked. "What was the personal favor you wished
me to do for you?"

Captain Noah, whose hand was in the pocket containing the letter he had just mentioned, looked a trifle disappointed. However, he made the best of the inevitable,
withdrew the hand empty, and began to talk, earnestly
and at some length. Miss Barstow listened, at first with
mild interest, then with apparent resentment and indignation, but at last with amusement and a faint smile.

"I see," she said, when he had finished. "It would help
your plans, of course. And I certainly owe you all the
help I can give. But," with a shiver of disgust, "it would
be very hard for me."

"So 'twould, so 'twould. But, in a way, knowin' what
you know, 'twould have a little mite of fun in it. And
if it did work out right, there'd be what the minister calls
a righteous retribution comin' for them that deserved
it, eh? Yes, I know 'twill be hard for you, Mary, but
'twill keep everything quiet and unsuspicious while I'm
workin' at the rest of my picture puzzles. As I see it,
there mustn't either of those swabs—excuse me; gentlemen, I should say—get a hint that I'm anything but the
most innocent green cabbage head in the back garden.
And there's still another reason for my hopin' you'll stay
here, a reason that's pretty important to me and somebody else you won't let me name, I suppose. . . . Oh,

well, all right, all right. Now what do you say, Mary? Will you stay?"

Her answer was not entirely satisfactory.

"I will think it over," she said, "and let you know to-morrow. And, oh, Captain Newcomb, you will forgive me if I don't thank you as I should. The fact is I am so —so disturbed and agitated—I have had such a shock and surprise— But I *am* grateful, I really am."

At the door in the hall the captain stopped to shake hands and say good night. And there, where it was so dark that he could not see her face plainly, he received an agreeable surprise.

"Captain," she said, hesitatingly, "there is one—one thing which—which might help me in reaching that decision I am to give you tomorrow."

Captain Noah turned.

"Eh?" he cried. "Eh? You don't say! What is it, for mercy sakes? If I can get it for you, you shall have it, I swan to man. What is it, Mary?"

"It is—well, it is that letter you have in your pocket. Not the one from the broker, the—the other."

CHAPTER XV

I T was, perhaps, a week later—that is, the week following that in which Captain Noah and Mary Barstow had their long and important interview, that Miss Sarepta Hatch first began to notice that Mr. Calvin Wentworth was calling more and more frequently at the Griggs home. Miss Sarepta, it will be remembered, was Balaam's next-door neighbor on the right as Mrs. Elvira Ginn was on the left. And there were few happenings in their vicinity which one or the other, or both, of these ladies did not notice.

In this case the discovery was probably simultaneous, although it was Miss Hatch who first mentioned it. She happened in at Mrs. Ginn's to return the cupful of sugar she had borrowed the month before.

"Well, Elviry," she said, knowingly, "I suppose you've noticed it, ain't you?"

Mrs. Ginn just then was noticing the fact that although Sarepta had borrowed a coffee-cupful of sugar she was returning a teacupful. So her reply was given rather absently.

"Eh?" she said. "Noticed? Noticed what?"

"What's been goin' on to the next house. Looks as

if 'twas a case of 'Get up, Jack; John, sit down' to me."

" 'John sit down?' John who?"

"Oh, that's just a sayin'. It don't mean nobody special. I mean it looks as if 'twas a case of 'When the cat's away the mice'll play.' Don't you think so?"

"What's cat's away? Balaam Griggs's? If you mean that old raveled-eared tomcat of his, it ain't away because I see it no later'n yesterday eatin' a chicken out back of the woodshed."

"Eatin' a chicken! Land sakes alive! What did you do to it, Elviry?"

"I didn't do nothin' to it. It didn't kill the chicken itself. 'Twas one that that Mr. Wentworth, who's stoppin' up to Obadiah Burgess's, run over with his automobile when he came to take Mary Barstow out to ride. And 'twas one of Balaam's chickens anyhow, not yours nor mine, Sarepta."

"Well, that's a comfort, although I bet Balaam would be mad if he knew it. So you see Mr. Wentworth take the Barstow girl out ridin', did you?"

"Yes, I see him. I stood behind my front-door blinds in the hall and I could see and hear 'em, too. 'Twas Cap'n Newcomb's auto they had, wan't it?"

"Looked like it to me. You don't know where they went, though, I guess."

"No," with reluctance, "I can't say's I do. And I guess likely you don't, neither."

"Yes, I do. They went down to the village, and she done some errands, and then they stopped in to Lathrop's and he treated her to ice-cream. It's the second time he's bought ice-cream for her—and she's let him, too. Don't that look kind of significant to you?"

Although she tried very hard to appear indifferent, Mrs. Ginn's envy at her friend's superior information showed itself in her tone as she said:

"Oh, yes, I suppose you might call it kind of significant—if you're sure it's so."

"Oh, I'm sure. Evelina Dodge told me herself and you know her Joshua is clerkin' to Lathrop's this summer."

Elvira could not successfully contradict such authentic information, so she merely sniffed.

"'Twas Mr. Wentworth and Mary I meant when I said the mice would play," went on Miss Hatch. "Irvin' Clifford's gone West, to Omaha I think 'tis——"

Elvira interrupted. "No, it 'tain't, it's Saint Louis. Ethelinda Doane down to the Mansion House told me 'twas Saint Louis. And she ought to know 'cause Mr. Clifford boarded there all the time he was in Trumet."

"Well, I don't care if he did. Peleg Bearse was round here yesterday peddlin' fish and you know as well as I do, Sarepta, that Peleg boards to the Mansion House just the same as Mr. Clifford did. And Peleg he says Mr. Clifford's gone to Omaha to work on some kind of a sawmill engyne or somethin'. I think 'twas a sawmill engyne he said; anyhow I know 'twas Omaha."

"Well, all's I know is that 'Lindy Doane told me he'd gone to Saint Louis to help put up machines for

16   235

makin' ice, or rice, or somethin'. Hello! Who's that comin' down the road?"

It was Captain Noah in his little car, a fact which Mrs. Ginn, running to the window, proclaimed the next moment.

"He'll know," she cried. "Him and the Clifford man was great chums. He'll know where he's gone."

She ran to the front door, followed by Miss Hatch.

"Cap'n Newcomb!" she screamed. "Cap'n Newcomb!"

The captain, who had already gotten a short distance past the house, heard the hail and turned. When he saw the two ladies standing in the Ginn doorway he slowed down the car, but did not stop. His sojourn in Trumet had not been a long one, but it had been long enough to make him wary of Sarepta and Elvira.

"What is it?" he shouted.

"We want to ask you somethin'," screamed Mrs. Ginn. "Where's Irvin' Clifford gone to?"

The car rolled slowly on. Captain Noah looked back over his shoulder.

"Eh?" he cried again.

Miss Hatch raised her voice. It was no shriller than Elvira's, but she prided herself on its carrying power.

"Where's Irvin' Clifford gone to?" she screamed.

The captain took his left hand from the wheel, made a speaking trumpet of his fist, and shouted through it.

"He's—gone—away," he shouted. Then he put on speed and the little car shot down Knowles' Hill. Mrs. Ginn and Miss Hatch returned to the house, where for twenty minutes they discussed the doings of their fellow townspeople, male and female, paying particular attention to Miss Mary Barstow, Mr. Calvin Wentworth and Mr. Irving Clifford. They agreed that Mr. Clifford's sudden departure looked very suspicious, as if he had received his dismissal from the young lady; also that Mr. Wentworth's more and more frequent calls, coupled with the auto rides, ice-cream treats and the like, were very significant.

"If it's so—I mean if anything comes of it," declared Sarepta, "she can call herself mighty lucky, that's all I've got to say."

It was *not* all she had to say, by a good deal, for she went on to dilate upon Mr. Calvin Wentworth's good points fluently and at length. "He's so polite," she said, "and so—so sort of superior and genteel. Anybody can see he's a gentleman. Course Irvin' Clifford was polite enough, far's that goes, but——"

"But," put in her friend, "there's a difference between buildin' cold-storage houses to freeze fish into and bein' so rich you don't have to pump water to wash your hands. No; what Mr. Wentworth can see in Mary Barstow the dear land knows, but if she gets him she'll be a lucky girl, as you say, Sarepta. But how will Balaam take it, I wonder?"

A good many people wondered that very thing during the next few weeks. Mr. Griggs' prejudice against marriage, when it involved his stepdaughter, was known from one end of Trumet to the other. The Hatch-Ginn conversation was but one of many similar discussions. Had there been a quarrel between Clifford and Miss

EXTRICATING OBADIAH

Barstow? Was the said quarrel the reason for the engineer's sudden departure for Omaha, or Saint Louis, or Salt Lake City, or Jericho, or Jerusalem—or wherever he had gone? And was Mr. Calvin Wentworth a candidate for the vacant place in the young lady's affections? And how, provided he was such a candidate, and a successful one, would stepfather Balaam accept the new development? These were Trumet's questions.

Clifford, although by no means unpopular in the village, had made no especial effort to achieve popularity. Nor had public curiosity at any time centered upon him as it had upon the mysterious and romantic invalid, Mr. Calvin Wentworth. Everyone in town knew of Mr. Wentworth's "debilitated" health, of his wealth—reputed to be a million at least—of his Fifth Avenue clothes and his highly genteel manners. Cousin Calvin was languidly polite and chatty with the Trumet fair sex, old and young. With its males he was condescendingly familiar. Mr. David Weeks, the village lawyer and director in the Harniss Bank, found it enjoyable and flattering to be consulted by the former frequenter of Wall Street concerning which stocks might be considered "good buys" at present. And Hannibal Thayer, who kept the billiard and pool parlor, liked to have Mr. Wentworth drop in, casually, to try a few fancy carom shots on the newest table. The prevailing opinion was that the ex-New Yorker was "a real swell and perfect gentleman, but not a mite stuck-up."

So the majority of Trumet was inclined to believe that, provided the affair ever reached the point where marriage was seriously considered by Calvin and Mary,

238

EXTRICATING OBADIAH

Mr. Griggs would not permit his long-cherished and deep-rooted prejudice to stand in the way.

"It's one thing." declared Ethelinda, standing, dish-towel in hand, gazing out of the Mansion House window. "It's one thing to be down on her marryin' the common run of everyday Cape Codder, like them that's been tryin' to get her and *she* wouldn't look at, let alone Mr. Griggs. And it's the same one thing—or—or next door to it—although after all, it is a different thing, ain't it, Mis' Hobbs, to be down on her marryin' even a nice young cold-storage man like Mr. Clifford. But when it comes to heavin' out objections to her takin' up with a perfect millionaire nobleman like Mr. Wentworth—*well*, that *would* be another thing, wouldn't it, Mis' Hobbs?"

Mrs. Hobbs, looking across the road where the "millionaire nobleman," leaning nonchalantly against a post, watched Sport chase a neighbor's cat up a tree—that is, the cat went up the tree while Sport fretted and pawed below—Mrs. Hobbs, watching the easy grace and perfect poise of the gentleman, sighed. Cousin Calvin had a habit of dropping in at the Mansion House occasionally, where he sat and smoked on the veranda and chatted affably with Mr. Bearse and Uncle Labe or herself. Captain Penniman seldom took part in these conversations. The captain had the bad taste not to like Mr. Wentworth, referred to him contemptuously as a "darned dude."

"That would be another thing, wouldn't it, Mis' Hobbs?" repeated Ethelinda.

"What would be?"

239

"Why, what I said. I said her marryin' Mr. Clifford would be one thing and Mr. Wentworth's marrying her would be another thing. And for Mr. Griggs to be set against her marryin' Mr. Clifford would be a different thing from his bein' set—I mean her bein' set—against her marryin' him—I mean him marryin' her—Mr. Griggs, I mean."

"Who marryin' Mr. Griggs? What are you talkin' about, 'Linda?"

"Nobody. Why, what an idea! I guess nobody'd want to marry old Balaam. It was Mr. Wentworth I was talkin' about. I do think he's just too lovely! Don't you, Mis' Hobbs?"

"Sshh! Don't talk silly, 'Linda."

"That ain't silly, it's sense. I think he's too good for her, don't you, Mis' Hobbs?"

"Nonsense, 'Linda," rather sharply. "You mustn't make such remarks. Very likely he hasn't the slightest idea of marryin' her. Probably he is just friendly, as he is with—with us, for instance."

'Well, maybe so, but— Oh, there she comes now! Look! look, Mis' Hobbs! See! There she comes now. Now we'll see how they act together."

Miss Barstow came down the street, evidently on a shopping expedition. Mr. Wentworth saw her, pushed himself away from the supporting post, raised his hat and stepped forward. The young lady saw him and appeared to hesitate. Ethelinda noticed the hesitation.

"Humph!" she sniffed. "She don't act so terrible glad to see him, does she now? Maybe there *ain't* nothin' in it, after all. Hello! ain't that Mr. Balaam Griggs

standin' in the door of the barber shop over there?
Yes, 'tis, I snum if it ain't! Don't he look sort of ugly
to you, Mis' Hobbs?"

It was Balaam, sure enough, and he looked anything
but pleased. His stepdaughter saw him, caught his eye
—and no longer hesitated. She turned, smiling, toward
the advancing Wentworth.

"Why, how do you do?" she said. "This is a surprise. Isn't it a beautiful afternoon?"

Mr. Wentworth admitted the beauty of the afternoon
and, whistling to Sport, sauntered on by the young lady's
side. Mr. Griggs stepped from the barber's doorway.

"Say, Mary," he hailed.

Mary turned. "Oh, it is you," she said. "Well, what
is it?"

Balaam did not seem to know exactly what it was,
at all events he seemed to find it difficult to speak.

"Yes, Mr. Griggs?" repeated the young lady, sweetly.
"What was it you wanted?"

"Why—er—why—er—" stammered Balaam; "I was
just wonderin' where you were goin', that's all."

"Oh, I'm just going to do a few errands. At Lathrop's and Snow's. Then I may take a walk, it *is* such
a beautiful day."

Mr. Griggs scratched his chin. "Umph!" he grunted. "Well, maybe I'll go with you."

His stepdaughter seemed surprised.

"You?" she cried. "Why, Mr. Griggs, you scarcely
ever take a walk—a long walk."

"Um-hm, I know. But maybe 'twill do me good.
Come ahead."

Miss Barstow shook her head.

"I am so sorry," she said. "If I had only known. But, you see, Mr. Wentworth here——"

"How do, Griggs," observed Cousin Calvin, casually.

"Mr. Wentworth has asked me to go with him. It was he that suggested the walk. You won't mind, will you? Another time, you know. Or you might walk by yourself. Good-by."

They strolled on together around the corner and out of sight. Balaam swore aloud. The barber came out of his shop.

"Say, Balaam," he observed, grinning. "What's happenin' there?" with a jerk of his head toward the departing couple. "Young Clifford's bein' cut out, ain't he? Say, first thing you know you'll have a son-in-law whether you want one or not. Eh? How about that?"

Mr. Griggs turned and snarled at the speaker as Sport had snarled at the cat.

"You mind your own dum business," he ordered. Then he strode off in the opposite direction from that taken by Mary and Mr. Wentworth.

If, instead, he had followed them he might have noticed that the "walk" did not materialize. Apparently Mary changed her mind. In fact, after rounding the corner, where her stepfather could no longer see them, her manner toward her escort was by no means as cordial and intimate. And when, as they came out of Snow's "general store," Captain Newcomb drew up to the curb in his little car, she promptly accepted his invitation to ride home and whizzed away, leaving the "millionaire nobleman" to walk by himself if he chose.

That evening Mr. Griggs was obliged to attend another lodge meeting, but he made it a point to leave early. He reached his house about nine o'clock and, before opening the door, peeped in under the sitting room curtain. What he saw made him grind his teeth. Mr. Wentworth was there, seated in the most comfortable rocker; Mary was with him and they were chatting familiarly and pleasantly.

Balaam entered softly and, tiptoeing in, stood silently in the doorway of the sitting room regarding the pair. There was a mirror upon the wall opposite the doorway and it is just possible that Miss Barstow looked at it. At any rate her manner toward Mr. Wentworth became even more confidential and pleasant.

"Oh, yes, Calvin," she said. Then, with a coquettish little laugh, she added, "I am calling you Calvin because you asked me to, you know. And, after all, somehow it does seem as if we were old friends, doesn't it?"

Mr. Wentworth smiled. "Indeed it does," he said. "And may I call you Mary? Now that we *are* old friends, of course. Mary," he repeated, softly. "The dear old-fashioned names, how I love them."

Mr. Griggs could contain his feelings no longer. They expressed themselves in an explosion which was a combination groan, grunt and snort. Both Miss Barstow and her visitor startled and turned.

"Oh," cried the young lady. "*What* was that? Oh, it is you!" with a sigh of relief. Then she asked, "Why —why, when did you come in?"

It seemed to Balaam that she appeared embarrassed

243

as well as startled. The lamplight in the room was rather dim, so he could not see whether or not she changed color. But he was willing to believe that she did; at all events if she did not he was sure she should. He glowered at her angrily.

"Evening, Griggs," observed Mr. Wentworth. "How was the gathering of the Grand Exalted Brethren of the Double Cross this evening? How many new victims did you hot-foot over the blistering sands this time?"

Balaam transferred the glower from his stepdaughter to her caller.

"I don't know what you're talkin' about," he growled. "I've been to the Red Men's meetin'."

"Woof, woof! Big Injun!" remarked Cousin Calvin, the imperturbable. There was no embarrassment on his part, not the slightest.

"But, Mr. Griggs, why did you come in so quietly?" asked Mary. "I'm sure I didn't hear you open the door, and I think Mr. Wentworth did not?"

"Not a sound," affirmed the gentleman. "He came in with the catlike tread of the untutored child of the forest. He has been on the warpath tonight, Mary. The noble red man has buckled on his tomahawk. Let the pale face tremble for his scalp."

Mary laughed merrily. Her stepfather did not even smile.

" 'Tain't no wonder you didn't hear me come in," he said. "You was too sociable for that."

Mary looked in puzzled fashion from him to Mr. Wentworth.

"What does he mean?" she inquired, addressing the

latter. "Sociable? Why shouldn't we be sociable? We are not enemies, are we?"

Mr. Griggs laughed. "Oh, no!" he exclaimed, loudly. "No, no, you ain't enemies. Anybody could see that. No, no! Enemies! that's a good one."

Cousin Calvin shook his head. "The child of the forest has been scorched by the firewater, I should say," he observed. "That is, I should say if I didn't know what a moral person he was. Your stepfather and I, Mary," he went on, "had a discussion concerning morals during our motor ride a week or two ago. I was much impressed. Mr. Griggs is a highly moral man— in spots," he added, with a chuckle.

Balaam may have felt that the subject of that motor ride was not one to be discussed in his stepdaughter's company. Or it may have dawned upon him that he was not likely to have the last of it in a game of repartee with Mr. Calvin Wentworth. At any rate, his next remark dealt with another subject. He drew forth his watch and looked at it.

"What!" he exclaimed, with great and most obvious astonishment, "almost ten o'clock! Well, I swan to man! Who'd have thought it was as late as that?"

Mary rose to her feet. "Ten o'clock!" she repeated. "Why, I can scarcely believe it."

Cousin Calvin looked at his own watch.

"No wonder you can't believe it," he said. "It will be ten o'clock in exactly twenty-seven minutes. Mr. Griggs' watch is running with the throttle open, I should imagine."

Balaam shook his timepiece and held it to his ear.

"She's runnin' fine," he declared. "That watch of yours is slow, Mr. Wentworth. It's a New York watch, I judge, and it ain't got acclimationed yet."

"Accli—which?"

"Acclimationed—used to the climate we have down here. When it gets that way it'll run smoother, same as mine."

Before the owner of the New York watch could speak again in its defense, Miss Barstow put in a word.

"Well, it is nearly ten, at all events," she said, "and I think, if you gentlemen will excuse me, I will leave you now. I am rather tired and—" She hesitated, and then with a twinkle in her eye, added, "I have a letter to write before I go to bed."

Mr. Wentworth looked disappointed.

"Oh, don't go—yet," he protested.

"Who are you writin' letters to?" demanded Balaam, suspiciously.

Mary smiled and shook her head at him.

"You are so forgetful," she said. "Didn't you ask me to write to that man in Boston about the land he was looking at?" Then turning to Wentworth she added: "Really I must go. As I said I am rather tired, and, besides, I am sure you and Mr. Griggs have many things to talk about. Good night, Mr. Griggs. Good night—er—Calvin."

She gave the couple in the sitting room one final glance and then, with the twinkle in her eyes more pronounced than ever, hurried out and up the stairs. Mr. Griggs looked after her and then, tiptoeing over, quietily closed the door. Cousin Calvin watched the door-shutting with a languid smile.

"Why the deep secrecy, Uncle?" he inquired.

Balaam came back to the chair Mary had just vacated and sat down upon it. He did not answer his visitor's question, but instead asked one of his own.

"Say," he demanded, sullenly, "what are you up to, anyway?"

Mr. Wentworth's smile broadened. "Well, Uncle," he began.

"I told you once I wasn't your uncle," broke in Balaam, pettishly. "I don't see as you've got no call to call me out of my name."

"So? Tastes differ, that's a fact. If I had a name like yours I'd much rather be called out of it than in it. Let's see, what is your name? Jeremiah? Nebuchadnezzar? Jonah? Why, of course, that's it—Jonah."

Mr. Griggs frowned. "No, 'tain't Jonah neither," he snapped. "And you know it well's I do. Look here, I don't care for any of your funny talk just now. I don't feel like laughin'. What I want you to do is to tell me what you're up to?"

"Up to? Well, Uncle—Beg pardon—Well, Jonah—Pardon again—Well—er—Rain-in-the-Face, Chief of the Wampanoags——"

"What in time?"

"What is your Indian name, Uncle? What do they call you around the camp fire up at the 'taown hall'? Eh?"

"Look here! I don't want no funny talk, I tell you. You come here to my house and everybody says you're

callin' on my stepdaughter. You've took her out ridin' in Newcomb's car—all hands seen you. You buy ice-
cream for her, and more'n once, too. This very afternoon you and she went walkin' together right down the
main road. More'n five million folks have been heavin'
out hints about your cuttin' out Irve Clifford and keepin' company along with Mary. I'm sick of it, I be.
Now what do you mean by it? I ask you again: What
are you up to?"

Cousin Calvin took a silver case from his pocket and
selected and lighted a cigarette.

"Join me?" he asked, proffering the case to Griggs.
"No? Too effeminate for the lips of a warrior, I imag-
ine. Only squaws should smoke such things. Righto,
Sitting Bull. But you don't mind if I do? Good."
He crossed his legs, leaned back in his chair, took a
puff or two and then said:

"What am I up to? Well, Uncle, I have heard it
said that I was pretty nearly up to the minute. Of
course I am too modest to say as much myself, but—"
He languidly waved the cigarette and beamed upon his
companion.

Balaam's teeth snapped together and he struck the
arm of his chair with his fist.

"Say," he growled, "this thing's got to stop, do you
hear?"

"Bless me! Is it possible? What thing?"

"You know what well as I do. This thing of your
carryin' on with my stepdaughter and—and sittin' up
with her—and buyin' ice-cream for her and——"

Mr. Wentworth laughed. "The ice-cream portion has

248

already stopped," he observed. "Twice she and I have eaten the frozen cornstarch and glucose they prescribe at the local drug store and it is sufficient, quite. Not any—no more—thank you kindly—a genteel sufficiency."

Mr. Griggs grunted. "Yes, and all the rest of it's got to stop, too. Why, the whole town's sayin' now— Do you know what they're sayin'? Eh, do you?"

"Sorry, old scout, but I do not."

"They're sayin' *you* are goin' to marry her, now."

Cousin Calvin blew a ring of smoke, watched it expand and widen, and then deftly blew another through it.

"How do you know I'm not?" he asked, gently.

Balaam's jaw fell and his eyes opened.

"How do I know?" he gasped. "How do I— Why —why, you——"

"There! there! Don't explode. Yes, how do you know? Mary seems to— Well, she doesn't spurn my society, exactly. In fact," with a slight smirk of self-satisfaction, "she actually appears to—er—like it. She's a pretty girl, a mighty pretty girl. She would make a very creditable wife for any man. Perhaps I am planning to marry her. Why shouldn't I?"

Mr. Griggs bounced from his chair. His face was flaming red and his fists clenched.

"Why shouldn't you?" he repeated. "Why shouldn't you? I'll tell you why you shouldn't. 'Cause I say no, that's why."

"Is that all?"

"All? Ain't it enough? Didn't I tell you I wouldn't

have her marry? Didn't you and me talk that over goin' to Ostable and back? Ain't we talked it over a
dozen times since? Wasn't it your scheme that got
rid of Irve Clifford? Eh, wasn't it?"

Mr. Wentworth did not affirm or deny. He merely
smiled, and upon Balaam Griggs watching that smile
a great light suddenly burst.

"Eh?" cried Balaam. "Eh? by godfrey's domino, I
believe— Did you help me get rid of him so you could
—so *you* could get her yourself? Did you?"

His visitor laughed quietly. Griggs swore aloud.

"Well, you won't get her," he declared, savagely.
"Indeed and indeed you won't."

"Won't I? Dear me!"

"I guess 'twill be dear me. Why, you dum idiot, do
you cal'late I'll have her marryin' you any more'n I
would him? I guess not."

Cousin Calvin tossed the stump of his cigarette into the
flower pot on the window sill.

"Aren't you rather loose in your reasoning, Griggs?"
he asked. "Excuse my mentioning it, but has it occurred to you that Clifford is—er—one sort of person
and I another?"

The effect of this speech upon Mr. Griggs was somewhat surprising. Instead of awing and impressing him
it seemed to do the exact opposite. He laughed loudly
and sarcastically.

"Haw, haw!" he roared. "You're another all right.
I cal'late that's so, sure enough. Irve Clifford is earnin' good wages, or all hands say he is, and you—you,
by time, you ain't earnin' nothin'."

"Possibly I don't need to, Uncle."

"Um—hm, possibly you don't. Long's Obe Burgess is fool enough to eat you and sleep you, and him and Noah Newcomb to lend you money, I don't know's you do need to work. But they don't know and I do." With a significant nod, "*I do*."

Wentworth looked at him keenly.

"What do you mean by that?" he asked. "What **do you** know?"

"I know about you. I've been kind of suspicious ever since you borrored that forty dollars off Obe six weeks ago when your dividend check didn't come. Haw, haw! a mighty good reason why it never come. Waitin' for it yet, I cal'late, ain't you? Yes, and I cal'late you're liable to be for *one* spell. Dividend check! Haw, haw!"

"What do you know?" demanded Wentworth, sharply.

"I know all about you, my fine feller, how much you're worth and all. I know how much Obe is liable to get when you die. Huh! I bet I do. I got suspicious, same as I said——"

"Figured that I might be asking you for a loan, I suppose."

"What if I did? Stranger things than that might happen. I've got it to loan, if I want to, I guess."

"I guess you have. I never heard that you lent any, except on a mortgage, but perhaps I don't realize how openhanded you are. They call you a tightwad down here, Uncle, but probably they're wrong. I was just thinking that I might ask you to help me out a bit financially—just till those dividend checks come in, you know."

"You was? You was, eh? Well, young feller——"

"Thanks for the compliment."

"Shut up! I'm goin' to tell you what I done when I got suspicious of you. I've got a friend who keeps store over to Bayport and he subscribes to Bradstreets'. I asked him to have your standin' looked up and he done it. I got the Bradstreets' folks' answer from him a couple of days ago. Ah, ha! Ah, ha! I thought that might make you look kind of sick.'

The thought was erroneous. Instead of looking sick, Mr. Wentworth, after a momentary pause, burst into a hearty laugh. Balaam, who was not expecting laughter, stared at him in utter amazement.

"Ha, ha!" laughed Cousin Calvin. "Looked me up in Bradstreets', eh? Well done, old scout! Bully for you!"

"Bully for *me?* Be you crazy?"

"Not a bit. Neither are you. You're as sharp as you are reported to be. So you looked me up, eh? I wouldn't have believed anyone in this burg had so much business sense. And what did you find?"

"I found out what you was worth—or what you wan't worth, and that comes to the same thing. Oh, you needn't look scared, I shan't say nothin' to Obe Burgess nor Newcomb nor the rest——"

"I know you won't."

"Is that so! I want to know! Well, you better let me finish. I shan't say nothin' about what I've found out to them fellers nor nobody else, partly because 'tain't

none of their business, and partly because I don't want
to be too hard on you——"

"Thanks, awfully."

"Be still, I tell you. I shan't say it to them if—*if*,
mind you—you stop callin' on my daughter or seein' her
or havin' anything to do with her. Just drop her right
off this minute and I keep mum—otherwise No."

He thumped the table to emphasize the "No."
Cousin Calvin leaned back in his chair, put his hands
in his trousers' pockets and whistled softly.

"Sorry, Uncle," he said, quietly, "but it can't be
done."

"Can't be done? What can't?"

"The 'dropping Mary' game, not on those terms it
can't. She's a nice girl, I like her. As to marrying her
—well, I haven't made up my mind about that yet,
but——"

"Ain't made up *your* mind? Well, I've made up mine.
You—you, struttin' round playin' the millionaire, when
you're only a good-for-nothin', next door to poverty-
struck, seedy——"

His companion waved a protesting hand. "Easy, easy,
old scout," he said. "Let's let it stand at 'seedy.' Seedy
is a word that interests me just now. I *am* a trifle seedy
around the edges, I'll admit; I need some new togs
and a general touching up and revarnishing. Suppose
you let me have—until the dividend checks show up, of
course—say, two hundred dollars. With that I'll take
a little flyer to New York and——"

"I let you have two hundred dollars! *I* let you have
it! By godfrey domino! you *be* loony. Here, you get

253

out of my house! Get right out! And don't you let me see you nigh Mary again."

"Dear me! But suppose you do see me near her; what then?"

"Then I'll tell her how you was the one that sicked the Emmons woman onto Irve Clifford."

"If you do then she may send for Clifford again."

"No, she won't. She's down on him for keeps. And tellin' her ain't the only thing I'll do. I'll tell Obe Burgess and Newcomb about the Bradstreets' report. I'll tell it all around town. I'll show you up, my fine feller."

Mr. Wentworth smilingly shook his head. "Oh, no, you won't," he said.

"Won't, eh? I want to know! Why won't I?"

"Because you will be afraid to, Uncle, dear. Because you will know that the minute I hear of your telling any-one anything about me I shall call upon your Mary —*our* Mary—and read her this bit of literature."

He took a folded paper from his pocket.

" 'But provided,' " he read, " 'my daughter, the said Mary Barton Barstow, comes of age or marries, the said trust held by her mother, my wife, and Balaam Griggs, my joint executor, shall terminate and the said twenty-five thousand dollars shall be hers, the said Mary Barton Barstow's, without let or hindrance.' Neat little sentiment, don't you think? I copied it my-self at the Probate Clerk's office in Ostable. . . . Eh? Why, Uncle, you look ill! Does the child of the forest need his medicine man?"

Balaam had collapsed into a rocking chair. He did look ill, very ill, indeed.

"No, old scout," went on Cousin Calvin, sweetly, "you won't tell anyone anything, I'm sure. And, provided you behave like a nice old dear, I won't tell anyone anything either. And when you lend me that two hundred, as I can see by your eyes you are going to, I will run away to Broadway and be gone two whole long weeks. Isn't that a pleasant prospect? And perhaps during that two weeks I shall decide not to marry Mary at all. There, it's your bedtime, Uncle dear, so I must be trotting. So long, Jonah. By-by, Sitting Bull. Good night, old·scout. I'll call tomorrow; meanwhile you think it over. Good night."

CHAPTER XVI

CAPTAIN NOAH was getting rather anxious and very impatient. Another fortnight had passed, full two weeks since he received the first letter from the New York broker, and each day of those two weeks he had gone to the post office with the hope of finding a second letter, a letter which should give him the information he desired concerning the Ostrich Mining and Smelting Company. But each day he had been disappointed—no letter came.

Obadiah was getting anxious also, not because of the non-arrival of the letter—he knew nothing of the New York correspondence—but because Captain Noah had not as yet performed some miracle which should either get back his five thousand, or, better still, prove that in turning over his capital under Mr. Griggs' guidance he had made a wise investment. The captain so far had done neither of those things; in fact, he had scarcely mentioned the subject since their momentous interview that night at the edge of the bluff. And each time that Obadiah mentioned it his friend and mentor either treated the affair as a joke or bade him keep on the course and say nothing until he knew whether it was land or a fogbank he was headed for.

On the most recent of these occasions the little man had ventured to protest. "But, Cap'n Noah," he demanded, "how am I goin' to n-nun-nun-know which 'tis until I can see? There ain't nothin' ahead, not even f-f-fog, yet."

"Don't let that worry you, Obe," observed the captain, cheerfully. "There ain't anything astern *but* fog, is there? So if there's fog ahead you're no worse off, and when you do sight somethin' solid, provided you do sight it, 'twill look all the better to you."

Obadiah looked puzzled. "Nothin' astern but fog?" he repeated. "I can't see what you m-m-mean by that. There was twelve thousand dollars astern of me once— yes, and abreast of me, too. What's that got to do with fog?"

Noah laughed. "The twelve thousand wasn't exactly what I meant, Obe," he answered. "I meant your investment in that Ostrich stuff was a sort of foggy transaction, seemed to me. You took Balaam's word for everything and set sail for where he told you, no matter whether you could see five fathom ahead of your jibboom or not."

"Well, I don't see as I'm seein' further now," observed Mr. Burgess, rather peevishly. "I did cal'late you was goin' to help me. You said you would. And all you do is talk about fog. I don't give a d-d-dum about fog. I want to know about my money. The five thousand I put in was solid cold c-c-cash."

"Sartin. Ice is solid and cold enough, too, but hot air

257

blowin' over it turns it into fog right off. Same way
with your cold cash, Obe. Balaam he got his hot air
to playin' on it and——"

"Aw, now, let up, won't ye? I don't feel f-f-funny
one bit. My Lord above! What'll I do? *What'll* I
do?"

He was wringing his hands, but the captain put his
own big hand upon them. "There, there, Obe," he said,
kindly, "what's this all about, anyway? You don't know
any more about this—er—poultry investment of yours
than you did at the beginnin', do you?"

"No, course I don't. I——"

"Sshh! And you thought 'twas a good investment
then, didn't you?"

"Sartin I did."

"Of course you did. Well, if the last you thought
you knew was somethin' good what are you wishin' for
—somethin' bad?"

"No, no, course I ain't. 'Tain't likely I be, is it? But
I want to know *somethin'*, and I want to know it pretty
soon. If I don't I—I—I swan to man, Cap'n Noah, I
believe I'll go ravin' d-d-distracted."

"No, no, you won't. Well, *I* want to know somethin',
too, Obe; you and me are just alike fur's that goes. But
there's this difference between us—I'm workin' hard to
find out somethin'. And I cal'late to find out afore long.
You just set still and hold your hair on—hold what
there is left of it on, at any rate. You just wait, same
as I'm doii. There's nothin' to be gained by frettin'."

But in spite of this philosophical preachment the captain did fret a good deal. He more than once sat down

to write his cousin another letter, but each time gave it up. He was asking a favor, and he had no right to hurry the person asked. No doubt there was a good reason why Mr. Chase had not written—but, why hadn't he?

Other letters came regularly enough. Of these the most recent from Chicago contained news which brought a broad grin to Captain Noah's face. He made it a point to see Mary Barstow soon afterward, and found that young lady in a state of mind which, so the captain opined, might lead a well-informed person like himself to infer that she, too, was hearing regularly from Chicago. She seemed quietly, blissfully happy, and said not a word concerning her recently expressed determination to leave her stepfather's home. In fact, she said that she would remain there, for the present at least.

She and Noah conversed on several subjects of mutual interest. Mr. Calvin Wentworth's name was among those mentioned; in fact, Cousin Calvin was mentioned a great many times.

"Did you know that he was going to New York?" asked Mary.

"Goin' to New York?" repeated the captain. "Who is? Not Cousin Calvin?"

"Yes. And he is going soon, on the Saturday morning train, so he told me."

Captain Noah whistled. "On the train?" he repeated. "On the passenger train or the freight?"

"Why, the passenger train, I presume. He doesn't look like a person who would travel on the freight."

"No, he don't, that's a fact. He's the kind of critter who, if he'd had a cabin passage on the Ark, would have

kicked at bein' aboard a cattle boat. No, he'll go fust-
class if he goes, I cal'late. But it costs money to go to
New York—or it used to when I was goin' there reg'lar
—and where does the Honorable get the wherewithal?
That's what puzzles me. He ain't borrowed any from
me lately, and Obadiah ain't let him have any, 'cause I
warned him not to."

"Perhaps he has enough of his own. He can't be
entirely without means."

"He isn't, I cal'late. You saw what Chase wrote—
that his dad left him a good deal, but that he'd run
through about everything. I imagine he has a little income, just about enough to buy him smokes and a few
clothes and such down here, provided he can live on Obe
and pay nothin' for room rent or eats. But goin' to
New York is different. He must have had a windfall
somewheres. How long is he goin' to be gone; did he
say?"

"A week or so, I think he said."

"Humph! Well, as the old woman said when her
grandson told her the white rooster had laid an egg,
that's interestin' if true. I can't hardly believe he's goin',
though. Well, if he should stay a couple of weeks instead of one he might be some surprised when he got
back, eh?"

Mary blushed, smiled, and admitted that that was true.

"Although I haven't actually made up my mind yet,"
she said.

"No, no, course you ain't. But I kind of hope you
will, for it does seem to me the most sensible—not to
say pleasantest—way of settlin' things. And it will set-

tle 'em, too, that's a fact. Ho, ho! And 'twill pretty nigh settle old— Humph! speakin' of the Old Scratch, are Balaam and Calvin as thick as they was there one time?"

"Mr. Wentworth is here a good deal," with a mischievous smile. "Perhaps he might be here more if— if I were more—more friendly. But, oddly enough, Mr. Griggs doesn't seem to like to have him here now; in fact, whenever I mention his name he is as cross as can be. At times he is scarcely civil to him, it seems to me."

"So? Well, probably he don't want him trespassin' around you any more'n he did Irve. I wonder if he knows Calvin read that will. No, 'tain't likely he does. The Honorable would be likely to keep that quiet till he's made sure of you. We'll see if he does go away Saturday. I can't scarcely believe he will."

But he did. Everyone at the Burgess house was surprised when on Friday he announced his departure the next morning, everyone but Captain Noah, of course, and he pretended to be. But, oddly enough, it was Joe Kenney, Mrs. Mayo's nephew, who seemed the most surprised. Joe seemed really anxious and perturbed about it, and the captain, noticing this, asked the reason.

He and the boy were together in the yard that Saturday morning, after breakfast. Young Kenney was working for Balaam Griggs in the afternoon of each day, but the forenoons he was supposed to have to himself. However, Balaam was quite as likely to be over about eleven loudly demanding the young fellow and intimating that the latter was cheating him of hours for which he had duly and liberally paid. The captain noticed that, on such occasions, Joe made his appearance, usually, from the woodshed. He idly wondered what the boy found in that shed to keep him busy, but Joe, when questioned, seemed reluctant to talk on the subject, and his aunt frankly said she did not know.

"He's up to somethin'," she said, during one of her conversations with Captain Noah—which conversations, by the way, were becoming more and more frequent. "He's up to somethin', some secret or other. He don't want to tell, I can see that, and long's he don't I ain't goin' to pry. I know 'tain't anything bad. He's a good-hearted boy, Joe is, and he's all the relation I've got in the world. His mother was my only sister, and when she died I promised her I'd bring her son up as if he was mine. And I have tried to, I certainly have. If she could have foreseen——"

She did not finish that sentence, nor did she refer to her dead sister again. The captain idly wondered what it might be that the latter had not foreseen. Something unpleasant, apparently judging by the look of distress upon the housekeeper's face. Noah did not like to see that look there, nor did he like to hear her sigh. He resented both look and sigh. Somehow or other he had come to feel a sort of proprietary interest in Melissa Mayo, and any trouble which she might be in he was inclined to accept as a personal affront. When she sighed he felt, as he might have expressed it, as if he wanted to lick somebody. This was a most absurd feeling, of course, and he probably would not have admitted its existence, but it did exist, nevertheless.

That Saturday morning, the morning of Mr. Wentworth's departure for New York, Joe and the captain were in the yard together, having finished breakfast at the same time. The captain was strolling leisurely toward the front gate when he heard his name uttered in a sort of shouted whisper. Turning, he saw Joe tiptoeing across the yard toward him. As he looked, the boy beckoned with one hand and flapped the other up and down, a pantomime which Captain Noah accepted to mean a desire for silence.

"Well, Joe, what is it?" he inquired.

Young Kenney tiptoed toward him. "Sshh!" he said. "I—I just wanted to ask you somethin', Cap'n Newcomb, and I didn't want Aunt Melissy nor Mr. Burgess to hear, that's all. Cap'n Newcomb," anxiously, "do you know how long Mr. Wentworth's liable to be gone? How long he's figgerin' to stay?"

The captain shook his head. "Why, no, Joe, I don't," he replied. "He never said nothin' to me. However, I understand he told somebody else he was cal'latin' to be gone a week, anyhow. If he goes to New York, as he says he is, he may like it well enough to stay a fortni't, 'twouldn't surprise me a mite."

Joe's face fell. He looked much disappointed. "And today's the seventeenth," he said, more to himself than to his companion. "If he stays two weeks it will come while he's away. It's the twenty-sixth, and that's a week from day after tomorrer."

"What is?" asked Noah. "What's a week from day after tomorrer, Joe?"

"Why," absently, "his birthday. Gee! that'll be too bad."

"What will?"

"Eh?" Joe seemed to come out of his trance. "Oh, nothin', nothin'," he said, hastily. "I was just thinkin' of somethin', that's all."

"So I judged. You was thinkin' of somethin' that was nothin', eh? Well, all right, Joe, you ain't lonesome. A good many folks in this world think nothin' most of the time."

He turned away, but again the lad spoke.

"Say, Cap'n Newcomb," he whispered. "Say, Cap'n Newcomb."

"Yes, Joe. Overboard with it. What's troublin' you?"

Joe shifted from one foot to the other, plainly hesitating between inclination and prudence. Inclination won.

"Say, Cap'n Newcomb," he said, "if—if I was to show you somethin' would—would you promise not to tell anybody?"

"Sure thing, Joe. Give you my word."

"And if I asked your opinion you'd tell me *just* what you thought?"

"You bet! Tellin's what I think is one of my strong p'ints—or my weak ones."

"Then—then you come with me."

He led the way and the captain followed, into the woodshed, out of it via the side door, into the barn, into the carriage room of the barn, and then up the ladder to the empty loft over the carriage room. This loft was, in the days when there was a horse on the premises, a storage place for hay. Now it was a receptacle for empty boxes, crippled shovels and broken rakes, a discarded bed spring, all sorts of odds and ends. There was a good-sized window at the northern end of the room, and by it was a chair without a back and an obviously homemade easel. Upon the easel was something covered with one of Mrs. Mayo's calico aprons. Joe carefully closed the trapdoor at the head of the ladder by which they had ascended. Then he threw back the apron.

"There, Cap'n Newcomb!" he declared, his tone a mixture of diffidence and triumph, "I've been workin' on it for pretty nigh a month now. What do you think of it? Pretty good likeness, seems to me."

The captain stared at the thing on the easel. Among the luxuries which Obadiah Burgess had purchased in the first flush of prosperity following his coming into possession of his Aunt Sarah's legacy was a camera. With this camera Obadiah had, until the novelty wore off, snap-shot almost everything of consequence, animate and inanimate, about the place. On one occasion he had "shot" Mr. Calvin Wentworth. The shot was anything but a bull's-eye if grace of attitude and beauty of pose were to be considered, but as a caricature of the ex-metropolite's languid manner and self-satisfied smirk it was a huge and glorious success. It was a bit out of focus, too, which made Cousin Calvin's thin, knickerbockered legs appear thinner and his nose longer.

With this photograph as a foundation Joe had proceeded to lovingly build a "crayon enlargement." In his desire to "get the likeness" he had copied the snap-shot with painstaking exactness. And, in a measure, he had got it, the enlargement was an unmistakable portrait of Mr. Wentworth; anyone having met the gentleman more than once or twice would be sure to recognize it. But in the process of enlargement the photograph's peculiarities were likewise enlarged and unwittingly caricatured —a caricature of a caricature, so to speak. And, in order to add a final killing touch to this outbreak of genius and probably also to insure against any possibility of mistake as to identity, the artist had drawn, from memory this time, a portrait of Sport, the Wentworth dog, lying at his master's feet. Sport, in the crayon enlargement, looked as if he had been badly stuffed by an amateur taxidermist, also as if the stuffing process had hurt exceedingly.

The young Raphael who had produced this masterpiece gazed upon it for a full minute without speaking. As Captain Noah said afterward, "You could almost see the pride oozin' out around his collar he was swellin' so with it." Then he drew a deep, satisfied breath and said: "Well, what do you think of it?"

Hearing no answer, he turned to find the captain reaching for his handkerchief. His face was red, and he seemed to be struggling with emotion, admiration doubtless.

"What's the matter?" demanded Joe. "You feel sick? Eh? You ain't *laughin'*, are you?"

Noah shook his head violently. Producing the handkerchief he wiped his forehead, blew his nose vigorously and replied: "Laughin'? What is there to laugh about? It's pretty hot up aloft here, that's all. Whew!"

"Um-hm. I suppose 'tis pretty hot, but I'm generally so busy while I'm here that I don't mind it. What do

266

you think of it, Cap'n Newcomb? Know who 'tis, don't you?"

"I sartin do. I'd know it if I sighted it through a thick fog."

"Um-hm," with the pride of the conscientious workman, "it seemed to me I'd caught the likeness pretty well. And that dog, now? What do you think of that dog? I did him free hand; tried to get him to stay still long enough for me to draw him, but he wouldn't. Pretty good, ain't he?"

Noah gazed reverently at the crayoned quadruped. "He's a wonder," he said, with feeling.

"Glad you like him. And now, honest, Cap'n Newcomb, how *do* you like that as a—as a picture of Mr. Wentworth?"

The captain waited a moment before replying; he was trying to frame an answer which should be both truthful and satisfying. Then he said, solemnly: "Joe, if I had wanted to pay to have a picture of Calvin Wentworth painted I couldn't have got one that satisfied *me* the way that one does. Not for *no* money I couldn't. It's just the way I'd like to have him painted. There! does that satisfy you? Now," he added, hastily, "tell me all about it. How long have you been to work on her? What are you cal'latin' to do with her? Tell me the whole thing."

So Joe told. He had been at work on the portrait for nearly six weeks, in his spare time, of course. The idea of making a crayon enlargement of Mr. Wentworth had occurred to him quite suddenly, had come as a real inspiration. He had kept it a secret because he intended it to be a surprise to the gentleman.

"I was goin' to give it to him on his birthday," he said. "And now he's liable to be in New York when his birthday comes. Ain't that too bad! I don't know what to do with it now; whether to send it to him or wait till he comes back, or what? That's why I got you out here and told you about it, Cap'n Newcomb. What would you do if you was me?"

The captain, still staring, as if fascinated, at the portrait, was seized with another heat attack. He mopped his forehead and eyes, choked once or twice and then asked: "What was you goin' to make him a birthday present of it for, Joe? What was the idea? Love him as much as all that, do you?"

"Why no, I don't love him exactly, as I know of. But he's rich, you know——"

"Oh, he is, eh?"

"Well, ain't he? Everybody says he's awful rich, got loads of money. I thought I'd make this enlargement of him and perhaps he'd—he'd let me have somethin'— somethin' I want."

"Somethin' you want? What do you want?"

"Well, I want some money, a lot of money."

"You want money? For that? I thought you was goin' to give it to him."

"So I am; that's what I planned to do. But I thought— Well, you see I thought maybe he'd be pleased with it. You think he will be pleased, don't you, Cap'n Newcomb?"

Captain Noah rubbed his chin. "I know I'd be pleased

if you gave it to me," he said. "But go ahead, Joe; suppose he is pleased, what then?"

"Why then I thought—I thought I'd ask him to lend me the money. I could pay it back a little at a time, I guess. Anyhow I'd try awful hard."

There was a look of determination on the lad's face which the captain had not seen there before. He had considered the young fellow a listless, almost lazy specimen, but at this particular moment he appeared eager and energetic enough. Noah was interested.

"What do you want the money for?" he asked.

Joe hesitated. He glanced at the closed trapdoor, then at his questioner and then at the floor.

"I can't tell you what I want it for," he said, soberly. "I—I need it, that's all. Do you suppose likely he'll let me have it? Gee! I wish he would."

"But what do you need it for, Joe? Goin' to buy somethin', was you?"

"No, I'm goin' to pay somethin'. 'And—and," with another burst of the same fierce eagerness, "then I'm goin' away. I'm goin' out West somewheres. That's where I want to be. Gee! I'm sick of stayin' around here, livin' on Aunt Melissy and—and doin' for—for *him*. I'm goin' out West. I want to be on a ranch or somethin' like that. And I'll be there, too. I will, you see if I don't."

The captain's interest had increased mightily. This sudden outbreak on the part of Mrs. Mayo's nephew surprised him. Now he remembered that early in their acquaintance the housekeeper had said that the lad's ambition was to go West and work on a cattle ranch. He had paid little attention to the statement at the time.

"Humph! so you want to be a cowboy, do you, Joe?" he asked. "I thought you was cal'latin' to be a painter."

Joe shook his head. "I like to paint first-rate," he said, "but I don't figger to make my whole livin' doin' it. You have to be awful good to do that, everybody says. I can do crayon enlargements pretty well, but that's about all, I guess. Anyhow, 'tain't what I want to do. I want to go West and work my way up on a ranch or somethin' till I come to one of my own."

"How do you know you'll like it?"

The boy's eyes flashed. "I know," he declared. "You bet I know! Gee! I dream about it nights."

Captain Noah reflected. "Hum," he mused. "I know two or three fellers out West there, men I used to meet in the old shippin' days in 'Frisco. One of 'em in particular was a good friend of mine—is yet, I shouldn't wonder. I presume likely if I wrote——"

He paused. The lad's gaze was fixed upon his face.

"You're in earnest in this, are you, Joe?" he asked. "Would you go right off if you had the job? Provided your aunt was willin', I mean?"

"You bet I would!"

"Um-hm. But what's this money you want to borrow from Mr. Wentworth? You're goin' to pay somethin' with it, you say? What somethin'?"

The fire died in the lad's eyes. The frightened look returned.

"I can't tell you," he muttered.

"Why not? Don't you want me to write to my friend out West there?"

"Yes, yes, I do. But—but I can't tell you."

"Can't, eh? Well, I'm sorry. I doubt if I'd feel like recommendin' a young chap who borrowed money to pay —to pay somethin' he didn't like to tell of. Eh? How about that?"

Joe did not answer. He stared sullenly at the floor of the loft.

"Does your Aunt Melissy know about this money you want to pay?"

The boy looked up. "Don't you tell her," he begged. "Don't you tell her a word. You promised me you wouldn't tell anybody anything. You know you did. Don't you tell."

"I shan't; I'll keep my word, Joe. Only I'm kind of sorry. I'd like to have tried to help along that ranch proposition of yours."

Joe looked down again. There was a little choke in his voice as he answered. "I know," he said; "and I'm ever so much obliged to you, Cap'n Newcomb. But—but I can't tell, honest I can't. Thank you, just as much."

Somehow or other Captain Noah felt conscience-stricken. He laid a hand on the boy's sleeve.

"Say, Joe," he said, "let me suggest somethin' else to you, will you? Don't send that picture to Mr. Wentworth in New York. You don't know his address there, anyway, so you couldn't very well send it if you wanted to. And don't give it to him here in Trumet nor ask him to lend you that money till you've come to me and told me you're ready to do it. Promise me that, will you,

Joe? It's your good I'm thinkin' of and nothin' else. Will you promise?"

The eager look had gone from Joe's face and the old listless, almost sullen, one returned. However, he promised. The captain lifted the trapdoor.

"I must be goin'," he observed. "Got to take another cruise up to the post office after that letter I've been expectin' for the last land-knows-how-long. I never seem to get it, but I'm always expectin'."

He was descending the ladder when an exclamation from Joe caused him to stop and look up. The boy was fumbling in his jacket pocket.

"What's the matter?" demanded Captain Noah. Joe continued to fumble. Then from the pocket he produced an assortment of crumpled papers, and from among them an envelope.

"I got it up to the post office three days ago," he stammered, confused and crestfallen. " 'Twas in our box and I took it to bring home to you. I've been so busy with that," pointing to the portrait, "and—and all the rest that I must have clean forgot it. I don't know when I'd have thought of it if you hadn't said 'letter.' Gee! I hope it ain't anything important."

The captain took the envelope. One glance at the handwriting, to say nothing of the printed name and address in the corner, was sufficient. It was the letter from Chase, the New York broker, the letter he had been awaiting so long.

"Humph!" he grunted. " 'Tis kind of important, that's a fact. How long have you had it in storage, did you say, Joe? Three days, was it?"

"Yes. I'm awful sorry. I guess," with a sigh, "you won't think I'm liable to be much good, out West or anywheres else, after this. Well, maybe I ain't. Sometimes I think I'm just no good and that's all."

Seventeen-year-old brains should not think in that fashion. Captain Noah protested.

"Sho, sho!" he cried. "Mustn't talk that way, boy. I'll forgive your forgettin' the letter. You put it in your pocket, and that's pretty nigh fatal, that is. Once let a letter, whether it ought to be mailed or delivered, get into a man's pocket and you've got a combination that's been responsible for more family rows than there have been wrecks in the Atlantic Ocean. I'll forgive you, Joe; I'm only too glad to get the thing finally and at last."

With the letter in his hand he crossed the yard and entered the back door of the house. Mrs. Mayo was in the kitchen, busy as always. She looked up from her ironing as he entered.

"Hello!" she exclaimed. "Back again, eh? You must have used your car, I guess. Don't tell me you've *walked* to the post office and back so soon."

"I shan't think of tellin' you any such thing for two reasons—the first is that 'twould be a lie, and the second is that you wouldn't believe it. There ain't a mite of use in lyin' when you can't get your lie believed. That's always been my motto, Melissy—one of 'em, anyhow."

Just when the housekeeper and he had begun addressing each other by their Christian names it is doubtful if either of them could have told. The use of such names early in acquaintance is a pleasant Cape Cod custom, and they had adopted it as their acquaintanceship ripened into friendship. The captain called all his friends, no matter of what rank in life, by their Christian names, and he had come to consider Mrs. Mayo a very good friend indeed. She was a mysterious friend and still the one refractory bit that would not fit into his "picture puzzle," but mysteries are always fascinating. And either Captain Noah's inclinations or reasoning, or both, had convinced him that, whatever Mrs. Mayo's part in the mystery might be, there was nothing disgraceful about it. No, indeed! It was odd how thoroughly convinced he was of that.

The lady looked at him and smiled.

"I wonder if you ever told a real lie in your life, Noah," she observed. "I don't believe you ever did."

The captain stared at her in bewildered amazement.

"For the land sakes, why?" he demanded.

"Because you don't look as if you ever did or ever could."

"My soul! Well, I'm much obliged. George Washin'-ton would have to shove over on that marble horse-block of his up to the Boston Public Garden and make room for me, wouldn't he, if that was true. He's safe from crowdin' for a spell yet, I cal'late. Never told a lie! If you knew how many— Tut, tut, tut! But, say, Melissy, what's become of all those breakfast dishes?"

"Become of 'em? Why, what do you mean?"

"I mean what did you do with 'em? When I went out of this kitchen a spell ago you was all walled in with dishes, like a scallop-opener in a heap of shells. Now they're all out of sight and here you are ironin'. What did you do with 'em?"

"Do with 'em? Why, I washed 'em, of course, and put 'em away in the pantry."

"You didn't! Not all of 'em, all by yourself?"

"Of course I did. There weren't so many."

The captain shook his head. "My, my, my!" he said, admiringly. "Well, long as you and George Washin'ton are such chums I suppose I've got to believe it, but I tell you this, Melissy: If ever I go to sea again I'm goin' to ship you as crew. I won't need anybody else. You could handle ship, stand all the watches, and have spare time enough left to cook in, besides."

The housekeeper laughed and declared he was talking nonsense, but she looked pleased, nevertheless. A moment later, however, her expression changed and she was grave enough when she asked:

"Noah, are you responsible for so many of our groceries and supplies comin' from Boston now?"

Captain Noah, who had not been expecting this, was rather flustered for the moment.

"Why—why," he stammered, "they have been comin' from Boston for quite a spell, haven't they? That is, the heft of 'em."

"You know what I mean. I don't mean comin' from Boston to Balaam Griggs and then here; I mean comin' here direct. Obadiah tells me he orders direct now, but I'm pretty sure he didn't have gumption enough all by himself to think of doin' it. It was you, wasn't it?"

The captain pulled his beard. "Well, Melissy," he said, "maybe you'll recollect one time when you and I had a little talk and you said—that is, you gave me to understand——"

"I know what I said. I'm not likely to forget it."

"Well—er—naturally then, bein' a friend of Obe's, I— But say, you don't feel bad because they come direct instead of through Balaam's commission agency, do you?"

"No, you know I don't."

"How about Balaam? How does he feel?"

Mrs. Mayo turned away.

"He doesn't like it," she answered, shortly.

"Don't, eh? What does he say?"

Her answer was brief, but its tone conveyed much to Noah's mind.

"He says— Oh, well, we won't talk about it," she said.

The captain's fist came down upon the kitchen table with a bang.

"Yes, we will talk about it," he declared. "It's high time we talked about it. What right has he got to——"

She held up a hand. "Please, please," she begged.

"But, Melissy, by thunder, it's——"

"Noah, do you want me to be very unhappy; to be in more trouble?"

"No, course I don't."

"Then—then don't talk about—about certain things, and don't ask questions. I can't answer them. I told you long ago what you should do; you should tell your friend the plain truth and have him get rid of the whole lot of us, of Balaam and that Wentworth man and Joe and me. That's what you should do."

"Well, I shan't. Not of you and Joe, at any rate."

"Why not?"

"Because I don't believe there's any reason why I should. I don't care what you say, Melissy Mayo, I know you're a good woman. I've knocked around some in this world and I've learned to judge folks. I *know* you're straight. And if Balaam Griggs——"

"Sshh! shh! Don't say any more, please. I mustn't let you. You don't know anything of the kind—you don't know anything about me—about us, at all. Some of these days, when all this is through with, if it ever is, and I've gone away, I—perhaps I'll write you and tell you the whole truth. I should like to have you think well of me, as well as anyone can, that is."

"Think well of you! Think well of *you?* Melissy Mayo, I—I—I swear I don't hardly dast to say what I . . . Here! Melissy!"

But she had gone into the dining room and closed the door. He drew his hand across his forehead and suddenly became aware that he was still holding in the other hand the letter young Kenney had given him. He turned, walked from the kitchen and up the stairs to his room. There, with the door closed, he sat down, tore open the envelope and began to read.

The letter was a long one, typewritten of course. Mr. Chase had much to say concerning the Ostrich Mining and Smelting Company of Lake Superior. Noah read on and on with increasing interest. At one time the property had promised great things. Then there was promise of a railroad being built to open up that section of the country, the ore could be promptly and cheaply gotten out to market, and so on. But the railroad was not built, the company lacked sufficient capital to go on, a period of stagnation set in, operations were discontinued, and for a long time Ostrich Mining and Smelting was, to all intents and purposes, dead.

But recently [wrote Mr. Chase], early last fall in fact, there was a sort of resurrection and revival of the thing. A big and powerful syndicate became interested in other properties near there and it was reported, and with reason, that they intended taking over the Ostrich holdings. There was quite a little flurry on the Curb for a week or so. The stock was sold, a number of blocks of it, for from thirty to fifty, one small lot even as high as sixty. For the Ostrich property is really valuable, or would be, were it not for the prohibitive cost of transportation. Then the syndicate decided not to buy, the deal fell through, and Ostrich fell dead again. Lots of people would like to sell, I presume, but of course no one wants to buy. There has not been a share sold on the Curb since last October. I had one of my men look into the matter and he tells me that there have been but one hundred shares transferred on the company's books since that time. Those hundred shares have been transferred twice and—here is where the odd part comes in—the three names involved in the transactions are those of people down in that heap of salt and sand where you are now, Trumet, Mass. On April fourth one Balaam Griggs—How's that for a name to be wished on an innocent child?—transferred one hundred shares to one Obadiah Burgess—And there's another name, if you like! And on the same day one Melissa Mayo transferred a hundred shares to said Balaam Griggs. Of course it was the same hundred. Melissa owned the stuff first and she sold or gave it to Balaam and he unloaded it on to Obadiah. But why on earth Obadiah should want it more than I——

Captain Noah read no further. He leaned back in his chair and stared helplessly at the wall paper on the opposite side of the room.

EXTRICATING OBADIAH

"Melissa Mayo! Melissa——"

He had been practically sure that Obadiah's wonderful "investment" was nothing but a swindle, a bit of sharp dealing on Griggs' part. And of course that was what it was, the *modus operandi* was childishly simple. Balaam had known his cousin, Mrs. Mayo, possessed this practically worthless stock; he had seen and grasped the opportunity to sell it at a high figure to his trusting friend and victim. All this was plain enough. But how much had Mrs. Mayo known? How deeply was she involved in the shady, contemptible transaction? That was the question Noah Newcomb asked himself over and over again.

"I should like to have you think well of me——"

She had said that; they were the last words he had heard her say. And as he sat there staring at the wall paper, the certainty was borne in upon him that he had come to think well of her, altogether too well for his peace of mind.

If she was a party to this——

He struck the table with his fist and rose to his feet.

"No, by the Lord, she ain't," he said aloud. A moment later he was on his way downstairs.

CHAPTER XVII

MRS. MAYO was in the kitchen, still busy with her ironing, when he entered. Her expression, as she bent over the table, was grave, almost sad, and she did not look up as he came in. Captain Noah hesitated, walked to the door, and then, pulling forward a wooden chair which stood by the window, sat down.

"Well, Melissy," he observed, "still hard at it, I see."

The housekeeper nodded.

"Yes," she said.

"Too busy to talk a minute or two, are you?"

"No, I guess not." And, then, looking at him for the first time, she added: "If it's anything important you want to talk about."

The captain pulled at his head. "Why, I don't know's 'tis," he said, "and I don't know's 'tain't."

"Well, if you don't, I don't know who does."

"So? Well, I didn't know but you might. Do you know anything about stock, Melissy?"

"Why, a little mite, perhaps. My father kept a dozen cows or so when I was young. He used to sell milk. If it's that kind of stock you mean——?"

"No, 'tain't. The stock I mean has more to do with lambs than it has with cows. I mean stock exchange stocks, stocks and bonds and that sort of thing. Do you know anything about them?"

"No, precious little. I never was sociable enough with 'em to know a great deal. I should think that was more in your line than 'twas in mine, Cap'n Noah. You own some, don't you? Seems to me I remember your tellin' me about some investments you had."

"Oh, yes, I've got some. Not enough to lame my wrists cuttin' off coupons, nor even enough to limber 'em up on the job—but some."

"Then why in the world do you ask me?"

"Because the kind of stock I was cal'latin' to ask about wasn't the kind I've ever bought or sold. It's a minin' stock, and minin' stocks are somethin' I've always steered clear of. I should be well to wind'ard of this partic'lar one only a friend of mine has put some of his money into it and has been askin' my advice."

"Oh, I see. What kind of a mine is it?"

The captain looked up at her from under his brows. "It's a copper mine," he said.

Mrs. Mayo's interest deepened. She put down her iron on the stand and turned toward her companion.

"A copper mine?" she repeated. "Why, isn't that funny!"

"What's funny?"

"Why, your askin' me about it. Copper minin' stock is the only kind of stock I do know anything about. And I don't know *much* about that; only I did own some once."

"You did, eh? Then I've come to the right port to load up with information, I should say. So you owned some copper stock, eh?"

"Yes. And for a good many years I thought it wasn't goin' to be worth ten cents a barrel. Then at last I sold it and got quite a little money for it—not anywhere near what it cost of course, but a good deal more than I ever expected. So it shows you can't always tell. Perhaps it'll work that way with your friend; although he may know his is all right," she added.

The captain smiled. "He thought he knew when he bought it," he observed. "Now he ain't so sure."

"Oh, I'm so sorry. What is the name of the stock?"

Noah looked at her more intently than ever. "The Ostrich Minin' and Smeltin' Company of Lake Superior," he said, slowly.

She looked surprised, very much surprised, but she did not look guilty or even embarrassed. The captain drew a long breath of—well, if not of relief, certainly of satisfaction. To possess a conviction is one thing, to have that conviction strengthened is another. Noah had been practically sure that Melissa Mayo had been merely an innocent participant in Obadiah Burgess's copper deal, now he was still more sure.

The housekeeper gazed at him.

"Ostrich Minin' and Smeltin'!" she repeated. "Why, Noah Newcomb!"

"My name," admitted the captain, cheerfully. "What's the matter, Melissy?"

"Matter? Do you mean to tell me that your friend has bought Ostrich Minin' stock?"

"Yes."

"Why, that's the strangest thing I ever heard of!"

"You don't say! I don't see anything so very strange about it. Folks are buyin' stocks like that every hour of every day, I suppose."

"That isn't what I mean. I mean it's so strange your askin' my advice about it. It's the one stock I do know anything about. It was Ostrich Minin' and Smeltin' I was tellin' you about, the stock I had so long and sold."

Captain Noah did not seem greatly astonished. "I want to know!" was all he said.

"You want to know! Is that all you've got to say? It seems to me the queerest thing goin' that you should come and ask me about that stock; and yet you sit there and say 'I want to know,' as if you'd been expectin' it all along."

The captain made no comment on this statement. Instead he asked: "How many shares did you own, Melissy?"

"A hundred. Why?"

" 'Twas one hundred shares my friend bought."

Mrs. Mayo, who had been standing by the ironing table during the conversation so far, slowly crossed the room and stood before him.

"Noah Newcomb," she demanded, "what are you drivin' at?"

"Who? Me?"

"Yes, you. What is all this talk leadin' up to; all this about those hundred shares of stock, my stock, and your 'friend.' Who is your friend?"

The captain smiled. "Someone you know," he said.
"Someone I know? 'Tain't you, yourself?"

"No. I don't often call myself my own friend, Melissy.
I ain't so sure I like myself as all that comes to."

"Then who is it? . . . Oh, I see! You've been foolin'
me all this time. Balaam told you about his buyin' it,
I suppose."

"Balaam? Balaam Griggs you mean? Was it Balaam
that you sold your Ostrich to, Melissy?"

"Of course it was, and you knew it was. You and
your yarns about your 'friend'! But why did he tell
you? Did he want you to buy it of him?"

"No. Balaam wasn't the friend I was mentionin', Melissy. You may find it hard to believe, but I ain't any
surer that I like him than I am that I like myself. And
he never mentioned Ostrich stock to me. Fact is, he'd
sold his afore I came here to live permanent."

"He sold it? Balaam had sold the stock he bought
of me? And before you came here? Why, he must
have sold it right off after he bought it of me."

"I shouldn't wonder. Er—Melissy, would you mind
answerin' a kind of personal question? Mind tellin'
me how much Balaam gave you for that Ostrich stuff
of yours?"

She shook her head. "I'm sorry, Noah," she answered. "I wish I could tell you, but I can't. You see,
I promised Balaam I wouldn't. Fact is, the stock, he
and I both agreed, wasn't much account anyhow and he
just bought it as a—a kind of favor to me, as you might
say. I owed him. . . . .Well, never mind that. I told
him I wouldn't mention the thing at all, and I shouldn't

only—only you kind of fooled me into it. What made you? Who is this friend of yours—always provided there is one at all?"

"There sartin is. Well, long's you can't tell me what Balaam paid for it, maybe you'd like to hear what he sold it for. He sold it for fifty dollars a share."

Mrs. Mayo groped for a chair and sat heavily down upon it. The color left her face.

"Fifty dollars a share!" she repeated, slowly. "Cap'n Newcomb, are you foolin' again?"

"No, Melissy."

"Then—then you must be crazy."

"I ain't, and neither was Balaam. The other party in the deal might stand a chance of bein' convicted on a charge of softness of the skull—that is the feller that paid the fifty per."

"Who—who was it?"

"Obadiah Burgess."

The effect of this name was to render her speechless for a moment. She grew paler even than before.

"Obadiah—Obadiah Burgess!" she repeated. "He sold it to Obadiah Burgess—for—for fifty dollars a share! That's—that's five thousand dollars, isn't it? He took five thousand dollars from him! Oh, Noah, you ain't foolin', are you?"

He shook his head.

"No, Melissy," he said, gravely, "I ain't foolin'. He sold it to Obe—let him have it as a particular favor to him—for five thousand cash."

"Oh! Oh! Oh! Noah, he—he paid me five dollars

285

a share for it. There! I have broken my word, but I don't much care."

The captain leaned back in his chair. He whistled, long and shrilly.

"Whew!" he exclaimed. "If that ain't—" He paused, laughed, and then added: "Well, in some respects I'll take off my hat to Balaam Griggs. In his line he's pretty hard to beat. Buy it for five hundred—of you, his own relation—and then sell it for five thousand to his particular friend. Tut! tut! tut! That's some tradin'!"

"But, Noah, are you sure he did it? I can't hardly believe he could."

"He did. And, Melissy, I cal'late he had as good as sold it to Obadiah before he bought it of you. The transfers of stock in the books were all together, you to Balaam and Balaam to Obe. I guess there ain't much doubt that he had made the dicker and fixed the five thousand price afore he actually paid you the five hundred. Let's see, you're his first cousin, ain't you? It's a good thing you ain't his sister, or you mightn't have got but two hundred and fifty."

She was silent, thinking, her fingers twisting in her lap.

"Noah," she asked, "is the stock worth—anything?"

"Why yes, somethin', I cal'late. Anywheres from five to seven dollars a share might be a fair price, I should think, to a person who was willin' to take a gambler's chance and wait."

"But I can't see— Noah, how did he get Mr. Burgess to pay so much for it?"

EXTRICATING OBADIAH

The captain sniffed.

"Melissy," he answered, "have you cruised along with Obe Burgess for the last four or five months and not come to know that he'd pay any price for anything, if the right person talked him into it? I'd undertake to sell Obe a dentist's license to fit false teeth into a hay-rake, if I could have a couple of days' time and a package of throat lozenges. And I'm a deef and dumb persuader compared to your Cousin Balaam."

He went on to tell of the reports of sales in the papers of the previous fall, expressing the opinion that it was those papers which had been shown Mr. Burgess.

"Obe thought he'd made a high old investment at first," he continued. "Then he got scared and wrote for me to come and help him out. After I did come he was scared to tell me, for fear of findin' out he had made an idiot of himself, and 'twas only a little spell ago I wormed the yarn out of him. He's mighty nervous, Obe is, and no wonder. His Aunt Sarah's legacy is fadin' away like a night's frost in a mornin' sun. About half of it's gone already, I judge."

She wrung her hands. "The poor man!" she cried. "The poor man! And I—" Then, as if the thought had occurred to her for the first time, she turned to him and asked anxiously: "Noah, you don't think I knew of this, do you? You don't think I was a—a partner in—in sellin' him that stock?"

Captain Noah put back his head and laughed heartily. "I knew you weren't from the first, Melissy. I've told you more'n once that I've learned to estimate folks, and

I made my estimate of you long ago. Here! My soul and body! Don't do that, Melissy! Don't!"

She had put her apron to her eyes and was crying softly. He sprang from his chair and came towards her, but she dropped the apron and motioned him away.

"Don't mind me," she said. "It—it ain't anything. I don't know why I cried, unless—unless it was because you said you trusted me. I don't see how you can."

"I don't see how I couldn't. If you ain't a good, straight, honest woman, Melissy Mayo, then there ain't any made."

She smiled pitifully. "And yet you know I've been helpin' cheat poor Mr. Burgess," she said.

"You ain't, neither. You ain't responsible for Balaam's——"

"I've kept still while Balaam sold him the household supplies at big prices. I've stayed on here when I knew he couldn't afford to keep me."

This speech the captain found it hard to answer. He made a brave effort, but the right words were not within hailing distance. She watched him grow red in the face and sighed.

"You know it's true," she said. "But I ain't goin' to let you think I knew what was goin' to become of that Ostrich stock when I let Balaam have it. I didn't. My husband bought those shares afore he died; we was livin' in Gloucester then and Joe's mother, my only sister she was, and her baby was livin' with us. John, my husband, had some friends up there in Michigan and they thought high of the Ostrich property and gave John a tip to get in on the ground floor. So he got

in, though," with a shrug, "it waä more like the cellar
than the ground floor, I'm afraid. But up to the time
of his death he had confidence in it and kept sayin'
he was goin' to hold on. I'd most forgot the stuff
through all the years since he died, and lately," she
sighed and looked wearily out of the window, "lately
I've had other things to keep me thinkin'. But along
that time in April Balaam came to me and said he understood I still had those shares. I said yes, I believed
I had, and he said, as a favor to me, he'd be willin' to
take 'em over as part payment. So I thought 'twas a
wonderful chance and I sold 'em. That's all the story.
Of course if I'd known what he meant to do with 'em
—cheat that poor, simple, good-hearted man out of his
money—I'd have cut my hand off before I let him have
'em, debt or no debt."

Her fingers clenched in her lap and her eyes flashed.
Noah said quietly, "So there's a debt, eh? I thought as
much."

She turned on him in alarm. "You thought as
much?" she repeated. "What do you mean? What
did you think?"

"I thought there was some reason why Balaam had
you workin' here, where you felt you hadn't ought to be,
and kept you here against your will. And the only
reason I could think of was that, somehow or other,
you'd come to owe him money. I know he'd rub his
own grandmother through a sieve if the old lady had
swallowed a ten-cent piece, and I know if, by hook or
crook, he got you under his thumb, he'd stop at precious
close to nothin' to keep you there. You owe him money,

Melissy. You just the same as said so. Will you tell me how much it is?"

She shook her head. She looked worried, almost frightened.

"No, no," she cried, hurriedly. "I didn't say I owed him anything. You mustn't ask me, Noah. Please."

"I shouldn't ask you if I wasn't your friend, Melissy. And I ain't askin' for curiosity, either. How much do you owe Balaam Griggs? Come now, tell me."

But she would not tell. He tried again.

"Of course it ain't of my business, Melissy," he began. She interrupted him.

"It isn't that, Noah," she said. "I don't mind you askin' a bit. I know you're doin' it just because you're interested and friendly. But I can't tell you, truly I can't."

"Why not? It can't be such a Scargo Hill of money that I'd be afraid to sight it through a spyglass. Would you mind tellin' me what you owe it for?"

This question seemed to trouble and alarm her more than the other.

"Oh, no, no!" she cried. "Please don't ask me, Noah. Please!"

He came close to her.

"Melissy," he said gently, "I hate to torment you. I hate to keep askin'. I'm doin' it not just because I'm interested and friendly, as you say, but for a bigger reason than that. I know you're in some sort of trouble, deep trouble, and I believe I could help you out. I'm sartin I could. I'm goin' to, if you'll give me the chance."

The tears were in her eyes again, but she still shook her head.

"No, Noah," she said, "you're awful kind and good and I'm—I don't dare tell you how grateful I am to you for wantin' to help; but you can't help, nobody can."

"I can, and I'm goin' to."

"You can't. It's a trouble I must get out of myself. I will, I hope and trust, give me time."

She was trying to be brave and to pretend a confidence she did not feel. The captain recognized the effort and realized also the discouragement behind it. He swallowed hard.

"Melissy," he persisted, "you needn't tell me what you owe this money for, if you don't want to. All I'll ask you is to tell me how much it is. Look here, you know I've got some money of my own. Course I ain't any Commodore Vanderbilt or anything like that, but I ain't liable to have to ship afore the mast in the poorhouse, neither. You tell me how much you owe Balaam; then I'll lend you enough to pay him. After that——"

"No, no, Noah. No."

"After that you can pay me a little at a time. Mighty little and any time. Come now, let me do this, won't you? It'll just be a pleasure for me, honest."

He bent forward and tried to look in her face, but she turned away. It was a moment before she spoke.

"You are a good man, Noah Newcomb," she said, quietly. "You're a good man."

"Who? Me? Rubbish! I'm just a—a capitalist, that's what I am. I'm a capitalist, same as Obadiah cal'-

lated he was, and I'm hankerin' to turn over my capital. Only," he added, hastily, "I pick my investments more careful than he does his, that's all. Now, Melissy, we'll just call it settled. You tell me how much——"

She turned to him now and, after one glance at her face, he knew that it *was* settled, and settled against him. She looked up into his face and once more shook her head.

"No, Noah," she said, quietly but firmly. "No, I can't do it and you mustn't think of it. If I had to borrow money I think I'd rather borrow it of you than anyone I know, but I can't borrow. That wouldn't help me any."

"Why not? I tell you I don't need——"

"Hush! Don't tell me any more. Just let me remember what you have told me. Be sure I'll never, never forget it. And thank you."

He was still rebellious. "But why not, Melissy?" he demanded. "All I want to do is to see you happy just once, that's all."

She smiled, although her eyes were brimming.

"I am happier than I have been for a good while," she said. "And you've made me so."

"And you can't tell me how you come to be in Balaam's debt?"

"No, Noah. Perhaps if it was my own story altogether I could, but it isn't, it's somebody else's, too; so you see I can't tell."

Noah clenched his fists.

"I've a good mind to grab the old landshark," he growled, "and choke it out of him."

This frightened her. She seized his arm.

"Oh, no," she pleaded. "Noah, you won't do anything to him, or say anything to him about it, will you?
For my sake you won't do that? It wouldn't do any
good and would only make more trouble. Please promise you won't."

And just then, as one more justification of the old
"Speak of angels" proverb, they heard the voice of
the very person they were discussing. Mr. Balaam
Griggs, somewhere on the premises, was shouting for
his young relative.

"Joe! Joe Kenney!" he shouted. "Jo-o-e! Where be
you?"

Mrs. Mayo shivered at the sound. "He'll be in here
in a minute," she whispered. "And I—I don't feel as
if I *could* see him just now."

The captain grunted. "I'm dum sure I don't want
to see him, either," he muttered. "It might be too hard
to put off that chokin' program if I did. I'll clear out,
Melissy, up street or somewheres. Guess likely I'll go
for a cruise in the Pancake—my car, I mean. You and
me'll have another talk pretty soon. I ain't given up
yet. You think that notion of mine over; do now. It
won't be the least mite of trouble and——"

Balaam went by the window, still roaring for young
Kenney.

"Joe!" he shouted. "Joe! Joash Kenney, where in time
are you, you good for nothin' loafer? Jo-ash!"

Captain Noah turned to Mrs. Mayo.

"What did he call him?" he asked. But Mrs. Mayo
had gone; the door leading to the back stairs was just

closing. The captain picked up his hat and headed for the dining room and the front hall, but before he could escape from the kitchen Mr. Griggs entered it. The dealer in antiques and copper stocks was decidedly not in a good humor.

"Seen anything of that everlastin' young relation of mine?" he sputtered, red-faced and out of breath.

Captain Noah filled and lighted his pipe. Balaam repeated his question.

"I say, have you seen anything of that Joe Kenney 'round here?" he asked.

The captain scratched a match. "That wan't what I heard you callin' him a minute ago," he observed, between puffs.

"What wan't?"

"Joe. You were yellin' the shingles loose callin' him some other name, wan't you?"

"Eh? Other name? I called him a good for nothin', everlastin'——"

" 'Twan't those I meant. You were callin' him 'Jo—Jo—somethin' or other."

"Humph! I called him Joash. That's his name."

"Jo—what? I thought his name was Joseph."

" 'Tain't. It's Joash. Did you ever hear such a name in your life? He hates to be called by it, and no wonder; but it was christened onto him just the same. Have you seen him? I want him to do some cratin' and cartin' over to my place and he's always off somewheres where I can't lay hands on him, lazy good for nothin'. . . . Eh? What are you lookin' at me so funny for?"

The captain was staring at Mr. Griggs with a puzzled

expression on his face. He seemed to be trying to remember something.

"What did you say that boy's name was?" he asked
again.

"Joash."

"Spell it."

Balaam spelt it, and added: "Have you seen him, I ask
you?"

Captain Noah did not answer. He walked briskly out
of the kitchen, out of the yard and down to the garage
where he kept the little automobile.

His ride was neither very long nor very enjoyable. He
narrowly escaped running down several indignant citi-
zens, afoot or in wagons, because he seemed to be quite
absent-mindedly unaware of their proximity. It was not
until he had progressed as far as the forks of the road
leading to South Trumet that the puzzled frown left his
face. He suddenly leaned back in the driver's seat and
whistled.

"That's it!" he exclaimed aloud. "Sure enough, that's
it!"

He turned the car about and, at a thirty-mile an hour
gait, whizzed back to Trumet and the Burgess front gate.
Before that gate he brought the automobile to a stand-
still, sprang out, opened the door softly and went upstairs
to his room. Then, having locked the door, he opened
one of the small upper drawers of his bureau. The
drawer was more than half full of papers, memoranda,
newspaper clippings and the like. The captain had a way
of loading his pocketbook with such things and then,
when it became too corpulent for comfortable transpor-

tation, unloading it into his bureau drawer or a compartment in the tray of his trunk. The contents of this drawer represented almost a year's accumulation in trunk tray and pocketbook.

He emptied the heap upon his table and, sitting down before it, began looking the papers over, one by one. It was some time before he found what he was looking for, but at last he held it in his hand. An oblong strip of cheap note paper, evidently torn from the bottom of a letter. Upon it was written:

sending you every cent ju
omptly as ever I can. For
d's sake remember how hard it
n't put Joash, poor boy, in state's prison.

Leaning back in his chair the captain tried to remember how that slip of paper had come into his possession. It had fallen from the copy of the *Herald* he was reading on that first night of his first visit to Trumet—first in recent years, that is. And in accounting for its presence between the *Herald's* pages he saw himself again sitting in the corner of the crowded Trumet post office, beside the peach crate waste basket, while Mr. Balaam Griggs savagely tore a letter into pieces and tossed the fragments in the direction of the waste basket.

He rose, walked over to the bureau, and returned with another slip of paper, a note written by Mrs. Mayo as a shopping guide when he had offered to do an errand for her in Wellmouth a few days before. Again sitting down at the table, he took this note and the other fragment and compared the handwriting upon each. And, as he did so, slowly an expression of triumphant and complete satisfaction began to dawn upon his face. He struck the table top a mighty slap with his open hand and rose to his feet.

No wonder he looked triumphant. The long, worrisome "picture puzzle" was, he believed, solved at last. The last troublesome fragment was fitting into place. Leaving the litter of papers upon the table, he hurried downstairs and out of doors.

He circuited the house and approached the barn from the rear, in order that no one in the kitchen might see him. He entered the carriage room and, softly ascending the ladder, rapped lightly upon the under side of the trapdoor. He heard a startled exclamation and the sound of a chair being scraped along the floor. Then a voice, Joe Kenney's voice, said quaveringly: "Who is it?"

"It's me, Cap'n Newcomb," whispered the captain. "Let me up, Joe."

A weight was removed from the trap-door and the latter was lifted. Captain Noah came up into the loft and closed the trap after him. The crayon enlargement of Mr. Wentworth was still upon the easel, and the artist's fingers, not to mention his nose, were smeared with chalk; so it was easy to see how he had occupied his time since the captain's former visit.

"Been hard at it, haven't you, Joe?" observed the captain, with a nod toward the easel. "Too busy to hear Cousin Balaam bellowin' after you like a bull of Bashan, eh?"

Joe looked frightened. "Was he?" he asked, fearfully. "I didn't hear him. Gee! honest I didn't."

"Course not, course not. Well, don't let that trouble you any. Time enough for him to find you when he does, I guess likely. But, Joe, I've come up here to ask you a question and I want you to answer it. Will you?"

"Why, yes, sir, I—I guess so. Course I will if—if it ain't——"

"And if you do answer it, will you answer it honest and straight?"

"Yes, sir."

"All right. Joe, what has Balaam Griggs got on you that would put you in state's prison? . . . Eh! Good Lord above! Here, here, boy, brace up; don't act that way!"

For Joe, after a gasp and a momentary stare at his questioner, had gone suddenly white and collapsed sideways upon a heap of empty boxes. Captain Noah pulled him to his feet, but he seized the captain by the arm and broke into a torrent of pleadings and protestations.

"I didn't," he cried, "I didn't. It wasn't my fault, Cap'n Newcomb, I swear it wasn't. I lost it; I didn't steal it. Don't let him put me in prison. I didn't do it, Cap'n Newcomb, I——"

Noah put a hand on the boy's trembling shoulder and patted it soothingly.

"There, there, Joe," he said. "There, there! Buck up; be a man. I don't doubt you didn't do it, whatever it was, and I ain't accusin' you of anything. I'm here to help you, and so I want you to tell me the truth, that's all, just the truth and nothin' else. There's nothin' to be afraid of. For all we know, this may be the first tack towards that ranch of yours. Anyhow, it ain't towards prison, I give you my word for that. I'm goin' to be your friend, Joe, if you'll give me the chance. Come on, now; spin your yarn."

And after a time, and little by little, Joe spun it.

CHAPTER XVIII

ISS BARSTOW had not exaggerated in telling Captain Noah Newcomb that her stepfather was "cross." For a period of several weeks Balaam had been as ugly as sin and woe betide the unlucky individual upon whom he could safely vent his spite and ill humor. During those weeks he had almost entirely given over his habit of dropping in at the Burgess house for a meal, and he and Captain Newcomb had seen comparatively little of each other. Their talks concerning Trumet real estate had almost entirely ceased. The captain had not seen fit to purchase any of the "bargains" pointed out to him by his enterprising friend, and the latter had about reached the conclusion that he never intended doing so. But he had not entirely given up hope; Balaam seldom did give up all hope where a trade was involved.

During the period of his "crossness"—that immediately preceding and following the departure of Mr. Calvin Wentworth for New York—Mr. Griggs had avoided the captain's society just as he avoided that of Obadiah Burgess and other business "friends." He was in the depths of gloom. The knowledge that the debonair Wentworth shared his secret concerning Ira Barstow's will, and the forebodings which that knowledge entailed, prevented his enjoying companionship. Cousin Calvin had already "borrowed" two hundred dollars on the strength of that secret. Balaam foresaw a dismal future replete with similar borrowings. His money was as much a part of him as his skin, and to be skinned a little at a time was an exceedingly painful process. He had felt the first pangs already in reality. He was feeling the others in anticipation. No wonder he was despondent and out of sorts.

But when another week began and Mr. Wentworth did not return from the metropolis Balaam's spirits began to revive. There was no real reason for this revival, in his moments of serious reflection he realized that there was not; but he was more optimistic and began to cherish a faint hope. As the week drew on to its close and still there was no sign of the missing society leader the hope became stronger. Something might have happened, some accident perhaps. Balaam had been in New York but twice during his lifetime, but his memories of the Broadway throngs were acute. He knew that he, himself, had been in momentary fear of being run over; perhaps Cousin Calvin had been run over. At the thought his countenance was contorted with emotion, which may or may not have been grief. Perhaps—this was another happy supposition—perhaps the missing one had committeed some crime, such, for instance, as requisitioning two hundred dollars from the earnings of a hard-working, frugal man, and had been arrested. Or— But never mind Balaam's other guesses and hopes, there were several, but the sum of each and all was that, for a reason unknown, Calvin Wentworth might—*might* be permanently detained in New York. Of course, common sense told him this was not in the least likely to be true, but he dared to hope and to feel more cheerful.

Another reason for his improving temper was the fact that his stepdaughter was giving him so little trouble. He had expected grief, tears and deep despondency when Irving Clifford was "exposed" and sent about his business. For a day or two Mary had been very pale and quiet, but only for a day or two. After that she had perked up amazingly and had been as merry and, to all appearances, as happy as she had ever been. Then Cousin Calvin came and went. While he was here she had seemed to enjoy his society, but now that he had gone she was not mourning for him, that was evident. Balaam was forced to believe that she really cared nothing for him, that she had cared little or nothing for Clifford, that she was, in short, a heart-free young lady, which, according to his view, was precisely what a stepdaughter with twenty-five thousand dollars in his care and unaware of it, should be. And, to add to his satisfaction, not once during the past fortnight or more had she mentioned the idea of going to Boston to earn her own living.

This particular morning she appeared to be in the highest spirits, singing at her housework in the kitchen and rattling the dishes with brisk cheerfulness. Balaam, out in the shed, rubbing with oil the battered panels of an antique dresser, heard her and grinned. The dresser was a new purchase; he had paid four dollars and a half for it and believed he could sell it for thirty at least, so he felt that he could afford to grin. Incidentally Mary's cheerfulness was a happy augury. If that Wentworth fellow did come back; or, at the worst, *when* he came back, he might find all his society wiles useless. Plainly Miss Barstow did not care two cents for him. Of course this did not change the distressing fact that Wentworth knew of the Barstow will, but—well, it was some comfort, nevertheless.

Mary's singing suddenly ceased. So did the rattle of the dishes. A few minutes later Balaam, through the shed window, saw her coming across the yard. Her eyes were shining, her cheeks were flushed and she seemed elated and excited about something. Incidentally, a susceptible person—Irving Clifford, for instance—might have thought her wonderfully pretty. Balaam did not notice; he was not susceptible.

She came to the open door of the shed.

"Mr. Griggs!" she called. "Oh, there you are! Cap'n Newcomb is here. He wants to see you."

Balaam looked at her, questioningly. "Who? Noah Newcomb?" he repeated. "What does he want to see me for?"

"He didn't say, except that it was a matter of business."

"Business, eh? What business?"

"He didn't say, I tell you. Aren't you going to see him?"

Mr. Griggs reflected. The only business Captain Newcomb could possibly wish to discuss with him would be that involving those real estate "bargains." Perhaps—

yes, doubtless the captain had decided to trade at last. He threw down the oil rag and turned to the door.

"I'll be right out," he said. "Where is he?"

"At the front gate. He is in his car. I asked him to get out, but he wouldn't."

"Humph! All right." Then, watching for the first time the young lady's manner, he asked: "What are you so lively and chirky about? Look as if you'd had good news. What is it; anybody left you a million?"

This last was a slip of the tongue, for any mention of a legacy was decidedly dangerous. But of this danger Miss Barstow was, of course, quite unaware. She laughed merrily.

"Oh, no," she replied; "nothing like that. I am enjoying this weather, that is all. Did you ever see such a marvelous day? It is as if it were made on purpose."

"On purpose for what?" demanded Balaam. She seemed startled and oddly confused for an instant, then laughed again and said:

"Oh, for nothing in particular, I suppose; just for us all. But you must hurry. Cap'n Newcomb is waiting."

The captain was on the seat of the "Panhard." He hailed Mr. Griggs cheerfully.

"Mornin', Balaam," he said. "Busy this forenoon, are you?"

Balaam looked at him over his spectacles.

"I'm most generally busy, or cal'late to be," he observed. "But I ain't too busy to talk with my friends, especially such a friend as you be, Cap'n. What can I do for you today?"

Captain Noah smiled genially. "Well, I was kind of

hopin' you'd feel like takin' a cruise along with me in the Pancake here," he replied. "Eh? How about it?"

Mr. Griggs looked doubtful. "I'm pretty busy, same as I said," he declared. "I like automobile ridin' first-rate—you know that, Cap'n Newcomb."

The captain nodded. "Wentworth said you was crazy about it," he observed.

Balaam glanced suspiciously at the speaker. "Oh, he told you I went along with him, did he?" he asked.

"Yes, he happened to mention it. Said you and he went over to Ostable together, I believe."

"He did, eh? I want to know! Did he tell you any particulars about the trip?"

The question was asked with an elaborate air of innocence, and it was answered with one just as childlike and bland.

"No," said the captain. "I believe he did say somethin' about your havin' the time of your life."

"Is that so!" with righteous indignation. "Do tell! The time of my life! I tell you right now a few more of them times and I wouldn't have any life. You never see such divilish fool drivin' in all your born days. Crazy, reckless lunatic! Says I, 'You never missed that post by *more'n* two inches.' 'What of it?' says he. ' 'Tain't your post, is it?' Did you ever hear such loony talk in your life? What in time did I care whose post 'twas?"

Captain Noah laughed heartily. "I shan't drive you that way, Balaam," he said. "Better come along with me. I've got a little matter of business I want to talk over with you."

Mr. Griggs appeared to consider. "Business, eh?" he repeated. "Where was you cal'latin' to ride to, Capn'?"

"Oh, I don't know. Down Trumet Neck way, I shouldn't wonder."

The real estate "bargains" were, some of them, located at Trumet Neck. Balaam twisted a side whisker reflectively. "Wa-al," he drawled, "I presume likely I *could* go. Little mite of time off wouldn't do me no harm, as I know of. I—er— Why, yes, Cap'n, I'll go, seein' as it's you."

He hurried into the house for his hat. Captain Noah regarded the center of the wind-shield and, apparently, found something amusing there, for he smiled.

The little car buzzed through Trumet and off along the South Trumet road to the junction of the road leading to Trumet Neck. This thoroughfare was merely "oiled" not macadamed, and was therefore somewhat bumpy, but it was an asphalted parkway for smoothness compared to the byway into which they presently turned. This was a narrow rutted lane through the woods and wound and twisted on through a desolate wilderness of scrub pines, beach plum brushes and sandy nothingness. Balaam, who had never traveled its jolty windings before, rattled loose a question.

"Wha—wha—what are you tu-turn— Ugh! Godfreys, what a bump *that* was?— What are you tur— Ugh!—turnin' in here for? This don't go to the— Ugh! —Neck, does it?"

"Short cut," replied the captain. "Hang on, Balaam. 'Tis kind of rough over the rips here, ain't it."

It surely was. Mr. Griggs' few remaining teeth bade

fair to leave him before that ride was at an end. And
the road, or roads—for the captain kept turning from
one to the other of the narrow overgrown tracks—seemed
to have no end. Half a dozen times the passenger started
to ask where on earth they were bound, but each time
his pilot merely grunted "Short cut" or "You'll see
pretty soon," and centered all his energies on the steering. Griggs gave it up finally, but he mentally vowed
to add at least ten dollars to the price of whichever bargain Captain Newcomb decided to buy, as a salve for his
own bruised feelings and person.

At last the car jounced out of the woods and into a
small clearing. There was a house in the clearing, a low
shingled building, evidently unoccupied. Between the
pines behind the house shone a gleam of sunlit water.

Balaam stared at the house and its surroundings.
"Where in time are we?" he demanded in astonishment.
"This ain't the Neck, is it? I don't remember no place
like this at the Neck."

Captain Noah laughed. "The Neck?" he repeated.
"We ain't within five miles of the Neck. This is Howell
Winslow's shootin' camp over at East Wellmouth. That's
the bay you see out yonder. His duck blinds are over
at the pond a hundred yards in the other direction. You'd
never do to go to sea without a compass, Balaam, if you
can't guess your latitude any nigher than to call this
place the Neck."

Mr. Griggs continued to stare. "But you said you was
goin' to the Neck," he declared in bewilderment. "What
in time did you lug me way over here for?"

The captain grinned, "I told you I *might* go to the

Neck," he said, "but I came here instead. Howell left
the key to this place with Irve Clifford last spring and
told Irve to use it if he wanted to. Irve turned the keys
over to me when he went away, and so I thought I'd
have a look. I've only been here once before, with Irve,
but I found my way pretty well, don't you think? Come
on, Balaam, let's go inside."

He sprang out of the automobile and slowly his passenger followed him. Mr. Griggs' disappointment was
keen.

"I thought you said you wanted to talk business with
me," he grumbled. "I didn't know you was goin' to
cruise way over here just to look at a shootin' camp. I
told you I was pretty busy to home and——"

Noah interrupted. "There, there," he said. "Who
said we weren't goin' to talk business? Not me, sartin.
This camp's for sale. You knew that, didn't you, Balaam?"

Mr. Griggs had known it, but had forgotten. Now,
as the fact was called to his attention, his spirits revived.
Perhaps Newcomb was thinking of buying the Winslow
camp, and had brought him along as a consulting expert.
In his mind's eye Balaam saw a prospective liberal commission to be paid him by Mr. Winslow.

"Let's go inside and look her over," he said, blithely.
"Pretty fancy lookin' buildin' outside, seems to me.
Feller that bought this outfit at a reasonable figger
wouldn't make no mistake. No sir-ee, he wouldn't."

His companion did not answer, but led the way over
to the building. It was not "fancy" exactly, but it was
pleasant and summery in a rough way, although the shut-

ters were up at the windows and the doors locked. The captain took a key from his pocket, unlocked the door and went in. A moment later he reappeared, having loosened the fastenings of two of the shutters, and proceeded to swing those shutters open.

"There," he said. "Now we can see somethin', I cal'late. Come in, Balaam."

He and Mr. Griggs entered the living room of the camp. Balaam, staring about him at the big fireplace, the heavy table and chairs, did not notice what his companion was doing. Therefore he did not see the latter lock the door on the inside and put the key in his pocket.

The captain walked over to the big table, took a memorandum book and a small packet of papers from inside his coat and tossed them on the table before him. Then he sighed contentedly and produced and lighted a cigar.

"Have one, Balaam?" he inquired. "Sho! No, course you won't. I forgot you was too moral to smoke. Well, here we are, snug and quiet and where nobody can interrupt us. What do you say if we talk business?"

There was an odd note in his voice which Mr. Griggs did not understand. He looked at the captain's face, then at the papers on the table.

"What's them?" he demanded.

Captain Noah smiled. "Those are part of the business I brought you over here to talk about," he said. "It's liable to be a pretty long talk, so sit down, Balaam."

Balaam looked at the captain's face and then at the papers once more.

"What's them, I ask you?" he repeated.

"Sit down and I'll tell you. Sit *down*."

Mr. Griggs sat. The captain took up one of the slips of paper and glanced at it.

"Balaam," he said, "as nigh as I can figger it out you claimed Melissa Mayo—or Joe Kenney, which is the same thing—owed you twelve hundred and fifty dollars in the beginnin', didn't you?"

Balaam's eyes and mouth opened. He leaned back in his chair, his face white and red by turns.

"That's what 'twas, twelve hundred and fifty, wan't it?" repeated Noah, calmly. "Twelve hundred and fifty was the amount Joe collected for you in Gloucester that time and then lost."

Balaam's lips moved, but he did not say anything. The captain continued.

"The way I got the yarn from Joe," he said, "it happened about like this—I wish you'd tell me if I'm wrong anywhere: Two years ago or more you owned some shares in a fishin' vessel and sold 'em out to a feller in Gloucester. He was to give you his check on a certain day and you was goin' up to Gloucester and get it and close up the deal. A week afore that day came you was sick in bed with rheumatism—sshh! don't interrupt for a minute. If I'm wrong you tell me afterwards—so, bein' sick, you wrote to Melissa Mayo, your cousin up to Pigeon Cove, and asked her to go over and see this Gloucester man on the day appointed and get the check or the money, whichever 'twas to be. She couldn't go so she sent Joe. Joe went and the feller paid him cash. Then somehow or other Joe lost the money——"

Balaam's face was no longer pale. It was a flaming red. He sprang to his feet.

"Lost it!" he shouted. "He stole it, and he knows darned well he did. . . . But that don't make no difference, not to you it don't. What are you talkin' to me about Joe Kenney's thievin' for? Did you cart me over here to talk about that?"

The captain blew a cloud of cigar smoke and nodded.

"Um-hm," he said, "that and some other things."

"You did? You *did?* Was that the 'business' you had along of me?"

"Um-hm. That and the rest of it."

Mr. Griggs stared at him suspiciously. "Is this—is this some kind of a comical joke or somethin'?" he demanded.

"Nary a comic, Balaam. I brought you over here on purpose to talk about your dealin's with Melissy—her and some other folks."

Balaam started for the door.

"You go to thunder," he snarled.

"Maybe I will later on. Where are *you* cal'latin' to go just now? You won't go far that way, the door's locked."

It was locked, and so Mr. Griggs found. He hastened to the two remaining doors leading from the room and found them locked also.

"Don't waste your time, Balaam," counseled Noah, serenely. "You won't get out of here until you and I have had this talk. That's why I brought you over here, five mile away from the rest of creation, so we could have it without anybody's else buttin' in or you're buttin' out. Now sit down like a sensible man and listen. I'll hurry all I can.'

"By godfreys, Newcomb, you unlock that door!"

"I'll unlock it pretty soon, Balaam. Soon as you and me have finished this business talk."

"I'll—I'll have you took up. I'll have you put in jail for this."

"All right. But while we're waitin' for the constable let's have our talk out. Goin' on with my story now: Joe, he lost the twelve hundred and fifty——"

"That's a lie. He stole it and then run away."

"He says he lost it and then ran away because he was afraid to tell you he had lost it."

"He lies. Besides, it ain't none of your affairs, Noah Newcomb. You open that door."

"Pretty soon, pretty soon. Even if I did open it you wouldn't gain any time. The only way to get out of here, except in my car, is to walk, and 'twould take you lots longer to walk six or seven mile home than our little talk'll take. Now suppose we don't argue about this not bein' my affairs. I know it ain't as well as you do, but you can't have lived in Trumet all your life without realizin' it's human nature to love to talk about other folk's private business. Eh? Ho, ho!"

He chuckled. Balaam did not chuckle. He looked as if he could have committed murder cheerfully, provided it could be committed without danger to himself.

"Regardin' that question of stealin'," continued the captain, scratching a match on the sole of his shoe and re-lighting his cigar, "I wrote to the chief of police up to Gloucester and he writes me that there wasn't a particle of real evidence that Joe took it. The boy did run away, but he was scared pretty nigh to death, and when they caught him he hadn't a cent on him. The chief seems to think the most likely thing is that some of the tough gang around the wharves knew Joe had been paid the money and that the youngster's pocket was picked. He says he told you that, but that you wouldn't have it so. You was all for havin' the poor chap put in prison. Now——"

Mr. Griggs interrupted. He turned away from the door, strode back to the table, jerked the chair to its feet again and sat down. Then, looking Captain Noah straight in the eye, he said, defiantly: "Well, what of it?"

"What of it? What of what?"

"What if I was goin' to have him put in prison? What if it's all true—except that about his losin' the money? What if he did steal twelve hundred and fifty dollars from me? What of it? You've got me here under false pretenses; you're keepin' me shut up here against my will; I'm goin' to sue you for damages. All that I *know* is goin' to happen. What I don't know is what is all this stuff about Joe Kenney's thievin' is leadin' up to?"

He emphasized his points with thumps of his fist. The captain was absolutely serene.

"Well," he observed, "it's leadin' up to two or three things. To begin with you made Mrs. Mayo and Joe think you could put the boy in prison and would unless the money was paid back to you. Ain't that so?"

"None of your business."

"And so she agreed to pay you, and has been payin'
you two dollars a week for a period of—say—about thirty
months—or, we'll call it, one hundred and twenty-five
weeks; that's two hundred and fifty dollars. She's paid
that on the principal, ain't she—or about that? Eh?"

"None of your business."

"Besides that she's been payin' you, I understand, ten
per cent interest on the whole amount, payin' it right
along, not takin' out any for what principal she's paid.
Is that so?"

"None of your business, I told you. If that fool-
head Melissy Mayo has been tellin' lies about me——"

"She ain't. And," the captain's voice did not rise,
but there was a new and icy quality in it, "if I was you,
Balaam, I wouldn't call that lady names. For one reason they ain't deserved and for another they might not
be—well, healthy for you. I hope you understand that.
I'd like to have this talk of ours just a quiet, sociable—er
—argument. I'm goin' to keep my part of it that way if
I possibly can. But—*but* you must do your part. If
you've got to call somebody names call me; I don't mind
—much."

He chuckled, his good humor apparently restored. Balaam glowered at him, but said nothing.

"She's paid you the ten per cent on the whole amount
for thirty months," went on Noah. "That's three hundred and twelve dollars and a half, there or thereabouts,
as I make it. Just check me up as I go along, won't
you, please."

Mr. Griggs did not answer. If he was "checking up"
he displayed no external evidence of the process.

"That's five hundred and sixty-two dollars and fifty cents actual cash she's paid you so far," continued the captain. "It's come pretty hard to pay, too, I guess likely. Hard afore you made her come down here to do housework for Obe Burgess and help you skin him——"

"By godfreys, Noah Newcomb, if there's any law in this state I'll have it onto you."

"There's law, Balaam, plenty of it. Maybe we'll talk about it later on. However, just now we'll talk about this money business between you and Melissy Mayo. And hard *after* she come, as I was just goin' to say. A spell ago you wanted to know what all this was leadin' up to. Perhaps now is as good a time as any to tell you. I'm cal'latin', provided you and I can make a reasonable dicker, to take over this Melissy Mayo debt, as you call it."

Mr. Griggs certainly had not expected this. His eyes opened.

"Take it over?" he repeated. "Take what over?"

"This debt you claim Melissy owes you. Cause I doubt if she owes you anything, and I'm pretty sure you couldn't prove anything against Joe Kenney. But all this time you've been scarin' the two of 'em almost to death with threats of state's prison, and rather than have that go on any further I'll take over the balance of the debt."

"You'll take it over? *You* will? You mean you'll pay me the rest of it?"

"Yes."

"For thunder sakes, why?"

"Oh, just because. That's as good a reason as I can give you."

Balaam shook his head. "Tut, tut, tut!" he exclaimed. "If this don't—! Do you mean you'll pay the twelve hundred and fifty to me and—and do it as a favor to her?"

"Not exactly. I'll pay the balance of your claim, get your receipt for it free and clear, and then—well, then Melissy, or Joe, can owe it to me instead of you."

"I want to know! I cal'late you think they'd rather owe it to you than me, eh?"

"Shouldn't wonder."

"Huh! Say, what's the matter with you? Are you gettin' stuck on Melissy? Cal'latin' to marry her, are you?"

Captain Noah's face was by nature florid, now it was more than that. His chin quivered, but he seemed to find speaking difficult. Balaam laughed raucously.

"Haw, haw!" he crowed. "Well, there's no fool like an old fool. If this don't——"

"Shut up!" The captain's command was given with a crisp crack like the snap of a whip. "Balaam," he said, "I'd hate to make that figgerhead of yours any uglier, but —you take my advice and shut up. . . . I'm helpin' Mrs. Mayo out," he went on, after a moment, "just as I'd be glad to help any decent, self-respectin' person out of the claws of a feller like you. You knew she thought as much of that nephew of hers as if he were her own. You knew she promised her sick sister that she'd look out for him. You knew it and yet you could take advantage of it to— But there, we must stick to our argument and not get complimentary. I'd just love to pay you compliments for the rest of the afternoon, but I haven't got time. I've got to get back home by noon or thereabouts. I've got a particular engagement. Some friends of mine are goin' to be married over in Bayport and I've promised to be there."

He chuckled as he said it. "I wouldn't miss that weddin' for anything," he added. "Not even for the pleasure of your company, Balaam."

Mr. Griggs scowled. "My time's a little mite valuable, too," he sneered. "I ain't hankerin' to sit here and listen to your hot air. What have you got to say to me? What offer have you got to make? Mind I don't say I'll take it, but I'll hear it."

" 'Specially as the door's locked, eh? All right. You've had two hundred and fifty of the twelve fifty. Melissy's paid you that on the principal. That leaves a thousand. You acknowledge that?"

"I don't acknowledge nothin'; but she paid it to me."

"Yes—well, that's almost as good as an acknowledgment. Then she's paid you three hundred and twelve-fifty interest. I might quibble about payin' interest on the whole amount when she was payin' it off every week, but we'll let that go. But ten per cent—ten per cent, Balaam, is too much, just four per cent over the lawful rate. So we'll deduct that extra four, call it one hundred and twenty-five extra she's paid on the principal, bringin' the debt down to eight hundred and seventy-five."

Mr. Griggs laughed again. "Oh, we'll do that, will we?" he sneered. "Well, we won't, I tell you that."

The captain paid no attention to the interruption, but went serenely on.

"That's eight seventy-five left owin'," he said, "or you pretend it's owin'. Then there's the other five hundred, that you agreed to allow her when you took over the hundred shares of Ostrich copper stock."

Balaam gasped. "Did—did she tell you about that, too?" he sputtered.

Captain Noah shook his head. "She didn't tell me much of anything," he said, "although she did speak of the copper stock when we was talkin' one time. But she don't know that I know all about the whole miserable business, and she don't know I'm havin' this little social chat with you. If she did I'm afraid she'd feel bad, so it's well she doesn't, eh, Balaam? Well, to get along: We'll take off the five hundred; that leaves three hundred and seventy-five of the twelve hundred and fifty. I'll give you my check for three hundred and seventy-five in exchange for your name at the bottom of this."

He selected a paper from those upon the table and handed it to his companion.

"What's this?" demanded the latter.

"Read it and find out."

Mr. Griggs adjusted his spectacles and, holding the paper with fingers that shook a little, read what was written upon it. It was a statement to the effect that he, Balaam Griggs, having been paid twelve hundred and fifty dollars, the entire amount which his nephew, Joash Kenney, had lost while collecting for him in Gloucester upon a date named, acknowledged receipt of that sum

318

and relinquished all monetary claim upon Joash Kenney or Melissa Mayo. Also he expressed his belief in Joash Kenney's complete innocence in the affair and that the latter had lost the money and not stolen it.

"If you'll put your John Hancock at the foot of that," said the captain, "I'll make out the check for three seventy-five."

Balaam's answer was to toss the slip of paper contemptuously back upon the table and tip back in his chair.

"You go to thunder," he said defiantly.

"Meanin' you won't sign? If I was you I would, Balaam, I would honest. It's the best proposition I'm goin' to give you this forenoon. The next one won't be so good, I warn you."

"You warn me? You warn *me!* I warn *you* to open that door and let me out of here. 'As I told you afore, Noah Newcomb, you're meddlin' with what ain't none of your affairs and your keepin' me here is a actionable matter."

"Then you won't talk trade with me? Dear, dear!" Captain Noah seemed disappointed.

Mr. Griggs noted the disappointment and grew more triumphant. "I'll talk business with any man, when it is business," he said. "What Melissy Mayo owes me is my affair, and she ain't goin' to gain nothin' by sickin' you onto me. Not much she ain't. I ain't at all particular about sellin' out that debt. It's pretty safe, long's I've got my eye on the two of 'em, and it pays good interest."

" 'Good' is good," broke in the captain dryly.

"However," went on Balaam, ignoring the interruption, "I'll always sell anything if I get enough for it, that's a—a motto, as you might say, of mine. You give me your check for a thousand dollars—that's the twelve fifty less the two fifty principal she's paid—and I'll call it square. Cause I won't sign no such durn fool thing as that," with a jerk of the thumb towards the paper he had just thrown down, "but I'll call the debt paid. After all, Melissy and Joe are relations of mine, I suppose, and I'd like to do the fair thing by 'em."

Captain Noah gazed at him in a sort of reverent admiration. Then he slowly shook his head. "By the everlastin', Balaam," he exclaimed, "you are a wonder. You ought to be framed and kept on the parlor whatnot, you had. Folks would pay money to see you if they knew what I know. And most of 'em that see much of you *do* pay, now that I come to think of it. Eh?"

He smiled, shook his head once more, and picked up the paper.

"So you won't sign this?" he queried.

"No, told you I wouldn't. I make it a practice not to sign much. Folks get into trouble signin' things."

"That's right, so they do. And sometimes they get into trouble by not signin' 'em when they have the chance. And you won't take off the four per cent interest, so as to bring it down to a lawful six?"

"I sartin won't. Why should I?"

"Well, anything above six is against the law, so they tell me."

"Runnin' off with stolen money's against the law, too. And folks go to prison for it—just whenever the charge is seen fit to be pressed against 'em. And in spite of other nosey folks buttin' in, too," he added, venomously.

"And how about that five hundred you was goin' to allow for the Ostrich stock? Wouldn't you take that off?"

"No."

"But you told Melissy you would."

"I told her I might. And maybe I will yet—to her. But I shan't do it to you, nor any other outsider. That Ostrich stock ain't worth nothin' anyhow. I only took it off her hands as a kindness, a favor, as you might say."

"And then you sold it to Obe Burgess for five thousand dollars. That was another favor, I presume likely."

CHAPTER XIX

MR. GRIGGS was taken aback, even embarrassed, but he recovered quickly. As a matter of fact, he had guessed what was coming. If Captain Noah knew of the purchase of the Ostrich stock he probably knew of its sale. So Balaam was, in a measure, prepared. But his voice shook a little as he answered.

"Maybe 'twas, maybe 'twan't," he said, defiantly. "Anyhow, that ain't your affairs no more than the other."

The captain looked doubtful. "You're wrong there, Balaam," he said. "This is my affair; fact is, it's the affair that brought me to Trumet. Obe Burgess and I are pretty good friends. He promised to call to me for help if he ever got into trouble. He called and I came. That's why I'm here."

Balaam looked surprised and rather discomfited at this piece of news, but he rallied bravely.

"I want to know!" he sneered. "So Burgess got cold feet and hollered for you, did he? You're helpin' him same as you be Melissy and Joe, eh? You seem to be kind of a general helper round here, seems to me."

Noah nodded. "Just about that," he admitted cheerfully. "As I told a friend of mine a spell ago I seem to have signed articles as the Good Samaritan. An old shipmate of mine, that's Obadiah, had gone down into a fur country, like the feller in the Bible, and fell amongst thieves, so——"

"Thieves! Thieves? Who do you mean by thieves, Noah Newcomb?"

"Well—er—I don't know as I mean anybody. I realize you're a moral man, Balaam, so of course you wouldn't steal; but buyin' chamber sets for ten or twelve dollars and sellin' 'em for forty, and buyin' groceries and house supplies for half again what you sell 'em for, and buyin' good-for-nothin' stocks for five hundred dollars, on credit, and sellin' 'em for five thousand cash—well, of course that ain't stealin', maybe, but if I was the feller in a free country I'd about as soon fall amongst thieves as I would amongst them kind of 'friends.' What do you think?"

Mr. Griggs leaned over the table. "I tell you what I think," he snarled. "I think you're a fresh nosey, same as I said in the beginnin'. I did sell Obe Burgess them chamber sets and things. If I bought 'em cheap and sold 'em high, what of it? Ain't that my job? Ain't that what I'm in business for? If I see a chance to get that stock for little or nothin' and sell it for—er—more, what of it again? Ain't that what's done in the stock exchanges every day? If your precious chum of an Obe Burgess is a soft-headed fool is that my fault? I know what I've done and what I ain't done, Noah Newcomb, maybe better than you do. I'm a good, sharp business man, if I do say it. I'll make a profit in a trade every chance I get. That's all I've done now, and

I stump you to lay one finger on anything I've done that ain't legal. I stump you to. You and Burgess and Melissy Mayo and all the rest of 'em can go to thunder. Now you open that door and let me out."

He was out of breath when he finished and trembling with nervous rage. Captain Noah, at the other side of the table, was still perfectly calm. But now he dropped his bantering drawl and spoke quick and sharp.

"Balaam," he said, "I won't argue about the legal end of it. I know you're a slippery old eel and a shrewd one. I believe I could get you found guilty of usury afore a jury, but I shan't try. I know if I did you'd tell everybody that Joe Kenney was a thief and probably ruin his chances and drive his aunt out of town. So we won't press the ten per cent interest matter, not in public—not now."

Griggs laughed. "I cal'lated you wouldn't," he observed.

"No, but we'll settle it on my terms, those I named to you. And, as for the Ostrich stock deal, you might be able to squeeze by in a court even on that, although I'd risk but what I could get you for obtainin' money under false pretenses, showin' year-old newspapers for new ones and the like of that. But, unless it's necessary, we won't go to law about the Ostrich trade."

Balaam laughed aloud. "You remind me of a loon," he declared. "A loon hollers like time, makes a dickens of a noise, and then ducks under. I admire the way you duck, Newcomb."

"Thanks. Well, I won't name the critter you remind me of, but folks that are so unlucky as to have any dealin's with it generally bury their clothes when the interview's over. But we wasn't goin' to pass compliments, was we." He looked at his watch and added: "It's time we was gettin' down to tacks, because I can't keep that weddin' waitin' much longer. Here," he took up the written statement which Balaam had discarded so contemptuously; "you're goin' to sign that," he said. "And here," taking a large envelope from his pocket, "is the certificate for one hundred shares Ostrich Minin' and Smeltin'. There is a power of attorney signed by Obe Burgess fastened to it, so it's all ready for transfer back to you. And here," taking another paper from the table, "is a blank check on the Trumet National Bank. I want you to fill that in for five thousand dollars—and sign it. When you do that I'll hand you the certificate."

Balaam glared at the certificate, the check, and the speaker in wrathful amazement.

"Are you plumb crazy?" he demanded.

"No."

"And you cal'late I'll buy back that Ostrich stock and pay five thousand for it?"

"Yup."

"I'll see you in hell first."

"Um-hm. Well, if I ever get there you'll be about the first one I shall expect to see. Now we've talked enough. I *believe* I could get you in any court for payin' and obtainin' money under false pretenses. I *know* you could be jailed on a criminal charge for cheatin' Mary Barstow out of the twenty-five thousand her father left her, and that you'd ought to have turned over to her when she came of age two years ago. And, so sure as

I live and breathe, I'll go to Mary and back her in puttin' you behind the bars—unless you come to my terms right here and now."

Mr. Griggs, who had risen to his feet and was shaking his fist, dropped back into the chair again. The red left his face. As Noah said afterwards he turned, not merely white, but blue. He gurgled in his throat.

"Well?" snapped the captain. "What do you say?"

Balaam, when he could say anything, made no attempt to deny the fact of the legacy and the will. The captain spoke with an absolute certainty which carried conviction with it and the uselessness of denial was uppermost. But he did attempt to deny criminal intent.

"I—I—I wasn't cheatin' her," he stammered. "I—I was just keepin' it for her. I—I was cal'latin' to give it to her. I was all ready to give it to her. She—she—" he swallowed, rubbed his hand across his wet forehead and added, "She could have had it by askin'. I—I just forgot to tell her, that's all."

And then Captain Noah, for the first time during the long interview, made use of what our foreign friends call the great American asset—"bluff." His next remark was merely a guess, but he made it as if it were based upon absolute knowledge.

"You forgot to tell her," he repeated. "And so that's why you paid Calvin Wentworth blackmail—so *he'd* forget to tell her, too, I presume likely."

Plainly this man knew everything. It was useless to fight him longer. Balaam groaned, collapsed, and surrendered.

Not that it was a complete and unconditional surrender

in the beginning. The defeated one fought for every point in the negotiations. When the Mayo paper of settlement had been signed the argument concerning the stock transfer began. Balaam almost wept when the blank check was placed before him.

"I can't do it, Cap'n Newcomb," he whined. "I can't. Besides," as a bright idea occurred to him, " 'tain't likely I keep a five thousand dollar balance in the Trumet bank every day, is it?"

The captain smiled. "Not every day, I know you don't, Balaam," he said. "But I know, too, that you've got it there today because yesterday you deposited the money you got from sellin' that Ostable property."

Mr. Griggs's anger blazed up again.

"Who told you that?" he demanded. "If them bank 'folks have been tattlin' about my account I'll——"

"There, there! nobody told. I was right astern of you in the line at the teller's window. You didn't notice me, I cal'late, but I saw you—and the deposit slip, too. I'd been waitin' for that money to come in, Balaam. I knew you was expectin' it, and so I was anxious to get hold of you this mornin' afore you could invest it again."

Balaam glared, growled, groaned and picked up the check.

"I—I think you're mighty hard on me, Cap'n," he said. "I never thought you could be so hard on anybody that's been as friendly to you as I have."

Noah laughed delightedly. "That's it, Balaam," he cried; "keep it up. I was expectin' somethin' like that 'from you, and I'd have been disappointed if you hadn't lived up to my hopes. You ought to be gilded and framed, same as I told you. Considerin' how soft and tender you've been to Melissy and Obe, not to mention Joe and a hundred other poor critters you've had business dealin's with, I— Here, you seem to find it tough to make out that check. I'll do it for you."

He took the fountain pen—his own—from his companion's fingers and rapidly filled in the five thousand dollar check.

"There!" he exclaimed. "Now all you've got to do is sign."

"But, Cap'n Noah, I——"

"Sign. That weddin' party's waitin'."

"I— By thunder, I won't!"

"All right. Balaam, was you ever in the Ostable jail? They say it's a nice cool place in summer, and the food ain't rich enough to give you dyspepsy. There's visitin' days every once in a while. I'll be over to look at you through the bars and I'll fetch the minister and— Ah, thanks."

Mr. Griggs had signed the check and thrown the pen savagely into the fireplace. The captain calmly stooped and picked it up.

"And here's your certificate for the Ostrich stock," he said. "Oh, yes, wait a minute, here's my check for the balance of Melissy's account."

He wrote the check and handed it to Balaam. The latter glanced at it and then shouted a protest.

"This ain't but three hundred and seventy-five," he cried.

"Well, that's what it ought to be, hadn't it, 'cordin' to the figgers as I gave 'em to you?"

"No. You've took off five hundred for that dum Ostrich Minin'."

"I know, but you've got the stock, power of attorney and all."

"I don't want it. It ain't no good. It belongs to Melissy Mayo."

"Oh, no, it don't. It belongs to you. You bought it. And, so far from bein' no good, it's a great buy, and the feller that get's it at fifty—to say nothin' of five—is mighty lucky. I know that's true, for you said so yourself to Obe Burgess. And you wouldn't lie, Balaam, you're too moral."

A moment later he unlocked and opened the door. At the threshold he turned, the key in his hand, and addressed Mr. Griggs, who was following him.

"Balaam," he said, "I hope you like this shootin' camp."

"Like it! No, by godfreys, I don't like it! And I tell you, Noah Newcomb——"

"Yes, yes, I know. Well, I'm sorry you don't like it, because——"

"Because what?"

"Because I'm goin' to leave you in it a spell."

Before Balaam could reach him he had stopped outside and slammed and locked the door behind him. His next remark was shouted through the crack.

"Don't be scared, Balaam," he roared. "I'll be back for you by and by. Fact is, I think maybe I'd better cash that check of yours afore you change your mind and have payment stopped on it. I'll drop in at the bank as I go by. Make yourself comfortable as you can. I wish I could open a window for fresh air for you, but I can't, they're all nailed. So long."

He hurried away to the car. Even above the roar of the starting engine he could hear bellowed pleadings and threats issuing from behind the closed door of the camp. The language was, from a moral person, somewhat surprising.

Captain Noah drove at a good clip back to Trumet. He smiled as he drove and occasionally laughed aloud. He made a short stop at the bank and then, instead of turning in at the gate of the Burgess home, kept on and stopped before the residence of the gentleman with whom he had spent the forenoon, namely, Mr. Balaam Griggs. Another car was waiting at that gate.

The captain went around to the side door of the house and knocked. Miss Barstow opened the door. She was very becomingly and prettily dressed in a new street costume and a new hat, and her blush, as she greeted her visitor, was very pretty and becoming also.

"Oh, here you are!" she exclaimed. "We were beginning to fear you weren't going to get home after all."

"Wouldn't have missed it for money," declared Captain Noah. "Now where's the other party to this underhanded, nee-farious piece of piracy and kidnappin'?"

The other party appeared at that moment. It was Irving Clifford, and he and the captain pretty nearly shook each other's arms off.

"How are you, anyway?" demanded Noah. "And how's Chicago? And are you prepared to sign away your rights as a free man and a bachelor for the privi-

lege of buyin' this young lady's bunnits and shawls the
rest of your life?"

Irving laughed. "First rate to the first two questions,"
he answered, "and yes and glad of the chance to the last.
And how are you, Captain?"

"I'm pretty fit, thank you. What I make believe is
my mind is a little mite water-logged from doin' picture
puzzles, but now that I've got the last one done, I'm in
hopes it'll dry out again."

Mary put in a word. "Where is Mr. Griggs?" she
asked.

"Yes, where is the old rascal?" asked Irving.

Noah grinned. "Told you I'd get him out of the way,
and keep him there, didn't I; eh, Mary?" he inquired.

The young lady nodded. "Yes, you did," she admitted.

"But you doubted if I could keep my promise? Well,
I did. Balaam is a sportin' man just now. He's spendin' the day in a shootin' camp at East Wellmouth."

"A shooting camp?" repeated Clifford. "What do you
mean? What is he going to shoot?"

The captain's grin became a chuckle. "Well," he said,
"if he had anything to do it with I cal'late he'd like to
take a shot at me. I'll tell you about it by and by, if
I get a chance; if not, I'll write. Speaking of writin',"
he added, "I see you've left him a note."

There was an envelope propped against the lamp on the
center table. It was addressed to Mr. Balaam Griggs.

Mary nodded. "Yes," she said, "I wrote that Irving
and I had gone to be married——"

"At Bayport? Did you say at Bayport?"

"Yes, I believe I did. Why?"

"Oh, nothin'. I happened to mention that I was tear-in' myself away from his company on account of havin' to go to a weddin' at Bayport. I'm afraid he's liable to guess whose weddin' 'twas. Dear, dear! Well, I'll face the music. I cal'late 'twill be a lively jig tune; he was tunin' up for it when I left him. What else did you write, Mary?"

"I wrote that after we were married we were going to Chicago to live. I said that I knew all about the money Father left me, and that I should expect it to be turned over to me at once. If this was done within a month I would not prosecute, nor would I tell anyone what he had done. Then I said good-by, that was prac-tically all."

"Humph! That note'll be somethin' of a shock to him, won't it?"

"Yes, I'm afraid it will. He is a scamp, I'm afraid, and he has treated me abominably in some ways, but— I can't help feeling a little sorry for him."

Captain Noah nodded. "I understand," he said. "Ba-laam's meaner than a vinegar pie and he'd cheat his deef aunt out of her ear trumpet. He's gettin' only about half what he deserves, and he'd ought to be put in jail. I let him off easy this mornin'—but, consarn him, *I'm* sort of sorry for him, too, and my conscience has been troublin' me ever since I left him. If I didn't have any more sense than my conscience has I'd apply for a berth at the Idiots' Home.

"But there," he added, "here we are floatin' around these moorin's and there's that Bayport parson waitin'

with his watch in one hand and his empty pocketbook
in t'other. Is this your satchel, Mary? Good! All
aboard for the rites of padlock, as the feller said."

A few moments later two automobiles, one containing
Irving, Mary and various suitcases and bundles and the
other Captain Newcomb, left the Griggs gate and buzzed
up Knowles' Hill and on toward Bayport.

Miss Sarepta Hatch and Mrs. Elvira Ginn who, with
noses pressed flat against their respective front windows,
saw them go, had enough to talk about—even for them
to talk about—during the rest of that day and for several days thereafter.

CHAPTER XX

WHEN Captain Noah returned to the Burgess home that afternoon he was in a state of mind which might perhaps be described as divided. He had said good-by to Mary—no longer Mary Barstow —and to Irving, and the thought that he should see neither of them for some time was not altogether pleasant. They were not very old friends; he had known them but a few months, but somehow or other they had grown into his affections astonishingly. He and they had promised to write and he had half promised to visit them at Chicago in that vague future popularly known as "some of these days."

They had been quietly married at the house of the Congregational minister at Bayport, and the captain had been the only witness of the ceremony. He had seen them aboard the train at the Bayport station and had waved his hat until the last car disappeared in the distance. Then he climbed into his own automobile and headed for the shooting camp and the rescue of the incarcerated Balaam. The other car, that in which Mary and Irving had journeyed to Bayport, was to be taken back to Trumet by one of the garage hands.

Mr. Griggs was voluble and threatening when Captain Noah unlocked the door of the camp and let him out. The captain listened to the torrent of vituperation for perhaps a mile of their trip homeward. Then he put in a few words of his own.

"That's all right, Balaam," he said; "go as far as you like. Have the law onto me, have me taken up, sue me for damages, do anything you want to. *Only*—and I want you to nail this to your main truck so 'twill stick there and you'll never forget it—don't you dare say one word to a livin' soul about Joe Kenney's stealin' that money or his aunt's backin' him in it. *That* lie's got to die a quick death and a quiet one, and there mustn't be any preachin' over the remains. And don't you ever dare hound another cent out of Melissy, either. As I say, go as far as you like with me for shuttin' you up in that camp this forenoon. Sue me, if you feel like it, and cal'late you can risk the fireworks that suit'll start up. But you let Melissy Mayo and her nephew alone; d'you hear?"

Balaam ground his teeth. "Suppose I don't let 'em alone?" he growled. "What'll you do? You won't dast to go to no court with it."

His companion turned his head and regarded him steadily. "I cal'late with that signed statement of yours I could have a pretty good time even in court," he declared. "But I shouldn't go to any court. I'd come straight to you and inside of ten minutes I'd——"

"What?"

"Drown you," said the captain. "Now let's change

the subject. Looks as if there was a breeze springin'
up; maybe we'll have rain tomorrow, eh?"

So, between sorrow at parting from Mary and Irving
and satisfaction at the complete overthrow of Mr.
Griggs, Captain Noah's emotions were, as has been said,
divided. But there was no division in those of Obadiah
Burgess when, after supper, his friend took him up to
his room and there restored to him the five thousand
which he had considered lost forever.

"But, Cap'n Noah," begged the little man, after his
first spasms of incoherent exclamations and thanks had
spent themselves, "for the d-dear land sakes how
d-d-dud-did you d-d-dud——"

"Cut-out's open again, Obe," interrupted the captain,
with a smile. "How did I do it—that was what you
had your popgun loaded with then, wan't it? Um-hm.
Well, I'll tell you. I says to Balaam, 'Balaam, says I,
'I know you wouldn't take advantage of another human
critter for anything in this world, not knowin'ly you
wouldn't. Obe has a kind of feelin' that he'd rather
have his five thousand than he would that pretty stock
certificate you sold him. I know you'd love to oblige
him by tradin' back.' And Balaam, he bust out cryin'
and said he hadn't been able to sleep nights for fear
he might have charged you fifty cents more than that
stock was worth and——"

Mr. Burgess interrupted. "Go 'long!" he exclaimed.
"He didn't feel as bad as all that, did he?"

Noah looked at him long and solemnly. Then he
slowly shook his head. "Obe," he observed, "do you
know why a blind man never reads a comic paper?"

"No, course I don't. What's that got to do——"

"Well, the answer is, because he can't see a joke."

"Can't *see* one! Course he can't! Can't see *nothin'* if he's blind, can he? I don't call that very sensible t-t-talk."

"Don't you? I'm surprised. Then let's be sensible. You know what Scriptur' says—somethin' about 'Come, let us reason together'? Um-hm. Well, that's what I said to Balaam. And Balaam, he came and we reasoned."

"Sho! I was kind of afraid he wouldn't listen t-t-to reason much as all that comes to."

"He did. And it came to five thousand, which is a pretty reasonable total, too. Are you satisfied?"

"Satisfied? Oh, Cap'n Noah, I don't know what to say to you. I don't know how t-t-to thank you. I swan to man, I——"

He was pretty close to tears and the captain saw it.

"There, there!" he cried, hastily. "I don't want any thanks. I haven't done anything—except live on you free gratis for nothin' all summer. Don't talk any more about it. Let's talk about yourself and your plans. Now that you've got your five thousand back, how much of your Aunt Sarah's windfall is there left?"

They estimated and figured for some time. When the last estimate was made and the last figure set down it was a certainty that Obadiah's twelve thousand had shrunk below ten and that if he continued to live and maintain his present establishment it would ultimately shrink to nothing. The little man was again in a state of nervous despair and woe.

337

"I don't know how I done it, Cap'n Noah," he wailed. "I snum I don't know how I d-d-dud-done it. I never meant to spend none of the principal, but she kept a-dribblin' away here and a d-d-dud-dribblin' away there, a leetle mite at a time, and—and, oh, my godfrey's domino, *now* look!"

He was wringing his hands as he had that night when the captain wormed from him the secret of his investment in Ostrich Mining and Smelting. Noah slapped him cheerily on the back.

"Brace up, Obe," he ordered. "You haven't got anything to sound distress signals for now. You're pretty nigh out of the fog, as I see it. Know how it happened? How it happened is as plain to see as a piece of white stickin'-plaster on a red nose. You've been tryin' to float all creation without the wherewithal to do it with, and nobody's got away with that proposition since Noah—my namesake—hove anchor for the last time. You've got to cut down your livin' expenses, that's all."

"Yes, yes. I cal'late most likely I have, but how'll I do it?"

"Well, for one thing, Cousin Calvin won't be with you much more. He'll leave you pretty soon, I shouldn't wonder."

"He will? He will? Then—then what's g-g-goin' to become of all the m-m-money he'll leave when he dies?"

"It'll go to buy water sieves to strain wind through, I cal'late. Don't set up nights thinkin' how you'll spend Cousin Calvin's leavin's, Obe."

He told what he had discovered concerning Mr. Wentworth. Mr. Burgess listened, his mouth open.

"Well, I snum!" he exclaimed, aghast. "Then—then his comin' t-t-to die onto me was just a scheme t-t-to live onto me, that's all."

"Just about."

Obadiah clenched his fists. "By—by godfreys," he exclaimed, "you just wait till he gets back from New York or wherever 'tis he's gone, I'll f-f-fix him. I'll g-g-give him somethin' he'll remember."

Noah grinned. "What'll you do to him, Obe?" he asked.

Mr. Burgess reflected. "I—I won't speak to him," he declared. "If he c-c-comes to the d-dinner table I'll get right up and go off and leave him."

He could not in the least understand why, at the announcement of this dreadful threat, the captain put back his head and shouted with laughter. But when his laugh was over Noah settled down to sober consideration of the problems involved.

"To be real honest with you, Obe," he said, "I'm afraid you haven't got enough income to carry on this place of yours. I cal'late 'twould break your heart to sell it, eh?"

Obe did not look broken-hearted at the idea.

"I don't know's 'twould," he replied. "I—I've been thinkin' maybe I might sell it. Fact is, Cap'n Noah, it's got to be a—a kind of c-c-cuk-care on my shoulders, lately, and I'm kind of sick of it, as you might say. If I sold it I could travel, I cal'late, and you know I t-t-told you I just loved to travel."

339

His friend smiled. "Um—yes," he said, dryly. "Well, Obe, I wouldn't travel too fur, not if you ever wanted to get back, I wouldn't. But suppose you did sell; who would you sell to?"

Obadiah looked knowing. "Oh, I've had offers," he boasted. "Them Bay Shore Land Company folks offered me twenty-five hundred cash only last July. I told you then, but you thought t-t-t'wan't enough."

"It wasn't. This house and land, with this view, is worth every cent of four thousand for just a summer place. I wouldn't swear but what you could get five for it, if the right feller came along."

Mr. Burgess did some more reflecting. Then he ventured, timidly, "You wouldn't want to buy it, yourself, would you, Cap'n? You know you've told me a good many times how much you liked it."

Cap'n Noah laughed. "What on earth would I want of it, an old hulk like me, driftin' round from Dan to Beersheba, and no home port in sight?" he asked. "I'll be haulin' out of here pretty soon, Obe, now I've got you out of your snarl, and then land knows where I'll be. But," with a wistful look out of the window at the bay, a-shimmer in the starlight, "if I was figgerin' to make fast and settle down I don't know of any snug harbor that would suit me better'n this. I could have consider'ble fun fixin' this place up and spendin' money on it."

Obadiah had a brand-new proposition to offer. "Cap'n Noah," he said, "I presume likely you wouldn't want t-t-to t-t-take care of my money for me, would you? I ain't fit to take care of it by myself and I know it.

C-c-couldn't you kind of k-k-keep it for me and let me have it, little at a time, like reg'lar wages, say? Maybe I could m-make it last then," he suggested, hopefully.

The captain shook his head. " 'Fraid that might be too big a responsibility for me, Obe," he answered.

Obadiah nodded. "Course I realize 'twould be consider'ble," he observed, "on account of the income bein' so small now. But," eagerly, "what's the reason I c-c-cuk-couldn't make some more; b-buy some stocks, or somethin'?"

His friend whirled in his chair to stare at him.

"Buy stocks?" he repeated. "You—buy stocks! For thunder mighty sakes, haven't you had enough stock buyin' to last you one spell?"

Mr. Burgess was unconvinced. "Well," he declared, stubbornly, "I got out of that all right. I got my money back. I d-d-didn't lose nothin'."

Captain Noah was silent for a full minute. Then he rose from his chair. "You go to your room and turn in, Obe," he commanded. "I'll think over that takin' care of your money notion. And say," he added, as the little man obediently turned to the door, "you don't walk in your sleep, do you?"

"No," indignantly, "course I don't."

"Well, all right. Then you probably won't get up and try to turn over any of your capital afore mornin'. Good night, Obe."

Mr. Burgess went to his room and to bed, but the captain did not retire, not then. He looked at his watch, found it to be only nine o'clock, and then descended the stairs to the sitting room. Joe—or Joash—had gone out. The housekeeper was sitting alone by the center table, mending stockings. She looked up, nodded and smiled when he entered, but she did not speak. Captain Noah took a chair and, after regarding her for a few moments in silence, went straight to his subject.

"Melissy," he began, "I've got somethin' to tell you—somethin' important."

She dropped the stocking in her lap and turned to gaze at him.

"Somethin' important?" she repeated, slowly. "Oh, it isn't—it isn't bad news, is it?"

"I hope it ain't. I'm kind of hopin' it'll be good news for you. The only thing that makes me hesitate about tellin' it is for fear you'll think I've been interferin' where I hadn't any business, meddlin' where it's none of my affairs. Part of it was my affairs, 'twas really what I came here to Trumet to do, but t'other part—your part—was just—well, I just felt I'd got to do it, no matter what you said. The truth had come to me little by little and it made me so bilin' mad that I—that I——"

Mrs. Mayo interrupted. "Cap'n Noah," she broke in, quickly, "what are you talkin' about? Don't explain or apologize any more; tell me what you mean."

So the captain told her, told of his receiving Obadiah's letter of appeal, of his coming to Trumet, of his discovery that his former cook was being systematically cheated, of his own suspicions and beliefs in the beginning, and then of his gradual unearthing of the truth. Then he went on to tell of his interview with Balaam

Griggs that forenoon and of the "settlement" between them.

"I hope," he said, earnestly, in conclusion, "that you won't blame Joe for tellin' me about losin' the money up to Gloucester and the way Balaam was squeezin' you for it. 'Twan't Joe's fault for tellin', really 'twan't. I had the ends of the strings all in my hands and I just scared the yarn out of him, I guess. The fact is, Melissy, I—I just *had* to know it, that's all. 'Twas plain as day that Balaam was grindin' you somehow or other; I've watched you sufferin' under it ever since I came here, and as I came to know you better and better the harder 'twas to watch. I swore to myself that I'd stop it, and the only way I could stop it was by findin' out the whole truth. So there 'tis; it's done. I hope you'll forgive me for doin' it, but whether you do or not, as I say, it's done—it's stopped. Eh? Did you say anything?"

She had not said anything, nor did she speak now. She was leaning forward, one elbow upon the arm of her rocking chair and her head upon her hand. Her face was in the shadow and he could not see it. He looked at her expectantly, waited a moment, and then went on.

"Here's the agreement I had him sign," he said, taking it from his pocket and laying it in her lap. "You'll notice it's a settlement in full and that he swears he believes Joe never stole the money. As fur as I can see, Melissy, he can't ever make any more trouble for you."

Still she did not answer, nor did she even look at the paper in her lap. He rose to his feet.

"Well," he said, "I cal'late that's about all there is to

say. I hope, after you've thought it over, you'll come
to realize that I did it just out of—er—friendship, that's
all. I'd ought to have asked your permission to do it,
I suppose likely, but, you see, I—well, I was pretty sure
you'd say no if I did ask. I thought it ought to be done
—and I haven't changed my mind. Er—good night,
Melissy."

He turned to the door. But now she raised her head
and spoke.

"Wait, Cap'n Noah," she said. "Please don't go—
yet."

He turned back. Then he saw that her eyes were wet.
It was the second time he had seen them so, and, as on
the first occasion, the sight stirred him to a fierce resentment. This woman must not cry, not only for her own
sake, but for his. And yet now it was he, Noah Newcomb, who had made her cry.

"Melissy," he pleaded, "I'm terrible sorry if I've done
what I shouldn't. I—I hope you won't feel too hard
towards me."

She looked at him in wonder.

"Hard towards you?" she repeated. "*I* feel hard towards *you?* What *can* you mean?"

"Well—well, you've been cryin' and I—I thought——"

She smiled through her tears. "You didn't make me
cry," she said; "at least if you did it was only because
you have been so good to me and—and I couldn't help
cryin'. Oh, Noah, what shall I say to you? What can
I say? And Joe, too, poor boy! You've lifted a load
that's been a heavy one, I can tell you. I don't believe

you can hardly realize what these last two and a half years have been to us both."

She went on to tell of her life since her husband's death; of her sister, whom she had loved so dearly; of the latter's death and the leaving of her only son in Melissa's charge.

"She loved him even more than most mothers love their sons, always seemed to me," said the housekeeper. "And when she died she charged me to keep him and bring him up same as she would if she'd lived. Well, I've tried to do it. And Joe's a good boy, too, and a bright one. He'd do well at what he liked, I'm sure. But that awful scare he had when he lost Balaam's money, and the thoughts of state's prison always hangin' over him, kind of broke his ambition, as you might say. He ain't been the same since."

"He'll be all right now," declared Captain Noah, heartily. "I've got some plans of my own for him. I'll tell you about 'em in a day or two, after I get 'em a little better worked out. Joe'll be all right, I'll bet on it. But what I want from you, Melissy," he added, earnestly, "is to hear you say that I did right in takin' your affairs into my hands and doin' as I did with Balaam."

Her eyes brimmed again at the words.

"Oh, haven't I told you?" she whispered. "I—I want to thank you, but—but I can't—not now."

"No, no, you don't. Nothin' to thank me for; I just——"

"There is everything to thank you for. Noah Newcomb, I think you are the best man I ever knew."

He laughed aloud. "Your acquaintance has been

kind of limited, I'm afraid, Melissy," he said. "Here, where are you goin'?"

She had risen and was on her way to the stairs.

"I am goin' to my room," she said. "If—if you don't mind I'd like to be alone a little while. Some other time—tomorrow, perhaps—we can talk about the money I owe you——"

"Owe me? You don't owe me anything."

"Of course I do. I owe you the money you paid Balaam when you took over the debt. I owe that and I certainly shall pay it, every cent of it. It may take some time, for after I leave here I may not be able to earn much right away, but——"

Captain Noah interrupted.

"After you leave here?" he repeated. "You ain't goin' to leave here, are you?"

"Of course I am."

"But what for?"

"What for? You know what for. You know that Obadiah Burgess doesn't need a housekeeper any more than he needs that Wentworth man to live on him. I suppose you'll get rid of Mr. Wentworth pretty soon, Cap'n; you seem to be able to do 'most anything. Well, you won't have to get rid of me and Joe. We shall go of our own accord."

"Melissy!"

"There, there! I didn't mean it, Cap'n Noah. I know you don't want to get rid of us. It's we ourselves that will feel we ought to go. Thank you. I—I wish I could thank you enough, but I can't—and I mustn't try; if I do I shall cry again. Tomorrow, perhaps, we'll talk it all over. I'm happier tonight than I've been for 'most three years and—and you— Good night."

"But, hold on! Melissy! I ain't——"

She had closed the door and he heard her going up the back stairs to her room. Soon afterwards he went up the front stairs to his own. He did not sleep well that night; his mind was a curious jumble of thoughts, some pleasant, some otherwise, some wildly absurd. He lay awake for hours, idly wondering and planning concerning his own future. Of course, now that the "picture puzzles" were done, now that Obadiah was extricated from his difficulties, he, Noah, would probably soon be leaving Trumet. There was nothing to keep him there. And yet he had come to like the quaint little old village. It seemed more like home to him than any other place on earth. But he had no home. What a useless, shiftless, shifting life his was, anyhow! And so on, and so on, until long after midnight. And when he awoke the next morning his first conscious thought was that Melissa Mayo was going away and going soon. And the idea was no more pleasant or reconcilable to him then than it had been the night before.

As was his custom when perplexed or troubled, he went for a ride in his auto that morning. He returned at dinner time to find Joash at the foot of the table where the housekeeper usually sat.

"Melissy's gone to Bayport," explained Obadiah. "She's been cal'latin' to go for 'most a week. Wanted to do some shoppin' over there at the hardware store, some kitchen things for the house, you know. Snow, up to the Corners here, don't keep no stock the way

they d-d-do over to Bayport. She went on the mornin'
t-t-train and she's comin' back on t-t-tonight's. What
makes you look so surprised, Cap'n Noah? Don't you
know she said d-d-d-day afore yesterday she cal'lated
to go today?"

She had said so, but the captain had forgotten it. The
table looked particularly uninviting and lonely without
her. After dinner was over he went outside to smoke
his pipe. Obadiah joined him, a broad smile upon his
face, and a gaudily wrapped box in his hand.

"H-h-have one, Cap'n?" he inquired, opening the box
and extending it proudly.

Noah regarded the box and the row of fat, banded
cigars with surprise and some suspicion.

"What in the nation?" he demanded.

"Fresh box of Liberty Maids," explained Mr. Burgess, proudly. "First I've had for a long spell. Now
I've g-g-got my money back, kind of thought I c-c-could
afford to celebrate a little mite. And Balaam didn't buy
'em for me, neither," he added.

The captain accepted one of the "Liberty Maids," not
because he wanted one, far from it, but because he did
not wish to hurt his friend's feelings. He delayed in
lighting it. however. Not so Obadiah, who began to
puff like a tugboat and to smell like a burning carpet
factory.

"Cap'n Noah," he observed, from the midst of the
fumes, "do you know what I was thinkin' after I
t-t-turned in last night?"

Noah shook his head. "No," he replied, "but I hope

for your sake your thoughts wan't as—er—promiscu's as mine was."

Mr. Burgess did not know what "promiscuous" meant, but he did not let that fact trouble him.

"No," he said, "they wan't. I ain't subject to—er—them things very much. But I got t-t-to thinkin' after I turned in, and the more I thought the more it s-s-seemed a p-p-pup-pity to me that you wan't goin' to be the one to own 'this house."

The captain smiled.

"I know, Obe," he said, "but, the way I look at it, it would be more of a pity if I did own it. What would I do with it?"

"Why, live in it, of course. That's what folks gener- ally d-d-do with houses, ain't it?"

"Not if they're all alone in the world, the way I am."

"Why not? I'm all alone just as much as you be and I've been l-l-livin' here, ain't I?"

His friend's smile broadened.

"I shouldn't say that you'd been livin' alone exactly, Obe," he observed. "And now that there's a prospect of all hands of us clearin' out, you want to go, too."

Mr. Burgess nodded. "That's 'cause I'm so dead sot on travelin'," he declared. "It's different with you. You t-t-told me more'n once that you'd like nothin' better than to spend the rest of your d-d-days right here in Trumet in this very house."

"But not alone, Obe, not alone."

"All right, and that brings me up alongside of what I was thinkin' last night. I was thinkin' why didn't you g-g-get married? You ain't old—that is, you ain't so

d-d-darned old. Why don't you get married, Cap'n
Noah. Then you could buy this house and live in it and
you wouldn't be alone. . . . What are you lookin' at me
like that for? There ain't n-n-nothin' the matter with
me, is there?"

For the captain was staring at him in bewildered and
blank amazement. Slowly he shook his head. "I don't
know," he muttered, "I declare I don't know whether
there is or not. You ain't a spirit medium or a mind
reader or anything like that, are you, Obe?"

"Eh? I ain't what?"

"A mind reader? One of those fellers who can tell
what another feller's thinkin' about?"

"One of them town hall, 'Now what do I hold in my
hand,' critters? No, course I ain't."

"Umph! And yet *you* was thinkin' that fool thing
after *you* turned in! Humph!" And then, with a sidelong glance at the little man's face, he added: "Didn't
go so far as to pick out somebody for me to marry, did
you, Obe?"

Obadiah looked important and wise. "Why yes, I
did," he said. "I run over quite a number of names.
Finally, though, I kind of settled down to one, as you
m-m-might say."

"Oh, you did, eh? Well—er—who's the lucky one?"

"Why, Miss Sarepty Hatch down the road here. She
ain't never been married and I shouldn't wonder if. . . .
Here! What did you do that for? Where you goin'?"

For Captain Noah at the mention of Miss Hatch's
name had risen, stared at his friend as if to make sure
the latter was serious, and had then, after knocking Mr.

Burgess's hat over his eyes, walked briskly off, his shoulders shaking. And he would not come back, although Obadiah shouted several urgent invitations.

But he did return later on, however. The ex-cook was in the woodshed chopping up pine boughs for kindling, when the captain looked in at the window.

"Say, Obe," he asked, and he seemed embarrassed, "think it's goin' to rain, do you?"

It was a cloudless afternoon. Mr. Burgess was, naturally, surprised at the question.

"Rain? No," he snorted, disgustedly. "Course 'tain't g-g-goin' to rain. What——"

"Er—what time does that down train get here this evenin', d'you know?"

"Same time it generally does, I cal'late. That's half-past seven, if it's on time. But you knew that. What——"

"Humph! 'Bout a twenty minutes' run from Bayport, ain't it? That would make it leave there about 7:10. And it's only half-past four now. That would give me time enough, lots more than enough."

"What ails you, Cap'n Noah? What are you mumblin' to yourself about?"

But the captain did not answer. A moment later Obadiah, peering from the woodshed door, saw him climb into his automobile, which had been standing by the gate, and drive away.

Mrs. Melissa Mayo, her shopping finished, was sitting upon the jackknife-scarred bench adorning the platform of the Bayport railway station. She was waiting for the train which was to take her back to Trumet, and the wait

351

was likely to be a long one, for it was scarcely half-past five. She was thinking deeply when her meditations were disturbed by the sound of her name. And the voice which called that name was, oddly enough, that of the very person of whom she had been thinking.

"Melissy!" shouted Captain Noah. "Hi, Melissy!"

He was seated in the little car, and when he saw that he had attracted her attention he opened the door and stepped down to the road. Then he beckoned to her.

"All aboard, Melissy," he said. "Heave ahead! Boat's waitin' at the dock."

She rose and, picking up her bundles, walked toward the car. He hastened to take them from her.

"Why, Cap'n Newcomb!" she exclaimed. "What in the world are you doin' way over here?"

The captain's embarrassment, so apparent when he questioned Mr. Burgess through the woodshed window, was still with him.

"Why—why," he stammered, "I—I was just over here and—and—I happened to see you sittin' there and——"

"Happened to see me! You couldn't have seen me when you first called. You hadn't come past the corner."

"Hadn't I? Sho! I want to know! Well—er—I didn't mean I happened to see you, exactly. I meant I knew you was over here to Bayport——"

"Oh, Obadiah told you, I suppose."

"Eh? Oh, yes, sartin, Obe told me. And so I—I—er—I was out for a ride—didn't have anything else to do, you understand—and I just thought I'd hunt you up and see if you didn't want to ride home along with me. This—er—Pancake of mine ain't quite so big as a train of cars, but it can go about as fast as some of the trains down here, and when you cal'late it's goin' to be at a sartin place at a sartin time it's 'most generally there. Which you can't always say of trains—our trains, anyhow. Eh, now? Eh? What?"

"Mercy on us, Noah!" exclaimed the housekeeper. "How fast you do talk today!"

"Do I? Want to know! Must be a little mite nervous, I guess likely."

"Nervous! I didn't know you could be nervous."

"Didn't you? So did I. I mean—well, never mind. What do you say, Melissy? Goin' to get aboard and take a cruise in the good ship Pancake, are you?"

She smiled. "Why, of course I am," she replied. "And I'm ever so glad of the chance. I was gettin' dreadful tired of sittin' on that depot platform. It's real kind of you to think of me, Cap'n Noah."

The captain did not answer. He stowed the packages, Mrs. Mayo's purchases, in various places about the car, helped her in, climbed to his own seat beside her and put his foot upon the button of the self-starter. The engine started, so did the car, and they soon left Bayport behind.

Mrs. Mayo chatted a good deal as they whirred along through the stretch of woods between Bayport and South Trumet, but her companion said very little. He seemed very much preoccupied and, as he had said—although it was a most unusual condition for him—nervous. After a time the housekeeper, getting no answers, or very absent-minded ones, to her questions and remarks, also lapsed into silence. Occasionally she, glancing at the captain's face, saw his lips moving. He seemed, so she thought, to be practicing some speech, rehearsing something, learning it by heart. She could not understand his manner, which was decidedly strange.

They passed through the hamlet of South Trumet, by the garage in which the "Pancake" had received its overhauling after the accident which led to Noah's first meeting with Irving Clifford, and entered the last three-mile stretch of hilly, curvy road separating them from Trumet itself. The last house in South Trumet had been left behind and there were pine groves on both sides of the road, dusky, shadowy pine groves in which the early September twilight was already deepening, when Noah suddenly spoke.

"Melissy," he said, "I've been thinkin' over what you told me last night and I can't have it so."

"Can't have what? What do you mean, Cap'n Noah?"

"Can't have you haulin' up anchor and leavin' Obe's house and—and all of us for good. You mustn't do it."

"But I must. You know I must. Surely you wouldn't have me sponge my livin', and Joe's livin', from Mr. Burgess any longer."

"Ain't any question of Joe's livin'. I've got some plans about Joe and his livin'. Don't you remember I told you I had? They may work out or they may not—although I think they will—but anyhow Joe'll be looked after. It's you I'm thinkin' about, Melissy."

She smiled a trifle sadly. "You needn't worry about me, Cap'n Noah," she said. "Earnin' my own livin' is no new trick for me. I've had to do it almost all my life. Don't you worry about me; I shall be all right."

"Well, then, how about me?"

"You? Why, what do you mean?"

"I mean what I say. Look here, Melissy, how am I— well, what's goin' to become of *me?* That's what I want to know."

She did not seem to understand. "Become of you?" she repeated. "Why, you—you will be no different from what you were when you came here, so far as I can see."

He shook his head. "Then you can't see very fur," he said, with decision. "I'm as different as a china nest egg is from the real article; they both look somethin' the same outside, but that's as far as the likeness goes. When I come here I was a sort of easy-goin', happy-go-lucky feller, who had made his pile—not a very big one, but enough—and all I was figgerin' on was sort of driftin' around from one port to another until I foundered. But ever since I got here to Trumet I've been changin' and my notions and ideas have been changin', too. My notion of happiness used to be no owners and no responsibilities, nothin' to own and nothin' to care for. Do you know what my notion of happiness is now, Melissy?"

Her attention had been attracted by the eccentric course of the car, which was veering from side to side of the narrow road as its pilot, in his growing agitation, jerked the steering wheel back and forth. So her answer was given rather absent-mindedly.

"No, I'm sure I don't," she said. "But—but, Noah, what makes us jiggle around so? Be careful, do."

The captain did not answer her question nor hear or heed her caution. He had reached the point he had been leading up to now, and nothing short of an earthquake could have diverted his attention from that point. The "jiggling around" continued and so did Captain Noah.

"I'll tell you what my notion of happiness is now," he said, earnestly. "It's to own that house and land that Obe Burgess owns now. To own it and furnish it new mostly, and fix up the grounds and have a garden, make a *home* of it, you understand. And—and this is the real important part, Melissy—to have you to live in it along with me. That's my idea of bein' happy. Do—do you cal'late you could—could help me to get that happiness?"

He had rehearsed this speech, or the substance of it, a good many times in the last few hours. And now, to his chagrin, he saw that she did not wholly understand.

"Me?" she repeated. "You want me—you want me to keep house for you?"

The captain gave a jerk at the wheel that sent the car almost into the sandbank at the side of the road. He jerked it savagely in the other direction and the automobile shot over the brow of a long hill and began the descent.

"Housekeep be darned!" roared Captain Noah. "I want you to be my wife. Will you, Melissy?"

"Oh!" she exclaimed, faintly, and that was all.

"Will you, Melissy?" pleaded the captain.

EXTRICATING OBADIAH

Still she did not speak.

"For the Almighty's sake, don't say you won't! If you say that I—I swan I don't know *what* I'll do."

"Oh, Noah, how can I? . . . Oh, look out!"

The last was a faint scream. If it had been a very loud one there was excuse sufficient. For Noah, in his eagerness to hear her answer, had permitted the car, as it ran down the long slope of the hill, to approach close to the bank on the left; and now, in his stress of feeling caused by that answer, he had jerked the wheel half around and the auto was shooting directly into the ruins of what, on the right of the road, had once been a rail fence. Mrs. Mayo was conscious of the splintering and cracking of wood, then of a succession of rockings and bumpings. She was also dimly conscious of the fact that her companion was no longer on the seat beside her, but was standing partially erect. Then came a final bump, a smash of glass, and a tremendous splash.

When the housekeeper recovered from the shock sufficiently to care where she was, or to realize that she was anywhere, this is what she saw: The car, with its windshield smashed to flinders, and its nose pointing back in the direction from which it had come, was standing with its broadside at the very edge of a little pond. The waters of this pond, black and forbidding in the evening dusk, were violently agitated. As for Captain Noah Newcomb, he was nowhere in sight.

Melissa was a woman of considerable presence of mind. She was not prone to hysterics and she seldom lost her head. As soon, therefore, as she could be sure that that head was not, literally, lost, she sprang to her feet and called her companion's name.

"Noah!" she cried. "Noah, where are you?"

There was no answer. The waters of the pond still rocked and splashed amongst the reeds on the edge, that was all.

Mrs. Mayo sprang from the car. She leaped out upon the side furthest from the pond, but she ran around to the other side.

"Noah!" she cried. "Oh, Noah!"

There was no answer, but then she saw him. He was lying in the water amid the reeds and he was lying very still. She ran in beside him. The water was shallow, fortunately, and his head was not below the surface.

How she ever did it she often wondered afterward, for he was a big man, but she managed to drag him ashore. Then she bent over him and tried to see where he was hurt.

"Noah!" she begged, distractedly. "Oh, Noah! Oh, my dear, my dear!"

She had his head in her lap, and now from that head came a faint voice.

"Say that again," it said. She was so overjoyed to find that he was not dead that she scarcely noticed or understood the words.

"Oh, you're alive!" she cried. "You're alive!"

The voice made answer.

"You bet!" it said. "Say that again, Melissy."

"Say what, Noah? What do you mean? Where are you hurt?"

358

The head in her lap moved, turned, and slowly Cap'n Noah sat up.

"I ain't hurt anywheres to amount to nothin', Melissy," he said. "I—I yanked the Pancake around so sudden to keep it from goin' into that pond that it hove me out and cracked my head on the mudguard. Knocked me out of time for a jiffy, that's all."

He struggled to his feet. She protested.

"Oh, you mustn't do that," she cried. "You're hurt."

"Tell you I ain't hurt at all," he declared. "I've got worse knocks than that fifty times a v'yage when I went to sea. But," with an attempt at a smile, "I hope I'm a better navigator on sea than I am on land. That's twice I've drove this auto of mine into a pond."

He stopped and stared about him.

"And, by the everlastin', it's the very same pond!" he exclaimed, in wonderment. "It's the same pond I dove into when I met Irve Clifford the first time. Well, I swan! Humph!" And then he added, fervently, "It's a lucky pond for me."

She had risen and was standing beside him. She was still fearful that he had been hurt more than he knew.

"Lucky!" she repeated. "What do you mean? Unlucky, I should say."

He put his arms about her. "Then you'd say wrong, my lady," he cried, exultantly. "The first time I took the Pancake in swimmin' here Irve Clifford fished her out. And Irve's come to be one of my very best friends. And now 'twas you that fished me out, and you —well, you're goin' to be somethin' more than a friend; you're goin' to be Mrs. Noah Newcomb."

359

She tried to draw away from him.

"No, Noah," she protested, "I haven't said that—I mustn't say it. Don't you see I mustn't think of it? I—I'm poor and I'm not young any more and—and you'd just have me to take care of, and it——"

He laughed aloud. "There, there, that'll do, Melissy," he said. "We'll argue all that out after we're married. You called me your dear just now and that's all I was waitin' to hear. That settled everything so fur as you and me are concerned, my girl, or if it didn't this will."

And he stooped and kissed her.

The remainder of the homeward run of the "Pancake" that evening was straighter, but considerably slower than that which had gone before.

CHAPTER XXI

A GOOD many happenings may take place in ten days, and Captain Noah was thinking that very thing as he leaned over the front fence of the Burgess place ten days after he and Mrs. Mayo rode home from Bayport together.

To begin with, the Burgess place was the Burgess place no longer. And it was not the "Badscom place," either, as it had been called when he first knew it. It was the Newcomb place now, for he and Obadiah had closed a deal and he had purchased that portion of Aunt Sarah Badscom's legacy for four thousand dollars. Both parties to the transaction were delighted, for the captain had a home at last and the home he most desired, and Mr. Burgess had in actual cash about fourteen thousand dollars, a sum which looked like a De Rothschild fortune to him. As a matter of fact, it was likely to be nearer fifteen thousand, for Captain Noah and Melissa would probably purchase the greater part of his furniture.

Obadiah had put the captain in charge of the said for-tune. Noah had hesitated about accepting the responsi-bility, but had finally decided to do so. He realized that

if his former cook himself took charge of it there would
soon be another letter summoning him to help extricate
the little man from new tangles. There were plenty
more helpful "friends" of the Balaam Griggs type in the
world, and the captain had worked out all the "picture
puzzles" he craved for the present.

Obadiah himself recognized the danger and strongly
urged that his friend act as his financial guardian.

"You take care of it, Cap'n Noah," he said. "You
t-t-take care of it and hang onto it for me. There's
about eight hundred dollars a year interest c-c-comin'
to me now, and that ought to be enough for any single
feller like me. A man that wants more than that is a
d-d-dum hog, the way I look at it. See here, Cap'n, you
send me that interest at such and such t-t-times reg'lar,
and if I write in between times and ask you for more you
tell me to go to t-t-thunder, will you?"

Captain Noah laughed. "Suppose you come yourself
and say you want it, Obe," he suggested. "What then?"

Obadiah did not hesitate.

"Have me p-p-put in the crazy asylum," he said.
"That's where I'd b-b-belong if I did that."

So it was arranged. And now Mr. Burgess, the first
installment of his interest in his pocket, had gone up to
Boston for what he called a "little vacation." It was not
likely to be a long vacation, for his supply of funds was
limited; but it was the first of the "travels" which he
was planning to take. The captain had urged him to
consider his former house as a sort of headquarters, a
haven to which he might return whenever the joys of
traveling grew stale or the traveling wherewithal scarce.

"You can call it your home just the same as ever, Obe," he said. "I'll be glad to see you and so'll Melissy, when she comes to be skipper aboard this craft."

Melissa, accompanied by her nephew, had gone back to their former home at Pigeon Cove for a few days' stay. There were affairs to be settled there before Mrs. Mayo left for good, furniture to be taken out of storage, and similar matters. When she came back she and Noah were to be quietly married, although no one outside the immediate household shared that secret yet.

So Captain Noah was temporarily left alone in Trumet and was sleeping in his own home and eating at the Mansion House. Just now—it was Sunday—he was considering going down to that hostelry for dinner. It was not a prospect to which he looked forward with eagerness, but he knew it was time, because he had heard the train whistle at the station a few minutes before, and that meant twelve-thirty at least.

He leaned over the fence, puffing lazily at his cigar—which, by the way, was not a "Liberty Maid"—when he became aware that someone was approaching along the road; a man, obviously not a Trumet "native" and yet someone whose walk was familiar, very familiar. The man drew nearer, swinging his cane, and languidly strolling on, and the captain whistled between his teeth. The languid gentleman with the cane was the missing invalid, he who had left Trumet to be gone a possible two weeks but had been gone nearly five—Mr. Calvin Wentworth.

Cousin Calvin was a sight to gratify a taste not too subdued nor yet too florid. His clothes were new, his

hat was new, so were his shoes and socks. His waistcoat was a cheerful check, his tie a dream of beauty.
Altogether it was quite evident that he had availed himself of the opportunity which his visit to the metropolis
afforded and had been, as he told Balaam Griggs he intended to be, "touched up and revarnished."

Captain Noah noted all those things and smiled. Mr.
Wentworth, becoming aware of the captain's presence,
smiled also. There was a touch of conscious superiority
in the Wentworth smile. The Newcomb smile might
have meant almost anything, or nothing in particular.

"Afternoon, Newcomb," hailed Cousin Calvin, with
languid graciousness.

"Hello, Mr. Wentworth!" exclaimed the captain.
"Well, well! Back again, eh?"

Mr. Wentworth admitted that he was back again.
Also he deigned to inquire concerning the captain's
health.

"First rate, thank you," declared Noah, heartily.
"Feelin' fine, I am. And you?"

"Top hole, old chap." And then, with the first appearance of real interest he had shown, he asked:
"How's Sport?"

Captain Noah repeated the name.

"Sport?" he repeated. "Sport? I don't seem to—
What's his first name?"

"First name? I say, what—? I'm talking about
Sport—my dog, you know."

Then the captain seemed to comprehend.

"Oh, your dog!" he exclaimed. "The yellow and
black one with the stepped-on face. Sartin, I recollect

now. Why, he's all right, I presume likely. Seems to me he was last time I saw him."

A little of Cousin Calvin's languor disappeared. He looked at Captain Noah with a new expression, not of suspicion exactly, but as if he were beginning to realize there was something peculiar in the latter's manner.

"Last time you saw him?" he repeated, slowly. "You speak as if you hadn't seen him for some time. Aren't you living here now?"

The captain nodded, genially. "Oh, sartin," he said; "I'm livin' here, all right, livin' here right along."

"Then don't you see the dog every day?"

"No, not every day."

"Why not?"

"Don't know. Don't get down his way so very often, maybe."

"Down his way? . . . See here, what are you doing, stringing me? Isn't the dog here?"

Captain Noah smiled in innocent surprise. "My, my!" he exclaimed. "I thought you knew that. But I suppose you didn't. 'Tain't likely you would know, come to think of it, because——"

"Know? Know what?"

"Why, know that your dog was down to the Mansion House. They're takin' care of him down there. It's all right. Mrs. Hobbs says she thinks a sight of dogs, and as for Ethelinda——"

"Who sent my dog to the Mansion House?"

Mr. Wentworth's composure was, for him, unusually ruffled. Captain Noah was mild and calm as a foggy morning in mid-summer.

365

"Why, I did," he answered, cheerfully.

"You did? You did? Say, look here, what——"

"Yes, you see, I tell you: He was a good enough dog of his kind, I presume likely, though he was so everlastin' homely. Course he couldn't help that, poor critter, but——"

"What in the devil are you talking about?"

"About your dog. I'm tryin' to tell you. You see, I could have put up with his homeliness, but he did eat so like the nation that I couldn't stand it any longer, and——"

"You couldn't stand it? *You* couldn't?"

"No."

"What business was it of yours? Did you have to pay for what he ate?"

"Why, yes."

"You did? Are you off your head? You don't own this house, do you?"

"Yes."

The answer was given in the same quiet, cheerful, conversational tone, but it seemed to knock the returned invalid completely off his mental pins for the moment. He stared at the speaker, at the house, and back again. His mouth opened and shut several times, but he did not say anything. Captain Noah did not say anything, either; he continued to smoke and to look cheerfully interested and anxious to please. At length the Wentworth mouth managed to form words.

"You own this house?" he demanded. "You own it? Do you know what you're talking about?"

"Yes, generally speakin'."

"You own this house! How long since?"

" 'Bout a week."

"You mean you—you bought it of Burgess?"

"Um-hm."

Cousin Calvin stared long and hard at the imperturbable and cheerful visage before him. And as he gazed, an uncomfortable conviction that what he had just heard was the truth began to steal upon him. If it was the truth——

"Where's Burgess?" he demanded.

"Gone travelin'."

"Traveling? Traveling where?"

"Don't know. Just travelin', I guess. Always wanted to travel, you know, Obe did, so now I guess he's just —er—travelin'."

"When is he coming back?"

"Don't know."

Mr. Wentworth seemed to reflect. Then he stepped forward and put his hand upon the gate. The captain, leaning upon that gate, and pretty effectually blocking it, did not move.

"Excuse me," said Cousin Calvin.

"Oh, sartin sure, I'll excuse you. I could see you didn't know I'd bought the place. I'll excuse you; no hard feelin's at all."

Wentworth laughed, uneasily. "I meant excuse me, will you, and let me open the gate," he observed.

Still the man blocking the gate did not move.

"Wanted to go in, did you?" he inquired.

"Why—why, yes, naturally I did."

"Um-hm. What for?"

"What for?"

"Um-hm. What for?"

"Why, to go to my room," hotly. "I've been on the road since twelve last night and I'm tired."

"That's too bad. Don't blame you for wantin' to go to your room. I'd go if I was you."

"Thanks. Then suppose you let me go."

"I wouldn't hinder you for nothin'. But you ain't goin' the right way. Your room's down to the Mansion House, I suppose. If it ain't there I don't know where 'tis. There's where your trunk and the rest of your dunnage was sent."

The invalid gasped. "You've sent my trunk to the Mansion House!" he shouted, wrathfully. "What for?"

"Didn't know where else to send it," was the mild reply. "Obadiah and I didn't know what you'd want done with it, so we made the best guess we could. Then again you'd been gone so long we didn't know but you'd decided to stay in New York altogether."

"Stay there altogether! What would I want to stay there altogether for? You chaps were pretty damned fresh, if you ask me."

"Thanks. I'll remember in case I ever ask you. Why would you want to stay in New York altogether? That's just what I said to Obe. 'No man with so many debts around New York as he's got,' I said, 'would want to stay there all the time.' You see, Mr. Wentworth, we'd looked up your record quite a long spell ago. How so many of those New York store folks ever trusted you beats me. It beat them, too, didn't it?" he added, with a quiet chuckle.

Cousin Calvin's fists clenched. "By gad!" he cried, "you——"

"Yup. Well, Obe kind of thought you might have married the Emmons woman and settled down. ' 'Cordin' to all accounts,' says Obe, 'he and she were thick enough to be married. Look at the game the two of 'em put on Irve Clifford.' Eh? What say?"

But Mr. Wentworth had not said anything. His usually rather pale face was a bright red and he was perspiring freely. Also he seemed to be tongue-tied, a condition in which very few people had ever seen him.

Captain Noah tossed away the stump of his cigar.

"So, you see, Mr. Wentworth," he went on, "we didn't know where to send your things, and just took a chance and sent 'em to the Mansion House. 'Tain't the Copley Piazza hotel exactly, but a healthy man can live there— with practice. I'm eating there myself just now, and I'm fairly healthy." He turned away from the gate and then turned back again. "In case you ain't got in those dividend checks you were always expectin' when you borrowed of me," he added, "maybe you could make some such arrangements as you made with Obe—fix it to put the Mansion House in your will, you know. So long, Mr. Wentworth. Maybe I'll see you again some time."

He strolled up the path and entered the house. Cousin Calvin, his face redder than ever, watched him go. For a minute longer the returned invalid stood there in the road, clutching his cane and swearing between his clenched teeth. Then, suddenly recollecting that he might be watched, and that it would be decidedly wiser not to advertise his discomfiture throughout Trumet, he turned

and walked back toward the village. He had no definite
idea as to where he should go, but he instinctively headed
toward the Mansion House. His baggage was there and
his dog was there, and it seemed to him that he might
as well join them.

Trumet's main street on a Sunday afternoon in autumn
is not a crowded thoroughfare. Nevertheless, in front of
Snow's drygoods and general store there were several
people standing. They seemed to be looking in at the
window. As he passed it seemed to Mr. Wentworth that
these people looked at him, then in at the window, and
then at him again. And they whispered among themselves. So he looked in at the window, too.

What he saw there, prominently displayed in the very
center of the show window, was a large "crayon enlargement" in a gorgeous, not to say flamboyant frame. It,
the "enlargement," was a portrait of a two-legged clothespin with a wooden face, its lower extremities clad in
thunder and lightning knickerbockers, standing above a
four-legged object which looked as much like a dog as
it did like anything else. Both man and dog appeared
to have frozen stiff and then warped out of shape while
thawing.

The new arrival from the metropolis gazed at this exhibit and gasped, gazed again and felt a shiver run up
and down his back. For, in spite of the atrocious color
and bad drawing, the likeness was there. The face of
the clothespin was a caricature of his own. And, to
avoid all possibility of mistake, beside the frame was a
large placard with the inscription: "Crayon Portrait of
Mr. Calvin Wentworth of New York. Done by J. Ken-

ney, 'Artist. Orders for Similar Work Received Here."

Mr. Wentworth stared and stared. Then he made a dash for the door of the store. It being Sunday that door was locked, of course. What the irate original of that crayon portrait might have done next if left undisturbed is a subject for conjecture, he might have broken the window perhaps. But before this rash deed could be perpetrated a hand was laid upon his sleeve and a voice, the voice of Uncle Labe Bassett, cried:

"Well, well, well! I do vum if it ain't Mr. Wentworth himself! When did you come back, Mr. Wentworth? Glad to see ye, sir. Say now, say, ain't that fine? Somethin' of a surprise to you, ain't it? I bet you! Cap'n Noah Newcomb had Joe Kenney put that in there for folks to see. The cap'n cal'lated that all hands would want to look at it, and, by gracious me, they do! I never cared much for Joe's paintin' afore I see this, I'm free to give in that I didn't, but when I see that there says I: 'That boy's a wonder, that's what he is, a wonder!' Look at it now; the very image of you, Mr. Wentworth. How many times I've seen you look like that. I says to Balaam Griggs t'other day, says I——"

Cousin Calvin never learned what Mr. Bassett said to Balaam Griggs. He tore his sleeve from Uncle Labe's detaining grasp without even explaining that he was obliged to go. Instead he told the old gentleman where *he* might go. He broke through the little group by the window and strode up the street, lashing the weeds beside the road with his cane and devoutly wishing that each decapitated burdock stalk was Noah Newcomb.

But, as he strode on, out of the jumble of his thoughts
a new idea began to shape itself, an idea suggested by
a name uttered by Uncle Labe.

"Balaam Griggs."

Balaam Griggs! Why, of course, Balaam Griggs!
There was his refuge. There was his Sunday dinner,
his night's lodging. Why not his board and lodgings
for many days and nights? He took out his pocketbook,
made sure that a certain paper was within it, and then,
his frown succeeded by a confident smile, walked briskly
along the lower road toward the Griggs domicile.

Balaam was a moral man, as he occasionally stated in
public. Also he was a pious, church-going man at times.
But, like some other pious men, he seldom permitted piety
and morality to interfere with his business. The day before he had come into possession of an old chair which
had originally been painted a bright green. On the mor-
row, Monday, a prospective customer was coming to inspect that chair. Therefore Mr. Griggs now, although
it was Sunday, was renewing the green paint which in
places had been knocked from the chair.

The door behind him opened. Balaam, mentally scold-
ing himself for not having locked it, turned, dripping
paint brush in hand. His mouth and eyes opened and
he gasped audibly.

"Ah, old scout," observed Mr. Wentworth, blithely,
"improving the shining hour as usual, I see, eh?"

Mr. Griggs did not answer.

Cousin Calvin stepped into the room, glanced about
over the crowded huddle of "antiques," and perched,
whistling, upon the corner of an ancient—or reproduction

of an ancient—table, having first dusted it with a spotless handkerchief.

"Still the busy bee, Uncle," he remarked. "That's the boy. Well, is there any honey in the hive today?"

Balaam, still clinging to the brush, which dripped oozily upon the floor, spoke.

"Where did you come from?" he demanded.

"From the broadest spot on Broadway, old scout."

"Huh! Been havin' a good time on my money. I cal'late."

"Your cal'lations are well cal'lated. I have."

"And what did you come back here for?"

"I came," Mr. Wentworth airily tapped his new shoe with his cane, "I came," he said, "because I could no longer stay away from you, Uncle, dear. I thought of you so often. Your bright smile haunted me still, so to speak."

He grinned as he said it, for Mr. Griggs' countenance was something to see, although there were no bright smiles visible upon it.

"Ugh!" grunted Balaam.

"I agree with you. Have you missed me? I'm sure you have. Well, you'll not miss me any more because— Oh, by the way, is it true that that Newcomb fellow has bought out Burgess, house and all?"

Mr. Griggs grunted again.

"Yes, darn him, I guess he has," he said.

"Darn him by all means. Darn him and repeat, I'm with you. But, as I was going to say, you won't miss me any more, Uncle, dear. I'm going to stay here now."

Balaam leaned forward.

"You're goin' to *what?*" he cried.

"I'm goin' to stay here, live here, spend my days—*and* nights—here. You'll take me in, of course you will. How can you refuse? Eh? A man with as tender a heart as yours is."

Mr. Griggs made no answer. The hand holding the dripping paint brush tightened a little, that was all.

Mr. Wentworth reached into the pocket of his new coat and drew forth his pocketbook. Opening the pocketbook he extracted a paper.

"I love to read this, Uncle dear," he said. "It's my meal ticket, my permanent meal ticket, so to speak. Want to hear it again? Do let me refresh your memory. 'But provided my daughter, the said Mary Barton Barstow, comes of age or marries, the said trust held by her mother, my wife, *and* Balaam Griggs, my joint executor, shall terminate and the said twenty-five thousand dollars shall be hers without——' "

He got no further. The dripping paint brush, flung by the Griggs hand, struck squarely in the middle of his chest, just at the lower point of the V in the new checked waistcoat. It struck, and spattered much and stickily.

Then Mr. Griggs reached for the paint pot itself.

CHAPTER XXII

A BOUT a year after the Sunday upon which Mr.
Griggs threw the paint brush Mr. and Mrs Irving
Clifford, still residing in Chicago, received the
following letter from Captain Noah. They had received
many from the same source. The letter began:

DEAR IRVE AND MARY: I haven't written you for a good
while, but that isn't all my fault. Melissa kept saying she
was going to write and so I didn't, waiting for her. Of
course she says she didn't write because *I* kept saying *I*
was going to and she was waiting for me, but you mustn't
pay too much attention to *her*.

Above this last sentence was written in Melissa's handwriting:

And I hope you know him too well by this time to pay
much attention to *him*.

The letter continued:

I don't know as there's much news to write. Things
here in Trumet are pretty much the same. Melissa and
me are well, and I tell her she gets younger and handsomer
every day. Of course it is natural she should, being lucky
enough to have me for a husband.

EXTRICATING OBADIAH

'Another interpolation here in Mrs. Newcomb's handwriting:

More of his nonsense. Besides, I tell him *somebody* in the family ought to be good-looking.

The captain went on:

We are busy cleaning house and getting the decks scrubbed and things lashed down and stowed aloft and alow for winter. We have built on a new ell on the port side of the house and, besides an extra stateroom upstairs, there is a new room on the main deck that *I* say is a smoking room. Melissa she says it is a sewing room, and so far it does seem to be, but some of these days I tell her I am going to bust loose and smoke in it if it turns out to be the last puff I draw. A six-foot-three man has to have *some* rights, ain't he? He can't be browbeat and pounded around *all* the time by a five-foot-three woman. However, joking to one side, the new rooms are tiptop, and Melissa and me get a heap of comfort out of them.

Joe's letters from out West keep coming all the time, and are as full of hurrahs and enthusiasm as ever. I calculate he has to work pretty hard there on Mr. Snowden's ranch, but it don't seem to sicken him of the job. I am real grateful to Mr. Snowden for giving him the chance. He did it to oblige me, of course, and my wife and I appreciate it. If we ever take that Grand Cañon, orange grove, 'Frisco cruise we've been talking about so long we mean to make port there at the ranch and see Joe and thank Snowden personal. But I do really believe the boy is making good. His boss wrote me that he was, and his own letters seem to bear out the statement. So long as he don't try to crayon enlarge any of the cowboys and get shot up on account of it I calculate he will do pretty well. I tell Melissa that I do hope he won't take a notion to paint a picture of any of the steers. He is liable to be tossed over the main truck if he does. No self-respecting beef-critter would stand one of Joe's portraits for a minute.

Speaking of Joe and his pictures reminds me of Cousin Calvin naturally. I *have* got some news to tell you about him, but I'll keep it for the last, and tell you about Balaam first. The old scalawag is about the same as ever. I met Captain Zeke Penniman down the road the other day and he had a new yarn to spin about Balaam and his antiques. Seems the old rascal had been to an auction over to Well-mouth. He never misses an auction, you know. Well, he had been to this one and he'd bought a lot of junk and some old silver and plated ware amongst it. Soon as he got the plunder home and stowed away between decks in his robbers' roost, the shed where he keeps his antiques, out he goes and hunts up Mrs. Ann Eldridge, who has got money and hopes she is a collector. Ann says she simply does love old curiosities and old things and she never lets one get away from her if she can help it. Probably that's why she married old Abner Eldridge, for if he ain't a genuine antique, and a curiosity at that, I never laid eyes on one. Well, anyhow, Balaam hunted her up and dragged her down to his thief's den to see the wonderful old silver he'd got a hold of. He had an old tablespoon there that he got up on his hind legs and fairly cried over. Said 'twas one of a set that Noah used aboard the *Ark*, or some such matter—used to feed little Japhet his porridge with it, he understood. Words to that effect anyhow.

Well, Ann she cried over it, too, until she turned it over; then she saw what Balaam hadn't noticed, or at least hadn't said anything about; that was the words "Ocean House" stamped in fine letters way up on the handle. It was a spoon that came from the hotel at South Bayport, the one that was burned down four or five years ago. But do you suppose Balaam was fussed when she pointed the name out to him? Not a fuss. Any other swindler would

have been tongue-tied, but Papa Griggs never turned a
hair. Instead he pretended to be more vainglorious than
ever. That *proved* it was one of Noah's spoons, didn't it?
"Ocean House" would be just the name the old chap would
call the *Ark*.

There was another interpolation by Mrs. Newcomb:

I do hope you won't believe all this. Part of that spoon
story is true, that about Ann's finding the name, but all that
Noah's *Ark* part is just more of Captain Newcomb's jokes.
I have got used to his jokes by this time, but I'm always
afraid other folks won't understand.

The captain continued:

So you see Balaam hasn't changed much. For months
and months he didn't speak to me when he met me on
the road, but day afore yesterday he came beating up to
windward of me and asked me if it was true I was thinking
of buying Solomon David's pasture land down on the lower
bay front. Said he heard I was, and if it was so he hoped
I'd buy it through him, because I knew what heavy losses
he had lately and how much he needed the commission
money. I calculate the losses was the twenty-five thousand
of Mary's money that he had to pay over to her. What
do you think of that? Balaam will get on in this world,
I shouldn't wonder, if he lasts long enough and the world
lasts. But I think the world is taking chances by associat-
ing with him.

Obadiah is off again on another traveling cruise. He has
gone to Providence this time. He won't stay long, because
I didn't let him have but forty dollars to go with, and
you can't stay very long anywhere on that these days.
He is usually about ten dollars ahead of his drawing account and, so far as I can see, Melissa and I will always
have him as a sort of permanent charge on our hands.

EXTRICATING OBADIAH

We don't care much, though. If it hadn't been for him I shouldn't be here alive today and, besides, I rather like to have him around and hear him talk. He sets off a bunch of firecrackers with every sentence, and when he gets real excited he talks like a corn-popper. But he is a good-hearted little soul as ever lived, and I think the world of him.

Did I write you in my last letter that he had been to Syracuse? You remember he always used to say he wanted to go on account of that second mate he sailed along with once. That mate used to get tight, you recollect, and then sing "Home, Sweet Home," to the tune of Syracuse. So Obe has been set on going to Syracuse ever since. Well, he went last month and came back some disappointed. He said it was a nice place, but it wasn't nigh so big as he expected, said it didn't seem to him any bigger than Boston. Seems that mate had given him the notion that Syracuse covered two-thirds of creation and had a building option on the other third.

And now I must tell the news about Cousin Calvin Wentworth. The yarn that is going about Trumet just now is that he's going to be married. Yes, sir, married. What do you think of that? I wrote you how he had been living at the Mansion House ever since he left here. Well, he has been star boarder there, too. Course he can't have paid any board, for I know perfectly well he hasn't got anything to pay it with. I imagined that he had worked the invalid game and the leaving everything in his will trick on Mrs. Hobbs, same as he had on Obe, but now I ain't so sure. Nigh as I can find out Mrs. Hobbs and Ethelinda and all the rest of the females at the Mansion House fell down and worshiped him when they first saw him. That high-toned way of his and his city clothes and that waxed mustache was too much for 'em. And he can be mighty convincing and persuading when he takes the trouble to set that oily tongue of his running.

379

EXTRICATING OBADIAH

Anyhow, they say he is going to marry Lavinia Hobbs. Sarepta Hatch told me, and she said Captain Penniman told her this very morning. I asked her what else Captain Zeke said, and she said she'd be ashamed to tell me, said his language was enough to bring a judgment on him. So I calculate the captain's bearings must have been pretty hot. Well, it is enough to make a decent man swear, the idea that any grown-up woman can be such a fool, but that kind of thing happens all the time, so perhaps it ain't so wonderful. He'll have a soft snap, a home, and somebody to work and support him. She'll have I don't know what, something to put on the parlor whatnot maybe, for Cousin Calvin is ornamental, I will give in. I wonder if he'll send wedding cards to the Emmons woman in New York. But say, if he is married I've got a wedding present to give Lavinia. I've got that crayon tintype that Joe did of Wentworth, and as sure as I sit here writing this I shall send it to the bride on the wedding day. I don't know how pleased she'll be, but I know her husband will be delighted. They say he wanted to murder Snow, the storekeeper, for exhibiting it in his show window.

There, folks, I guess I've written the longest letter on record or thereabouts. Melissa and I talk about you pretty often, and some of these days we may be coming out to Chicago to see you. And of course we are counting on your spending at least a month of next summer with us here at home. We want to see you, you may be sure of that, but we especially want to see that new Clifford. Judging by his picture he must be considerable of a fellow. Tell him to hurry up and grow because I want to ship him as second mate aboard that new catboat I am planning to have next summer.

Melissa says she knows I have written you a pack of nonsense, and that she shall look it over before she lets me mail it. I expect she will, for she looks me over pretty careful afore I do much of anything. Well, I never took her advice yet that it didn't turn out to be a good thing, so I am not complaining. She sends a shipload of love and good wishes and so do I. Take care of yourselves, both of you, and of that second mate of mine. And write soon.

Yours right straight along,
NOAH NEWCOMB.

THE END

www.ingramcontent.com/pod-product-compliance
Lightning Source LLC
Chambersburg PA
CBHW030355030726
47497CB00002B/346